Dear Anna,

Bon Appetit

Shadi Hamadeh

Food Wars

MAIRI MCLELLAN

AND

SHADI HAMADEH

authorHOUSE®

AuthorHouse™ UK Ltd.
1663 Liberty Drive
Bloomington, IN 47403 USA
www.authorhouse.co.uk
Phone: 0800.197.4150

Published by AuthorHouse   09/12/13

ISBN: 978-1-4918-8479-9 (sc)
ISBN: 978-1-4918-8478-2 (hc)
ISBN: 978-1-4918-8480-5 (e)

Permission to use the fictional character Jimmy Olives was kindly granted by Jamie Oliver's PR Team.

Perfect Songs kindly gave permission for the usage of lyrics from the song The Power of Love.

Contents

You are what you eat.

To Lynn Molina – M.McL.

To Karim and Nadim – S.H.

ACKNOWLEDGEMENTS

Mairi: I would like to thank Shadi Hamadeh for giving me the opportunity to discover my passion for writing. My heartfelt thanks go to Soad, Ezzat, and Carmen for being behind me all the way. And, of course, to Jamie Oliver for being an inspiration.

Shadi: My heartfelt gratitude goes to my family: Basma, Karim and Nadim for their love and support. I am grateful to my grandmothers and many old women in the Lebanese mountains who taught me that food is precious. Special thanks go to all the small farmers around the globe who inspired me to develop the story behind Food Wars. Finally, my deepest thanks goes to Mairi McLellan for bringing the story to life.

PROLOGUE

At noon on September 14, Philip McGregor, of 22 New Market Gate, Glasgow, bit into his third cheeseburger. At the same time, a report appeared in the national news: "Scotland now ranks third in the world for obesity figures. In another decade 1 in 3 people will be obese." He glanced up at the clock on the school canteen wall; plenty of time to eat before the end of break. *Physics next*, he thought, groaning. Still, if he got a seat near the radiator, he could have a quiet snooze. He finished the burger in two bites. *Okay, still got time for another one,* he thought, congratulating himself. Up he got and shuffled slowly, swaying first to one side and then the other as those huge legs of his propelled him forward. He was aware that heads looked up when he walked by, just as they did today, accompanied by the usual sniggers, whispers, and pointed fingers. But he was used to it by now.

"There you go, Porky Chops," the dinner lady said as she popped another cheeseburger onto his plate. "Don't overdo it now, sonny," she added kindly, reaching out and patting his mountainous belly.

"Don't worry about me—me champion!" he said, putting down his tray momentarily to beat his chest, Tarzan style. "Me eat four burgers in one sitting!"

This brave display attracted giggles and stifled snorts from a nearby table. But Maggie, the dinner lady, grinned and gave him a wink. What she liked about Porky was that even in the state he was in, he could still laugh at himself. She had been first to call him "Porky Chops," in the full hearing of other students too; the name had stuck and was then shortened to just "Porky."

It took several minutes for Porky to reach his place again, he walked so slowly. He took up two chairs instead of one, which was awkward. Once settled, he quickly started munching. Time was running out. After the first few bites, he began feeling a bit dizzy, and his tummy gurgled dismally. He shrugged to himself; he should probably stop now, but hey—he was a growing boy! He needed his nourishment. After all, he would be known as the boy who ate four burgers in one sitting. As he raised the burger to his lips for another chomp, he swayed in his seat and, without warning, suddenly fell off and crashed to the floor with a thump. In the few seconds before he passed out, Porky saw Maggie frantically grab the phone and start dialling. Then a wave of blackness covered him, numbing his senses, and he knew no more.

♦

At six o'clock on September 14, Kitchi had just woken up and was staring at the ceiling. Two hundred years ago on that date, white settlers had returned home, tired and dusty after a week's sport; behind them, strewn on the plain, lay thousands of slain bison. Today was the day of the Buffalo Dance. Kitchi sighed; he didn't care. He hated the annual Pow Wow celebration on the reservation in Wind River, Wyoming.

♦

At one o'clock, Porky groggily opened one eye, dimly aware of someone standing over him. He felt strong arms lift him up and put him on a stiff board. After strapping him onto it, the board was lifted unsteadily (not very high) and carried towards a sort of wailing noise. Porky felt a tingle dancing down his vertebrae; was he in an ambulance? But . . . wait. There was nothing wrong with him—was there? These people had no right, interrupting him in the middle of a meal. He started to struggle but felt a large, firm hand press down on his chest, and a face appeared above him. The face was speaking in muffled tones, and he thought he could just make out the words "you" and "okay." Porky tried to nod, but that was when he felt the plastic mask on his face with tubes dangling. "Euhhh," was all he could manage. Then he felt a touch on his forehead, and his mother's face looked down at him. He blinked up at her and saw that she was rocking backwards and forwards and blubbering into her hands. He'd never seen her cry like that before.

◆

At three o'clock on September 14, Abala, having run into the Ethiopian highlands, crouched behind the prickly undergrowth and waited till the soldiers had gone. At the same time in Addis Ababa, local officials shook hands with foreign investors after signing away 2,500,000 hectares of land in the heart of Ethiopia. Scratched and dazed, Abala crept slowly over to where the soldiers had dragged the boy's body. He was lying on his back with his eyes open, staring at the sky. They had cut his tongue out. He must have died of shock.

◆

At half past one, the ambulance carrying Porky and his mother stopped at a traffic light. "Bloody hell," swore the driver. Porky felt his wrist being held; a face peered closely into his.

"Get a move on—we're losing him!"

Next came an ear-splitting sound, and the vehicle jolted forward and raced ahead. Everything inside shook. Porky was aware of his mother making a noise similar to the ambulance siren. As they came to an abrupt halt outside the hospital, he braced every muscle in his flabby body for what would come next.

♦

At eight-thirty on September 14, just as *Amelia Witheria*, the last of the orchid species, breathed its last breath, wilted, and died, Amy Wong started work on her class presentation, "The Face of China." For once, Amy's mind drew a blank. But she had to excel—or she wouldn't be first in the class.

♦

At one o'clock and thirty-three minutes, Porky was wheeled into Accident and Emergency; he was aware of many people clustered around him. In the next moment they were all running alongside the trolley as he travelled at a great speed along the corridor. Then he rounded a few corners and was taken into a dim room, where he was placed on a bed almost as hard as the uncomfortable stretcher. A gaggle of people were in attendance, all muttering about drips and oxygen. When they had finished fixing things around the bed, they put a mask on his face and told him to breathe deeply. Then he was pushed into a room labelled "Operating Theatre." And that was when his heart stopped.

♦

At five o'clock and thirty-five minutes on September 14, while shoppers in supermarkets all over the United States selected bags of frozen french fries for their evening meal, Bina sat on her bed, wailing while she clenched the bedcovers in her fists. Her little dog jumped up to lick her tears. "Oh, Pluto, it is impossible," she sobbed. "Move away from India to marry Ajit? I cannot do it."

♦

At one o'clock and thirty-six minutes, Porky watched from above while three theatre nurses and two doctors battled to revive his failing heart. He wouldn't remember any of this afterwards, of course. It was one of those inexplicable psychological moments (or perhaps it was supernatural) that happen to only a few. And now Porky was one of them. He thought it remarkable that there was so much activity in that small room, while he lay so perfectly still. But most of all, he was shocked by his enormous bulk as he lay on that operating table. He looked more like a huge animal than a human being, and he was only a sixteen-year-old boy! In a way, it was the first time he'd ever really seen his whole body. He had always avoided looking in a mirror, unless absolutely necessary. Certainly never a full-length one; what agony that was! Of course, sometimes he'd catch a glimpse of his reflection in a shop window and feel truly horrified. But now the truth was laid bare. And on top of it all, he was dying! A surge of anger coursed through his veins, making him shake. *No! No more!* Porky decided to live.

♦

At eight o'clock and thirty-seven minutes on September 14, Mr. Corporate of Food Masters Inc. was busy at his desk banking his millions of dollars online interrupted only by incoming messages to his phone, each one announced by a resounding chime. Yet it was a softer, but more urgent, noise which finally got his attention. A simple cardboard box on the windowsill was vibrating and moving ever so slowly towards the edge. Mr. Corporate glanced up just before it fell to the floor. An object rolled out on impact, travelled across the floor and stopped at his feet. It was glowing deep purple. At the same moment a strange scorch mark appeared on the map of the company's global empire. The brown smudge, accompanied by a burning smell, was visible over Scotland. Mr. Corporate's chest grew tight, so tight that he could hardly breathe.

◆

At seven forty-five in the morning of September 14, just as another 2,500 acres of cleared rainforest was being burnt to make way for beef farming, Serenity was crouched down on her hands and knees at the edge of the estuary to see what was making that eerie squeaking sound. She found a sea turtle with a plastic bag lodged deep in its throat, choking for air.

◆

At one forty-five, Porky opened his eyes. The light was dim, and there was no sound except for some light chattering far in the distance. Apart from realising he was now awake, the immediate sensation Porky felt was terrible, excruciating pain in his stomach. The pain was tearing him apart and threatening to engulf him completely. It took all the little strength he had to open his mouth and call for help. His weak pleas went unnoticed. No one came; the tinkling chatter in the background continued.

◆

At six o'clock on September 14, while tons of unused food from the FairPrice supermarket chain in the United Kingdom was loaded into garbage trucks, Jasmine was watering her camels. She was being ultra-careful with every drop, and the camels didn't like that.

♦

At exactly the same time on September 14, as the huge carcass of the second last whale in the world was being picked over by scavenging piranha fish, Lastro lay huddled, his teeth chattering, among the fishing nets for warmth. A spurt of water went up in the distance against the brightening sky. A lonely whale lingered in the shallow waters. That was Dobi, his only friend.

♦

At two o'clock, Porky was being given a morphine injection. He lay back, sweating and exhausted, from his fight to attract someone's attention. He had miraculously overturned the bedside table by pushing for twenty whole minutes with his massive shoulder; the table lay on its side on the floor, its contents scattered. Another nurse was picking up broken pieces of glass, and the two nurses continued their conversation as if Porky wasn't even there. He was feeling angry and confused and didn't know what to do about it. He let his eyes wander around the room, which was brighter now that the curtains had been drawn back. It was an average sort of hospital room: plain white walls, a TV screen positioned high up in one corner, the obligatory picture or two. Some long dappled shadows played on the walls, indicating trees outside. For some reason, this blurry image of normality made Porky want to cry. But just in time, the morphine kicked in, and he relaxed as the room began to drift away. But one thing remained: a picture on the wall. It was getting bigger, not smaller, and then Porky recognised it. It was Van Gogh's *Sunflowers,* and its petals were fluttering in the breeze from the open window. Were they waving at him? *Is this drug-induced?* Porky felt himself smiling. But as the pain receded, he distinctly heard a voice saying, "Don't worry, Porky. Don't worry."

CHAPTER 1

Porky

Porky refused to come out from under the covers. He kept his eyes pressed shut. *Maybe they'll just go away,* he thought hopefully. *There's no way I'm talking to* them*!*

"Phil, you'll be back on your feet in no time, luv," his mother offered.

"Hey, lad, a month from now and we'll be off to watch the football," Dad said, enthused.

No answer.

"Maybe later this week I can sneak you in some ketchup-flavoured crisps—just a treat, eh?" Mum tried again.

His parents were promising him **food**? Were they complete idiots? There was a bit of whispering with a nurse before the door closed. Porky came up for air.

"Yeah, and good riddance!" he growled under his breath, but the nurse heard and threw him a strange look.

Ever so slowly, he turned on his side, grimacing as he edged himself into a comfortable position. He stared at the rain hitting the window, watching all the little trickles as they made their way down the pane. Nothing else to do anyway. The TV was on the other side of the room; four hours on each side, the nurse had said. The whole of the Glasgow skyline was visible against a grey sky, and all he could do was gaze at it while waiting for the pain injection to

1

wear off. Not a pleasant prospect, really. Sure, he had gifts: cards, flowers, and a few games and CDs, but for now, all Porky wanted was silence.

But he couldn't stop himself from thinking all kinds of things at full speed, mostly the events of the last few days: collapsing at school, the ambulance ride here with Mum snivelling beside him, and then preparing for the operation. Wow—it was so hard to empty his mind. Should he say, "Ommmmmmmm" or something?

He nearly laughed at his own joke when his eyes found the card his class had sent him displayed on his bedside table. He hadn't really had a chance to read it before now. It was handmade with a computer clip art picture of a cartoon elephant (bad choice there) in a hospital bed and "Get Well Soon" pasted underneath. Everyone in his class had signed it, but only a few had written personal comments: "Get well soon," mostly, "Get better," "See ya soon," "Lucky you—no homework!" (yeah, ha ha). Then he saw Beaver's name: "Chin up, mate," he'd written. What was this? "We'll miss you, Philip," signed Allie and Greta. Two quite cool girls really . . . A lump rose in his throat.

He hadn't known he had any friends, well except Beaver, but Beaver had no friends either, because he was fifteen and still in the Cub Scouts. Nobody knew why. (He was in the beaver group, so that's why they called him "Beaver." He kind of looked like a beaver too.)

Porky felt himself smiling. Then stopped. That means he must look like a pig.

Well . . . of course . . . yes . . . he supposed people might see him like that. His heart felt heavy. His thoughts went back to his parents. Ketchup-flavoured crisps! Typical! They'd always just let him stuff his face. No limits. *It's their fault,* he decided. *Why have they done this to me?*

A nurse came in and interrupted his train of thought.

"Hello, Philip," she said. "If you need to use the bathroom, I'll show you how to walk with your drip stand."

So with some help, he rolled himself out of bed and onto the floor. Then slowly, with one arm gripping a chair, he managed to hoist himself onto his knees and finally his feet. He felt a little shaky but shuffled slowly along the corridor, pulling the stand carrying his drip bag carefully so as not to tangle the tubes. Whoever passed by couldn't help but look him up and down because of his enormous size. He knew that. He lived with it every day. Once, a bus didn't stop to pick him up. Probably thought he'd be too heavy. He'd always made a joke out of it before, but now, in this vulnerable state, it wasn't funny anymore; something was giving way inside him—he'd had enough.

As he lumbered unsteadily along, still musing on Allie and Greta's words ("miss you") and enjoying the warm feeling it gave, a smell jolted him out of his daydreaming.

What is that? It's horrible! But weirdly, along with the smell came a familiarity which was strangely comforting in this sterile place. He turned the corner and reached a dead end—the nurses' common room—and there, tumbling out of an already over-full bin, were the polystyrene boxes containing remnants of food that he knew only too well—McDollar's takeaway meals. But now the sight and smell of those empty cartons disgusted him, making him feel a revulsion he'd never known before. He stopped and stared at them for a long time. How many times had he spent Friday and Saturday nights in front of the TV, gobbling down one of those dinners? Waves of horror and regret flooded over him.

What a disaster, he thought. He caught sight of himself in a glass door as he made quickly away from the scene. *Crime scene, more like,* he thought, smiling weakly. Even now, Porky could enjoy his own jokes. But the shape he glimpsed gave him such a start that he made a slight choking sound. Whether there was something wrong with the glass or not, Porky looked enormous. *Nothing's changed at all—I'm just the same,* he agonised in dismay.

Now all he wanted was to get under the bedcovers again, so he tried to find his way back. But, just then, a group of kids, younger than him and dressed in pyjamas, came careering round the corner, narrowly missing him. Porky's drip fell and got tangled in his ankles, and there was an embarrassing moment as he realised there was no way he could bend over to pick it up. Those little kids weren't at all fazed, though. One of them got on his knees, straightened the tube, and handed it back with a shy smile. Porky was surprised there weren't the usual sniggers; strangely enough, they seemed kind of in awe of his size, as if he were some giant whale or something. It was then, as they moved off, that he noticed they were all bald.

And there was his nurse again, come to fetch him back.

"Why are those kids bald?" he asked.

"Oh, they're from the Terminal Ward," she said. "They've got cancer."

Porky felt a shock go through his body. *Terminal? What, as in Terminator?*

"What made them so sick?"

"Don't you go worrying about things like that," she said in a sickly sweet voice. And then she patted his head as if he were a dog.

The doctor was waiting in his room. No chance of getting under the covers now.

"How are you, Philip?" the doctor boomed.

"All right."

"Just all right?" Still booming.

"Well, I'm still fat, aren't I?" Porky glowered. He eyed the bed; he just wanted to get in and not talk to anyone.

"But still alive!" Of course he was still alive.

"It was only a gastric band op. Why am I still here? It's been over a week."

"Philip," the doctor said, lowering his voice at last, "your heart stopped during the operation."

Porky's heart did stop again for a split-second at those words, and then he half leapt; half threw himself on the bed, causing nurses to scuttle in all directions to try to save him from falling (because it wouldn't be easy to lift a patient like Porky from the floor).

"I think we should talk this over with your parents," he heard the doctor saying.

"I don't want to *ever* see my parents again!" Porky screamed at the top of his voice.

Night fell. Porky was still under the covers. At last the lights went out. He resurfaced, and slowly, gradually managed to sit up. A huge wave of nausea had enveloped him all afternoon. Maybe the smell had brought it on. He was free from it at last and hungry, but for once not for food—for knowledge. He pulled out his laptop and got online.

Okay, where to start? He started with "terminal"; the word that really spooked him.

"Terminal—a definition." He typed the words in decisively.

Terminal: undergoing the last stage of a fatal disease. He wondered if his disease was fatal.

"Cancer."

Cancer is a leading cause of death among children in the United States. *Wow!*

Tomatoes contain lycopene, an anti-carcinogenic substance which is only released when cooked. *Strange, but interesting.*

Turmeric, the yellow spice commonly found in curries, has been found to have anti-carcinogenic properties. *Should feed the terminal kids turmeric-flavoured tomatoes then!*

Porky chuckled, but stopped himself—that wasn't fair. This wasn't a joke. But rather life or death. He thought of the terminal kids sleeping in their ward, the moonlight shining off their bald heads. He shivered a little and felt somehow scared. Was the food in hospital all right for them? Would it help them? He didn't know, because he was on liquid food only. What about the school meals which millions of British children ate, day in, day out? No, not good. Definitely not good. Burgers and chips ad infinitum.

"Fast food." He typed quickly, feeling tension rise through his body.

Top carcinogenic foods to avoid: 1. potato chips and french fries 2. hotdogs

Top anti-carcinogenic foods to eat: 1. berries 2. green vegetables

What was the Pesco's slogan? "Five a day." Eat five raw fruits and vegetables a day. Now he remembered—hadn't someone campaigned about all this years back? Tried to change the school meal menus in schools. Yeah—Jimmy Olives, the cool chef on telly. But nobody paid any attention; he was beaten down. But why, when it made so much sense? Porky slept then, his mind swimming with images of giant burgers bigger than him, falling on him, and threatening to smother him to death.

He awoke to find a young woman standing at the bottom of his bed. "Ms. Sophie Grayling" said her name tag.

"Good morning, Philip," she said. "I'm Ms. Grayling, your councillor. You've slept late—what were you up to last night?"

How did she know? How did she know that he'd eventually drifted off after researching every possible site on fast food and how it's made? So he had to go to her office in half an hour. Councillor? What, another diet?

Porky really didn't want to go. These days, he just wanted to be on his own. Once he reached Ms. Grayling's office, there was a fifteen-minute wait. Luckily, the waiting room wall had a map on it; Porky loved nothing better than to get lost in a map. So he was disappointed when the door opened and a kid came out—a terminal kid! Porky's gaze followed the kid as he walked down the corridor. He was lost in thought for a moment. Ms. Grayling looked bemused when he finally turned to look at her. She motioned him to go inside.

"Why are those kids bald?" Porky's voice was hushed now.

"It's the treatment they get for cancer, it makes their hair fall out." She answered so easily and with a smile, as if it wasn't scary at all.

"What made them have . . . um . . . get so sick?"

"Well, there are many factors. Nobody knows for sure why one person gets cancer and another doesn't."

"But I read last night on the Internet about foods that are anti-carcinogenic," Porky offered, feeling pleased and hopeful, "like cooked tomatoes and turmeric, for example."

"Yes, yes, that's all very well—*but* none of it has been proven. Far too few reliable clinical tests have been done on food." (She emphasised *but* very nasally, as if talking down to him.) "The only way forward is to research into new drugs, to manage and . . . eventually cure cancer. Up till now the medicines we're administering are by far the best treatment for those children."

"But some foods are clearly cancer-causing, aren't they?" Porky tried again.

Ms. Grayling clearly wasn't interested in this topic; she looked directly at him and said, "What about *you*?" (Again with a nasal emphasis.)

"Oh. Well, we all know why I'm so fat!" *Might as well get to the point,* he thought.

"And why is that?" Ms. Grayling looked him straight in the eye.

"Maybe someone stuffed me so full because they wanted me to burst!" Porky's voice was rising.

Ms Grayling didn't bat an eyelid as she said, "It's normal to be angry with your parents, Philip." And then she added, "For a while, that is."

There was a long silence. Porky felt confused; there was so much inside of him rolling about, images he couldn't control, stuff he didn't understand.

"Yeah," he said finally, "yeah . . . but . . . you know—it's more than that." He faltered, trying to grapple with his thoughts. "It's everything."

"Everything?"

"Yeah—the shops, the supermarkets—the things they make us eat."

"Make us?" Ms. Grayling interjected. "No, I don't think so, Philip . . ."

"They do," he interrupted. His voice was raised, almost tremulous.

He looked at his hands on his lap; they were shaking.

"Look at the adverts, everywhere," he began again. "For sweets, crisps, drinks—full of sugar—even energy drinks. Caffeine for kids—give us a break!" He was flushed now.

She stayed calm, looking at him as if to say, "Let it out."

"You may have a point there."

"And . . . and . . . why do our parents . . . ?" He couldn't continue.

"Why do your parents what?" she asked quietly.

"Why is it called a frigging 'Cheery Meal'?" Porky shouted. He wanted to punch a hole in the wall.

A long pause.

"Well, I can't answer you on all of those, Philip, but they're insightful questions to be asking."

Another pause. Porky was breathing loudly and too fast.

"It's not always somebody *else's* fault, Philip."

"Oh—so it's *mine* then, is it?" shouted Porky, imitating her increasingly irritating habit of emphasising words.

She narrowed her eyes then; he could tell she didn't like him very much. "Until you stop being angry with your parents—and everyone else for that matter—we're not going to get very far."

His first session with his councillor was already a disaster. He had to get out of there. He felt shaken up and in need of fresh air, so he made his way towards the glass door at the end of the corridor. It was a fire escape, with old-fashioned iron stairs leading down. He had to descend really slowly, but eventually he made it. He flopped down onto a wall. Now where was he?

It took a while for him to make out where he was, because it was all so beautiful. Everything was so, so green and waving slightly in the wind. He looked up and saw apples bobbing. He was in a garden, as if from another time; at least that's what Porky felt, as he'd never seen anything like this before. The greenness and the breeze soothed him, and he shut his eyes just to listen and to feel.

This is the kind of place anyone could get better in. He almost spoke aloud but stopped short, as he was aware that someone was watching him.

And when he opened his eyes, indeed there was something gazing at him. He looked up into the face of a large sunflower, nodding its head up and down at him as if to say:

"*Yes, Porky, yes.*"

CHAPTER 2

Kitchi

T he school yard was perched on the edge of a cliff. It must have been the most uniquely positioned playground in the whole of America. Superlative in terms of stunning landscape all around and, at the same time, perhaps the most precarious, breaking all health and safety regulations. Of course, there was a high fence bolstered with concrete supports, but Kitchi was glad of this blip in the planning, because it gave him the best view any school kid could wish for at break time! He liked standing in the farthest corner, which projected out over the precipice; he felt that if he could jump, he would fly . . . over the wide plains, circling the dark green fir forests to the right and then swooping down across the silvery lake on the left, before rising high up the mountainside fast enough to be back in the yard before the end of recess! The land that his forefathers, free and proud, had roamed centuries ago was wild and beautiful. But Kitchi never thought of anything like that; he didn't see it that way. His only thought was of what lay beyond, of where he could fly to.

But today, everything reminded him of those ancient times. Couldn't shake it off. It was a week until the big Pow Wow in neighbouring Hot Springs. The whole population of Wind River Reservation in Wyoming, both young and old, took part in this yearly festival. It started with Culture and Customs Week at school and culminated with the grand Buffalo Dance in their own reservation the day after the Pow Wow. Preparations were already under way; he caught sight of two of his classmates practising some dance steps at the far end of the yard. *Idiots!* he thought. *I'm going for a smoke.*

Behind the toilets, all manner of things went on at break time. Here you could buy cigarettes and any kind of second-hand stuff for computers: music, films, games—you name it. Kitchi was always on the lookout for magazines, particularly ones on cars; even fashion would do, because he liked the photographs, which he cut out and made pictures of his own at home. But definitely nothing to do with sport, especially wrestling, which all the boys were into in a big way. It was important to be strong on the rez. Toughness counted. For most, there was no other choice. Nobody got rich here. (Except sometimes in the casino that the white folks attended.) There was no chance of building your own business. Most kids didn't finish school. Conditions were bad, too. Some neighbours didn't even live in proper houses. You could hear everything they said through the walls as you walked past. The place was a mess. There was no making it here. No wonder people wanted out.

Things were changing, though. Last year, a dozen or so kids left to go to university. Next year, there'd be more. Maybe in four year's time, he'd be one of them. The elders disapproved of all this; said it was the disease of the youth. Yeah, the youth were to blame for everything. Was wanting new things and looking ahead such a bad thing? Wasn't it better than being addicted to whiskey and playing cards?

The reservation made you like that. Restless.

He'd study design. Not engineering or medicine, like most kids wanted. He liked shapes and colour. The blues and yellows, sometimes purples of a butterfly's wings. The curve of an eagle's beak; the majestic sweep of its wings. In perfect symmetry, exact lines—such balance! Yes, these were good things, the things that Nature showed us—but to propel us into the future, to be more productive and useful.

His dream was to design aeroplanes; maybe even fighters! He regularly saw them fly overhead, because there was an air force base at Loon Lake nearby. Sometimes, when there were drills, the planes would fly really low, and he could even see the colours and the numbers. He'd run home and try to draw parts of those planes. They were so beautiful: noses like cones, gentle curved bodies, and wings with moving parts. (He knew Father had been called to meetings with the elders on account of those pictures.) *But so what?* he thought. *If we Native Americans, had the money we'd have planes, wouldn't we? We could put eagles' heads on the fronts or something, and paint chief logos on the sides. Yeah, it'd still be cultural!*

The school bell brought this wacky daydreaming to an abrupt end. *Ugh—more culture coming up,* he groaned inwardly. And so he dragged himself reluctantly towards the classroom again, for another gruelling session on the legend of the Buffalo Dance. As if he hadn't heard it a million times over.

The students of grade nine were preparing for Parents' Night, which was held prior to the Pow Wow and was a preview of the float and performance the school would put forward. Mr. Helaku called on Dyani to finish reciting "How the Bison Were Released on Earth." Kitchi's classmate stood up.

"This is an ancient Comanche and Apache legend," she chirped, smiling brightly.

Oh no—not this again, Kitchi thought, yawning. He wished he could look out the window for some relief, but the room had no view; it looked out on a brick wall. It was brightly painted with a mural, though, and he found himself following the lines and curves of a giant sunflower. The heritage of sunflower production had been last year's project for the lower grades, and Kitchi had enjoyed watching the kids paint it. He traced the large yellow petals round and round. Beautiful curves. And good perspective on the rows and rows of sunflowers in the fields in the background. Once he'd scanned the whole mural, he saw something he'd never noticed before: the words of a Native colour legend:

"Every time you look at a sunflower, the whole world starts to smile."

Yeah right, snorted Kitchi to himself.

"And Kitchi," Mr. Helaku said, raising his voice, "the story of the Buffalo Dance is a legend from which of our Nations?"

"Blackfoot," Kitchi said in a deadpan voice. He didn't even look up. He could have given the answer in his sleep.

"Correct. Now, Leotie, could you and your partner come to the front and tell the class the famous story of the Buffalo Dance? Thank you. Don't forget to do the actions."

The girls sprang into action. No shortage of enthusiasm there.

The Buffalo Dance. He remembered last year's as if it were yesterday. He winced as the painful memory resurfaced, because Etchemin had been chosen to dance with the warriors. His younger brother. Why not him? Maybe due to disapproval of his love of art and design? Not very "brave-like" behaviour, he supposed. But he had felt pangs as he watched his brother dancing; pangs of jealousy? No, it was something else he had felt—a strange thrill, as if his whole body throbbed with the beat of the drums, and an electric charge coursed through his veins. He hadn't admitted this to anyone, of course, least of all to himself.

"What good is the annual re-enactment of this dance doing for our people these days?" a voice interrupted, challenging the teacher. "We don't hunt bison anymore. We buy our food from supermarkets!"

Euuhh? Kitchi was startled out of his reminisces. *True. So true. My thoughts entirely,* he silently agreed. He sat up straight now, nodding. Everyone was looking around to see who had spoken. It was a student who'd joined the class half way through the year, from another reservation. *Little Rock Rez,* he thought. But he didn't look very Native. His features did; perhaps his cheekbones weren't as wide as Kitchi's, or his eyes as almond shaped and dark, but it was the way he dressed that marked him as different. He was smart and trendy, and relaxed. You felt that he didn't need to prove anything, like everyone else did by pushing each other around.

"I mean," the new student went on, "this attachment to the past isn't feeding us today, is it? We're not learning anything new, moving with the times."

Kitchi kept on nodding, despite the grumbling that was growing louder around the class.

"Our legends are rich in wisdom and knowledge," shouted Guyapi, a popular student.

"Then why are you all so poor?" came the insulting answer.

Guyapi was up and out of his chair in an instant, shoving the new boy's desk into his chest with considerable force. It must have hurt, because the boy's face became almost purple as he tried not to cry out.

Once Mr. Helaku regained control of the class and calmed everyone down, he announced that this was certainly an interesting argument, which would be debated in class by two teams in two days' time, on the eve of the Pow Wow. Hands shot in the air, begging to be chosen for the team in support of the legends. Two were duly selected, and then the teacher looked straight at Kitchi and declared, "Kitchi, you were nodding strongly in agreement with John. You will join him on the second team."

So he doesn't use his Native name, he thought. He was shocked more by this than by being chosen for the debate.

"Listen up, everybody! In two days' time, our class will consider this question: The Buffalo Dance—relevant or not to our people today?"

It was official. It was in two days. Kitchi's mind went blank. What was he going to say?

"Hey, well done," John said. "Pleased to meet you, Kitchi, isn't it? I think we'll make a good team. Two heads are better than one, eh?"

And with that, John walked away, without offering any help. Kitchi's heart was thumping; he was really in a mess now.

After dinner, when most of the men gathered inside to play cards and smoke, Kitchi found solace in the quiet of the empty wooden veranda. It was cool out there. *Two days,* he thought, panicked. And that guy John had such confidence in him. His partner had obviously seen something of life, maybe he'd even travelled. In contrast, Kitchi knew nothing about anything! How the class were going to laugh. He shrunk inside himself at the thought.

Grandma came out now and sat down in her rocking chair. She was smoking her old pipe and rocked and smoked, watching Kitchi carefully. "You should go and talk to your uncle," she said. "He wrote a book about the bison and our Ancestors. He can help you."

Kitchi sighed. Obviously, Grandma didn't know that he was on the *other* side of the debate.

"Yeah, sure. He can help. I'll talk to him," he promised, just to keep her happy.

And just then, as if to make matters worse, Kitchi's brother, Etchemin, and his friends descended onto the veranda. They began polishing the bison horn he'd won as an award at the dance last year. There was a lot of monkeying about and laughing, as they each took a turn holding the revered horn aloft and breaking into some dance steps and howls. Now this was more than Kitchi could stand, so he slunk off into the shadows of his bedroom.

The next day, however, he did call on his uncle. He found him in his little office, packing a suitcase.

"Hello Kitchi!" he said, smiling. "A little bird told me you're going to be the star of the class."

"I wouldn't exactly say that," Kitchi said quietly, and then he ventured, "Where are you going?"

"On a tour of the United Kingdom, and then onto Europe to promote my book. I'll fly first to Glasgow, Scotland. I'm going to visit some schools there too."

"Why, Uncle?" Kitchi blurted out. "Why is it so important for others to know about our people and their history? It's over now. Shouldn't we look ahead? Prepare for the future?" His voice was so strained that his uncle looked thoughtfully at him for a moment and then motioned him to sit down.

Uncle sat opposite him and began, "It's not about the past or the future—it's about now. Our legends remind us about who we are, now and forever. It's not wrong to be proud of it, Kitchi."

"Proud of what?" Kitchi sighed. And then he felt something rise in his chest. "Of this?" he said, jerking his arm in the direction of an open window, half rising from his seat. "Of all the squalor and hopelessness our people have to live with?" When he turned back to his uncle, his face had a crazed look about it.

"People have done this to us—it's not who we are. Instead, we are a proud people because Mother Earth is our soul."

Words like those always made Kitchi frustrated. "I don't know what you're talking about!" he shouted, almost seething.

"Do you know who you are, Kitchi?"

"Huh? Of course I do!"

A silence followed. Maybe Uncle allowed it, or maybe he didn't know what to say next. Kitchi was thinking hard.

Suddenly, Uncle reached forward and grabbed Kitchi's knees playfully. "Hey! I want you to help me choose a headdress to take."

"Are you actually going to wear one of those? That's so naf!"

Uncle wasn't going to back down. "No, Kitchi, people love it when they see me in a chief's headdress!"

Kitchi looked over at the collection hanging on the long wall. There were some impressive arrangements, but to him they looked faded and old—just like their stories. But one stood out; it had green, black, and white feathers laid out in stripes, the colours alternating as they moved around in an arc. They were the colours of the fighter plane that had flown low over the valley only yesterday.

"I know who I am," he almost whispered.

"Oh?"

"I want to design aeroplanes. I want to fly." Kitchi's voice was stronger now.

"Kitchi, that's not who you are. That's what you want to do."

There was another long pause.

16

"That one," Kitchi said, pointing to the "fighter plane" headdress. "Take that one." He began to head for the door.

"See you at the Pow Wow!" called his uncle.

"If I'm still here!" Kitchi joked back. But deep down, he meant it. He would have given anything to be a million miles away. Away from the class debate, away from the Pow Wow—away from everything.

On the morning of the debate, Kitchi woke up early. It took him half a second to remember what day it was and another quarter of a second for his stomach to start churning. He'd tried to prepare last night, but his mind wouldn't cooperate. He couldn't come up with the right words; even a clear argument escaped him. A slight movement outside told him Grandma was in her rocking chair. He pulled himself up slowly from his bed; his papers still occupied half the floor.

"You awake, Kitchi? Come out here for some milk," the old woman commanded from the veranda. Grandma had the good sense to leave her pipe unlit till the family had finished breakfast. But she was itching to start smoking, hence was hurrying everyone along. "Kitchi," she said after she had cajoled him through all his preparations to leave, "today, in your class, whatever it's called— just be true to yourself. Do you hear me?"

"Yes, Grandma." *I don't know what you mean, but yes, Grandma.* He felt so despondent.

"Be true to yourself, I say."

The classroom was brimming over with excitement. This debate was the first of its kind in Wind River Reservation School. Even the principal was in attendance. Kitchi sat next to John at the front of the room; the other team was on the other side. A sea of faces was in front of him, bobbing up and down, smiling, whispering to each other. He felt sick. His legs trembled under the table.

Once the teacher had explained the rules (each team member would speak once, for three minutes, with team members taking alternating turns), the debate opened with Guyapi. And he was powerful.

17

"We are a proud people," he began, "and we have survived what the white man did to us. We were stripped of all that we had: the Bison. But they did not know that even without our Bison—we still live on!"

His delivery had force, and each word crackled with tension— you could feel the sparks fly out from him into the classroom. As students recognised those ancient truths, murmurs of approval spread around like a fire catching. A few clapped and some others started beating on the desks in a mock drumbeat.

"The Buffalo Dance . . ." His voice went an octave higher, and then he paused for effect. The class became hushed, waiting. ". . . honours the relationship we had with the Bison. They were taken away, but they live on—in our souls! Our dance drives away the evil spirit of famine!" He was shouting now, and the class loved it. Glorious whoops and thumping of desks accompanied the cheers.

Now John stood up. Gradually, the noise died down, but then someone laughed out loud in a taunting way, as if to say, "Beat that!"

John wasn't fazed in the least. He quietly scanned the room, looking into the faces of his classmates, and said simply, in a steady voice, "There are no bison." And then he sat down.

What? That's it? Kitchi, aghast, watched the students first hesitate for a second before breaking into uncontrollable laughter. *You're leaving it at that?* He felt himself near to internal collapse. John, in his desire for theatrical effect, had left it all up to him. But his mouth had just dried up.

Fala was on her feet now, looking supremely confident. "To walk in the way of the Natives is to be in harmony with Nature and the circle of life." She smiled contentedly. "In our re-enactment of the Buffalo Dance, we remember how our ancestors trusted in Mother Nature to provide them with life. They felt this oneness with the Earth and the Bison. They felt it in their *souls*." She managed to draw this word out with great emphasis. "So be proud of who you are and carry on the spiritual traditions of your forefathers." The clapping had already started, but she stopped her classmates by raising her hand in the old style of Native greeting, holding her open palm out vertically. And then she finished triumphantly with, "Tread lightly and walk in peace."

The students were completely won over. All of them answered by raising their palms back at her. Thunderous applause followed.

Their teacher struggled to get everyone calm again and then said, "Now you, Kitchi." He threw him a sympathetic look.

Everything seemed to be in slow motion; the students were still jostling themselves back into their seats, but all eyes were looking his way. He felt himself rise and clear his throat, almost involuntarily. He knew he had to speak, but his mind was totally blank. And suddenly he was saying, "Hello, I'm Kitchi."

There was a roar of laughter at that. His voice had sounded tremulous. Their noise filled both the room and his mind.

He swallowed hard and tried again. "A lot of what has been said already is interesting and . . . um . . ." He searched for a word. ". . . soulful." Another pause. "But is it applicable?" *Applicable?* he thought. *Didn't know I knew that word!*

He could sense that there were many listening who weren't quite sure of what "applicable" meant either. It got a bit quieter. "What I mean is: how do these traditions affect our lives today?" *Affect? Will that work?* "Does the Buffalo Dance change, um . . . make anything different?" He looked at his classmates and could tell that perhaps some were confused as how to answer. *Okay, what next?* He thought of Grandma. *Be true to myself.*

"I'm only asking because I ask myself all the time!" Someone in the front row smiled. "Do we think of this when we raise our chickens? Or sheep or goats? I don't know. All I know is that we buy food from shops . . . and . . ." *Be honest*, he urged himself. "I mean, I don't feel this soul thing. I don't understand a lot of what is said about being in harmony with Nature." The room was silent now. He hesitated and then went for it. "All I want is a job and a future in the real world." Kitchi could swear he saw glimmers of recognition . . . maybe even agreement? He relaxed slightly and had a thought. Could he pull it off? "And . . ." he braved a smile, "there are no bison!"

It ended with smiles and claps. The girls were smiling at him *a lot!* But when the vote came, Fala held up her hand in the old Native salute, and her team duly won massive applause and (almost) all the votes. It was over. They'd lost. He was disappointed but felt good somehow.

Dyani and Leotie waved goodbye to him. "Good job, Kitchi— see you at the Pow Wow tomorrow!" they chorused.

But late that night, as he lay on his bed, Kitchi knew he couldn't face the Pow Wow. He didn't want to go through the motions anymore. To wear a jaded costume, paint his face like a clown—no, he wouldn't do it. He would say he was sick.

It worked. He was left alone. Except for a dozen or so of the very old and some newborn babies, the reservation was empty that day. Peace and quiet. But it was a bleak place to find solace in. No inspiration here to soothe a troubled mind. Kitchi turned left at the bottom of the main road and headed up towards the school. His aim was to reach his favourite spot: the far corner of the school yard. Once there, Kitchi pressed his body against the fence and closed his eyes. A strong wind was blowing that day, and it blew the smells of the plain, the forest, the water of the lake into his face. After breathing it all in for a moment or two, he felt himself lift his arms to either side of him, his fingers stretched wide open, and press them with force onto the fence. *What am I doing?* he thought. But it didn't matter; there was no one to see. He must have stayed like that, arms held out, eyes closed, for an age, till his muscles ached with the exertion. Finally, he looked up at the sky.

I'll do it one day, he thought. *I'll leave this place. I'll be somebody and do something that matters!* He almost spoke to the blue expanse of another place, another time.

"Go down on the plain."

Kitchi heard the voice as clear as day. He dropped his arms quickly and stood still, looking around nervously. Had anyone seen him? The place was deserted and silent; only the wind whistled gently.

"Kitchi—go down on the plain."

He was scared now, because he really *had* heard a voice. And yet there was no one there. Then a strange thing happened: his fingertips started tingling ever so slightly, but enough for him to notice. The voice came again as the tingling increased.

"Go down on the plain. I'm waiting for you there."

A strong gust of wind blew on him now; his long black hair tangled in his face, his shirt flapped. Okay, he would go. The wind wanted him to fly. Maybe this was his answer? Then Kitchi was running, fast, to a place in the fence where he knew there was a broken part. He squeezed through the gap and began stumbling down the slope, using his hands to steady himself as stones and earth were dislodged and tumbled down ahead of him. For the last several feet, he slid on his bottom till he reached flat ground. He raised himself up and looking a very different Kitchi now: clothes, arms, and face were smudged with brown earth; face flushed and panting, he gazed around him. The plain was empty and quiet. He walked a dozen steps or so. *There's nothing here. What was I thinking?*

And then he saw it. Less than a hundred feet away, standing in a little glade near a dead tree, was a bison. It was grazing, lifting its large hairy head intermittently and chewing, shaking it from side to side to ward off the flies. It was real, all right. He could smell it—a pungent smell that made his nostrils itch. He desperately wanted to scratch his nose but, frozen with fear, he dared not move.

The bison saw Kitchi. And their eyes stayed locked on each other for what seemed a very long time. Each stood motionless. The tension was broken finally when the buffalo let out a loud snort, and then the beast began to stamp its front hoof up and down. Kitchi watched as little clods of earth were flung in the air. One landed not far from him. *Oh my God—it's going to charge!* Kitchi couldn't think what to do next.

It didn't, though; it only moved closer to Kitchi's left side, away from the dead tree. He knew that dead tree. As a young boy, he and his friends had dared each other to run onto the plain as far as the tree and touch it. It was magic, they said. It gave you power, they tempted. But Kitchi had never got as far as this. And now here he was.

His fingers were tingling again, stronger now; they felt so hot. And, as well as the fear, Kitchi was aware of another sensation— hunger. For some reason he couldn't understand, because he'd had breakfast not long ago, he felt very, very hungry. The feeling grew until it became an ache in his stomach, and he could bear it no longer. It took over his whole being till he was only conscious of that awful pain, his hot and tingling fingers, and his beating heart. The bison's eyes were on him again. It was moving slowly closer.

"You need me, Kitchi. You and I are one."

Kitchi had one, terrible thought. He was going to have to kill it, or be killed. A sudden movement to his right made his eyes dart in that direction. There, dangling from the dead tree, was a bow. He had to get it. But where were the arrows? So many thoughts raced through his mind, but there was no time. He made a dash for the tree. The bison started stamping his feet; it was moving faster and was nearly behind him now. Kitchi could only just still see its brown mass far to the left. He sped and almost leapt to take hold of the bow; he'd never moved so fast in all his life. Something was on his back; a weight jiggled up and down. What was it? But there wasn't a moment to find out as, once the bow was in his hands, the great beast was upon him. He looked straight into its eyes.

"You need me, Kitchi."

Was it going to charge? Did it want to kill him?

And somehow, in an instant, without a moment's hesitation, Kitchi's right hand, fingers tingling and throbbing all the time, reached behind his shoulder and pulled an arrow from a quiver he'd not known was there. He pulled the bowstring tight, placed the arrow, and shot. How he did it, he would never know. In that moment, there were no thoughts—only action. Once delivered, he restrung in a flash and shot another. The bison gave a great groan and thudded to the ground.

At that sound, Kitchi turned and ran. He ran until he could run no farther. He ran up the rocky slope, through the gap in the fence, back to the safety of the schoolyard. At last he dared to look down. His trembling hands gripped the wire in an attempt to keep his weak legs from buckling under him. As his chest heaved painfully up and down, he scanned the horizon. He quickly found the dead tree. But there was nothing else there. The plain was empty.

Tears were flowing now. Unstoppable. Not until he found his bed again. Until he slept a little from sheer exhaustion. Till his family were back from the Pow Wow and peeked into his bedroom to see him sleeping, just as they'd left him.

♦

The Buffalo Dance was here at last! The most important day of the year for Wind River Reservation; a huge tent had been erected in the centre, as usual. That evening, the same routine would be taking place in every home: costumes that were worn year after year were being taken out of plastic bags or battered suitcases, dusted down, and ironed out a little. Mothers were dressing their children, who wouldn't stay still but laughed and jumped in front of the mirror. Fathers were solemnly brushing out their long hair; daughters helped to braid it. If the family had the privilege of having a warrior under their roof, everyone would be looking on as he applied war paint to his face, all gazing silently in awe at the transformation.

Kitchi could hear the commotion in the other room. No one had disturbed him. He guessed they must have accepted by now his stand on things and presumed he wasn't interested. He sat up; he could just see the outline of the great tent against the grey, dusky sky. People were streaming towards it in crowds, some holding loft torches. The excitement in their voices drifted in the open window. He caught glimpses of shining faces. The beauty of the scene struck him unexpectedly, and a lump came into his throat. *To walk in the way of the Natives is to be in harmony with Nature and the Circle of Life.* He remembered Fala's speech. *Is that what these people are doing?*

He stood at the open window, watching, until he became aware that he was the only one left at home; in fact, the only one left outside of that tent. *These people—or my people?* Kitchi was feeling strange. He tried not to think while grasping at this new sensation.

Bewildered, he reached into the back of the cupboard for last year's costume. And without turning the lights on, he got dressed slowly in the moonlight. It was a young brave's outfit; the white feathers marked him out as an apprentice. His mother had chosen blue cloth to match the sky that Kitchi spent so much time gazing up into. As he moved quickly around the room, because he was now very late, the pebbles and bones that Grandma had sewn onto his waistcoat bounced off his body. He noticed and smiled. And suddenly, there was his image in the mirror, and it made him gasp. A boy from another age stood there, with strong burning light glinting in his eyes; those eyes that had flooded with tears only hours ago. What had happened to him on the plain? He had killed a bison. He could hardly believe it. But no time for thinking—he was late.

At the entrance to the tent stood a man who knew his uncle. When he recognised Kitchi, he smiled and said, "Tread lightly and walk in peace."

"Em . . . yes, same to you," Kitchi said, awkwardly returning the greeting.

He'd missed the official opening formalities. The dance was about to begin. There was so much smoke from pipes that it was hard to see anything. Kitchi pushed himself to the front. Drums began to beat slowly, softly, and in the light of the blazing torches, with all that smoke around, there was an atmosphere of danger. Kitchi could feel his own heart beat; he had started to feel really nervous.

The drumbeat quickened now and was accompanied by ghoulish screams and high-pitched wailing. This was the song of the Buffalo Dance—and it was truly frightening. Out of the smoky gloom, from four directions, suddenly sprang four tribesmen. Their human form looked totally outlandish, covered with circles and semi-circles of long white, black, and yellow feathers. Two even longer, and strikingly red, feathers stuck up from each head, unmistakeably emulating bison horns. The dancers' faces were painted stark white, with a blue band of colour over the eyes. The result was meant to be terrifying, to scare the evil spirit of famine away and draw the bison in for the kill (except that everyone, including Kitchi, knew who the warriors were).

The one on the far right was obviously Tall Stork, the foreman at the chicken factory, instantly recognisable by his protruding and crooked teeth. Next to him was the gas pump handler; Kitchi knew that double chin and fat belly anywhere. It didn't escape his notice that the third dancer still had his competition number from the Pow Wow yesterday stitched onto his sleeve, number 1517. Somehow, this took the magic out of the scene.

Still, as the drums beat on incessantly, as the screeching and yowling became more urgent, as the men's feet lifted and fell again and again in perfect synchrony with the music, as the huge feather circles twirled and whirled, as the ribbons and tassels swung to and fro, as the bells and rattles jingled, the faces of the dancers changed from those of the men he saw daily on the streets to those of wild creatures—eyes staring, heads jerking, and mouths grinning. They became creatures of the plain, hunting and the hunted, strong yet terrified, bound together by a will to survive, a will to find a bison or die. An urgency in the drumbeat flowed through the floor, through the soles of Kitchi's feet, up his legs, upwards still to his own torso, where he felt again a gnawing hunger—a tormentor dancing to the drumbeat of his heart. *They felt this oneness with the Earth and the bison.* Fala's words were in his head again. It was clear now. He thought he understood. The dancers had communicated it to him without a word. *They felt it in their souls.*

A nudging on his arm distracted him; someone was pushing a small piece of meat into his hands. All around him, people were popping the morsels into their mouths. There followed a thimble-sized glass of hot, fiery liquid. He closed his eyes and chewed on the meat, hoping it wasn't real buffalo. Once gulped, the drink almost set his mouth on fire. Dizzy now, he opened his eyes again. Everything had changed. The dancers were still swirling, drums drumming, but directly in front of him, only two or three feet away, stood the bison of the plain. Its head was massive. He would know those eyes anywhere. There was a mark on its neck where his arrow had gone in, but it was healed over and pink now. *It's still alive!* Kitchi thought. He looked around him. Nobody seemed concerned by the appearance of this huge, snorting creature and its overpowering smell.

"Yes, I'm alive. We are One."

"The Cycle of Life?" offered Kitchi. There was no answer, just a long silent stare that Kitchi took as a yes. Then the bison was speaking again.

"You will be honoured tonight. Take your prize and let your uncle give it to the one you will dream of. He is in pain but is brave. This boy will lead the Keepers."

Keepers? His first reaction was of confusion; who were they, and what had this to do with him? His second concern was a burning question. But he was afraid to ask. The answer came in an instant:

"You *will* fly, Kitchi. You have an important part in this—in time to come."

And now what? Two hands were on his shoulders: "Go on, Kitchi—it's your turn now." An elder presented him with the bison horn and firmly pushed him into the circle.

To his amazement, the dance was easy to follow. Once he'd mastered the basic steps of lifting one foot, then the other, then twist and turn, he moved effortlessly around the circle, flitting in and out between the other dancers. Round and around he turned, all the time clutching the bison horn close to his chest. His feathers, bobbing lightly up and down, took on the appearance of wings at either side of him. So he spun round and round, delighting in their flapping movements: at his sides, at his back, on his head. And soon, having lost all awareness of the crowd looking on, forgetting that his school friends and family were there, he was laughing. Spinning and laughing. Flying round the dance floor with feather wings. Flying. *This is who I am.*

It was to be a very long night. Celebrations went on unabated till almost morning. When Kitchi woke up, still lying in the corner of the veranda where he'd finally passed out, he surveyed the debris strewn everywhere: streamers, empty bottles, and burnt-out fireworks; he knew they'd had a really great party, even if he could hardly remember any of it! Suddenly, he fell serious, recalling, instead, his dream.

So vivid. It was as if he'd been with the boy in the ambulance and then beside his hospital bed. Able to touch him, speak to him. But the boy with the pasty face wasn't conscious; he groaned in pain. Just before Kitchi woke up, an oxygen mask was placed over the boy's face. His features were hard to figure out, but one thing Kitchi could be sure of—he was enormous! Like a great bear of the forest.

This boy will lead the Keepers. The bison's words rang out like an alarm clock. He could have lain there all morning, savouring the details of the dance . . . That had to wait—he had something to do. Reaching out to find the horn, his prize, carefully wrapped up in his clothes, he called out to Grandma, "When's Uncle leaving?"

"About now, I think. I just saw the taxi arrive."

Next he was hurtling through all the shortcuts he knew between the small wooden houses and camper vans, jumping aside to avoid the piles of old junk cluttering back yards.

Guyapi came into sight, sitting on some caravan steps. "Hey Kitchi," he called, "*cool* dancing, dude!"

Couldn't stop—he had no time, but he turned and waved. There was the taxi. Uncle was standing on the steps of his house, flanked by various important members of the community, shaking hands. Kitchi bombed up, breathless.

"Kitchi! You've come to say goodbye?" Uncle said, surprised.

"You've got to give this to someone," Kitchi panted, holding out the horn. "He's a boy . . . I don't know his name . . . he's ill . . . in hospital." The words tumbled out between pauses as Kitchi got his breath back.

"Your prize? Are you sure?" One look at his nephew's face told him he was sure. "All right. But who is he?"

Kitchi thought about this for a second; his fingers had begun to tingle again. "You'll know him when you see him. He's very, very, very fat!" And they both laughed. Looking tenderly at him, Uncle said goodbye.

"Goodbye, Uncle." Kitchi, fingers throbbing now, handed him the horn with a smile. "Tread lightly and walk in peace."

He watched from the edge of the school yard as the yellow taxi meandered down the winding road onto the plain below, wishing the horn safely to its destination; into the hands of the boy who would lead the Keepers in their quest.

CHAPTER 3

Lastro

Somewhere out in the depths, a whale was singing. Nothing unusual about that, thought Lastro, turning over in his sleep, curled up among the smelly fishing nets. He strained to hear better and finally murmured, "Dobi—hey, you still around? I love your low song. Helps me sleep well in this wet, wretched forever-bobbing God-forsaken boat!"

Already roused, there was no more sleeping tonight as a sea hawk's screech made him jump into full alert. Lastro groaned, all too aware that this meant a long night shivering and scared while the others snored. And wet! Why could he never stay dry? From where he sat, low down at the end of the boat, he could see the dark, rounded shapes of his uncle and cousins—they could sleep through a storm, so hardy and tough they were. Lastro wasn't like them; too soft. "Jelly Belly," he was called, because he was so scared of jellyfish. "Sensitive," his mother would say in his defence, her soft eyes resting on his, smiling broadly, seeming so pleased with him. Well, that didn't help—it wasn't enough.

He scanned the coastline; the dim and distant village lights now appeared, one by one. *Oh, to be at home, in bed, in a room with four walls!* he inwardly screamed. Under the pale orange sky, the vast expanse of sea rose up and down, inky black and threatening. Like a huge menacing beast.

You can't tame the sea, Lastro thought with resignation, but not entirely passively, for anger welled up in him—the heat surging through his body caused him to sweat and breathe fast. If only to be free from this, not to be at the mercy of the punishments the sea dished out so relentlessly: gigantic, crashing waves always threatening to break their boat to pieces with one mighty swipe; jellyfish stings which left you with aching, swollen limbs for days and nights; the ghoulish fish faces of their catch, staring up at him from the deck with dead, empty eyes. He felt lonely half of the time and scared the rest. Nothing was friendly down in the deep.

He shuddered when he thought of tomorrow's dive to pick up the lobster baskets and draw in the nets; there were always shadows. Anything could be lurking down there, waiting for him. Like the time he got caught by an octopus, its long, strong tentacles twirling and tightening around his legs and not letting go. He closed his eyes and wished himself far away from here. Why didn't they just throw explosives in the water, like he'd heard the mainland fishermen had been doing for years? Then they wouldn't have to stay up all night. Was that why the fish appeared weirder these days, so . . . twisted . . . with alien-like faces? And they smelled different, too. The smell had been bad enough, but now it was almost metallic. Lastro sank back down, heavy with worry. At that moment, a long note rang out, followed by four or five more.

"Dobi," he whispered, strangely comforted and relieved. He loved those lullabies. He lay still, waiting to enjoy the rest of the song that would follow:

Six notes, then repeated. Six more notes, a little louder this time and repeated; the whole two parts then sung over and over, sometimes for hours. *Oh, please sing now. Don't leave, like the others.* There had been five, and they had sung to each other, a continuous song, never changing. And he knew them all by name: Dobi, Mobi, Gogi, Nono, and Jojo. But this was Dobi, and he was alone now.

Like Lastro.

He thought he was dreaming when he heard the whale sing next; the note was higher, repeated, sure, but faster than before. The eerie sound came closer and then rang out higher still. Lastro felt the hair on his arms stand on end; all his senses heightened. The whale was nearby, he could tell from the way the boat was rising and falling sharply, urgently.

Dobi? Lastro could scarcely breathe. "What is it, Dobi?"

CHAPTER 4

Serenity

Serenity turned over in her bed and checked the clock. Groaning, she hunched herself up on her pillows just in time to catch sight of her mom and aunties disappearing into the forest's edge at the bottom of their garden. She hadn't woken up in time. But, on feeling a sharp pang of pain shoot through her stomach, she thought that maybe her mom had been right to leave her behind. Sunbeam patterns dancing on the walls announced a beautiful day outside; such a relief after the weeks and weeks of humid rains. She pulled back the curtains, and blinding sunlight flooded the room, forcing Serenity undercover again. But only for a moment, because the day was too delicious to resist. Why, oh why was she in bed on such a day? This was impossible to accept. She would get up right away and follow them. Once on her feet, Serenity wobbled over to the bathroom and soon found herself in a crumpled heap, crouched over in pain.

Okay Mom, she thought, *so you were right,* and at that, she remembered the medicine at her bedside. Mom had prepared it last night, and it tasted foul. Serenity had watched, as she always did, while her mom worked. Mom supplied shops in the local towns with natural remedies. First, she had cut, stripped, chopped, and boiled some *Echinacea Officinalis* root. Serenity had helped dig that up only last week, so it was really fresh.

"Boosts immunity," Mom always said; she repeated the plants' uses every time she used them, as if Serenity hadn't heard it a hundred, no hundreds of times over. Other leaves were added, but although Serenity recognised them, she didn't know all the names. Two different leaves were torn roughly up. One was long and a very dark green; it stained Mom's fingers as she worked. "It is the oils," Mom had told her. The other was shiny and light, almost transparent, and sometimes carried little bunches of strong-smelling white flowers. "The flowers will help the cramps most of all," Mom said as she smashed their little heads with a pestle. Then the roots, leaves, and flowers were heated together in a pot and simmered. Once cooled, it made the healing tea that sat, waiting for her to drink it right now. Serenity smelled it, grimaced, shut her eyes, and knocked some back. *Ugh . . . it needs honey or liquorice,* she decided and went to search for some in the kitchen. If you could call it a kitchen—more like a cross between a factory workroom and a laboratory!

Serenity's family lived on the edge of the Amazonian rainforest. Her mother was an indigenous native from the Tupinamba tribe, and her father was Norwegian. Her passion was medicinal plants, and his was conserving wildlife. They were an unusual couple, and Serenity was an incredible mix. She had the bright blonde hair of her father and the unruly wiry curls of her mother; she had Nordic height and deep brown Amazonian eyes and light brown skin. Locals along the river called her *Perniqui,* after an unusual bird of the forest with a large yellow plume.

She settled back into bed, waiting for the fever to abate. It wouldn't take long; Mom's medicines always worked. She clicked on her tablet. The usual silly stuff posted by friends: photos of cats and babies. Things like that drove her mad; Serenity lived a life of serious passions. Now that she was ill, she remembered a blog she'd looked in a few days ago. *What was his name?* She got it— Porky's Blog. He was sick in hospital or something. Now what was this? Porky had posted a picture of himself; no, it was a video— she wanted to laugh when she saw him. Wow—was he huge! And she could only see his top half. It was clear he was sitting up in a hospital bed; she could see a drip attached to his arm. He was singing or something—boy, he looked angry! She popped in her earphones and caught the end of the song:

Gonna have another burger?
What ya trying to do?
Kill yourself?
Go on, have another burger,
One, two, three
Extra fries too?
Go on
What ya trying to do?
Kill yourself?
Yeah, go on—kill yourself!

Porky acted out the song in true rap style, complete with arm movements. Serenity didn't know whether to laugh or cry. Maybe it was meant to be funny, but she didn't think so. She recognised the anger in his tone, because it matched the anger of the Native Amazonians when they talked (and sang) about their habitat being destroyed. She saw that he was online and quickly typed in *Cool song, Porky!* . . . what to put next? But he replied straight away: "It's not meant to be cool."

Ouch. She hadn't meant to annoy him. *No, I mean it really works. I'm as angry as you anyway.*

"Oh—why?"

Because—did you know that for every burger eaten, twenty trees are cut down in the rainforest? Here in Brazil anyway.

"I don't get it. Burgers need trees—what?"

No! But big beef farmers need land. So they bulldozer their way in and sometimes burn it too. We know from the animals and birds making their escapes. I can see them too. Serenity's eyes followed a long, low barge heavily loaded up with logs pass by on the river.

34

"You can see them?"

Yeah, I can see a logging boat now, sailing past my very eyes.

"Wow!" There was a long pause. "McDollar's." Another pause. "It's a good name for a fast-food chain, don't you think?"

Yeah. So, think of it this way: Every time you refuse a burger, 20 trees are saved.

"I'll remember—don't worry. Hey, what's your name?"

Serenity. And I'm sick in bed like you today.

"Cool! Okay—not cool."

But then the connection was lost, as was common in the Amazon. She smiled—she had a new friend who would surely talk about the injustice to the trees. Yes, he looked the type.

What Serenity didn't know was that Porky was about to receive a very special present. A present that would make him well and promise never to touch a burger again. His promise would, in fact, bring about all that Serenity had jokingly predicted.

A noise at the kitchen door startled her out of her reverie. The women were back from their collecting trip. "Why are you out of bed?" scolded her mother at once.

She jumped back over the tiny living room into her bunk and watched instead. The barks, roots, and branches of leaves and flowers were laid in mounds on the kitchen floor. Neighbours arrived with their children to help pull the leaves and flowers off. They all sat in a circle and chattered as they worked. Serenity listened to the usual moaning and occasional angry rant about the loggers and what they had illegally done next.

She sipped her medicine and drifted off to thoughts of Porky and his song again. Mom brought her a piece of bark to suck. As soon as she held it in her hands, her fingers began tingling and wouldn't stop. It was the weirdest sensation. *Must be really ill,* she thought. She looked at the bark carefully, turning it over. *Or is it something to do with this?*

A welcome breeze wafted in through the window. The fresh weather indicated that holiday time would soon be here, and

Serenity carefully cradled her dad's promises, in case they flew away. He'd promised a long time ago that one day she would accompany him on a trip to Africa, where he went once a year to check on migrating sea turtles arriving from South America. This was his work. He checked the wild turtles out for their migrating patterns and injuries. The Great River Basin Turtle Sanctuary was her dad's life dream realised, and as her mom always said, he was *obsessed* with it. But the more she helped out at weekends, the more Serenity understood her dad's obsession, because she had one too: Sergio.

Sergio was not a tall, dark, good-looking Amazonian guy (much to her parents' relief)—he was a turtle. And the love of her life. She would sneak out to see him tonight, whether she was better or not.

CHAPTER 5

Porky Discovers His Secret

Porky was in the supermarket with his parents. The weekly trip bored him silly. There was only one thing that made it worthwhile—the stop at the café just before checkout. Today, he had chosen a large strawberry sundae with chocolate chips, which he was savouring slowly while his parents drank lattes and read the papers. Porky's sundae was just sliding down nicely when his mum realised she'd forgotten sausages.

"Philip—be a dear and go and get a pack of sage 'n' onion sausages, will you, pet?"

So, off he reluctantly plodded into what looked like miles and miles of aisles. Soups . . . Canned fruit . . . Preserves . . . Coffee . . . Tea . . . Frozen foods. His eyes flitted rapidly up and down frozen foods, and pizza caught his eye. And he found himself drawn to the massive freezers with glass doors that lined the walls. Ah, pepperoni with extra cheese . . . mmm . . . his favourite . . . maybe just one. *Mum won't mind—she'd eat half of it anyway! Better get a couple.* He opened the door and reached inside. *What's this?* Octopus tentacles and yak's milk cheese. *Some weird flavours these days,* thought Porky. Bat's wings and sweet corn. *What? Can't be!* Porky scanned the shelves: Curried wombat? Shredded gecko scales with pineapple?

Porky suddenly felt very cold. He looked around; there weren't many shoppers about. Although he'd been here umpteen times, there was something eerie about the place today. Shuddering slightly, he turned to the long open freezer running down the centre. Nothing was recognisable; there were french fries, but in every shape and colour imaginable. Blue, pink, green . . . well, they're not french fries any more, are they? Who'd eat them? Is this some kind of new promotion, or a joke? *Better find the sausages,* Porky decided firmly.

"Need help, young one?"

Porky whirled round at the sound of that voice. Because it wasn't human. But somehow, he knew it. The masked face was impenetrable; not even the eyes showed. This giant of a man, maybe seven or eight feet tall, wore a silver suit, a curved helmet, and huge gloves. It was unmistakably Sondero, a character from his latest computer game.

"Don't touch!" the mechanical voice ordered. "It is forbidden to touch any frozen material. Read the rules. Read the rules." The Sondero look-alike was pointing to a sign. And how could Porky have missed it? There was a large red skull with a speech bubble illuminated by neon lights; it read: "Do not touch freezers containing Genetically Modified Foodstuffs. Let a member of staff handle all GMOs."

"Sorry, didn't know it was genetically modified," Porky muttered under his breath. And then, frustrated, he added, "Just lost my appetite, mate."

"Leave area immediately," Sondero instructed, raising an enormous hand.

Determined not to be scared, Porky piped up, "Keep your gloves on, mate. I'll just choose some french fries instead." And he turned to closely examine the contents of the middle freezer, picking up each bag one by one and squinting closely at the different colours.

"Move out of area." Sondero gave Porky a shove, causing him to fall sideways onto the freezer; he struggled to regain his balance.

"Hey—I'm only looking for friggin' sausages!" This sounded odd, now that he was halfway inside the french fries freezer. But Sondero had his gun out now—a snappy, robot-style little number.

"Leave freezer area."

"Okay, okay." Porky backed away, his hands half raised. He appealed to the other customers now, arms outstretched this time, palms upwards, and pulling a funny face while jerking his head back at the robot. But no help there; everyone looked so . . . scared? No. Then what? Passive, lifeless.

What the hell is going on? Porky's mind raced as he tried to take in the scene. A tall, silver-suited man, complete with helmet, pushed each customer's trolley. Trolleys piled high with boxes, cartons, polystyrene containers, plastic cylinders. There was not a scrap of anything that resembled food.

"Where's the sausages?" Porky yelled at the top of his voice.

Porky heard himself shouting as he woke up; his legs and arms were thrashing around, throwing off the bedcovers. His body was drenched in sweat; he couldn't bear to be in this airless, lifeless room any longer. "We're living in hell, a foodless hell . . ." he mumbled madly, a remnant of his dream still having its effect.

And so he found himself stumbling along the corridor, having wrenched the wretched drip tube from his arm, doing his best to get away as quickly as possible. But two nurses were after him now, and Porky, so incensed by the message in that hideous dream, half turned around, swung his arm in an arc, and actually landed one of them a whack in the face! It was enough to halt his pursuers and allow him to lumber off, like a large bear, in the direction of the fire escape door. He had to get there. He had to see if it was real.

The garden. His sunflower.

And there it was, all green in the morning sunshine. Branches and bushes swaying to and fro in a gentle wind, just as he had left it. Except there were people there now. Porky hesitated. Maybe this meant he couldn't go down? He squinted hard; it was difficult to see without his glasses. They were wearing white dresses, each one the same, and most were bent over close to the ground.

"Okay Philip—game over!" The nurses had caught up with him. "Back to base for breakfast and medicine," barked the male nurse he'd hit. Porky glowered at them both; he'd promised himself that he wasn't going to talk to anyone. But his curiosity about the garden overcame him.

"Who are they?" he pointed.

"Oh, the Sauranine sisters? They tend the hospital garden."

"Sisters?"

"Philip—they're nuns," the less surly nurse said, smiling and winking at her colleague.

"Can I go down and . . . um . . . meet them?"

"*After* breakfast and medicine!" came the reply.

The nurses exchanged looks, raising eyebrows. Porky was becoming a most unusual patient.

On the way back, flanked by his two guards, he was marched past the schoolroom. The terminals were already at their desks, sitting attentively and smiling, excited. At the front of the class stood the reason. They had a visitor, who was making a presentation. Porky pulled on the arms of the nurses and strained to see. The man was bending over, putting something on his head. When he stood up, the children spontaneously cheered and clapped. He was wearing a Native American headdress. The effect was stunning. And the Native American himself was playing the part well, standing very straight, arms crossed, staring into the distance with a proud, regal look on his face.

But it was the feathers in the headdress that had caused such a collective gasp: white, black, and green—arranged in a pattern even more beautiful than a peacock's plumage. The chief's face broke into a smile now at the sight of the terminal kids' beaming faces. In the same moment, he noticed Porky standing in the doorway; his eyes flickered with some kind of recognition; his face became serious again, and he bowed his head in greeting. Together, everyone stopped and looked at Porky, who had blushed self-consciously and was looking down at his fingers. The tips were tingling ever so slightly.

It was another strange moment in what was becoming an altogether very strange day.

However, it wasn't long before the mystery was solved: while eating breakfast, or rather sucking breakfast (liquids only), Porky heard the sombre stranger being interviewed on the hospital radio. He was talking about some interesting topics related to the customs of his people of long ago, but particularly those concerned with the bison, or buffalo; he was saying that whether we liked to admit it or not, the white man had almost completely wiped them out. Of course, he was plugging a book he'd written: *Yearning for the Bison Years. Might make a good Christmas present for Granddad,* mused Porky.

But his mind didn't stay on that for long; it was firmly fixed on the garden expedition, and as soon as permission was granted, off he went. At last, he was escorted down the fire escape steps and left to his own devices, under the supervision of one of the sisters.

"Are you interested in gardening then?" Sister Gandhali asked.

"Oh . . . no, I just . . . I dunno . . . I just like it here. Makes me feel better."

"Yes, I totally agree," she continued, in a lilting Indian accent. "This garden reminds me of home—India, of course, not Glasgow! In my village, many people have gardens like this one, and everyone understands the healing power of plants."

"Healing power?"

But she had moved away to talk to another visitor, and Porky was left to wonder. The leaves of the trees were rustling in the breeze; it was enough just to listen and watch. "Healing power." The words had a magical ring to them. They were exciting and thrilling, yet soothing at the same time. Like the sound of the leaves above his head. It was a new idea, but somehow familiar. The framed drawings of herbs that had been on the walls of Granddad's poky little bedsit popped into his mind. Had Granddad believed in the healing power of plants?

He strayed further along the gravel paths, between rows of shrubs and bushes and the zillions of little pots that lined them. Some plants had name tags: *Hypericum Officinalis.* Porky screwed up his face trying to decipher the scientific name. *Why do humans have to complicate things,* he wondered, *when in reality it's all nice and simple?* And that thought brought Porky back to his dream, where his day had begun. *What was all that about? Sondero—in the supermarket?* Suddenly, he grew worried about his state of mind. *I guess Ms. Grayling would have a lot to say about that.* Well, he didn't have to tell her. But he had to tell someone, because there was something wrong. Something very wrong. Not with him, but with all the reasons why he was ill, and not just him, but all those poor terminal kids too. And how many other millions of people? Was he the only one who knew that food was making mankind sick— killing it? He thought of McDollar's. *Huh! And at the same time, making others very, very rich!*

He sat down then on a low wall, shoulders hunched forward, feeling utterly overwhelmed. As soon as he let out a low, long sigh, he felt the tingling in his fingertips start up again. *That's weird,* he thought and looked up abruptly, scanning his surroundings, thinking that the Big Chief must be looking at him again. But nothing, no one . . . unless . . . and there it was again; waiting, watching, and gazing down at him. The sunflower.

"And you must be *Sunflower Officinalis,* I presume?" Porky said out loud, quickly realising that he'd just spoken to a *plant*!

"*Helianthus annuus,* actually." Sister Gandhali was back. She was laughing softly, but not *at* him. "Would you care to give me a hand?" she asked.

She pointed to some small pots and showed him how to put in just enough soil till the pot was half full. "Then place this seed into the middle, cover it up with more soil, add a few drops of water, and that is it!"

"Wow! It's so simple!" He picked up some seeds. "And what are these? What are we planting?"

"Why—sunflowers, of course!" And she laughed again. "You mean you do not know that this is a sunflower seed?"

"No, I've never seen one before," Porky confessed, but he wasn't embarrassed in front of her; she wasn't like Ms. Grayling, who was full of hidden things.

"Ooh, you British kids! All you know is to pick up the phone and order delivery! Any Indian child can tell you what kind of spice should be used in which dish, and what kind of tea is good for digestion."

"Yeah, I guess you're right," Porky answered shyly. Then he remembered something. "That's what Jimmy Olives said."

"Who?"

"You know—the Bare-It-All Chef?"

"Bare-it-all?" Sister Gandhali repeated; she had turned a little pale.

"Oh, never mind. He had a TV programme and went to Italy and found out that all Italian kids, even really little ones, knew what an asparagus is!" Porky threw a sunflower seed in the air and caught it, as if to prove his point.

"Exactly. And you see this wonderful sunflower?" She waved her hand up at it, as it majestically surveyed them from above. "You know what this plant gives us?

Porky shook his head rather pathetically.

Sister Gandhali raised her eyebrows, but only in jest. "Oil to cook with," she said, "and it is very healthy for salads too. Full of vitamin E—all from this wonderful little seed! And you know who we have got to thank?"

Porky stared back at her blankly.

"The Native American Indians," she informed him. "They were the ones who domesticated this flower for food production, oh, nearly three thousand years ago."

Porky's eyes were wide with intrigue as he asked, "Really?"

"That is right," the sister said, beaming, pleased that Porky was so interested in what she had to say. But Porky wasn't listening any more, because he was thinking about how the Indian chief in the classroom this morning had met his eyes and seemed to *know* him. About how his fingertips had tingled, just as they were doing now. He picked up a little sunflower seed and looked at it closely, turning it over and over. Mesmerised, and aware that his fingers were throbbing now—so hot—almost burning, without hesitation he filled one of the little pots with soil, popped the seed in, and covered it up. After he'd added a drop of water, he blew on it and whispered something.

"Yes, very good," Sister Gandhali said, slightly puzzled.

Porky turned to her and smiled broadly, his first real smile for a very long time. Then he looked up into the large, brown face of the sunflower, which was watching him intently.

"I'm going to do something to put all of this right again," he vowed in a low and steady voice, knowing that the sunflower understood even if he, himself, didn't. He couldn't begin to really grasp what was stirring deep inside of him—right now, he only *felt* it. He tenderly picked up the little pot and began to climb the fire escape steps.

Before he'd even reached the second step, a bird began to sing. Two long notes. Within a few seconds, he heard it again, repeated a little way off. And again. It sounded remarkably like a signal.

♦

It was Monday morning; the start of a new working week. Mr. Corporate glanced over at the world map on the wall of his office. The Food Masters Inc. Empire was shaded in purple and had extensive coverage; areas like Greenland, Alaska and Siberia stood out like sore thumbs. The burnt-out hole over Scotland irked him, but the scorch mark over Ethiopia troubled him more. He picked up the phone. "Ms. Grayling, please," he said gruffly and waited, drumming his fingers impatiently on the desk. He listened to her for only a moment before interrupting sarcastically, "Look, my *dear* Ms. Grayling, it's been weeks," and he added, his voice sounding increasingly strained, "I want to know what's going on there. And I want results. Remember—I'm paying you a *fortune!*" He slammed the phone down angrily and sat gazing at the city skyline for some time.

Finally, his eyes came to rest on the box.

What had his grandmother said to him just before she died? The moment all came back to him: the weight of the crystal in his small hands and the burning heat too. Something about Africa . . . *A rich and powerful man you will be, but don't ignore Africa, my son. There lies the heart of the Earth.* At the time there had been no further explanation. But he still had the scars. He looked down at his trembling hands; scar tissue marked the spot where Grandma's crystal had burnt through his skin. As a boy he'd heard the story of how his great-great-grandfather had removed the precious stone from a mine in Africa and secretly brought it with his slave ships to the New World. Mr. Corporate's mouth was dry so he ordered tea. He walked slowly over to the windowsill and hesitated, his hand hovering above the box. Then he quickly opened it and picked up the crystal, turning it over and over in his hands. Light reflected off each of its facets onto the walls. There—it was nothing. *Pretty harmless,* he concluded.

At that moment an alarm went off on his mobile. *Damn!* He'd forgotten about his morning meeting with Mr. Deal.

Minutes later Miss Featherstone entered the room with a tray of tea. On noticing Mr. Corporate had gone she placed it on his desk and turned to leave. She caught sight of some strange lights moving on the wall and lingered, marvelling at how beautiful they were. But as she stood there wondering, the lights became a dark shape—a dark growling shape. The low growl became louder till suddenly the shape jumped from the wall into the room, circling it quickly as if searching for something. Miss Featherstone screamed and darted out. The beast with the blazing eyes took up a position on the sofa and waited for its new master to return.

♦

The Conference of the Birds

Over the Cairngorms Nature Reserve in the Highlands of Scotland, near Windhorn, the sky was almost completely darkened by a monumental number of flying birds. It looked like they were playing games as they swirled and swooped, first forming shapes and then instantaneously breaking them up. Anyone wandering on those lonely moors and wooded hills would have covered their ears against the unbearable noise.

It took some time for the multitudes to settle, but finally all were perched, waiting. A long silence followed until two red kites glided into view, their huge wings fully extended. They took their places on a high branch, graciously surveying the scene.

It took less than fifteen minutes for the Conference of the Birds to reach its objective; in the same instant several members left. One gigantic albatross set off in the direction of the South Pacific and a cockatoo and a stork made for East Africa. Only a black and white northern lapwing was to remain in Scotland, and it duly headed towards Glasgow. The others hunkered down for the night before resuming their migration routes.

◆

CHAPTER 6

Abala

It was a clear, still morning the day it happened. There had been rumblings all week, sounding just like thunder in the distance. Except it wasn't the rainy season.

Abala had noticed that the elders met more often, sometimes daily, grouped under the wide branches of the shifara trees on a mound near the well. Raised voices, sometimes a shout or a defiant fist in the air, made passing villagers stop and glance up at them, before continuing on with pale and worried faces. Grandfather was too weak to walk to the mound, so he didn't join them this time. Instead, he sat against the house, looking into the distance. Abala wondered what he could be thinking about and finally decided that he was back in the past. Because Abala used to go back there too . . .

He had always taken the goats out first thing, and on coming back, Grandfather would be sitting like a king, at the head of the low table set out in the courtyard in front of the house, resplendent in his tribal headdress of red and gold tassels (he insisted on wearing it at mealtimes), waiting for his subjects to gather beneath him so he could preside over the proceedings of . . . breakfast!

Then, early morning chores done, all the family members gathered around, jostling and nudging for the best places: his five brothers and sisters, Auntie Melkam and her two fat twins, Father and Mama, and a neighbour or two. And suddenly Grandfather's voice would cry out, loud, clear, and shrill, raised in prayer, like a bird singing to the heavens:

"Thanks be to God that we live another day and share this bread, which He has ordained the land to freely give, as a symbol of our bonds."

Noises of agreement from the adults sounded from around the table: "Alun." But some kids always loved to join in, giggling. Auntie Melkam's twins shouted, "Alooooon," causing smiles all around. Until Pika, the parrot who guarded the house, would join in: "Aleeen Aleeen, Heyo Aleeen." And then everybody laughed, the early start and the aching limbs forgotten, as the taste of *injera* bread dipped in spicy beans with garlic and ginger and *Quanta fir fir*, beef in fresh herbs and seasoned butter, smoothed away grumpiness and even the scariest dream.

Then they'd trudge off to school, an hour's walk—a long line of kids in different colours, so they could be seen from afar, said Mama, who watched them until they dipped behind the hill and out of view. And before he turned into the bend in the track, Abala would always look back for one last wave from Mother—and Grandfather would raise his stick.

Grandfather. How he hated that stick, and being confined to the house, not able to help. He tried to hide his wounded pride by telling jokes, but his eyes told more. What a strong farmer he had been! They had all heard the stories, over and over, told by relatives over dinner outside in the courtyard, all eyes admiring the large dish of sizzling spicy meat in the middle of the table. Between mouthfuls of *Kaey Wot* stew wrapped in *injera* bread, remembrances flew from one to the other across the courtyard. The stories were sometimes as spicy as the food!

"No! Tell us again."

"He carried three injured lambs over that mountain, two on his back and one on his head!"

Abala wanted to laugh at the thought, but couldn't because he'd just plopped a dumpling in his mouth and it would splosh out all over his shirt, or even worse onto the table. Then Mama would give him a stern look, and he'd be filled with shame in front of his elders.

"What about the time Grandfather saved the baby calf when it was stuck in its mummy's belly?" shouted Abala's little sister, Almaz. There was a loud hum of approval for that story.

"Yes, yes, tell us!" the twins cried, bobbing up and down. This time, Uncle Abraham recounted the gory details while Mama and Auntie Melkam screwed their faces up in disgust.

"Noooo, please no more!" groaned Mama. "You're making me sick! I've got half a bowl of *Wot* left, and I don't want to waste it!"

"All right then . . . the day Grandfather saved old Farmer Guma from being crushed under his own badly built wall!" Sniggers rose up. "No—shhh, his daughter's here!"

Mama was just finishing off telling about when Grandfather solved the mystery of the orchard thieves, when Father nodded at Abala meaning *go get the goats,* and so off he slipped across the fields against a backdrop of village fires, dotted here and there, and the wild calls of hyenas in the distance, like night music. Once back, their own fire had just gone out as he crept off to bed.

"Don't sleep in your clothes, Abala," Mama called out from the kitchen as he drifted off to sleep, smelling the sweet aroma of *injera* dough that she was preparing for the morning.

Those were the days. For their bellies, and their neighbours' bellies, and their neighbours' neighbours' bellies had been rumbling and aching with hunger for many years since then.

It was a perfect, clear, still morning the day it happened.

Abala woke to take the goats out, as usual. There was no smell of *injera* bread baking. His father announced in a very stern voice that there was to be no school that morning.

"And no chores. And no going out to the fields." Abala could sense that nobody knew what to do.

"Must be time for breakfast then," Grandfather said, taking his seat at the head of the table, arranging his red and gold scarf over his head and shoulders. For the first time ever, he looked absurd. And then flushing suddenly, ashamed at the thought, Abala fumbled about, helping Mama place what was left of yesterday's bread on the table. It was hard, so they dipped it in *telba*, a flaxseed drink, to soften it up a bit. Everyone huddled closer than normal around the table; the adults' faces were very tense, the children unusually quiet. Black smoke not a long way off covered half the sky.

Grandfather, his head held high, eyes closed, raised both arms with his palms flat, receiving their meagre breakfast with thanks. "Thanks be to God that we live another day and share this bread, which He has ordained the land to freely give, as a symbol of our bonds."

They ate silently; the bread was stale, and the *telba* had gone a little sour.

"Abala—go and see if Auntie Melkam is all right."

It was only next door, but Abala didn't want to go. He couldn't bring himself to rise from the table, from this breakfast that held them together. There was a horrifying sense of impending doom.

Grandfather nodded gravely, "Go on, boy."

As soon as he'd turned into the dirt track, before anyone knew what was happening, they arrived. First one came on horseback, firing randomly around the square, and then many, many more. Loud bangs and horrendous screams followed. Confusion . . . people running in all directions. Bloodcurdling screams. Shouts. He could see villagers being surrounded by green-clothed men. The soldiers were lashing out at people with machetes. He saw blood. He was sure his heart was going to stop. *Mama and Father!* He ran back to the house, but everyone was gone. Only Grandfather remained, sitting very still.

"Wh-at . . ." Abala wanted to scream and shout. "Come on—get up!"

But Grandfather stopped him with one hand pressed against his chest.

"Run, Abala," he said. "Run for your life!" His stare was painful to see. Eyes like flint.

He turned back just before he entered the wood, one last look, though he was afraid to stop. Grandfather was still sitting there; he could just make him out. And then he raised his stick.

Run, run, run . . . Abala crashed through the woods. Trees were few and far between; there was nowhere to hide. *Run—just keep going . . .* But his body was taking a battering, scratched and torn, especially his feet. *Run, run, run . . .* He repeated Grandfather's words like a mantra. *Run, run.* But he had to stop, he had no more breath. He threw himself into a thorny thicket, flinching in pain. And lay still. For how long he would never know; it felt like hours. Till he heard—something. There were people coming. Some soldiers were thrashing about, dragging someone, a boy. From where he hid Abala recognised him, he was in the class above him at school. He was whimpering, his voice hoarse from crying, "No . . .no . . . please . . . let me go home."

Abala was frozen, tense with disbelief at the unspeakable sounds of slapping, jeering, laughing even. The boy screamed, and all was silent. His heart thumped like it would burst out of his chest. He tried not to breathe; it was impossible for them not to hear his heart. *Don't hear it. Don't hear it. Don't hear it.* Some more crackling in the undergrowth. Voices, then he smelled cigarette smoke.

He walked all night and reached the mountain town at dawn. But he was afraid to enter, so he hid in a barn a little way out. An hour or so must have passed; the sun was up now, but nothing, no sounds, nothing. Was there no one here? He dared a peek; only chickens pecking in the dirt road. One became aware of him and started running, causing them all to skitter and scuttle in all directions, squawking. "Oh no . . . shhhhhh!" Instinctively, Abala raised a finger to his lips. He chanced a dash across the road and crept slowly onwards, keeping to the shadows. The buildings were empty, and nearly all of them burned. Belongings lay everywhere: kitchen utensils, bedding, even a pair of boots. His mind was stretched tight from all that had happened, so that he couldn't begin to take all this in. No questions filled his mind, only the sharp fear of being discovered. In the same instant, a hand was clamped over his mouth, an arm gripped tightly round his waist, and he was lifted in the air by someone who smelled strongly of many days of sweat.

He must have passed out for hours, because when he opened his eyes, it was nearly dusk and he was wrapped in a blanket, lying a short distance away from a huddle of people. They were in a garden, sheltered by a wall and a few trees. For a while, they were too busy to notice him, so he could observe them at ease. There seemed to be a mix of ages, he even glimpsed a couple of children running around. What was going on? At last he realised they were gathering food and dumping their offerings on the ground on a rough cloth. Someone was building a fire.

"What have we got then?" said a broad shouldered, heavy-set man who Abala could smell from where he lay. *That's the one who picked me up,* he thought. The man's long robe was different from anything Abala had ever seen. His white headdress sat tightly on his head.

"Tomatoes, squash (little ones), potatoes—great—some onions, chillies (yes, *very* important!). Okay, that's it, is it? Mmm, well, it will do—it will have to do," he announced importantly.

Was he a cook? A woman, squealing with delight, scurried in, holding two chickens by their feet. "Got them at last!" she yelled triumphantly and proceeded to pluck all the feathers out, then rub them all over with stuff from a bottle. He knew the smell . . . it was *berbere*. Mama used it all the time; it was made of red chilli peppers, garlic, and other spices. Suddenly, Abala realised he was very, very hungry.

The two kids ran up excitedly, carrying apples bundled in their shirts. What could he bring? On putting his arm out to pull himself up, he realised the ground he was lying on was strewn with hard pods. He picked one up and smelled the long, black, twisted thing. He'd never seen one before. It had a strange, sweet smell.

"Hey, the boy's awake," someone said, and a woman came over and gently coaxed him towards them.

"There, there," she said, "it's okay, come and have dinner with us."

He grabbed a few pods, walked over, and thrust them at the man in the white cotton headdress.

"And a good guest always brings an offering," he laughed. "I'll show you what to do with these in the morning."

Abala smiled, not afraid of him anymore; still gripping a carob pod, he sat down in the circle as the food was served up. And what a meal it was! The steaming hot chicken in *berbere* sauce sat in the middle with little bowls of vegetables all around. Some *injera* bread was passed around; it smelled old and was hard, but nobody minded because they just wanted to start dipping into the chicken dish with it. The oldest man there raised his hands, palms upwards, and said simply, "Thanks be to God that we live another day and share this bread." There was a long pause, so long that Abala thought that the old man had forgotten what came next.

". . . which He has ordained the land to freely give, as a symbol of our bonds." Abala's voice was surprisingly loud and shrill, and everyone stared at him incredulously, until some soft laughter bubbled up.

"What's your name, boy?"

"Abala Alemayehu Zerihun," Abala said, holding his head high.

"Ah, Zerihun . . ." Murmurs went around the campfire at the mention of Grandfather's name. But at the sound of this name and those familiar words, a tremendous pain rose up in Abala's chest, and for the first time since all this began, he felt hot tears rising up and choking him. So he ran over to his blanket and, at last, sobbed and sobbed and sobbed.

Later, when he was more relaxed and the adults were sipping the thick, black spicy coffee that follows every meal, he looked intently at all their faces. They were ordinary farmers just like his own folk. He saw faces which were so care worn, but not from their way of life, no—from drought and famine, and now *this.*

"They'll drive us all out, you know," one man was saying.

"That's the third land grab this year," another sighed.

"Haven't they got enough that they want our land too? It's all we've got."

Who's taking our land? And grabbing it too? These thoughts were new to Abala. He tried to listen hard, but he was so sleepy . . .

"Where will we head for now?"

"Across the border is our only hope."

What? Leave Ethiopia? Leave my country? The pain was rising up again, and he held himself still; he didn't want to cry again in front of these people. And it was then, out of the corner of his eye, that he saw something flash in the trees and a dark shape move first one way, then another. He strained to see, his body tense. There was a pair of eyes watching him, steadily, holding his gaze. But not human eyes. Taunting him, threatening him.

"Which He has ordained the land to freely give, as a symbol of our bonds," a voice mocked. **"Abala Alemayehu Zerihun, you had better hold your tongue or you will have it cut out—just like the boy in the woods—remember?"**

The words were not spoken, but Abala heard them loud and clear. What was this new enemy, and how did it know him?

CHAPTER 7

Bina

Mr. Rajeev Khan
12, New Market Gate
Glasgow
Scotland

Dear Respected Brother Rajeev,

God be good to you and your family.

Greetings from all your family here in Carrunder. And from India, the country that will forever be your home. I trust your work is going on well and that of your sons too.

My letter may come as a surprise to you, for as you know I had closed my heart to the matter which we discussed six months previously. But now I have reconsidered. You are aware of my situation since the tragedy, which grows more painful by the day. We are struggling here since my fields were forced out of my hands for such a pittance! My new job as a caretaker at the tea-packing factory cannot support my family. You know I have only daughters and my wife is old in years, there is no one to help me. I cannot bear to go on failing my family; I want them to maintain their dignity. Of course, my daughter Mira is not marriageable and, regrettably, a destroyed life—but there is Bina. I have thought deeply again about your proposal and have decided to accept. I, therefore, give my consent to the marriage between your eldest son Ajit and my second daughter Bina.

Most honoured brother, please allow Bina one month to say her goodbyes to her family.

Your dear brother, Darshan.

The letter was sent by the first post.

Darshan told his daughter at breakfast. Holding his emotions inside, dry-eyed, he steadied himself by secretly gripping the underside of the dining table. Would she ever know how much it hurt him too? Good, sweet, obedient Bina bowed her head. It wasn't like her to make an ugly display in public. He knew instead that she would save it for later. Her dog, Pluto, would bear the insane screaming and lap up her tears, or her sister, Mira, would sense an angry heaviness in her touch today and every day until she left at the end of the month.

One month!

Only thirty more days of seeing golden-eyed Bina move silently, sweetly around the house. Flitting in and out of rooms: dusting, washing, carrying dishes to the table, making tea, patiently feeding her sister. Would she ever know he had her best interests at heart? She had stopped going to school; she had too many chores at home. No, her mornings were spent lugging the heavy plastic gallons of clean water home by tuk tuk and then heaving them up the stairs of the building. In Britain, with her uncle's son to care for her, she wouldn't have to work so hard. Maybe she could receive an education. She deserved it. Would she ever know how much he loved her?

But what would home be like without her? An empty shell.

Bina took a drop of myrrh oil and played with it between her fingers. There wasn't much left, and she didn't know where she was going to get more from. And it was so expensive.

But poor Mira needed it; the oil calmed her so that her limbs didn't jerk so much, and Bina believed that the myrrh instilled a deep sense of peace in this young woman who had lost so much. But today—today it was Bina's turn to feel loss; so much that it crowded out all empathy and responsibility for her elder sister. Today, she didn't want to massage Mira's limbs, to tenderly caress her and whisper to her as if reassuring a hurt animal. No, today her own wounds were too deep.

But after a little while, she began, because this is what she always did, robotically at first—pressing a little too hard, angrily even, till the tears flowed, heavy hot drops onto Mira's neck and shoulders. Her sister let out a groan, and her head jerked back. She shouted—unintelligible sounds—not different from any other day. Or were they? It was hard to tell. Pluto, her little wiry-haired dog, was tilting his head to the side, listening intently. Maybe they *were* understandable then. What was she saying? Was she saying, "Don't cry" or "Be strong"? Bina would never know. No one would know what Mira thought and felt. Not since the disaster left her like this. A jerking cripple, mute and blind; not in this world.

So Bina resisted the urge to cry out, to wail, to scream. Wasn't Mira's life worse? But now that she'd be leaving, who would massage her sister every day and sleep next to her at night? Who would change her diaper every morning? Mother couldn't; she could hardly move around herself. It dawned on her then that these services could be paid for with the money sent by her husband-to-be, and much more besides. *I guess that's the point of it all anyway,* she thought, as if it had only just occurred to her. *It's all about money. It's always about money.*

As soon as the massage was over, it was time to go shopping. She would take Mother; her daily walk was important. They had to pass by the school on the way to the busy shopping street. All the windows were open, and familiar sounds of school life floated down to the street: the high-pitched children's voices and squeals, the clatter of moving chairs, and the loud shouts trying to maintain control. Or further along, the rhythmical chanting of little voices learning rhymes. To Bina it was a magical world that had escaped her. She'd briefly tasted the excitement of classroom friendships, serious tests, the colours on the walls, future hopes. But it was not to be for her—her family needed her. They were so poor, like so many in the region since the disaster. And she had no brothers who could bring money in. A bell rang. It was time for recess. She felt herself flush with embarrassment. *Oh please don't let them see me!* Her shame curled up into a tight knot in her stomach. She tugged on her mother's hand and hurried her away a little too fast.

Lunch was to be a big one. Her father was bringing back some guests (a rare occurrence at their house), but today was important. There had been a large demonstration in Koornipal outside Pharma Chemical's Head Office, and some relatives had come from towns in the neighbouring province who had suffered another leak from a pesticides plant recently, just as Bina's village had years ago. There would be up to fifteen people. Half of Father's monthly salary would go on this meal! But what to cook? She scanned the baskets laid out in front of the local grocer. There were lots of things there she couldn't afford. Like cauliflowers and mangoes. A curry with those would have been marvellous. Potatoes would have to do. And ginger, that was cheap. She'd spice it up a bit and add a little tomato for colour—they'd love it and wouldn't notice it was only potato. Purchases made and feeling pleased with her idea, and her thriftiness as well, they turned around for the slow walk home.

But was ginger the right thing for people that were sure to be angry and upset after a demonstration? Bina suddenly thought. *Surely it would fire them up more?* She wasn't sure but the thought continued to niggle. What should she do? The lunch would be all wrong. A street vendor was approaching slowly, his cart piled high with coconuts. *Ha—got it! Coconut milk will soften the dish and line their tense stomachs like a balm.* She then thought that coriander would be "sweetly hopeful" and bought two large bunches for the price of one. A super bargain!

And into the kitchen she went. The hard work of peeling the potatoes, mashing up the coconut flesh for milk, not to mention fetching extra water, kept her mind from the earth-shattering news of this morning. Bina liked to have a project, a mission, and the people coming today were heavily burdened; each would have his tragic, pitiful story to tell. Serving them helped her too.

But they were late. The potatoes in coconut milk had bubbled for too long and were becoming sticky and congealed. Bina's heart was slowly sinking with every extra minute that was ticking by. Thoughts of her father's news flooded in. *What was her cousin's name again? Ajit? Had she ever seen him? Where was Britain?* But the thought that mattered most, the one that burned inside of her till it hurt, was, *Would she love him?*

Shouts outside indicated father's homecoming, along with his honoured guests. Suddenly the house was in chaos—there were so many people! Bina was lost in a muddle of bowing politely, handing out bowls of water containing marigold flowers for hand washing, serving cool lemonade drinks, and avoiding tripping over the mounds of shoes at the doorway. She couldn't remember anyone's name. But that didn't matter, nobody would speak to her—she was only a girl. It was clear that the mood was sombre; any exchanges were tense. She stole a glance at their guests' faces; the men looked tired and unhappy. Food served, Bina placed herself just inside the kitchen opening, hidden by a curtain, and waited. It would be a long afternoon. Pluto padded over and placed his head in her lap. At last, a rest and some comfort. And, at that, the tears welled up again, but she quickly choked them down. Just as well, for the next moment there was a commotion in the adjoining room.

"How can you say such a thing to your uncle, Ashram-Ji?" A plate smashed to the floor, and the sound of a scuffle followed. Raised voices all at once, so Bina couldn't tell who had said what to whom. She dared a peek around the curtain. A large burly man was holding a young (and handsome, Bina thought) man by his collar and pressing him against the wall.

"Look, I'm free to give my opinion!" protested the young man.

"And your opinion is an insult to your family!" The older man turned and spat at the floor. "That is what I think of your new-fangled opinions."

Father was quickly on his feet and laid his hand on the offended uncle's arm. "Let him sit down. We are all over-wrought. It is not his fault." He turned to Ashram and said, "Son, we are right to fight for compensation. Their neglect ruined our lives. Many men in this town are now blind. They cannot earn money to feed their families."

"And the managers, those son-of-a-bitches, got two years in prison. Two years!" Ashram's uncle was shouting again.

"Come on, come on. Let us not disturb the neighbourhood. Please, it has been a long day; let us eat." Father motioned to the plates and called out. "Bina, another plate of . . . um . . ."

"Potato and coconut stew," Bina said, smiling and filling a new plate, before clearing up the broken pieces from the floor. Repositioned behind the curtain, she was pleased to notice that the room grew quiet. They were enjoying it. Some low chatter resumed, and someone let out a long sigh. Bina secretly smiled; her plan was working! Then Father called for tea, and she was on her feet again, boiling water and setting out cups. Father was speaking again, this time quietly.

"Take me as an example. You all know my situation. I'm no longer a farmer, but a factory caretaker. My daughter was born damaged. We all know why. And I have received no compensation. But I have some news: I will have a new son-in-law, Ajit, my brother Rajeev's son. Bina will travel to Britain next month."

Some murmurs of congratulation, then:

"Ajit? But wasn't he . . . ?" It was Ashram who spoke.

"No, it is over now. Everything is fine again." Father cut him off quickly, almost in a whisper.

Bina held her breath. *What? What was over?* But Father was calling for the tea. *Oh no! How can I go back in there now?* She felt all eyes on her as she handed round the teacups. Only Ashram said thank you, and when she momentarily raised her eyes, she noticed that he was looking at her strangely.

It was late before everyone left to get the last train. In the quiet of the dark house, Father was drinking tea. She had made up her mind; she hoped he wouldn't refuse her request.

"Father, I want to travel north." And when she saw his face change, she added quickly, "Only for a few days. I must get some more myrrh oil. I can't leave Mira without knowing she has the oil."

How could he say no? He wondered if she had heard their conversation at lunch. Would she be strong enough? Of course he would not refuse her. Not now.

"My dear Bina, you can have whatever you want."

"Well, you know the village they all talk about? In the north?"

"You mean Karna, the one with the giant . . . what was it . . . watermelons?" Father answered with a disbelieving smile. "Why there? Why so far away, Bina? I don't want to miss you for so long." And he nearly bit his tongue at the irony of those words.

She was to go the next morning.

The driver turned up bright and early at five. "Long drive," he explained. "Nearly ten hours." He sat down while Bina gathered her things. The ruddy-cheeked man refused tea. Not the right time of day, he said. "Only this?" he asked, nodding at her small bag. He accepted a plate of small winter oranges though. Father and Bina looked on, astounded, as he peeled them and then ate the skins only! He stopped mid-mouthful when he saw them both staring at him. "Got a cold coming on."

"Oh." Father raised his eyebrows at Bina as she passed through the doorway and hugged her goodbye.

They didn't say much on the way. Occasionally the driver would point out a landmark of interest. It was when they stopped for lunch that he surprised her for a second time that day. He took one look at her chapatti stuffed with lentils, grabbed it, and tossed it into a ditch!

"Here," he said. "Eat this. You need it, little pale one."

A sharp, tangy smell hit her nose, and it was hard to tell if it was good or bad. But the taste was delicious! Meatballs in a fresh tomato sauce dotted with pomegranate beads. *What did he mean, I need it?* After wolfing the dish down, her stomach was warmed and contented; Bina slept for the rest of the journey. Till the driver announced their arrival: "Here we are!"

Still sleepy, she noticed a conglomeration of blue and yellow roofs ahead, hugging a green hillside. The sun was already getting low in the sky, rendering the whole view with a pink-orange hue. It was the most beautiful scene Bina had ever seen. She thought she must be in a dream. Except . . . for a really bad smell. "Ugh! What's that?" she said, fumbling for the window handle.

"Don't worry—we'll soon pass it—just a bit of marshland," the driver said while accelerating so sharply that Bina was almost tossed out of her seat. For the first time, her companion seemed to have lost his cool; he was glancing anxiously from side to side. But Bina soon forgot all about that when she saw the trees. A country road, long and tree-lined, led up to the village. They were so tall! All the leaves were fluttering in the wind—strange, pale blue-green in colour. The whooshing sounds filled her ears, and she couldn't help but stick her head out of the window, grinning stupidly—just like a tourist!

"What are they?"

"Eucalyptus" came the reply.

"Euca . . . ?"

"Now that you mention it—I need some of that." The car screeched to a halt; the driver jumped out and grabbed some spindly branches, and they were off again. He turned to Bina with a cheeky smirk and repeated, "Got a cold coming on!"

Bina couldn't help smiling at this funny man of few words, who seemed so in tune with his stomach.

Dropped off at the only guest house in Karna, Bina settled herself in a central courtyard and waited. Lusciously abounding in greenery in pots of all shapes and sizes, some earthenware and elegant and others simply old tin cans, which had once contained ghee or cooking oil and were now painted in pastel colours, the courtyard was a mass of tangled, tumbling leaves and flowers. It was striking and wildly beautiful in its chaos—and the smell! Bina closed her eyes and breathed in deeply. Truly, she had never smelled anything like it; sweet fragrances mingled with wafts of strong heady ones till she felt almost dizzy. And all of this was being serenaded to by a mass of busy insects: dragonflies, bees, and butterflies, which flitted and fluttered and dived all around. Every one of her senses was being bombarded and, slightly stunned by this colourful explosion of life. Bina relaxed and leant back with her face to the darkening blue and pink sky, soaking it all in.

And that was how the landlady, Mrs. Luta, found her when she made her noisy, bustling entrance, overwhelmed as usual by all the day's chores. She looked upon the young girl with her eyes closed and a dreamy smile on her face and sighed. *Another one to be looked after.* As if she didn't have enough to do! So many visitors thronged to Karna, and hers the only guest house! Of course they all wanted to see the giant cucumbers and tomatoes in her garden, not to mention the famous watermelon patch at the other end of the village. And the water! Crowds sometimes clamoured at the spring source and village wells to taste the water. But, of course, it didn't take long before they settled down and found the calm and solace so desperately sought. She'd heard of the sickness and misery elsewhere in the region. But it wouldn't come here, that she could be sure of; the inhabitants of Karna knew how to keep it away. But the increasing numbers of visitors were wearing her down. She looked over at Bina again, and her heart softened. *She's so pale.* Something moved deep down in Mrs. Luta's heart. *There's something else. An aching pain.* But not being able to clearly put her finger on it, she woke Bina up instead.

"Najib—take this young lady's bag to her room, please. And get these cats out of here! Shoooo!" Her angry tones roused Bina, and she noticed the cats for the first time as they skittered away in all directions. One made a dash past Mrs. Luta with its mouth stuffed full of something, green tendrils trailing onto the ground. "Sorry to disturb you, dear, but they nibble all the wild garlic, you see, till there's none left. And we can't do without wild garlic, can we?" she explained in exasperation.

"No . . . I suppose not . . ." Bina's voice faltered as she noticed how strange the cats looked. She'd never in her life seen cats like them. "Wow—they're so fat and shiny!" she couldn't help exclaiming. A far cry from the dirty, skinny creatures which searched for scraps around her house back home.

"Well, yes they *would* be, eating from *my* garden, wouldn't they, dear? Now I've got a meal to prepare for twenty-two people tonight. And Mr. Sangrit doesn't like mushrooms, Baveeta and Meena are vegetarians, and what about the couple who arrived yesterday and their little baby . . . ?"

On and on she rattled, and it seemed that she had forgotten Bina's presence as she chopped mounds of vegetables (and they *were* huge, Bina noticed). The air was cool and clean. Bina was feeling different. It was difficult to place the feeling and put it into words, except to say that she felt bright and alive. Not tired in the slightest from her journey; she could have set off at that very moment on the long hike out of the village to where the myrrh trees grew. The visit was scheduled for tomorrow, however, and so there was nothing to do for now. As she leaned back and raised her face up to survey the twittering birds bouncing from branch to branch above, Mrs. Luta's eyes were on her again. "Hmm . . . my dear . . .

I was wondering," she said, hesitating momentarily and then continuing, "Have you had a shock recently?"

Taken completely aback, Bina didn't know what to say. And before she could catch herself, tears were filling her eyes and dropping one by one onto her cheeks and her chin, and even plopped into her hands, neatly folded on her lap. Mrs. Luta did nothing to stop her, but instead picked up a fat long-haired white cat and placed it gently in Bina's lap. Instinctively, the tabby nuzzled into Bina's neck and purred loudly in her ear. Bina sniffled and remembered the words she'd said to Pluto. *No matter what happens, I'll never leave you.* Was it only yesterday?

"I know just what you need!" Mrs. Luta was beaming over at her, while at the same time getting into action as she heated some butter in a small pan, tearing off some curly green and purple leaves, throwing them in, and stirring madly. Next came pounded garlic, shredded stringy cheese, and a squeeze of orange juice; lastly, she began grating a very large round brown nut into the steaming mixture. Mrs. Luta was able to do all this while barking out orders to what seemed like a legion of helpers. Girls were flying to and fro at dizzying speed, their bright saris dazzling Bina. Now that she had her attention, Mrs. Luta tossed something in Bina's direction. Bina managed to catch what she thought was a ball before it bounced off the cat's head! However, it wasn't a ball—it was the smooth brown nutmeg that Mrs. Luta had used in her cooking. She'd seen nutmegs before at home, of course, but nothing compared with this. It was absolutely *huge* and filled the whole palm of her hand! Where it had been grated, a glorious spicy smell exuded, one that made her remember celebrations her family had enjoyed years ago when they served milk and rice puddings and sweet yummy cakes. She saw her mother young and strong and smiling in the kitchen as she pulled the heavy tray from the oven with ease. She saw her father, coming in from his fields, tired and drenched in sweat, instantly light up at the sight of the house adorned with paper lanterns, glowing candles, and those sweet peppery-smelling cakes on the table. A lump rose in her throat—how different it all was now.

But there was Mrs. Luta at her side, pushing a bowl into her lap. "There, there now. No more tears. Let this warm your heart." And charged off to attend to her next job.

The food was incredibly yummy and . . . hot. Beneath the bowl, her legs were getting *so* warm. Yet the bowl didn't feel at all hot. Bina hadn't eaten a dish like this since she was a very young girl, maybe at her grandmother's house? She couldn't remember. The nutmeg spice combined with the cheese and orange juice perfectly sweetened the slightly bitter kale leaves. It was almost intoxicating. As she munched her way through the dish, she felt her head swimming. Had people forgotten these age-old recipes? Or maybe they just couldn't afford the ingredients? Bina didn't know. But certainly she hadn't seen a garden as lush and productive as Mrs. Luta's in many, many a year. Bina let her eyes wander around the courtyard and beyond into the garden and orchard again. So much splendour! Like an Aladdin's cave of treasure: precious stones, jewels, money, and gold—but in the shape of fruit, nuts, herbs, berries, and seeds.

These wondrous dreamy thoughts were cut short, because not only were Bina's legs feeling hot, the rest of her body was too. Not in an uncomfortable way, though; rather like being immersed in a warm and pleasant bath. It was the onset of tingling in her fingers that began to cause some concern. What was happening? Was this normal? She looked down at her hands and realised that it was her right hand only, the one still clutching the massive nutmeg. Her fingers began throbbing, and she instinctively and lovingly tightened her grip on the large nut, whose smell had made her think of her mother and father. *This is important,* she told herself. *I don't want to lose this feeling. Maybe . . . maybe we can live again?*

Only the chilly mountain breeze coming through her bedroom at night could calm Bina down. But nothing could cool her down. She stayed hot, and her fingers tingled, and although comfortable, she drifted into a fitful sleep. *What did all this mean?* Her dreams were confused: her sister Mira standing and walking like a normal girl, helping with the housework, herself at a school desk, carefully turning the pages of a shiny new textbook. But the one picture that dominated and kept Bina from sleeping: the faceless image of Ajit, a garland of marigold flowers around his neck, at the altar.

It was dawn when they set off on the trek to Pradesh Peak, where the myrrh trees grew. Bina was accompanied by Mrs. Luta's niece, Amina, and Najib, the porter from the guest house. It was the first time she'd been out into the village since arriving, and her eyes nearly popped out of her head. The beauty of the place was astounding; there was no doubt about that. The multi-coloured roofed houses that she'd seen from the taxi were even prettier close-up. Yards were well kept, overflowing with thick bushes and shrubs, pots of flowers, trees of all descriptions, many even bowed over, heavy with fruit. She could see fields in the distance, under cultivation by the villagers themselves. But it was the people who Bina could not help staring at. Faces, round and fat, smiling broadly, greeted her wherever she looked. People were genuinely happy here, it was obvious. *What was it about this place?* The question nagged inside her as they made their way across the market square and then towards a long path leading to high ground outside the village. And there wasn't a single deformed person to be seen. No blind. No beggars. What a contrast to the pitiful sights of despair Bina lived with every day in Carrunder. *Why hadn't the disaster affected them here? Karna was still close enough.*

Bina was aware of Amina tugging on her sleeve. Did she want some pumpkin cakes for breakfast? Of course she did! Bina now awaited each meal with anticipation. What would the effect on her be this time? She looked down at the nutmeg still clenched in her fingers. She daren't let it go. It seemed to be giving her something, but what? Her fingers still tingled, and that was enough of a clue for now that something very special was happening, and whatever that was, it came from this village. A stall came into sight, piled with pumpkins the size of huge boulders. The stall holder's three children were all sitting cross-legged on top of an enormous pumpkin, watching while their mother served sizzling hot pumpkin cakes from a griddle. The sight made Bina giggle till she couldn't stop.

"Now that's the first time I've seen you smile, Miss Bina. You always look so sad," Najib remarked.

This made Bina laugh all the more, shake her head, and wonder.

"It's this place. It's Karna. It's magical! I love it!" She began to twirl round and round and dance along the path, attracting smiles from those passing by. "What is it, Najib? What's going on here?"

"Well, we know how to grow and choose our food, that's all."

"That's all? No, I don't think that's all. There's magic here. Why didn't the disaster come here?"

"Oh no, it came all right," Najib answered her. "But we know how to fight the toxins, and we stay clean." He paused for a while, and she noticed that he was looking into the distance at the village's borders, where there was some marshland. There followed an awkward silence, and Najib seemed nervous. She decided to try to change the subject when he suddenly said, "We've got to keep it like this, you know. All these visitors—they mustn't take anything away from here."

Bina remembered her nutmeg and tightened her fingers around it.

"Are those the myrrh trees up ahead?" she asked. The conversation was forgotten and they trudged onwards up the hill. It was a long way up, and not so far from the top, a row of eucalyptus trees was swaying in the wind, just like those Bina had seen at the entrance of Karna. As they passed by, Bina ran her free hand through the waving branches of pale blue-green leaves. "Mmm, what a smell!" she said, breathing in deeply. What happened next was very odd; somehow, Bina felt her head expand. Not so much her head as her thoughts, or the space that her thoughts were in. She glanced upwards at their destination and back at the trees. "Um, could I just stay here awhile? I don't know why, but I want to keep on breathing in this euca . . . what are they called?"

"Eucalyptus," Amina said, smiling and looking at her with some scrutiny. "Najib, can you go up and buy the oil?"

Bina handed over all the money her father had carefully saved that year. "As many bottles as this will buy." And she slumped back against the white trunk of a eucalyptus tree with a long, weary sigh. Bina played with the fallen leaves, gathering them into a pile. "This time next month, I'll be gone from India."

A long silence followed, and Amina observed this slip of a girl with the sad honey eyes and careworn hands, frowning at the ground, picking the leaves up, and rubbing them under her nose.

"I know what you need," Amina offered, taking the leaves from Bina's hands.

"Why does everyone keep saying that?" Bina tried to joke, but she really wanted to cry. Finally the words came tumbling out: "I'm going to marry someone called Ajit, who I've never met *and* I think there might be something wrong with him. He lives in Manchester. I don't even know where that is. My family needs me here, especially my sister. She's damaged, deaf and blind and crippled—by the disaster, you know?" She looked up at Amina, who was staring wide-eyed at her. "No, of course you don't know. Because everything's so wonderful here—but outside we're living in hell!" Bina's voice had become high and desperate. "I wish . . ." but she couldn't continue.

Amina picked up some eucalyptus leaves and rubbed them between her fingers. Then she began to gently massage Bina's neck and shoulders. "This will make you feel better." But Bina didn't hear; she was only aware of a strong peppermint smell that was penetrating her mind. "I know this is what you need because you *chose* it."

"I did?" Bina was only half-listening; the smell was making her think of things that were far away.

"Yes," Amina continued to explain. "That's how it works here. We know what to eat and when to eat it. What herb or plant to use and when to use it."

"Just like the cats in Mrs. Luta's garden?" Bina murmured in a small voice.

"Just like the cats in Mrs. Luta's garden."

Amina's voice sounded faint and distant; Bina was now thinking of Glasgow and what it might be like. She imagined the streets and houses based vaguely on a film of London she'd once seen on television. Everything was very neat. There were hardly any people on the streets (not like India). She saw parks with lots of space and children playing. Large department stores with lit-up windows full of things she could buy. And then a house with a garden she could call home. Amina knew just how much time Bina needed to take full advantage of the oil's properties, but not more. "Najib's coming back now." Bina opened her eyes and smiled.

"Thank you." She didn't know what to say next, because she wasn't sure what had happened. Except that she felt more positive, and she didn't feel afraid. And her fingers were tingling again. "I think I might be all right—going to Britain, I mean." And then more to herself, as she looked down at the nutmeg, she added, "I think I'm going to like it there."

The time to leave came, all of a sudden. When they got back to the guest house, the taxi driver was waiting. He was picking some berries from one of Mrs. Luta's plants and popping them into his mouth. "I know," laughed Bina. "You got a cold coming on?"

"No—got a cough!" he chuckled.

And on this happy note, Bina left Karna. A crowd of onlookers, including Mrs. Luta and Najib, waved her off from the guest house. Amina ran alongside the taxi, holding Bina's hand through the window, wishing her well and asking if she had the little bottle of eucalyptus oil safely packed. Once they started picking up speed, Bina leaned back and sighed contentedly. What an amazing trip! She felt so happy and squeezed the nutmeg, still secured in her right hand, as if to say, "Thank you."

At the same time, she was aware that the taxi was travelling a little too fast, and there was that horrible stench again. As she made to roll up the windows, she caught sight of the driver's face in the car mirror. He looked absolutely terrified. Immediately, a chill crept over her as she realised something was very wrong, and that it had been kept from her all along.

"What is it? Wh . . ." But before she could get the words out, the taxi swerved suddenly and something heavy hit it on the left side. The driver swore as the car was spun round and round; he struggled to stay in control. Then to her horror and disgust, something long and slimy, like a snake, entered the car window and was twirling and stretching in the direction of her face! Bina heard herself screaming.

"Get out!" She heard the driver's frantic command but couldn't move. The long thing, which she now saw was an octopus-like tentacle (or was it an eel?), had grabbed her right arm. And now there was another, and another entering the car, long tentacles wrapping around everything and anything. The driver yelled as he was picked up around the waist and thrown to the other side of the road. There were too many now; maybe four or five had her pinned down on the seat, and she felt their grip tighten round her arms. And suddenly she knew. It was the nutmeg. They wanted the nutmeg. Skinny, razor sharp tendrils were wrapped round her hand, trying to prise open her fingers. But she would not let go. Not now. Now that she had *new life* tightly held in her hand, she would not let go. Through gritted teeth, she held on. And next she was moving rapidly to one side; the world was turning over. The sound of glass breaking told her she'd hit the road. Now she was jolting back and forward, and all the time, her head bounced off surfaces till she thought the pain would kill her. She felt one of the slimy things pull back one of her fingers. Shouts from outside told her that someone else was there. She thanked the gods, for she knew she was not able to hold on any longer. With a sudden jolt, her hand was free; the long creatures retracted with a flash of pain, as one left a laceration on her forearm. She was being pulled out of the vehicle and helped to her feet. "Now run!"

And so they ran. A loud crash made her look back. The others stopped too. The giant tentacles had completely surrounded the taxi and crushed it until all that was left was a tiny cube. They stood motionless in their disbelief, watching the long fingers slide back into the stinking marsh. Bina felt the nutmeg hot in her hand; stunned and in shock, a child's song that she'd heard in the streets at home played in her head:

Paradeesh, Paradeesh
I've come for your gold
Paradeesh, Paradeesh
I've come for your home
Paradeesh, Paradeesh
I've come for your health.

CHAPTER 8

Amy

A my had only three more days to complete her class presentation. And it *had* to be better than Chang Lee's. That's all that mattered.

On TeenNet, her friend Kim was rattling on about boyfriend troubles. *Who cares?* thought Amy. She turned on her computer with a sigh. *What stupid things people think are important!*

For a long time, ever since Amy could remember, the most important thing in life was to be number one. How much of that was her parents' doing and how much Amy's true belief was hard to tell, but for all she knew, she'd always felt it. In fact, at times she found her parents to be backward and silly. Almost on cue, her mom put her head round the door: "You okay, Amy? How's the presentation coming along? You finished yet?" She offered a plate of cookies— presumably to help with the thought process.

"How can I be finished if I've just started?" Amy whined in a voice clearly meant to indicate that she wasn't to be interrupted again. *How can I be finished? The music teacher's just left. How dumb can you get?*

She typed in her password (t-h-e-b-e-s-t-1-6). "The Face of China." What kind of presentation topic was that? It was so broad . . . or was it limiting? She had to admit she was puzzled. Surely China had many faces? Which was the most important?

And what were they in the first place? Any brief beginnings she'd made on this lay scratched out and crumpled on the floor. In the canteen earlier that day, she'd overheard a group of boys from her class discussing the topic. Chang Lee had announced his choice: "The Chinese Work Ethic and Progress." Lots of nods and grunts of approval resounded around the table. Amy had shrunk away, in case they noticed her and asked for her opinion. She wasn't going to risk losing face in front of Chang Lee. *Why do I care so much?* she asked herself as she applied her thumbs to the pressure points on the back of her neck. Why was life so tiring?

Her computer screen flickered on. There was breaking news: "Police broke up a demonstration today, in Jixi of Anhui Province, protesting the rise in deaths from starvation in rural areas." What was all this about? Amy stared at the screen for a few minutes before gathering her thoughts. She was amazed to read such a thing about her own country. *Starvation? Deaths?* How come? Her family always had enough to eat. And everyone else she knew. Just that evening, they'd had duck and chestnuts with rice, and for lunch: egg-fried rice, and even rice cooked in milk for breakfast. Rice and more rice . . . if there was nothing else, there was rice. So—why were people dying? Amy scrutinised the podcast carefully; the camera rested on one of the banners just long enough for her to make out: "Save our rice!" *Save our rice? But from what?* The question had captured all her attention; hence Amy didn't even notice her mother's next entrance or her words: "Amy—you working hard? Yes? Good."

Amy closed her eyes. Why were they always nagging at her? To become a doctor like her cousin, or a lawyer like Mr. Chang Lee Senior, whose new Hummer 3, tinted windows and all, was the new dinner table talk? *Well, bummer! I'll turn out just the way I want! And I'll start with a killer presentation.*

If she could find out what the rice of China needed saving from, maybe she'd have found something cutting-edge. And if need be, she'd stay up all night. But suddenly, someone was at the door again.

"Mom, pleeese!"

The next day at school found her very sleepy indeed. And horror of horrors, on such a morning, Chang Lee sauntered over at break with a bold, "So what's your presentation on?"

Sometimes rivals have to get straight to the point. He had made Amy feel nervous, so to buy time, she tossed it right back.

"I heard yours is on something about work and . . ." but she trailed off, somewhat miserably.

"The Chinese Work Ethic and Progress, actually. You know, of course, that our country now plays a major role in world economics?" Of course she knew; did he think she was stupid? "What's your presentation on?" he persisted.

"Oh . . ." Amy felt her face reddening. *Rice. Okay—exactly what about rice?* But she regained her composure ultra-quick, flashed her perfect white smile, tilted her head slightly to the side, and at the same time narrowed her eyes a little. She held this pose for a fraction of a second and said confidently, "Rice." *Why am I flirting with him?* Her inner voice was quite aghast.

"Rice? It's not a cooking project for Home Studies! Ha!" He looked around to see if he had an audience.

"Oh, don't be confused, Chang," she said off the top of her head, pretending she was a well-researched expert. "China, rice, the economy—you know they're all interconnected; all facets of the same polished diamond. You see what I'm talking about?"

"Wh-uh?" He was momentarily taken but didn't buy it. "Ha— girls! No good for anything. Go back home to the kitchen!"

Now Amy was raging. She marched off; head down, so no one would see her bright pink face. Once she reached the girls' locker room, she let rip: yelling, screaming, and bashing the locker doors with her fists. "Chang Lee got you in a steam again?" Kim teased, knowingly. "When are you going to admit that you like him? All this competition; it's a little more than academic, don't you think?"

Some other students overheard and giggled as they passed by; on hearing the bell ring, they skittered off to class. Amy stared after them (a bobbing mass of pink Hello Kitty) with disgust.

"*Me* like Chang Lee? That's *so* ridiculous!" But when she turned, Kim had already gone, and the supervisor stood there instead.

"Amy Wong—you're late for class. Detention. Thursday." Could this get any worse? The presentation was due on Friday morning! Today was Tuesday, and she was no further forward. Staying behind on Thursday was a disaster.

There had been a famine in Sichuan Province less than five years ago, and another one in Guizhou Province only two years later. At that time, thousands of people were wiped out in Hua-ch'i alone. Other areas had suffered terrible losses, too. Amy glanced at the time. It was way past midnight. It was getting too late to concentrate, but she couldn't stop. There were too many pressing questions, starting with, why was this not common knowledge? These tragedies had happened because the rice crop had failed. But why? Search as she could, there were no answers to be found. The door handle turned; it would be Mom again, begging her to get some sleep. But it wasn't her mom this time, it was her father.

"Amy, pack some things and get yourself to bed. We need to leave before dawn tomorrow. My cousin, Jiuliang, has died. We go to mourn his needless death. It's a long way. Sleep now."

"But—my presentation!" she wailed. Mr. Wong just stood there, staring with big sad eyes. That look made Amy feel like a prize idiot.

They passed her school at about 5.30 a.m., just as a large, bright green Hummer drew up at the far end of the railings bordering the grounds. *That's odd,* thought Amy, because the car unmistakeably belonged to Chang Lee's father. *Why so early?* she wondered and craned her neck round for a better look before they turned the corner. She saw Chang get out of the driver's door and walk a few steps to greet someone, who had been hidden from view under a tree. The person gave him something, which Chang looked at for a moment, and then he bowed and turned back to the car.

It was all over in less than a minute, but Amy's heart, much to her annoyance, was beating wildly. Why, she couldn't really tell; was it, one, because she hadn't expected to see him; two, because she didn't know he could drive and admired him all the more for it; or three, because it was a strange thing to be doing at five-thirty before school? The correct answer, of course, was one, but Amy wasn't to know that at the time. What should have got her nerves jangling was reason number three. But Amy wasn't to know that either. Later she would find out why.

Once off the highway, busy with commuters, the road to Anhui Province stretched out endlessly before them. After an hour of watching row upon row of residential complexes, large malls, shops and industrial lots go by, they left the cityscape of high rises in-the-making, flanked by their massive cranes, behind. Now their way led them through smaller towns, boasting traditional architecture, pretty villas, and gardens, with green branches waving at them over walls. On and on, until soon there was nothing to see. Vast spaces of emptiness either side soon served to empty Amy's mind of all thoughts—till school, Chang, and the presentation were like things of another world and time. So small and insignificant. Unlike China—vast and huge. Here was a face of China; this enormity. Going from one province to another was like visiting a different country.

They stopped at a roadside café and were served by a lady they couldn't quite understand, due to the dialect of the region, which sounded so rough to city dwellers like the Wongs. They ate miso soup and pickled cabbage rolls. *Doesn't seem to be a famine-stricken area,* thought Amy, as they were brought pumpkin and honey cakes and jasmine tea for afters. As they set off again, she lay back, her tummy warm and full, and listened to her parents talking. She found out what had happened to Jiuliang. There had been famine in her father's hometown for months on end, and not enough had been done to help. It was the first Mr. and Mrs. Wong had even heard of it. They argued and disputed over all aspects of the story, as parents on a long car journey are apt to do. Finally, Amy had to yell at them to stop—but by this time, they had gone and gotten themselves well and truly lost.

Navidrive having run out of battery, out came the maps and, while her parents hunched over them disagreeing about where they were, and—more importantly—*who* had got them lost, Amy wandered off the road to get a better look at the valley below. She'd heard of this valley; everybody knew it as the "rice bowl" of Anhui Province. What she saw was surprising—no, shocking. The rice fields were empty. Where there once would have been multitudes of workers farming the water-filled paddies, recognisable by their stooped postures and straw hats, there was no one.

Intrigued, Amy slithered down the slope, her sights set on reaching the first field. A quick glance back assured her that her parents were still in deep conflict. It was wetter than she'd thought it'd be, and her feet were soon covered in mud. A sudden gust of cold wind made her shiver. This was silly, she decided, and thought to get back to the car. That was when she realised that all around her lay some strange shapes. Withered rice plants, all twisted and contorted, littered the paddies. She lifted one up; it was far too pale to be a healthy shoot, and she noticed that it was covered with sort of black patches—a mould maybe?

But before she had time to think about it any further, she was aware that the wind was blowing even stronger; in fact, it was making her clothes flap uncontrollably. She struggled to hold her shirt and skirt down with one hand, while with the other, she tried to snatch her hair out of her face and eyes. This was ridiculous! What must she look like? But almost at once, all thoughts of herself were banished when she heard a voice calling from a distance. Was there someone out there? She rapidly scanned the empty horizon, but no, nothing. She was just thinking that it could have been her parents when it came again.

"Amy . . . Amy!" It sounded like a long whistle. And then she clearly heard the words, "Look upon the death."

Look upon the death? The words echoed around inside her mind. *Look upon the death.* And overcome with eeriness that chilled her to the bone, and suddenly afraid, she whirled around to get out of that place as quick as she could. It was hard to slosh through the flooded paddies at speed, and she arrived back soaked up to her knees. After Mom had thoroughly fussed over her wet feet and she was settled back in the car, dry and wrapped in coats, the journey commenced once more. Amy, still shaken up, gazed out of the window as the acres of empty rice fields floated by. *Ghost paddies,* she mused. *What ghost spoke to me out there?* As if to answer her own question, Amy looked down at her hand. There lay the dead and diseased rice plant: limp, pathetic, useless. Just how Amy felt at that moment. Scared and useless. She looked at the rice shoot again. *This is how the rice feels.* She knew it now for sure. What it all meant. This is how the rice felt. This is how the land felt. This is how the people felt. *Look upon the death.* She knew those words from somewhere.

She racked her brain, murmuring aloud, "Look upon the death, and . . . at the empty hearth. The rains . . ."

"will come no more, no grain inside the store," finished her mother. "Are you studying Ning at school these days?" She hadn't realised she'd been speaking aloud. Her mother knew poetry? That was the second shock of the day.

"No. We did it last term. I was just thinking . . . don't know why."

Her father continued solemnly, "O some mercy show, dear God to us below." He paused for a long time and then went on in a trembling voice, "Before all love is gone, behold an empty dawn."

Mom reached out and touched his hand on the steering wheel, and he let her hold onto him like that all the rest of the way, while he wept like a little child.

The brass band announced the start of the funeral procession; they were just in time. Amy's parents were immediately recognised and ushered to the front with the other close relatives, leaving her a little way behind. Amy didn't mind, as she didn't much like funerals, so keeping a distance was way more comfortable. The traditions followed in these remote villages usually meant that the body would be uncovered, waiting for all the mourners to file past and say a final farewell. She hated this part and was hoping to hide behind someone and, in this way, avoid looking. As she walked slowly along, the scene around her gradually came into focus, until she felt bad about feeling distaste at the ceremony. Misery abounded everywhere: on the gaunt and tragic faces contorted with grief, in the state of health most people were in, so thin and pale they looked. She overheard mutters of disbelief and shock at the number of funerals being held weekly and whispers of more to come. Worst of all, she became painfully aware of her well filled-out body and smooth round face.

What had happened here? But, of course, she already knew. She'd seen for herself the diseased rice plants, even held one in her hand, and surveyed the empty rice fields, endless rows of them. And so, deep in thought, she suddenly found herself at the entrance to the temple, with nowhere to hide. There was Jiuliang lying only two metres away! Amy broke into a sweat and started to breathe too fast. But onwards she was being forced to shuffle, people pressing in from behind. Where to look? *Just look straight ahead, straight ahead, straight ahead,* repeated inside her head. So she fixed her gaze on a banner which hung from the ceiling, engraved with elegant Chinese lettering. And froze. Uncannily, the poet Ning was quoted in exquisite gold: *Look upon the death.* Her head was swimming; people started gruffly urging her to move. The gold letters of *Behold an empty dawn* danced from the banner into the air, causing Amy to audibly gasp. People were annoyed now and started pushing. A voice and an arm round her shoulders were the next thing she knew.

"Hey—you all right?"

Amy came to her senses immediately; she hated appearing weak. Trying to shrug off the offending arm, Amy whirled around and . . . looked into the most beautiful face she'd ever seen. The traditional long trousers and tunic suit with epaulettes indicated an official, and a black sash, a mourner. With long black hair that almost touched his shoulders, and in that outfit, he could have belonged to another century. "Come on—let's get out of here!" He took hold of her hand and was pulling her away from the crowd. "It's going to take hours—do you really want to sit around, staring at a dead body?"

Amy flinched at this outspokenness and lack of respect, considering his position *and* being in mourning. She didn't know if she should go with him or not. A quick glance around proved that no one was paying attention to them anyway. Before she could reply, he was off, walking away so fast she had to run to keep up. The fact that he still held onto her hand, thereby breaking yet another convention, sent a thrill charging through her whole body. *Wow—someone who doesn't care!* she thought gleefully. His hand was warm; his grasp firm. She wanted to hold onto it forever. But protocol demanded that at some point, and at some point very soon, she would have to let go. As they cleared the crowds and began to walk side by side, she did. He spun round sharply at her, facing her square on, eyes unwavering, staring straight into hers. Amy didn't know how to relate to this—it was so unusual. She fidgeted, her face flushed. "So—what made you gasp back there?"

"Oh, that." She relaxed. "Those words. You know the ones on the banner above the body . . . I mean . . . Jiuliang." He frowned, not understanding. "You know, the poet's words."

"Ning?" His eyes sparkled a little.

"Yes, you know, *Look upon . . .*"

"*the death, and at the empty hearth. The rains will come no more, no grain inside the store,*" he finished it for her. "That one?"

"Yes." There was a moment's silence between them. Out of respect for the poet, for Jiuliang, or just for the gravity of the meaning, she didn't know. She remembered how his hand had felt in hers and longed to hold it again, but took a deep breath to banish the thought. "I heard it."

"Heard it?"

"Yes, those exact words. In the rice fields, in the valley, on the way, it was a voice—but the rice made me sick. I felt so cold, I . . ."

"Stop, stop! You're not making sense."

"Oh, sorry."

But he was smiling, not mocking her. "I'm Seung-Yub, by the way," he said. "And sorry for the fancy dress. Tradition, you know? I'm the mayor's son, *unfortunately*." He made a funny grimace at the "unfortunately," making Amy laugh.

"Oh no, it's nice. I mean . . ." Feeling flustered, Amy bowed in greeting in the correct and polite way. "Amy Wong."

Seung-Yub duly bowed back and, on raising his head, gave her a cheeky wink.

"So—you like poetry?" he asked.

"Well, not really. Of course, I've studied Ning at school, but I'm more scientific minded, really. Right now, I'm working on a presentation called 'The Face of China.'" She laughed out loud then, because now it seemed ridiculous how stressed out she'd been about it. "It's about rice and the famine that's been happening . . . here, actually." She stopped, suddenly aware that her project was about his people's suffering.

"Want to know about those ghostly rice paddies?" He leaned in, a mysterious look on his face. "Come on—I want to take you somewhere."

"Oh? Where?"

"To meet my grandmother," he answered excitedly, without a trace of embarrassment.

"Oh." Her heart sank a little. *Village boys!*

He turned around then, his eyes gleaming. "*And* I want to show you something!"

Yeah? Your pet goat? she thought; all her previous excitement was waning now—and fast.

"Follow me, my lady!" he said, strolling nonchalantly towards a row of motorcycles parked at the side of the road. "Hop on." Amy wondered if she should. Her parents would soon miss her and be worried. He sensed her reticence. "Nobody will notice. Believe me. They've all got their eyes closed!"

She was shocked at such obvious disregard for the feelings of the mourners, including her own family.

He must have seen doubt cloud her face. "Hey, don't feel like that! Look, I believe in being *real*. Jiuliang's dead. It's over for him. What about the rest of us? What about the future of my village—my land?" His voice got louder as he started the engine. "You'll see. C'mon—get on!" He motioned to the back of the bike. Amy had never ridden one before, but faking cool confidence, she positioned herself behind him. "Hold on, Amy Wong!"

For the second time that day, she was touching him; her arms wrapped around his middle as she leant onto his warm back. His long hair flew in her face. What did it smell of? She breathed in. Peculiar. Pine cones? Or . . . a wood at night? Eyes closed, she knew she was smiling, because this had to be the best day of her life.

And the visit to his grandmother didn't disappoint.

The motorbike climbed higher and higher, round and round the mountain roads (if you could call them roads, that is). They were often precariously close to the edge, but Seung-Yub seemed to know the tracks well; at times he would even raise an arm to point out something of interest. She saw Mt. Huang Shan, far ahead of them, cloaked in mist. And the vast, wide valley below them, the former Rice Bowl, the ghostly rice fields occupying a great swathe of land. Amy thought it took on the shape of a giant lizard, the individual paddies its scales, all in various shades of green. Then, suddenly, Seung-Yub swerved the bike sharply to the left, driving under a wooden archway decorated with carvings and the Chinese inscription in bright yellow letters: *Peace and Plenty.* They'd arrived.

They were in a spacious courtyard (pretty much covered in mud), with low wooden buildings set out in a semi-circle, leaving an open view over the sloping hills of the farm below. The place was a hive of activity, people moving in all directions: some with hoes over their shoulders, some carrying water buckets on poles, others pushing carts laden with vegetables. Among them, ducks and geese waddled leisurely. She even saw some piglets dart across, sliding in the mud. It looked to Amy like a scene from an old picture book she had had as a child. It was strange to see a farm like this really existing in present time.

Seung-Yub pulled her by the elbow towards the main house, where they climbed onto a wooden terrace festooned with long bunches of dried red peppers, onions, and garlic. Through the open door, an amazing smell drifted out. "We're just in time for lunch," Seung-Yub said, grinning. "Come on!"

People were taking their places at several long tables. As she sat down, the farm workers were eying her curiously, probably due to her trendy city getup. (Leggings and a tight short dress, which had made the motorbike ride a tad difficult!) And out came the food: large bowls of steaming rice; deep iron woks, their contents sizzling noisily and steam billowing into the air behind them; platters of vegetables swimming in a sauce of whole red chillies. The rustic beauty of the table and its dishes took her breath away, and she almost jumped up, phone in hand, to take a picture, when just in time, she realised how ridiculous that would seem. And it was a good job she hadn't, because someone was now standing and saying a few solemn words about Jiuliang's death: on how the circumstances were tragic, yet avoidable, on how much his visits to the farm would be missed, and regret that he hadn't been helped more. After the prayer, everyone dived in, chopsticks clicking, and Amy asked Seung-Yub where his grandmother was.

"Oh, she's still in her clinic . . . she's never on time for meals."

"Her clinic?"

"Over there." He pointed to a yellow wooden house to the far right. And, sure enough, the painted letters said "People's Clinic," and as if to prove it, there were people grouped around the entrance, some carrying children. Most looked pitifully poor and bedraggled. A woman appeared in the doorway at that moment and waved over, smiling. She didn't look like a regular grandmother to Amy, except perhaps for her white hair, but even that was cropped short, uncharacteristic for an elderly rural Chinese woman. After talking to the people for a little longer, she made her way over. Amy watched her approach; she was wearing a simple red dress and many necklaces, which swayed as she walked.

"Is she a doctor or . . . ?" Amy had never seen such an unusual-looking woman.

"A traditional healer," Seung-Yub answered mid-mouthful.

A quack, you mean, Amy thought scornfully. She had no patience for non-scientific things.

Grandma took her place at the table, saying, "I'm late, and I'm sorry." She bowed to Amy. "My name's Xi, by the way. Always late, but what can I do?" She glanced back at the small crowd. "They're always waiting, sometimes for days." She scooped up a portion of rice and spooned the hot pork stew on top.

"Waiting for what?" Amy couldn't follow what was going on.

"Well, herbal medicine for one thing, and food. We hand out portions of rice every day to those affected by the famine."

"But . . ." Amy thought there was something strange about this. "If there's a famine here . . . I mean, a failed rice crop," she remembered the ghost paddies, "where does yours come from?"

In the momentary silence that followed, the two looked at each other and smiled strange compressed little smiles. Seung-Yub continued, avoiding her question, "Amy—what were you telling me about Ning's poem? You heard something in the rice fields? Heard what?"

"Oh, okay. Well, I heard the words of the poem that's written on the banner in the temple. *Look upon the death . . .* the wind said something . . . or I think it was the wind . . . but then I felt sick, like the rice shoot I found, and then at the funeral . . . the same words danced off the banner into the air . . ."

She trailed off, realising how stupid it all sounded. But when she raised her eyes, Grandma Xi and her grandson were staring at each other. Xi gave a short little nod, and Seung-Yub was on his feet.

"You'll need to be back soon, won't you?" he asked. For a second, Amy wondered if she'd done something wrong. But he was smiling gently as he added, "Come on, time to show you something. Like I promised, remember?"

Grandma Xi stood up and, to Amy's surprise, pulled her close to her chest. She was so short, Amy had to bend down. Xi was whispering something, a prayer maybe. Amy thought she heard the words *keep her*, and when she finally let Amy go, there were tears in her eyes.

Within minutes, they were on a path leading down the other side of the mountain, towards the farm's rice fields. She noticed that Seung-Yub kept looking nervously back over his shoulder. He led the way into a cave and, holding a torch in one hand, began feeling the rock face with the other. "That's it!" he murmured and, screwing his face up with the effort, pulled at a rock till it came loose. From the space in the cave wall, he carefully drew out a package. He sat Amy down; leaning in very close, so close that she could feel his sweet breath on her face, he pressed it into her hands. "Amy, this is for you. You're the Keeper. Take care of it."

"Wha . . ." she started to say, but Seung-Yub put his hand up to her mouth.

"You have to wait for a message. Do you understand?"

Amy was shaking her head and mouthing "No," when the tingling began. Her hands were getting hotter and hotter until they were almost on fire—but it didn't hurt. Then the tingling was accompanied by a tinkling sound, like hundreds of tiny bells ringing. It was obvious that Seung-Yub neither felt nor heard what she was experiencing, because he kept on talking. She knew she was staring at him open-mouthed, but she couldn't help herself. He was undoing the package now, revealing a little pile of rice grains. They were of various colours, ranging from white, through cream, brown to dark black. On looking down at them, she realised the shrill tinkling was coming from them—from the grains of rice!

Seung-Yub warned, "Don't tell anyone about this. We want you to get our precious wild rice out of here before it gets into the wrong hands. And remember—wait for the message!"

She understood this time and kept on nodding, though she was lip reading, as the rice grains' ringing filled her whole head! Before they left the cave, Seung-Yub helped Amy to hide the small package in her dress pocket, and as they straightened up, they were suddenly face to face, looking into each other's eyes. Amy was to play out that moment in her mind hundreds of times over the next few months: seeing how shocked her face looked, Seung-Yub cupped her cheeks in his hands and kissed her lips ever so lightly. And it was over, and they were out in the bright sunlight, and they were walking quickly up the path.

She thought of two things on the way back home in the car: the look in Seung-Yub's eyes just before he had kissed her, and the word "*Keeper.*" So it was *Keeper* that Grandma Xi had said in her prayer. What did it mean? These grains had been entrusted into her care, that was for sure, but what was she meant to do with them? In response, her pocket started to throb until she was sure there must be a hot, red patch on her thigh. A gentle tinkling sound, like chimes in a breeze, began again until she succumbed. *Okay, okay . . . wait for the message.* And she fell into an exhausted sleep.

But that was when the dreams began. Dreams that would haunt and disturb her for nights on end. On that long journey through China's vast spaces, as evening drew in, the ghosts of the sick paddies wailed and screamed in their torment and would continue all night.

By the time Thursday's detention came round, Amy had her presentation all worked out. She was so confident, in fact, that the humiliation of standing in the detention line with kids from lower grades didn't bother her at all. She was just going over the final details in her head when Chang Lee happened to walk past on his way to the library. He hadn't seen her, but Amy was annoyed to find her heart beating just as strongly as before. During the ride on the motorbike and in the cave, her heart hadn't beaten like this. It suddenly occurred to her that maybe Seung-Yub had used a romantic ploy to get her to do what he wanted. Her hackles were raised then, and a hot surge of anger followed, especially when she caught sight of Chang Lee coolly flicking through his papers as he queued up for photocopying. Her competitive streak aroused, there was no stopping her—she was like a warrior. She knew what she would do. Because now she had an edge. She knew what she would do, and she'd come out number one.

The bell rang for the end of detention, and Amy marched in the direction of the school gates. But if she had stuck around a little longer, she would have seen Chang Lee leave the library, walk up to a boy waiting on a bench, hand him a wad of paper, and give him a five hundred yuan note.

Amy was last to give her presentation. Several of the parents were in attendance, including Chang Lee's, who were, at that moment, beaming, thanks to his superlative performance. At last her name was called, and she was in front of the class. She began with a sweeping announcement: China's great heritage is going down the drain! Amy Wong was in action again, and every twist and turn was impressive. Her maps, graphs, and pie charts informed the audience how China's rice crop was in danger of dying out from disease unless . . . the only remaining grains of wild rice were located and the healthy practice of diversity encouraged again.

"And," she paused, ready to play her trump card, "I have a specimen to show you here today."

With a flourish, she produced a little glass container holding the rice and proceeded to walk around, showing it off. Instantaneously, two things happened at once: one of the parents rose to his feet, taking his phone from his pocket as he left the classroom, and Amy felt a sharp stab of pain in her abdomen. It was hard for her to make it back to her original spot next to the teacher's desk. She struggled to wind up with the few clever sentences she'd prepared. *What were they?* She'd rehearsed them over and over this morning on the bus. Glancing down at her notes on the desk didn't help either; the pain was increasing, making her dizzy so that the notes became a blur. To make matters worse, when she finally looked back at her audience, she was mostly aware, through the glass door, of the parent who'd left abruptly as he walked up and down, talking on his mobile phone, glancing back in at Amy at rapid intervals.

Chang Lee was beginning to notice that something was going wrong, and a self-satisfied smirk appeared on his face. Of course Amy saw this and felt her insides crumble. How could this be happening? She was gripping onto the tiny vial containing the precious wild rice as if her life depended on it. She'd never before lost face in front of the class, never failed like this. It was then she realised that she couldn't feel her fingers tingling like they always did when she held the rice. Nor were her hands hot, and no sound could be heard either, except for a classroom of people holding their breath, and an unfortunate snigger or two. With a chill that almost made her heart freeze, Seung-Yub's words came back to her: "Don't tell anyone about this . . . before it gets into the wrong hands." What had she done? Oh no—what had she done?

She was, literally, saved by the bell. Because at that sound, everything became motion. She was aware of the parent re-entering the classroom and making a beeline straight for her. There was laughter in the corner, where Chang sat with his parents. The teacher's voice was shrilly thanking everyone for coming and at the same time warning students against running from the room. As usual, no one listened and kept pushing their way to the door. And, suddenly, Amy bolted. She left everything behind except the vial of rice, which she shoved into her trouser pocket. There was that throb of heat again, spreading warmth across her thigh. For the first time ever, she mouthed a prayer of thanks. To whom or to what, she had no idea, but the chiming noises emanating from her pocket were her answer. *Wait for the message.* She remembered now as she ran down the corridor, pushing kids out of the way left and right. Why was she running? This was crazy.

Once out in the playground, she didn't stop. Sure enough, the loud footfalls behind her proved someone was following, and not far behind. A sharp look behind proved it. There he was, sporting sunglasses, and *still* on the phone. She broke into a sprint; this was no problem, he didn't have her training. She jumped onto the bus as he reached his car. But the bus was slow in the rush of school traffic, and soon he was directly behind. Amy peeked at the car and its driver in the bus wing mirror as they crawled along. She was racking her brain for a plan of what to do once she got off. What had she done? She'd made the wild rice public for her own benefit, to get an A and be first in the class. And to get Chang to admire her. But what did that matter now? She cringed at the thought of Seung-Yub ever knowing this about her. Her hands were shaking. Instinctively, she reached into her pocket to touch the precious treasure. As she gripped it, tears pricked her eyes; she'd have to be strong for Seung-Yub, for Grandma Xi . . . but it was more than that. Of course it was. The starving people she'd seen, too. The future rice crop depended on her. But the bus was stopping now, and instead fear overtook her thoughts again.

The stop was only fifty or so metres from her house. She could make it by the time he parked his car, surely? She chanced a quick look behind but couldn't see him. Looking only ahead now, she gathered speed, and then a familiar figure came into view. There was Mom walking towards her, carrying shopping bags. Amy felt a surge of pleasure at seeing her mother as never before, but fear quickly followed to check it. The sidewalk on their side was empty—good—there was nothing keeping them from the door of the apartment building. But Mom could be slow. Her pursuer was behind her now and coming up fast; a pizza delivery person on skates had appeared behind her mother. *Could be useful,* she thought, her martial arts training clicking into gear. She decided to trip up the skater, grab Mom's arm, and make a dash for the steps.

But just as the moment arrived, as Amy was beginning to move her leg out to the right, something weird happened. The delivery person threw the pizza box in Amy's face. Amy saw it all as if in slow motion: her arms rising up to push the box away, pizza slices falling past her face onto the ground, her mom slipping forwards with arms stretched out, a look of extreme shock on her face as she lost her balance. It was the sensation of someone tugging at her jacket that snapped her into action. She saw red.

With a shrugging of her arms, he loosened his grip and she twirled full circle on her opponent. A fast left kick took care of those sunglasses and stunned him, his hand reaching up to hold his jaw. Hardly a split-second later, Amy had struck again, this time with her fist under his chin. Stepping back to reposition for a knee-in-groin move, she caught sight of a disconcerting look on his face: fear and shock—but he wasn't looking *at* her, instead beyond her. Following his stare, on whirling round, she saw Mom lying splayed out on the sidewalk, her face deathly pale with a small pool of blood moving outwards from her head.

Like any trained fighter, she kept her composure until the enemy had been dealt with, although inside she was screaming. She needn't have bothered, because he was off like a shot, before she could even get a good look at his face. There was no sign of the delivery boy either; he must have already scarpered. Like a good warrior, her next move should be to call for help, so she pulled out her phone, fingers trembling. She couldn't see her mother clearly any more; a small crowd of onlookers had gathered around her, some kneeling, and one holding her hand. Amy pressed the button for Dad and waited, wailing loudly inside.

Finally he answered, and she yelled, "Dad—Mom's been hurt!" Her eyes were fixed on a box of broken eggs that had fallen from the shopping bag.

CHAPTER 9

Bina Goes to Glasgow

B A 202 London Heathrow: Gate 9

Placing one foot in front of the other and counting her steps, counting all the time, and taking deep breaths, Bina slowly but steadily made her way towards Gate 9. Through that gate was the pathway to a new and different life. As she walked down the tunnel to the door of the aircraft, she was suddenly aware of how different she looked to the other passengers. She wasn't the only one wearing a sari, but she felt she wasn't wearing it right. The other Indian women had flashy jewellery and shiny bags. They wore a lot of makeup. She stood apart in her village dress—the colour was too bright, but she had chosen yellow to match the sunflowers in their backyard. On top, she wore a Nike sweatshirt that a neighbour had given her, saying that everyone wore these in America. (She wasn't going to America, but never mind.) On her feet was a pair of new clumpy, white trainers. She had thought she looked trendy and Western, but in reality, she looked a mess. Once settled in her seat and ready for take-off, she stared down at the hennaed hands that marked her out as a bride, focussing her eyes on the whirling patterns and gathering strength.

For once, her right hand wasn't clutching the nutmeg. It was packed carefully in her hand luggage—but never far away. She thought of it now and wished she was holding it, but too late, the plane was racing down the runway and then jumped unnaturally into the air as she closed her eyes and said what felt like a hundred prayers.

Soon she was above the clouds and there, far below, was another plane flying in the opposite direction, trailing white smoke. How incredible to be part of traffic in the skies! The enormity of this new experience left her light-headed, and she instinctively reached for the little bottle of eucalyptus oil in her pocket. The aroma helped to settle her and, as she pushed her seat back and closed her eyes, she saw a garden. *A house and a garden to call my own,* she mused. And she remembered the last time she had thought about this. It had been in Karna, that amazing village where everyone was healthy and strong. Where the gift of a nutmeg had been thrown into her hands and where . . . her hand touched her right arm, stroking the place where there was a wound . . . where . . . an enormous thing had attacked her, trying to take that gift away. Had it all been real? But here were the marks of the ugly laceration, healing now, thank the gods. *What* did it all mean? She had puzzled for hours over that question during the last few weeks. If something wanted the nutmeg, wouldn't it still want it now? And how could a thing *know* anything, anyway? Or was it a "someone"? There had been no explanation at the time—only fear. What had Najib said? "They mustn't take anything away from here." But she had. What had she done? What about the kind people she'd met; had she put them in danger? Of . . . what? She thought of the nutmeg in her bag; was *she* in danger? Bina had to admit to feeling afraid, but there was no one to tell.

Uncle Rajeev met her at the airport, along with a few other relatives she didn't know. It was a relief to hear her own language spoken again. For the last few hours, and for the first time in her life, Bina had been in an English-only bubble. Now they were in Uncle's car, driving across Glasgow to 12, New Market Gate. Many polite greetings and pleasantries were exchanged, as was the custom. They were trying their best to put her at ease, Bina knew that, but nothing could help her now; her heart was as grey as the murky skies above. *Why so little colour?* She was surprised; she had thought Scotland to be beautiful and green. New Market Gate was no different. A row of grey brick houses, all joined together. *And* there was no garden, only a concrete backyard. This disappointment hit Bina hard, and she could no longer keep smiling at all those people. There must have been almost twenty of them squashed into that tiny living room, and all looking at her! A silver tray, on which sat two lumps of pink gelatine sweet dusted with white sugar, was brought in and placed on the coffee table. What—was the engagement ceremony to take place right there and then? But which one was Ajit? They hadn't been introduced yet, but it became obvious to Bina, after another hour had passed and yet another two rounds of tea, that he wasn't there. From the tension in the room, betrayed by too many whispers and fake smiles, she deduced that he was somehow missing or very, very late.

A sudden knock at the door produced long exclamations of delight and undisguised relief. "Ahhhhh! The groom! The groom is here!"

Bina's heart froze, and she held her breath, for in the next moment, she was to see her destiny, in person.

He didn't look at her at all. Not a glance. The young man walked quickly in, bowed to his father, lit a cigarette, and then dragged a chair over to the window and sat smoking, looking out at the street. Any tension there had been in the room now reached a new height, resulting in several people starting to talk at once to compensate, which only added to the embarrassment. Bina, sitting still as a statue, humiliated by this unexpected behaviour, her eyes fixed on the two pink and powdery sweets in front of her; suddenly stood up.

"I want to see Auntie Gandhali."

CHAPTER 10

Abala at the Refugee Camp

On waking, it took Abala two seconds to realise where he was. He usually remembered before the smell hit him. Never before had he known that human beings could smell so much. The stench was unbearable; there were just too many people. On top of this, it was his misfortune that the toilets and washrooms were very close to the small tent he shared with seven other people.

Nobody in the tent had stirred, except for the baby, so it was a good time to slip out before its mother woke up. He'd been placed in a family with five children, probably because they had a boy his age. They were kind people, but they didn't know each other. It was awkward to be so close to strangers, especially in sleep, for a body to touch his, one that wasn't Mama or his brother or sister. Hence, he couldn't sleep at all for nights on end; lying awake, listening to breathing that didn't sound like Mama and Father, he'd even have preferred Grandfather's snores. That thought sent a vicious jolt of pain to his heart: *Grandfather must be dead now. And Mama and Father? And . . .* But he stopped himself, because it was more than he could bear. He was left instead with the moaning of those having bad dreams; worse still were the screams of those who couldn't forget.

He liked to get out on his own, except there was nowhere to go and nothing to do. The other day, while he'd been walking around the camp, as he was accustomed to doing out of sheer boredom, he saw an elderly man sitting at the doorway to his tent, staring into the distance, looking out at the horizon like Grandfather used to do when there was a problem to solve. Motionless. Just staring. What problem was this man grappling with? Lost loved ones? Losing everything? Another few laps of the place, and Abala had passed this man three times. There he was. Still sitting. That's what it was like at the camp. Two things prevailed: Boredom (which was almost bearable) and hopelessness (which was not).

The refugees were given enough to eat, certainly. The food was bland, though. It was not the food of his country. There was no joy in eating a plate of food that was not a meal, lovingly prepared at home. It was not spicy. There was no *berbere* or *injera* bread. People here ate in rows, in silence, after they'd queued for hours. Some who had found family members sat in groups and talked. They were the lucky ones. The rest ate only to stay alive.

As the days wore on, Abala found that the best place to hang out was the children's area. You couldn't really call it a school, as there were no specific classes, there being a mix of too many ages and children who'd never been to school—but it was a hub of activity, nevertheless. The children drew and played games and even watched films. Abala had watched *101 Dalmatians* and thought that he'd have headed up a rescue mission if those hundreds of puppies had been goats.

This was definitely the place to be, and it was here that he first saw the red-haired girl. She wasn't African, and her father was in charge of the children's area. She was the only white child in the whole camp. Abala felt bad for her. How lonely she must feel to look so different! When she got tired of playing with the little kids, he noticed that she would tug on her father's elbow, and he'd nod and hand her a thin book, which lit up when she opened it. She would sit for hours, smiling into the bright light, until her father called over, pointing to his watch. He guessed it must be like playing cards; Mama always got annoyed if he and his brothers spent too much time playing and not doing chores. Oh, how he wished he could see inside that book and find out where the red-haired girl escaped to!

One time, when he'd sneaked out of the tent to go walkabout after dark, he saw that there were lights on in the workers' building. Curious, he crept up for a closer look. Crouching under an open window, Abala dared a peek. He saw the workers sitting round a table, playing a game of some sort; the red-haired girl was among them. She was throwing a die, and cheers went up: "A six for Sally!" her father shouted, patting her on the back. Her face was glowing in the light of the paraffin lamp. Sally. Lucky Sally. But she looked up suddenly and noticed him there. Abala froze and just stared back. Sally made to say something, but he turned and ran.

Back on his mattress, he struggled with pain and resentment. *It isn't fair.* He'd seen fresh fruit in that room. Mangoes and bananas. They never got a banana in the dining area. Not since he'd been there, anyway. Not able to sleep, he searched his mind for comforting thoughts. That didn't work. Something was making him uncomfortable; finally he found the offending object under the mattress—it was the carob pod he'd picked up on the night he was found. Still with him after all those weeks! Warm memories flooded in of that dinner he'd shared with the other survivors in front of the campfire. He could almost smell the roasting chicken . . . the looks on those people's faces when he'd prayed Grandfather's prayer! He fell asleep smiling, but a few minutes too soon, or he would have felt the burning sensation in the fingers which still held onto the pod. *Thanks be to God that we live another day and share this bread . . .* He was dreaming now . . . *as a symbol of our bonds.* His new tent family were sitting on the floor, grinning widely at a mound of colourful fruit in the centre. "Go on—eat!" Abala was saying, picking up a banana and tossing it into the lap of the youngest little boy. "Thank you, Abala Alemayehu Zerihun," someone said. He smiled.

The next morning, Sally sat with her eyes on the opening of the children's tent, waiting for Abala to enter. She hadn't been able to sleep either at first, but finally had dreamt of the boy who she'd seen at the window. He was sitting at the head of one of the groups of people in the dining tent, with a crown of fresh berries on his head. The juice was dripping down onto his forehead, and he wiped it away, laughing. A huge platter of fruit was on the mat, and the other refugees crowded round, helping themselves and calling out the boy's name. Three names: Abala Alemayehu Zerihun.

There he was! She rose and strode directly over to him, saying, "Hi, I'm Sally." Abala couldn't get over his shock in time:

"I'm sorry I was looking in your window," he blurted out.

"No worries! Hey—you speak English, that's cool!" her voice sounded funny to Abala. (Later he was to learn she was American.)

"Auntie Melkam taught me."

"Do you want to play on my iPad?" she gestured excitedly at the book in her hand. Abala nodded, his eyes open wide. Yes, that was exactly what he wanted.

After they had played several games, Sally was getting restless; Abala, on the other hand, could have played on and on for days! Eventually, she asked, "Do you want to see my blog?"

He didn't but nodded anyway, pretending he knew what she was talking about.

But the blog turned out to be a lovely thing, like a picture book, but with real photos. Sally was writing a story about the camp—like a diary, he thought. He saw pictures of many refugees there. "Put my picture," he said, pointing to himself.

"Good idea!" Sally said enthusiastically. Suddenly, the book was taking his picture! That was when Abala started giggling. Sally's fingers slid across the screen in all directions, which Abala found even funnier. Then—there he was! Smiling back at himself. This caused Abala to finally explode with laughter. Sally caught the laughing bug as well; her father came over, looking amused.

"Hey guys—what's going on?"

"Abala's going to write in my blog!" Sally sounded very positive about this.

"That's so cool, little dude!" her father agreed, slapping a firm hand on his shoulder. Abala felt a little afraid, like he was being forced into a corner by these two very enthusiastic people. *Write what?*

"Hey—it's okay," Sally said; she must have sensed his alarm. "Just write about what you think. What's going on in your life—that sort of thing." She made it sound so easy. Abala promised to go away and try. Which he did. And the next day, he came back with this:

I Am Hungry
I am hungry
for Mama's food
for berbere and injera bread
for wot and khat
for laughing faces round the dinner table
for the smell of my goats
and wood fires burning
for my life to go on as before
for Grandfather's prayers
to have fields full of wheat
and plenty to eat

"Wow—that's so awesome!" Sally was ecstatic. She began typing straight away. "There—done and posted!"

"Posted? Like a letter?"

"Yeah! Faster than a letter—look." And there it was on the screen, like a page from a book.

"Who will read it?"

"The whole world, if they want to!" she said, smiling. "Hey, there's another blog I was reading yesterday, it's by a guy called Porky. It's crazy—he wrote a poem just like yours . . ."

But Abala had sunk deep into thought, his poem having stirred him up inside. What was he really hungry for? What did he want to happen? Stay like this? He'd cried all he could cry. He was empty of tears. He knew he wanted to go back to his old life, before the land grabs, before the fighting, before the famine. To when they had sat round the table, listening to Grandfather's stories. To when he had woken up to the smell of *injera* bread baking. When there had been enough for everyone.

"Here it is." Sally moved closer to show him. Abala snapped out of his reverie. "See—Porky's Blog."

"Por-ky? Funny name."

"Yeah, like a pig or something! But he's one cool, angry dude! He's in hospital—he's sick but he writes every day. Look, a poem—just like yours! *I Am Hungry* by Porky McGregor:

> *I'm in hospital and I'm hungry.*
> *Not for hospital food—no way!*
> *Not for McDollar's—that's for sure!*
> *Not for packets of crisps or chocolate bars.*
> *Hey! I'm fat and I'm hungry.*
> *Not for liquid soup—which I'm fed every day.*
> *Or even a treat of fish and chips.*
> *No! I'm hungry for change,*
> *My friends.*
> *I'm Hungry for Change.*

"Isn't that cool?" Sally said, practically screaming. Abala nodded gravely and read it over and over. *Hungry for Change.* And he began to understand.

Later that afternoon, Abala found himself, for once, alone in his tent. His mind was preoccupied with everything that had happened that morning. He twirled the carob pod between his fingers in an effort to relax. "For my life to go on as before." The words of his own poem haunted him. *But it can't. How can things go back?* He liked Porky's poem. *I'm hungry for change, my friends.* Porky was right. But how? How could he change his future? He was a young boy, not educated yet, not skilled in anything—except looking after goats! He had nothing. No power. Nothing.

That was when he became aware that the carob pod was vibrating in his hands; his fingers were tingling in just the same way. Abala felt a little afraid but remembered his dream and thought perhaps this had something to do with Grandfather's prayer. The same instant he had that thought, his eyelashes started fluttering uncontrollably. It was weird but not uncomfortable. Abala was enough in tune with the land to recognise a sign when it came. So, it wasn't true that he had nothing. He had something. He felt that he had something. *And share this bread, which He has ordained as a symbol of our bonds.* The familiar words of the prayer spoke of a truth, a truth that he knew and believed—and wanted to live out! Everyone has the right to have enough to eat. *Was that it? Was that what Grandfather's prayer meant?* He was thinking fast now. His whole body was vibrating. *And sharing food together strengthens us. Yes, that's it.* He was feeling all warm and peaceful now. The gong rang for the last meal of the day. And he was ready to go.

He endured the boredom of the long queue, his body quivering ever so slightly, in anticipation of what might happen. What that was, he had no idea. But he felt on the brink of something, and he couldn't wait. *Hungry for Change;* Porky's words were becoming like a mantra. He picked up his bowl and bread ration and looked for a place to sit among the long rows of people eating. He saw his tent family and made his way over to join them.

"*Dananacho!*" he cried brightly.

A few people looked up at the happy sound of his greeting, but they looked back down at their bowls again and continued eating. Abala positioned himself in a spot where he could be seen clearly; he put down his bowl, raised his hands palms upwards, and uttered Grandfather's prayer in a loud voice. People were looking over now, whole groups turning their heads. There was a ripple of quiet laughter and smiles all around. Then silence followed; the usual blanket of silence which accompanied mealtimes. Abala also fell silent and bowed his head, shy now at his bold demonstration. *What if he was wrong?*

A cry rang out then, quickly followed by the rumble of many voices, all exclaiming and shouting at once. Someone's bowl was full of steaming hot wot stew, another with *berbere*-soaked chicken! Yet another found himself eating spicy khat and lentils! The wonderful smell of freshly baked *injera* bread was wafting around the tent. A child ran by, laughing, and dropped a banana in Abala's lap. "Thank you, brother!" he almost sang.

This made others turn and look at Abala. Some called out sweet sentiments and others saluted.

"It's not about me," he started to explain over the din.

All the camp workers came running in then; Abala smiled at their baffled faces. For what they saw, no man would believe. Platter upon platter of the most delicious Ethiopian delicacies were spread out on the floor mats, the people tucking in as if there was no tomorrow! Baskets of fruit lined the walls. Jugs of fresh juice appeared too—out of nowhere! Children were running and whooping as if at a wedding. It was truly amazing! Women were coming up to Abala and kissing him on the top of his head. Someone in the far corner started singing an old folk song about ushering in the harvest. Another banged the floor like a drum. Soon everyone was singing along. Abala saw Sally out of the corner of his eye, just as he was being hoisted up on a young man's shoulders.

She called out, "Way to go, dude!"

He shouted back, "Hungry for Change!" and raised his fist in the air, laughing. "We have to tell Porky!"

She gave him a thumbs up. And still the food wouldn't stop coming; people were now gathering it up for the next day's breakfast. The revelry went on far into the night, until people slowly wandered to their tents for a good night's sleep. Abala was much too excited though, so he went for a walkabout around the edges of the camp. Elated, he hummed the song sung that evening: *Draw in the harvest, pull in the carts. Overflowing with kindness from Earth's very heart!*

He had just fifty metres more before his own tent would come into view. He heard a growl from out in the adjoining wilderness, alerting him that a wild animal was close. The massive dark shape was visible now, lurking on the other side of the fence. The snarl that followed stopped him in his tracks. And then he heard a voice:

Do not repeat that spectacle, Abala Alemayehu Zerihun, or you will never speak again.

Abala stood frozen on the spot. His mouth was suddenly very dry. The beast drew closer to him, its eyes glinting.

What—tongue-tied already?

CHAPTER 11

Porky meets Bina in the Garden

It was a perfect sunny Sunday, cold for November. Only Porky didn't think it was so perfect. His parents had had the bright idea of visiting him and bringing Uncle Billy and Aunt Jean with them. *No way!* Porky had glowered at the nurse when she brought in the phone and refused to speak a word. He pulled the covers over his head like he usually did. *Just how long are you going keep this up?* He heard Ms. Grayling's stupid words again. He was getting tired of those twice-weekly sessions; nothing was changing, and she knew it. He just wished everyone would leave him alone. Except Sister Gandhali; she was nice. She didn't talk down to him or tell him what he should or shouldn't be doing (or eating). He was still on liquids anyway—it was so boring. He lay like that for a while, till he felt that uncomfortable mixture of laziness and guilt, which usually stirred him into action, even if it meant just turning on the TV. However, eventually it was the strange sensation of being watched that made him surface double-quick. He half-expected to see his friend, the sunflower, at the window, or the Van Gogh waving at him again. But what he saw caused all his hair to stand on end, and he had no idea why. Standing at the end of his bed was the Native American, but he wasn't a big chief any longer, he just looked like an ordinary man. Except a real-life Native American was extra-ordinary to Porky!

"Hello," the visitor said simply (*shouldn't that be "How"?* Porky thought, a nervous giggle threatening to bubble up).

"Hi," answered Porky, feeling suddenly shy.

"You are sick," the stranger said, stating the obvious.

"Yes," said Porky, feeling suddenly very fat and lowering his eyes.

The stranger's frightening look softened a little. "I have a nephew about your age. You are like him—in your distress, that is."

"Hey, I'm sick, but I'm not . . ." objected Porky, tired of the judgemental sessions with Ms. Grayling.

"No, no. Don't misunderstand. Your *distress* is a special quality, it marks you out. Not to conform sometimes leads to great things." Porky surveyed his visitor for a moment while trying to take this in. Why was this weird person here anyway? And talking to him like this? As if reading his mind, the man said, "I was told to give you this." He held out a package that had been concealed inside his coat.

"By who?" Porky refrained from reaching out. This was all too unnerving.

"My nephew," he replied, as if that would make sense. Porky was beginning to feel irritated.

"Look, I don't know your . . ." His fingertips began to tingle, just as they had in the garden. Now he knew that something strange was going on, way out of his control. And, even stranger, it felt good. Somehow, better than good.

"Okay," Porky said, struggling to sit up. "Thank you."

Kitchi's uncle placed the package carefully on the bed, gravely nodded his head, and made towards the door. He remembered something then and turned.

"Wait for a message, young one. Okay? Don't forget."

"Sure, of course." But Porky could only think about how his toes were burning where the package touched them, even through the sheets.

As suddenly as he'd appeared, the Native American visitor was gone. In the silence that followed, Porky sat staring at the package, a bit afraid to open it. *My God—it could be a bomb!* Panic rose up inside him, and in response, so did the tingling in his fingers and toes, as if to say, *It's all right, Porky. It's all right.*

He would open it in the garden. Of course. Everything was *all right* in that place! And he'd show Sister Gandhali. That's what he would do. And so the long process of washing and dressing began. As he descended the iron fire escape, he could hear the bells ringing for the end of church. *Great! Just in time.*

Wood pigeons were calling out to each other, as if announcing his arrival. The sisters didn't work in the garden on Sundays, but he would catch them leaving the hospital chapel. And there they were! He could see them clearly, white dresses flapping in the brisk wind, through the bare, black branches of the tall hedge, hurrying along the path that led from the chapel and skirted around the edge of the garden. And there was Sister Gandhali! She was trailing behind, talking on her mobile phone. Good—they'd meet up on the path. But she took off then, rushing ahead, pushing past the other sisters. Porky's heart sank; he'd never catch up with her now.

He started running forward, his feet shuffling noisily through the golden brown leaves beneath. Very soon, he was out of breath completely and had a sharp pain in his side. He tried to call out but emitted only a rasping moan. Dismayed, Porky saw Sister Gandhali moving ahead of him, soon to disappear from view. Suddenly, a loud squawking noise burst out of the trees above them. A large black and white bird was thrashing about in some high branches. Sister Gandhali turned round abruptly and caught sight of Porky. He was bent double, clinging onto a bamboo pole, panting rapidly and very red in the face.

"Porky!" she gasped. "What are you doing here?" Her voice sounded slightly annoyed. She also looked agitated, but not wanting to brush him off, she added more kindly, "It's a cold day—you should be in your room."

"I wanted to show you something," he puffed.

She hesitated and glanced sharply round in the direction of the main road in front. "Well . . . right now is not really . . ."

She's too busy for me today. His mood of excitement was deflating—fast.

The big black bird was circling above their heads, cawing loudly. There was a pause as they both looked up at it. Sister Gandhali looked towards the main road again. A taxi had pulled up and a bright yellow figure got out and started walking quickly down the path. As the streak of yellow came into focus, Porky saw it was a girl, an Indian girl, wearing a sari. She was running now, with her face all screwed up. When she reached Sister Gandhali, they embraced and held onto each other for what seemed like an age. So long that Porky decided he'd better make himself scarce. But when he tried to straighten up, he let out an involuntary yelp. The girl's eyes blinked open, and she peered at Porky over Sister Gandhali's shoulder. As their eyes locked, Porky cringed with embarrassment and just wanted to disappear. He knew he must look ridiculous.

"Oh, Porky, you're still here . . ." Sister Gandhali was speaking now. He could see she was flustered.

He began to mutter something about being about to leave, when the girl stepped forward and held out a hand.

"Please—can we help?" She was looking at Porky with a pained expression. For a moment, he was mesmerised by her loveliness, and then he blurted out the first thing to come into his mind:

"Aren't you cold like that?" *What a jerk! Why did I say that?*

But she just gave a little laugh and answered, "Yes, I am!" With a loud squawk, their new companion flew down, passing right in front of them, and settled on a bench nearby. "Come, let us sit," she said, gesturing towards the bench. "You can rest."

Her English was slow but clear. She was smiling at him now, and Porky noticed that her face was puffy, like she'd been crying. So the three of them sat down in a row, in silence, because nobody could think of what to say next. Porky wished he could ask why she had been crying, and he guessed that Sister Gandhali was upset about it, too. The black and white bird was on the ground, facing them now, pecking at a discarded sandwich. Porky noticed that its jagged plumes were a kind of metallic-blue.

"What kind of bird is that, Sister?" he asked. "We haven't seen one like it here before, have we?"

At this, Sister Gandhali seemed to come to her senses and she said, "Oh Porky—I am so sorry! This is Bina, my niece; she has just arrived from India. Bina, this is Porky."

"Por-ky. It is nice to meet you." Bina nodded her head from side to side in a most endearing way.

"Yes, you are right, Porky. We have not seen one. It is a northern lapwing on its way from North America to Africa."

"Oh!" Porky cried out, instantly remembering the mysterious package. "I've got something to open!" He placed the parcel on his lap. Bina watched Porky with fascination. He started tugging at the tape, but with no success.

"Let me help," Bina offered and began pulling too. A wrestling match with the parcel followed, making Bina giggle. The tape gave way at last, and laughing, they both rummaged inside the box together. They pulled the bison horn out at the same time, each holding an end. Porky gave out a loud snort—it was such a weird gift! And Bina laughed aloud at Porky's snort, until they were both laughing uncontrollably.

Their hysteria was broken by the lapwing. Flapping its huge wings, the bird soared abruptly into the air, passing so low over them that Bina let out a gasp and Porky actually ducked. Suddenly serious, Porky and Bina, each still grasping their end of the horn, looked gravely at each other. Because their fingers were hot and tingling again. They looked at one another, knowingly, and Porky smiled his *second* real smile in a very long time.

In supermarkets in Glasgow and across the country, shoppers—without realising or understanding why—began avoiding the frozen foods section and gravitated instead towards

vegetables and fruit. Thousands that day selected fresh produce instead of their usual choice of ready meals.

♦

Mr. Big pushed open the door marked *Mr. Corporate CEO* and took up his usual place on the leather sofa. After placing his cowboy hat carefully on the coffee table, he flicked open his tablet to read the financial news while he waited for his coffee. He wasn't really a cowboy; he liked to call himself a *rancher,* but in reality he was neither: he owned 80% of the world's beef farms. If farm was the correct word to use. No coffee came and he was aware of a strange smell in the room. "Miss Featherstone off today?" he asked.

"She resigned," Mr. Corporate sighed audibly.

"Resigned?" Mr. Big looked up, "But she loved her job!" On catching sight of his partner's perturbed face he added, "Hey— what's up?"

"Take a look at the news," Mr. Corporate nodded at the tablet in Mr. Big's lap and walked over to his world map to examine the two new scorch marks that had appeared (over India and China). While reading a report about a substantial loss in frozen foods profits in the UK earlier that week, Mr. Big's attention was disturbed by Mr. Corporate who started talking to the wall.

"A horn. A horn. How did I miss that? And the soldiers got the wrong Ethiopian boy—how did that happen? But the beast *will* get him—it *must*. Grandmother warned me . . . yes . . . yes she did."

At this Mr. Big got up and bounded over to Mr. Corporate's desk. He picked up an empty glass and sniffed inside. It smelled strongly of whisky. "What's going on here?" he shouted. No answer. Mr. Corporate was back at his desk gazing into his crystal. Mr. Big whirled his partner's chair around until Mr. Corporate faced him. "Look Buddy, you should be staring at your computer screen instead. Call in the head of our sales team, listen to what she's got to say and you'll be laughing! Profits can only increase. I've got orders from all the major meat manufacturers in Europe, and Christmas is just round the corner! Things can only get better. Quit worrying about all this nonsense. Kids! They're only stupid kids."

He decided to go and get some coffee and added, "And keep that thing in its box, it gives me the heebie jeeebies."

♦

CHAPTER 12

Lastro's Journey with the Whale

Dobi wouldn't go away. *What's wrong with him?* thought Lastro. *What does he want?* The new singing went on and on. Lastro was surprised the other fishermen didn't wake up. The whale's movements were making the boat rock violently now. "Hey—stop it!" Lastro finally shouted. He was going to end up in the water. In response to his protestations—or so it seemed—the huge mammal soared unexpectedly (and scarily) out of the water, directly hitting the boat. It capsized. Lastro was plunged deep, deep down, dragged farther and farther by a strong current he'd not known was there. Up above, he could see legs flailing, his uncle and cousins becoming entangled in their fishing nets.

But where was Dobi? The water was settling, becoming still; had the whale gone? He rose easily now towards the surface but noticed the dark shadow below him a second too late. The dark shape rose up suddenly with tremendous force, taking Lastro with it. He was bumped up into the air, only to land again, with a thump, on the whale's back; but he hardly had time to take this in before Dobi was curving forwards into the water again, making his descent. Lastro heard himself give out a desperate scream: "Noooooooo!" And then nothing—just the whooshing sound of gurgling currents.

Now Lastro was at the side of the great whale, clinging on for dear life to the thick skin of its left fin. But he was also rapidly running out of air. He could hold his breath under water for four whole minutes and swim five kilometres easily, but to his horror, Dobi was leading him away from shore—he could see the ever-brightening horizon above through the water. Lastro wanted to let go, but how would he get back now? He couldn't swim that far. The whale continued to forge ahead at breakneck speed. It was too late. A terrible feeling of dread was replacing the panic in Lastro's chest. He was going to die today. These were his last hours. Soon tiredness would overcome his ability to hold on; even now, his fingers were numb from gripping. Soon he would be left, a tiny speck, alone in a vast ocean.

And then he did let go, but it wasn't his own doing. Instead, Dobi flipped his fin sharply, causing Lastro to lose hold. He somersaulted backwards into the turbulent currents churned up by the whale's movement. *I'm gone* was all he heard in his head. Yet he fought hard to keep holding his breath, till a horrific sight loomed up before him. The black, gaping hole of the whale's mouth was open like a cave, and he was rushing towards it. Nothing could stop him. Even the frantic thrashing of his arms and legs. He entered and was engulfed in darkness. *This is it* he heard in his head. He was thrown into a tunnel and down a chute (as if in a swimming pool attraction), falling, falling, round and round until he hit the bottom and lay still. The absence of water made him raise his head. *Oh—this is not it.* And then, ironically, he passed out.

On coming round, he just lay still with his eyes open, scanning his surroundings, afraid to move. Afraid of what he might see if he turned around. He may have lain there for hours; he had no idea how much time had passed. But to his enormous relief and satisfaction, for once he was enjoying being warm and dry. He felt sure he was in Dobi's belly—or in a cavity somewhere inside the whale. Its lining was like a kind of soft rubber, pale blue in colour and spongy to the touch. In the dim light, he could make out that the whole of the inner cavity was arranged in ridges, gently descending to the floor, where there was a shallow pool. Lastro had landed mid-way up one side and fit snugly within one of the ridges. Apart from him, the space was empty. He could see movement in the pool, though, shifting colours and glints. Fish, of course. Everywhere was draped with seaweed in all shades of green, some piled up on the base, near the pool. The effect of the greens on the pale blue was, funnily enough, just like trees and sky. The place began to feel not so strange. The air was warm and sweet; he could breathe easily. He finally decided that the whale had not eaten him and was not going to eat him (which was a huge relief.) A gentle vibration at all times indicated the whale's movement. Swimming onwards. But to where? And why?

Now rested and calm, Lastro was hungry; not hungry—ravenous! He looked around at the clumps of seaweed. How on earth was that going to be enough? But amazingly, after the first few tentative mouthfuls, it proved to be so delicious that soon he was gobbling up handfuls of the stuff like a crazed seaweed monster! Hardly able to move after his feast, Lastro sank on his knees to drink from the pool, but to his dismay, the water turned out to be salty. It was so warm, though, and so inviting that he stripped off and took a bath! As brightly coloured fish darted in and out between his legs and tickled his toes, Lastro realised that he was experiencing a new and unfamiliar feeling—but a very nice and welcome one. He was happy.

Later, he had the good sense to chew on a particularly succulent weed that was full of juice. His thirst quenched and still warm from his bath, Lastro drifted off to sleep without another thought as to where he was or where he was going. Some time later, though, he woke up. Everything was still. The cavern looked different too. Dimness had been replaced by a red light, deepest in one corner and becoming a rose colour nearest the roof. The place was warmer, and vibrated, but not like before; this time, deep and regular throbs emanated from the red corner. Lastro lay awake and pondered this for a while. He crawled over for a closer look; the wall where the red colour was the strongest shook intermittently and regularly. He lay down and felt heat and strength. *Of course! This must be Dobi's heart!* Knowing that the whale had placed him in such a safe place made Lastro feel choked up. But then he was moved to puzzle over the reason he was there, travelling with his new friend—and in his belly! Only, for now, he found no answers.

It was then that Dobi began to sing. Again, it was the new song. This time, the whale took the notes higher still, invoking an urgency that sounded like a cry. A plaintive crying, singing and lamenting on and on. *Why are you crying, Dobi? What's wrong? Please, please stop!* Lastro curled up and covered his ears; it was too much to bear. Suddenly, he felt his fingers and toes tingle.

The sensation increased till they were almost burning. The rest of his body vibrated ever so slightly; he felt like a dragonfly suspended in mid-air, vibrating yet staying still. Was this his answer? If it was, it made no sense. But Lastro felt peaceful, more peaceful than he had ever felt on his fishing boat, when he would look back at the shore and gaze at the lights of the villages, when he would imagine one of those lights to be a warm room with four walls that would hold him and comfort him. Peaceful, because now he had his own warm room which made him feel perfectly safe and contented.

The next morning (Lastro guessed so, as Dobi was moving again), he was overcome with terrible, unbearable thirst, and he had no idea what to do about it. Finally, all he could do was holler. After several minutes of this, resulting in a very sore throat, nothing happened. But just when desperation began to give way to panic, Dobi lurched forwards, doing a downturn. Lastro was thrown upwards; he crashed against a spongy wall and went helter-skelter down another tube he'd not noticed before. This tunnel was narrower than the first and squeezed him unbearably tight. Another sudden about turn, and Lastro was . . . out in the open air! The light blinded him at first, but worse still, he was bouncing precariously up and down, soaking wet. Dobi had emerged from the water, ejecting Lastro with the spray from his blow-hole! Unable to stop himself from screaming (and feeling ridiculously like a girl), he jumped, landing on the whale's large, broad back. It was then he noticed it was raining, pouring even. And now he was sticking his tongue out, looking like a complete idiot, lapping up the fresh rainwater from wherever it landed: his hands, his arms, puddles on Dobi's back.

Next he was on his knees, bent double and laughing, overcome with the joy of drinking again, of staying alive, of being carried along in the middle of a vast ocean on a whale's back, of not feeling afraid of the sea, of being cared for by this huge mammal who had chosen him and only him to accompany him on this adventure! To where? He gradually sobered up as the unanswered question resurfaced. A more serious mood settled on Lastro as he sat there, still moving slowly along, and he stared all around at the deep blue of the sea and the lighter blue of the sky, a uniformity broken only by the white of breaking waves and the retreat of some grey rain clouds. He cried then, not from dismay, or fear, or a desire to be anywhere else, but from the sense of being held in the palm of something greater than him, and a certainty that he had been chosen for this journey, not by Dobi, but by an all-knowing force, for a purpose. They had been chosen together for a purpose—he was sure of it.

CHAPTER 13

Kitchi and the Bison Become One

Every time you look at a sunflower, the whole world starts to smile. Kitchi didn't grimace this time; he had a lot more respect for the Legends since the Buffalo Dance. But he still didn't feel much like smiling. Things had changed a lot though, he had to admit. Winning the horn had gotten him a whole new life—in a way. A new status, that was for sure. Everyone wanted to be his friend now: Leotie, Fala—even Guyapi! It had felt great for a while, but here he was in class again—staring out of the window, bored stiff by the lesson. Nothing else had changed. He stared at the face of the sunflower. He remembered the words of the bison: *The brave boy in pain. Lead the Keepers.* Why did everyone else get the excitement in life? Who was this boy anyway? He hadn't heard anything from his uncle. What had possessed him to give his horn away like that? He wished he still had it now. He could have showed it off. Kept the popularity thing going. People would be losing interest in him soon.

In the classroom, a buzz of conversation started up while the teacher dealt with a call at the door. It seemed ages since the dance. Had that bison been real? How could a bison speak? No, that was crazy. His eyes scanned the rows of sunflowers receding into the distance on the wall outside. So many shades of yellow. *Pain!* Kitchi thought angrily. Well, he was in pain too! A different kind of pain, sure. Restlessness made his soul ache. He was stagnating. He had to get out of the rez. How would he ever make it out of this place? Mr. Helaku was addressing the class now; Kitchi turned reluctantly away from the window. But a sudden movement outside brought his gaze straight back there. It was as if streaks of yellow were dancing all about. His mouth fell open at the sight of scores of sunflower petals fluttering, waving at him, and all the time, a growing feeling that this was an answer.

"Kitchi!" Mr. Helaku had noticed him and was addressing him with that familiar tone of exasperation. "If you continue looking out of the window instead of paying attention to my lesson, you'll be paying a visit to . . ." Kitchi didn't even wait to hear him finish. He pushed back his chair noisily and was on his feet before the teacher could say another word. He flung his books into his bag, slung it over his shoulder, and made for the door. "Kitchi! Come back here at once!"

Without looking back, he kept on walking till he was out of the main doors and striding down the street. He stopped momentarily, as if having second thoughts about something. Then he took off his bag and flung it into a nearby garbage bin. And he was off again, faster now—then breaking into a run. He didn't know where to, but he just kept on running. Past his house. Past the stores. Past the football field. Where to? But all the time, deep down, he knew where he was heading. Of course he knew. To the plain.

Kitchi scanned the vast, wild landscape. Nobody would think of looking for him down here. Today he would make his escape—today he would leave. He could feel it. But from where? Where should he make for? The unmistakable shape of the dead tree stood black against the sky. That would be the place. Wasn't that where he'd found the bow, dangling there, appearing from nowhere? And where a sling of arrows had mysteriously happened to be on his back? Never mind finding a real live bison. Kitchi didn't want to think of the bison. He was scared to see it again. He reminded himself again and again that it was dead. But at the Buffalo Dance, it had spoken to him. Was it dead or wasn't it? He reached the tree. A little flock of birds that were sitting on the branches became agitated and flew up suddenly, their cries echoing around the wide, open place. It was spooky out there. Kitchi glanced this way and that, anxiously. His heartbeat was thundering. A wind blew up and whistled through the branches. Suddenly his fingers were tingling again—just as they had before when he'd first heard that voice telling him to go down on the plain, and again when he gave the horn, his prize, away to his uncle.

You will fly. The bison's words came back to him. He'd forgotten it had said that. He was going to fly today. *Fly away from here,* he told himself. He was sure of it. He surveyed the sky for the plane that was coming to get him. Nothing. So he waited.

The sun was mid-way down the sky. *They'll have left school by now.* He imagined his classmates filing out and talking about his abrupt exit. A chill was descending onto the plain. Doubts were clouding his horizon now. Just how long was he going to wait? A tingle in his fingers started up again, reassuring him that he wasn't a complete idiot. That had happened last time he was down on the plain too. What else had the bison said? *You and I are one.* Those words made him remember Fala's: *They felt this oneness with the Earth and the Bison. They felt it in their souls.*

The hot, tingling feeling in his hands grew and grew until Kitchi was forced to glance down at them. The shock at what he saw caused him to take a few steps backwards, as if to get away from himself. For over his hands and all the way up his arms, thick sandy-coloured hair had sprouted and was growing at an alarming rate, even as he looked at it. Kitchi held his arms as far away from himself as he could, in an attempt to get away from the horror story unfolding before his eyes. Next he was turning round and round, his head shaking vigorously from side to side. With utter disbelief, he felt two horns spearing out of his forehead, boring through his skull, each one making a terrible scraping sound! He mouthed

"Noooooooo!" but no sound came out. He tried to yell but was silent while his screams reverberated inside his head.

All at once, his circling movements were cut short by a force that hit him in the middle; it was like being punched in the stomach, but without the pain. And thus he fell forwards onto his knees, startled as his feet and hands turned into hooves and stretched away from him. Was he rising up or were his legs elongating? His head felt really heavy now; great puffs of white smoke appeared in front of his face. An incredibly pungent smell filled the air. It was only when he let out a loud and ugly-sounding snort that Kitchi realised the smoke was actually his breath! Soon he was stomping and kicking, pieces of turf flying off in all directions. He ran to and fro, emitting loud groans and growls as he did so. The long howl of a wolf somewhere in the distance suddenly stopped him in his tracks. He stood still, head cocked to one side, sniffing the air and listening. And then, he raised his great animal head, the call of the wild having told him who he was. Head erect and muscles quivering, ready for action, Kitchi stood. A proud and glorious bison.

The very moment the sun slipped behind a mountain, his hooves left the ground. He bicycled in the air in a desperate attempt to stop himself from falling. But no need for that; soon he was climbing steeply upwards, up, up, and up. He tried swimming movements with his front legs to keep himself afloat. No need for that either, because he was well and truly off—flying high in the sky, without a plane, without wings, his only vehicle the body of a bison! If he was honest, he didn't feel the least bewildered at being a bison. Not for a moment had he felt disgusted or revolted—even at his smell! Nor did he have a sense that it shouldn't have happened. He felt safe, flying in the bison's body. But was that really true? Wasn't *he* the bison? He couldn't tell which was which anymore. Was he having Kitchi thoughts or bison thoughts? He didn't mind being a bison, put it that way. It felt natural. Even the flying bit. However amazing that must sound.

He flew all through the night, without once feeling sleepy. His thick shaggy fur coat kept him warm enough. There were other night creatures making overnight journeys. All feathered and winged, of course. Whole flocks of migrating birds. It was good not to feel alone up there, so high in the dark. And the migrating birds knew the route and guided him all the way. Miraculously, the birds weren't afraid of him; they just took one curious look and kept on flying. The stars looked closer than he'd ever seen them. Almost close enough to touch. After what must have been many hours of flying, he instinctively started his descent. Through the clouds, falling, falling. So many clouds! And there were the lights of Glasgow, shining brightly below. Taking care to avoid high-rise buildings and church spires, he slowly circled lower and lower. The large expanse of a hospital and its grounds came into view, elevated on top of a small hill. Kitchi landed splat on top of the hospital's helicopter pad! It was a very clumsy landing; the bison's legs buckled under, and he rolled over on his back. He lay still in that position, panting loudly. He would have stayed like that till he'd recovered his breath, only shouts of what had to be security guards could be heard somewhere below. The voices were getting closer; there were flashlights, too. Kitchi clambered to his feet and trotted off in the direction of some trees to his right. It was dark in there. He could hide.

Finding a soft spot proved difficult; the ground was covered in little pots! Finally, he settled for a space under an iron staircase against a wall. He huddled into the corner, and yet still the moonlight fell across Kitchi's face. Torchlight appeared on the path, followed by heavy footsteps. A pang of fear made the fur on his back stand up in a ridge. But just in time, before the footsteps reached his hiding place, the huge head of a sunflower bent slowly over and hung there between Kitchi the bison's face and the moon, shading him from view.

CHAPTER 14

Serenity Has a Dream

T hunder resounded over the forests, only split-seconds after lightning illuminated a dark and forbidding forest. Serenity had forgotten to draw the curtains, but she was afraid to cross the room to do it. She buried her head far beneath her covers. She'd seen such a strange sight before she woke up; not out of the window but in her dream.

First she'd dreamt of Porky doing the rap song, only this time he was singing:

Why would you wanna kill a whale? A whale. A whale.
Why would you wanna kill a whale?

Porky disappeared and was replaced by a gigantic blue whale that was bleeding and moaning. It swam slowly forward and ended up in shallow waters, where it got stuck. The whale's moaning increased until it became too agonising for human ears, like someone's nails scraping down a blackboard. Just when the sound was unbearable, something appeared: something she recognised. It was Sergio. He was beautiful. He shone like gold. And he had a phial of her mom's medicine round his neck. The whale's crying subsided. But then the phial turned into a droplet of gold; the droplet, in turn, became eight drops, and then they took on human shapes. Four boys and four girls, flying through the air. At this point, Serenity woke up to find her heart beating rapidly. What did it mean?

Dad came in and closed the curtains. "You okay?" She nodded from under the covers. He kissed her blanket-topped head and asked, "You coming with me to the sanctuary tomorrow? We're releasing the turtles at dawn. You'll be ready?" The lump in the covers nodded again.

By dawn, the storm was moving away; it could be seen far away over on the horizon as a swirling, dark mass. Only a fresh wind remained, and the sky above them glowed pink with promise. The little group of volunteers huddled together at the river's edge, drinking their first coffee of the morning out of tin cups. Serenity smelled the coffee enviously and rubbed her eyes; she wasn't used to being up this early. The first batch of migrating turtles that year had made a stopover, and it was time to send them on their way. Her dad oversaw the insertion of microchips into their thick necks. They used something similar to a staple gun. This way, the turtles could be traced by computer in her father's office. He would know if they made it on time, if they were using the age-old migration routes, or if there were any changes happening. And if a turtle got hurt, they'd know about that too.

Serenity watched the turtles push their way out of the underwater cage at the moment of release. They were all on top of one another in the panic and excitement to get out. She thought of Sergio, all alone in his shallow pool. He was an old turtle, like a majestic king—in Serenity's eyes, at least. She went to look at him and he swam over to her immediately. She stroked his massive, golden brown head. His shell reflected glints of orange, green, and, in places, a mottled red. His gentle brown eyes looked deep into hers. And that strange thing happened with her fingers again. As she stroked her dear friend's head, her hands shook, and her fingers were all tingling and strange. Her dream flooded back and filled her mind; Sergio had a mission, she was sure of it. Somewhere, a whale needed his help—*their* help. She ran to the kitchen and filled several plastic phials with her mother's medicines. She knew which ones: the blackberry tasting one that stopped bleeding, and there was a yellow bottle somewhere for the one that fought infection.

Running back to Sergio's open-air pool, she placed the phials securely round his neck and tucked under his shell, and then she pushed him out and guided him to the river bank before anyone noticed her. Now her whole body quivered and throbbed with a heat she didn't recognise; it wasn't like a fever. Sergio didn't complain at all when she shot the microchip into his neck. He nuzzled his big wrinkled face into hers, and they rubbed noses. And then he was off. And quickly! She hadn't known old Sergio could move that fast.

She felt pleased she was giving him the adventure of a lifetime and was envious, too, as she watched him disappear down the estuary that would lead him to the open sea. *I never go anywhere,* she thought as she trudged slowly back to the sanctuary, now brightly lit up inside as her dad's team got down to work. *Dad!* How was she going to explain this to him?

CHAPTER 15

Jasmine

"Hey! Flying Carpet! Where are you *now*?" A string of red tasselled reins lay scattered on the ground. So she was right; she *had* heard some bumping noises as she was surfacing out of a sound sleep. The other camels, tethered side by side, shifted nervously from hoof to hoof, grunting and chewing. They avoided her gaze, keeping their long eyelashes in place so she couldn't see what they knew—Flying Carpet had, in fact, flown! All except Abdul, of course! He looked at her straight in the eye with that familiar cheeky grin. If he could have spoken, he would have told her how Flying Carpet had spent half the night struggling free to go visit her sweetheart in the outskirts of the town they'd just passed. Jasmine sighed, understanding Abdul's look immediately. *Not again—that flirty, flighty beast!* She couldn't charge after her now; there was too much to do first thing in the morning. Especially the last morning before a journey. (The tribe were due to travel onwards to an oasis in the east.) She had to collect the camels' urine for one, from bags tied round their rear ends, which caught it during the night. Today, all the kids would have their hair shampooed with this urine. They used everything here. Nothing was wasted.

She was so angry! Flying Carpet hadn't been given that name for nothing—she was a fast mover! Later it would be too hot to stray far from the dark shade of their tents. She couldn't send someone off to look for her in the raging heat of the day. And how to find her? Footprints (and hoof prints) disappeared in the sand anyway. So later this afternoon, when everyone would be chewing qat, she'd have an exhausted, dehydrated camel to deal with—and no help from the "numb heads" she called cousins.

She was the one who did everything around here. And she was known for being bossy. Some were even scared of her. Even male youths older than her jumped at the sound of her voice! Maybe it was because she was a perfectionist; she'd thought about it often—as to why she was like this. Constantly checking and double-checking other people's work. Not resting until she was sure everything had been done properly. She just could not trust others to get it right. They would waste things. The tribe could not afford to waste anything. Why? Because they had to conserve—constantly. Take water, for example. Every drop counted. Every precious drop. What wasn't drunk had to be re-used—in myriad ways. The same water was used to wash almost everything and finally ended up rinsing the camels' bottoms! And nobody cared about this process as much as she did. Jasmine knew what the consequences of not looking after things could mean: Disaster! (Yes, with a capital D.) Like what happened four years ago in another part of Yemen, in the mountains to the north, where all the slopes are terraced and every available space farmed. One family hadn't looked after their terrace wall, and the result? The soil eroded, causing water to simply run through, taking the whole mountainside with it. Scores of families' livelihoods collapsed in one instant, into a big muddy pile.

Here's what her morning schedule looked like:

1. Morning prayers. (After first waking up the herd boys for morning prayers or they would never get up.)
2. Tell the herd boys to get sheep and goats out of the pens and lined up for milking.

3. Supervise the collection of water from the well. (Tip: don't fill the buckets too full or water will spill with carrying.)

4. Milk sheep and goats. (Supervise her sisters and cousins milking sheep and goats, because she knew that they either let drops leak or drank some secretly.)

5. Supervise transportation of milk to the tent. (Tip: again, don't fill the buckets too full.)

6. Help her mother and aunts make yogurt and cheese from milk. (Tip: don't ever let them do it by themselves, as they hide some in their aprons to feed their favourite children.)

7. Tell the herd boys to take sheep and goats out to pasture. (Tip: search each one for hidden stores of water or milk.)

8. Finally: feed, water, and tend her beloved camels. (Tip: don't come near Jasmine's camels, because they bite everyone but her!)

Sub-schedule for looking after camels (Jasmine's favourite task):

1. Collect their urine from bags tied round their rear ends. (Tip: tie the bag ends and transport all in a small cart, minimising drips.)

2. On the morning of a journey, lead camels to well and line up at water trough. (Tip: tie the camels together to make sure they all drink. A camel which has not drunk enough will collapse on the way.)

3. Supervise the camels' drinking. (Tip: time them—not a drop too much! Camels can last a very long time on only a little water.)

4. Check hooves. (Tip: apply frankincense balm to any sores on base of feet or on humps where saddles have rubbed.)

And yet these schedules still do not include the tasks involved in the care of donkeys, doves, and falcons. Jasmine could not cover everything, though she wished she could. She was not Supergirl, though others called her so, using the Arabic word: *Jabbara,* meaning "wonder woman." Certainly, the camels thought so. For at the ripe old age of sixteen, she was the tribe's camel expert. Maybe more of a camel psychologist, or *whisperer,* as it is called these days. It really looked as if they were talking together! All she had learnt about camels came from her great-uncle, Sheikh Nabil Khaled Ali Hareeb. He'd noticed this gift in her from infancy and always joked that she should have been born a boy, calling her Jado. And Jasmine's retort had become her catchphrase: *A girl's as good as a boy any day!*

Which she generally sang at the top of her voice, especially when she spotted a group of men passing by.

The only other thing Jasmine and her late uncle had disagreed on was concerning the camels: they had never found a cure for a skin disease that bothered the camels' ankles, making it painful for them to walk through the sand for hours on end. He insisted on using donkey dung mixed with honey; Jasmine was convinced that the dung stung the camels, because Abdul had told her so! Of course, Uncle Nabil only scoffed at this, and so the wrangle had gone on and on, trying out cure after cure that never worked.

As the sun climbed higher and higher in the sky, the family had to work faster and faster to finish their chores before the fiery blaze of midday. On making a full retreat into the shade of the tent, or trees or an old wall—anything—the qat chewing would commence. And, after that, *nothing* would be done *at all* till dusk. This sight of group upon group of lounging men (and women, cleverly hidden behind curtains), chewing madly with bulging cheeks, full of the green leaves which so stupefied the senses, made Jasmine swing between anger and despair. And when the loud playing and philosophical talk reached dizzying heights, she would be practically seething. She hated waste in all of its forms, and this represented a huge waste of time.

It was as the same song was being played for the fourth time that she saw a black speck on the darkening horizon. Within seconds, her keen eye could see it was a single camel, and not the falconry party returning from their early morning sport. *Flying Carpet! God is great!* She felt the uncoiling of her nerves as relief swept over her. She sensibly resisted the urge to rush out and meet the camel but waited for it to reach within fifty metres, thereby conserving her energy and preventing overheating. But when she saw Flying Carpet's pathetic limping gait, relief returned to anxiety. And as she had predicted, not one of her numb head qat-chewing uncles or cousins were willing to help. They hardly turned round to look at all, in fact. *I'll get you back for this,* she vowed silently.

While dressing the cuts and bite wounds on Flying Carpet's legs, neck, and mouth, she got an idea. *Ha! This'll shock them out of their stupid slumber!* She smeared some of the camel's blood on her face and hands, dishevelled her black headscarf, and tore one shoulder of her dress. Trying not to smirk, but instead look traumatised, she ran in front of the tent sheltering her immediate family, groaning and staggering, even falling to the ground. Despite their sluggishness, all the men were instantly on their feet, yelling and shouting, wielding the gigantic swords that had been resting inside their ornate sashes. "Who has done this to our daughter?"

"We'll get the beasts!" One great fat man tripped over his robes in the kafuffle to leave the tent.

"No one will hurt the tribe of Hareeb and live!" Two of her cousins ran into each other, having circled the tent from opposite directions.

It was all too funny for Jasmine, and unable to hide it any longer, she collapsed in a giggling heap, laughing uncontrollably. Until she looked up. She was surrounded by angry faces. Without a word, her father pointed to an overturned pitcher, its contents spilled and still shining on the ground. Four litres of fresh mint lemonade. Wasted. Jasmine's father knew how painful it would be for his daughter to clean the spilled precious water up. She scuttled off, almost crawling on her belly, afraid to look at him; she tried to put everything right again. She straightened the tent, the cushions, and the broken dishes; washed the blood off her face and hands; and changed her dress. But nobody cared. She was treated to looks of disgust and stony stares. Not a single person would talk to her, and she found herself taking refuge among the camels, curling up on the tummy of Flying Carpet as the camel rested her wounded legs. Sometime later, an older cousin came in to inspect Flying Carpet's dressings. He didn't register Jasmine's presence at all, but as he moved away, she was sure she heard him growl, "Idiot!" under his breath. Her chest was getting tighter the more she regretted what she'd done. She was in big trouble; she could feel it in the air.

Perhaps it was time to apologise. Something Jasmine had never done. She was always making others feel guilty. *Okay, here goes,* and she crept out from under the awning.

The sight that met her eyes came as a terrible shock. The camp was all packed up. And then she remembered. *Of course!* They were due to move on that very evening, to travel through the cool of the night, two hundred kilometres east to Al Bayda. She stood stupidly staring, as the last package was strapped onto a little donkey that would be the tail of the long caravan. It wore a "flower" in its bridle that someone had made out of a plastic bag.

Her father stepped forward. "Flying Carpet cannot travel. Her legs have not yet healed. You must stay here with her." He pointed over to a scruffy-looking little boy. "Hassan will stay as a help. And you can keep Abdul too. Murad Tribe will arrive in the near future. Travel onwards with them."

She nodded, too scared to speak. But inside, she was yelling at her father. *Hassan—a help? Some help!* He'd chosen the laziest boy in the whole tribe. What a punishment!

She stayed stock-still, watching the tribe walk away, getting smaller, until they became blurry and disappeared into the constantly moving horizon, shimmering with the rising heat. *Near future? What does that mean exactly?* She plonked herself down against a palm trunk and just stared at the empty space in front of her. It was hard to believe anyone had been here at all, not a sign, nor a trace—of anything. There wasn't the usual pile of garbage that you saw in towns. This was so typical of nomads—even the sand had been swept clean. Jasmine felt a swell of pride at her people, but it was almost immediately quenched by thoughts of her recent telling-off. Her cheeks burned with resentment. Hadn't she always worked hard? Harder than everyone else? She knew how to run the camp better than anyone. She even deserved to be a leader. And now, look at her; dishonoured and left behind. She waited till Hassan had dropped off to sleep, curled up in his blanket. Then, despairingly, she let her head sink between her knees. She knew she looked a pitiful sight; she would never let herself be seen like this. Except by her camels. Abdul plodded over and, bending down, nuzzled the back of her neck. She managed a weak smile and raised her head up to plant a kiss on his snout, when she saw a date that had fallen on the ground. She raised it to her mouth, but remembering the bowl of yogurt and lamb she'd eaten only five hours ago, she stopped herself from taking a bite. *What am I doing? I'll save this for tomorrow. For breakfast.*

She looked at the date and rolled it between her fingers, pleased with her self-control, with her knowledge of measured eating, with her sound management of the tribe's supplies. Her fingers grew hot, making the date sticky. But soon, her fingers tingled so much she had to let the date drop, and she held her hands, palms up, just looking at them in amazement. How weird! What did it mean? Was she sick? In the same moment, a wind blew up, which was uncommon at this time of year. It made everything rustle and flap: leaves, branches, the awning protecting the camels. What with the deep blue darkening sky and the whistling of the wind and the tingling in her fingers, Jasmine felt a little spooked. The wind whistled in her ears, and she held her breath when she distinctly heard a silvery voice whisper, "Wait. Wait and see."

Wait? Wait for what? Jasmine didn't expect an answer, so she jumped out of her skin when it came.

"For the *others*. Wait for the other Keepers."

The wind died down as soon as it had come. Jasmine sat in the dusk, rubbing the date between her fingers and saying the word over and over in her mind. *Keepers, Keepers, Keepers.* What did it mean? What was a Keeper, and what did they keep?

There was no easy answer to that. Jasmine stayed propped up against the tree, watching dusk engulf the sky and descend into night. A movement in the sky caught her eye. Something was flying and getting closer. It was coming straight for her! Could it be her favourite falcon got loose and was flying back to find her? But as it got nearer, she saw that it wasn't flying, but fluttering like a paper, or rather swaying from side to side yet still travelling forward. It got closer; it was bigger and heavier than paper. Was it a kite? She tried to widen her eyes in the dark. No, it wasn't a kite—it was a—the thing landed just in front of her; it was a carpet! A carpet? *A flying carpet!* Jasmine scrambled over on her hands and knees and knelt in reverence before it. She was smiling from ear to ear. She could just make out the markings; a map of Yemen was woven in many rich colours of wool. It was incredibly beautiful. She peered over it, but it was getting too dark. Somehow, she'd need to get a light. She brushed against the edge of the carpet in her effort to pull herself up, and it lit up!

"Wow!" Jasmine gasped out loud. Abdul raised a sleepy head with a grunt that sounded like a "wow" too.

The tapestry on the carpet was stunning in its beauty. Just as Yemen is. She followed the pictures on the map as if she were flying over the surface of the country. First one part would light up and expand, and then it would recede, allowing another section to glow brighter and fill the expanse of the carpet. She saw the high scorched brown rock face of the mountains surrounding fertile valleys below. Terraced fields were miraculously carved out of the sloping sides, abundant with all shades of green and coloured produce: grains, vegetables, coffee, melons, and pomegranates. Not to mention the scores of palms in gardens on the plains. She could see baskets and baskets of dates, ready to take to market in the towns. And the towns! Tall brick houses lit up now; their exquisite stone markings made them look like gingerbread houses from fairy tales. Colourful mosques came into view, their domes blue and green, sitting amidst lush green gardens filled with tropical flowers, palms, and cacti. She could hear the sound of water flowing. It was truly a land of honey. Along the coast in the south, she noticed a caravan of camels and donkeys wind its way slowly along rocky paths. It looked like her tribe, but she couldn't be sure. As she peered closer, the carpet suddenly went dark. "Awwww!" Jasmine was audibly disappointed. Abdul grunted in sympathy.

She wasn't sure what to do now. The night was pitch black. She waited for several long minutes. *Wait,* she remembered, *for the other Keepers.* The *other* Keepers? But that surely meant . . . that *she* was a Keeper?

Suddenly, the carpet lit up again. Jasmine was attracted like a moth to a lamp. But it was all different now. There was the map, yes, but this time the terraces weren't abundant with produce; instead, they were planted with trees bearing the green leaves of qat. She saw water basins emptying and pouring into the qat fields. The water wasn't replaced. She saw the red lights of bullets flying through the air—people in the towns fighting for water. The wind whispered in her ear: "Will the people of Yemen be the first in the world to die of thirst?"

Jasmine became frozen on the spot with horror as more scenes were played out in front of her. She saw the terrible poverty. She saw that the food wasn't enough to go round. Off-shore, she spied oil refineries nearby, and naval bases, too. There were so many problems their government couldn't solve. Jasmine felt angry and saddened at the same time. Something rose up inside her; if *she* was president, she wouldn't allow this to happen! As soon as this thought entered her head, two things happened simultaneously. Her fingers started tingling furiously, and the lights on the carpet went out. She was left in the dark. What now? Gradually a corner of the carpet began glowing, brighter and brighter. On looking, Jasmine could see a picture of a queen, recognisable by her crown. It was the queen of Sheba, who once ruled over the ancient kingdom that was now known as Yemen. Jasmine lay on the carpet and studied the glowing tapestry. Her whole body was tingling and hot now, just like her fingers. A light breeze blew over her, cooling her down.

"You have the answer, Jasmine. You know something. Wait for the other Keepers."

♦

At Food Masters Inc. Mr. Corporate was on his hands and knees checking his office wall for mould or insects or for whatever was causing areas of the world map to discolour. Nothing. Nothing unusual. He was puzzled, but preferring anger to confusion, stormed over to the window sill and poured a double scotch. He popped a blood pressure pill into his mouth and washed it down with a slug of whisky. *Ahhh that's better,* he thought. Bolstered up, he was now ready to take on anything. He reached for the box on the sill beside him, but just as he was opening it, the phone rang.

It was China Head Office on the line, from Beijing. He took the call and listened to a tale about a runaway schoolgirl in possession of wild rice. The last grains of wild rice in China. "Wait a minute—did you say a girl?" His face broke into a smile and then he laughed out loud. Another kid. This was becoming a joke. He knocked back the remains of the golden liquid in his glass. The whisky coursed through his veins and he laughed again. Nothing to worry about. "Just make sure you catch her," he continued. "Find out where she got it and secure the lot. I want her found, right? You've got two days." And before he closed the phone added, "Or else."

Mr. Corporate sat on the sofa, placing the crystal on the coffee table in front and crossing his arms behind his head. He was feeling pleased with himself. Kids! Dealing with kids was easy. Couldn't be easier. It had been easy enough to send an official to shake things up at the border refugee camp in Kenya; they'd soon deal with that blasted boy.

Kids were scared of so many things. He saw Porky in his mind's eye, fat and bumbling. *Bet he was bullied as a child,* he thought. And Bina. Now there was a tough nut to crack. Without her Philip McGregor would be nothing. What was she afraid of?

On the coffee table the crystal began glowing. It emanated an eerie tune like one from an old-fashioned musical box. A voice began to sing:

"Paradeesh, Paradeesh . . ."

♦

CHAPTER 16

Porky Gets a Visit from Friends

"**M**ornin', Romeo . . . rise and shine!" The nurse pulled back the curtains with a flourish, her greeting a fanfare. Porky groaned, only too familiar with the style of joking which was now rampant among the nurses. "Breakfast?" She handed him a mug. He managed a weak smile. "What? Is that all you can do? C'mon, Prince Charming can do better than that, can't he?"

Oh please go away, thought Porky. *I can't stand this a moment longer.*

How could simply talking to a girl have caused such a reaction? Well, he guessed he had talked to her every day over the last two weeks, sometimes even missing lessons. And he supposed the girl in question being Indian might have raised a few eyebrows. Or more likely . . . he cringed at the thought . . . maybe it was because he was fat? Because they felt sorry for him? Fat boy miraculously finds love. He could just imagine how they must talk about him and Bina. Hospital romance. Beauty and the Beast.

The next nurse to come in, however, surprised him. She picked up his mug and frowned, saying, "Still on liquids?" She looked him up and down. "But you've made such good progress recently!" She went over to check his chart. "Yes, as I thought. Well, Philip, you'll be pleased to know that as from tomorrow, you're on solid

135

food." She grinned at him. "It'll still be a special diet, of course. The nutritionist will be in to see you this afternoon."

"This afternoon?" Porky asked, a look of deep concern on his face.

"Yes. Why, Philip? Meeting your sweetheart?" And with a chortle, she was gone.

Ughh! But his annoyance didn't last for long. How could it when he had Bina to think of? He closed his eyes and saw her beautiful, smooth skin and chocolate-drop eyes.

Before Bina, he'd have dreamt of the breakfast he'd be having tomorrow. In his past life, he thought only of food—his comforter. But now . . . he was becoming a new person. He looked in the full-length mirror. The nurse was right; he'd lost loads of weight in . . . it must have been in the last two weeks. How odd; so quickly! Could love do this? But he hadn't even been exercising! And he felt stronger too. Much stronger.

A text message jolted him away from his self-examination. It was Beaver. He wanted to come and visit that afternoon with Allie and Greta! *This afternoon?* Bina was coming. He thought fast. It'd be all right. She'd meet his friends. Get to know more about his life. He texted back: *Yes, sure.*

A knock came on the door. A lady in a white coat peered round. "You ready for a visit now, then?"

It was his first ever serious talk with anyone about food issues. The nutritionist wasn't a bit like Ms. Grayling. She had a big smile and introduced herself as Kelly. She didn't make him feel bad or chastise him for his old way of life. Because that's what it was now. The past. And whatever the reasons were that he had eaten badly, feeling so ill and nearly dying had brought him around to the truth that really mattered: the modern diet was killing people and something had to be done.

Actually, Porky added the part about *something had to be done.* The nutritionist was happy enough if Porky understood that he should avoid fast foods, crisps, fried potatoes, and sweets and eat fresh fruit and vegetables (especially of many different colours). But Porky wanted the whole world to know this! And there was more he wanted to do. But he didn't push it because, if he was honest, he didn't really trust adults anymore. Those in charge, anyway.

Kelly must have sensed this, because after some hesitation, she was bold enough to bring up his parents. "I know it's none of my business, but . . . wouldn't you reconsider talking to your mum and dad?" He looked away. "I mean, it would greatly help with your healing, look at it like that."

After thinking for a bit, he answered, "You're probably right. It's not altogether my parents' fault—they're only pawns in the game."

"In the game?" Kelly repeated quizzically, looking at him directly, willing him to make eye contact again. He wouldn't. "You know what I mean," he said, in such a low murmur that it sounded like a growl.

After lessons, he made his way down to the garden to ask Sister Gandhali what time Bina would be coming. As usual, he greeted his friend, the sunflower, with a "Hey ho!" The sunflower duly bowed its majestic head. Then it was his custom to touch all the little sunflower seedlings on their heads with the tips of his fingers as he walked by. He'd once tried to explain this morning ritual to Sister Gandhali, after she'd invited him to attend chapel. "I'm not religious," he'd said. "I just touch all these little sunflowers we planted and think about how wonderful they are, like little kids, growing from seeds. And I say 'thank you' for them."

That afternoon, when Sister Gandhali saw him approach and say hello to all his little kids, her heart went out to him. Today would be the day. She'd tell him now. So she sat him down beside her and began.

"You know, Porky, about Bina . . ." And he waited to hear confirmation of the bad news he was already grieving over. Bina had told him the day before. It had come as a shock, to put it mildly; a bombshell was more accurate. "She is engaged to be married. To her cousin. That is why she came here, to Glasgow." There was a long silence. Porky ran his hand along the tops of the little sunflowers and back again. The massive sunflower nodded with sadness at the facts.

"But," said Porky at last, "why would Bina agree to such a match? To someone she'd never met? She's not weak. I know she's not."

"Porky, there are things that happened in Bina's hometown, in the whole region, in fact. A chemical disaster. And afterwards, many people were hurt, and now they cannot work. Bina's father is very poor now."

"So you're saying that what Bina's doing is a necessity—to help her family?"

Sister Gandhali nodded. Porky didn't know if that made him feel better or worse. If she didn't marry her cousin, her family would be poor forever. But *he* loved her, not her cousin. There was nothing left to say.

He sat in the same spot, close to his beloved sunflower while Sister Gandhali did a little weeding nearby. In his mind, he hoped the sunflower would give him some strength or an answer. But neither came. Instead, he became aware of a horrible stench, something like wet wool. It was unbearable to stay there any longer. He excused himself to Sister Gandhali, saying he'd be back down soon. He had friends coming he told her, and, of course . . . but he couldn't finish. He couldn't bear to say her name.

So he made his way quite quickly up the iron stairs (now he moved more smoothly than before). But if he'd glanced down, he would have seen a pair of deep golden eyes looking up at him. Desperate to tell him something, to imbue him with strength, and to empower him with a purpose.

Beaver was early. He and the two girls, Allie and Greta, waited for him in the lounge. The moment Porky entered the room, he felt their nervousness. There was an awkward few seconds as they said hello. He wondered if they noticed how different he looked now. "Hey mate!" Beaver beamed, coming forward like he wanted to hug his fat friend, but feeling embarrassed in the presence of the girls. He lifted his palm for a clumsy high five instead. Greta and Allie were giggling.

"But . . . you're still fat!" Allie blurted out, suddenly regretting it and clasping her hand over her mouth.

Greta nudged her and said, "That's not fair! He's a teeny weeny bit thinner."

Beaver butted in. "Okay, girls!" He gave them a sidelong look and added, "You look great, mate!"

"Thanks." Porky looked uncomfortable. "Actually, I think I've lost a lot of weight, but I know there's a lot more to go. It could be a long time before people really notice."

Beaver made a rather unsuccessful attempt at changing the subject. "Really miss you in the canteen, mate! Ha ha ha!"

Porky looked at him blankly. "Oh, why?"

"Well—you know! Four burgers in one sitting!" Beaver beat his chest like Tarzan. "You were soooo funny!"

Porky grew increasingly irritated as he looked at. "Beaver— have you any idea why I'm in here?"

"Okay—so you ate too many burgers!" And they all burst out laughing.

Porky's face contorted in pain and disbelief. "And I'll *never* be doing that again!" he said, his voice rising in anger.

"What—never eat a burger again?" Allie commented stupidly. Greta nudged her, giving her a warning look.

"Eh . . . DAH!" Porky looked at them, his face darkening. "And why? Because they nearly killed me, that's why!" A hush fell over the room. They'd never seen him like this before. "And . . . do you know that *these* can kill you too?" he shouted angrily, snatching a bag of crisps that Allie had taken out of her backpack and throwing it in the bin.

"Hey!" protested Allie. But Greta dealt her another sharp nudge.

"Can't you see he's upset?" she hissed.

Porky was looking at his hands; they were trembling. He sat down again and tried to start over. "Do you know there are terminal kids in here?"

"Terminal? You mean they're going to die?"

"Yeah. They've got bald heads from the radiation." His classmates didn't know what to say to this. Beaver looked at his friend. He wasn't the same. He was much more serious now. At that moment, he caught sight of trees swaying through the window. "What's down there?"

"It's the hospital garden. I spend a lot of time there. C'mon, I'll show you my seedlings!" Porky was suddenly brighter.

And the garden soothed him as usual. Porky greeted the sunflower silently. But it heard him loud and clear and bowed its great head.

◆

They didn't know it, but they were being observed while on their way down the iron staircase. Ms. Grayling was watching them from a window. She was on the phone. "Yes Kelly, thank you. I suspected it all along. No, don't worry. I'm on to it. We're keeping an eye on him."

◆

"Wow—look at this place!" Beaver was craning his neck up at the trees as if he'd never seen one before.

"Wicked!" cooed Allie. "Better than St. Gregory's Recreation Ground any day!"

"Why are we whispering?" Greta whispered, and they all laughed. The tension was broken. Porky relaxed.

"You see all those little pots?" Porky said, animated again. "I planted them."

"Isn't that what they call occupational therapy?" joked Beaver.

"No, seriously, mate. I'm not sick in the head. I have school lessons in here, you know. And I don't fill pots for fun. We grow vegetables too; I'm learning about organic gardening."

Allie picked up one of the little sunflowers and absent-mindedly started pulling off its leaves.

"No!" Porky rose quickly, bounded over, and snatched it out of her hand. The others exchanged looks.

"Wow! You're a quick mover these days!" Allie tried to make a joke out of it. But she had noticed his renewed vigour.

Just then, Porky spied Bina at the entrance, a flash of orange sari this time.

"Hey, there's someone I want to introduce you to."

"Oh yeah?" The girls looked at each other with raised eyebrows, and Allie winked at Beaver. They turned in the direction Porky was facing. And their mouths fell (slightly) open. Bina floated in like spring after winter. Or, at least, that's what the look on Porky's face communicated.

"Everyone—this is Bina," he said as he stepped forward and unashamedly took hold of her hand.

Bina made a little bow.

His three friends just stared till Greta whispered to Allie, "What's she wearing?" Greta dug her in the ribs with her elbow but giggled just the same.

After some mumbled "Hi's" and "Pleased to meet you's," they found some logs to sit on. Sister Gandhali rushed up with a tray of plastic cups filled with elderflower cordial. The girls were trying hard not to laugh. Porky acknowledged that the sight of an Indian nun in white robes suddenly appearing in the middle of a wood with drinks was actually funny, so he forgave them. As he sat there, presiding over this strange little meeting, he found himself caring less and less about what his friends thought of him.

Bina was trying her best. "Porky always talk about you, Beaver. He tell me you are in the Cub Scouts. Yes?"

Beaver blushed beetroot red. The girls erupted this time.

"Sorry, forgot to tell her it was a secret!" It was Porky's turn to laugh now. He turned to Bina with a smile and said, "Thank you, Bina!"

"Actually," Beaver said once he'd recovered, "I'm in the Beaver Group." Nobody laughed at this, because it was such an old joke. He successfully changed the subject this time. "But what about you, mate? What's this blog you've been writing?"

"Oh yeah. The blog." Porky stopped for a moment; it was hard to know where to begin. Greta came to his rescue.

"I liked your poem, 'I Am Hungry'—really good! Miss Webster read it out in English class."

"Really?" Porky looked stunned.

"Yeah! And everyone clapped."

"Hey! I'm fat and I'm hungry!" chanted Beaver.

"Not any more!" Porky shouted, laughing. The others joined in.

"I'm hungry for change, my friends, I'm hungry for change!"

They were clapping now and repeating it over and over. "Hungry for change! Hungry for change!" Beaver started beating an old rusty barrel. Porky's face was beaming. They got louder and louder and faster and faster until they all collapsed in the grass, laughing.

"What does it mean?" asked Allie, after they'd got their breath back. Beaver groaned and banged his hand on his forehead. "Well, smart ass, what does it mean?" glared Allie, shoving Beaver on the shoulder.

"What does it mean? It means . . . um, change the way you eat or you'll get fat?" Beaver sounded vague. He wasn't quite sure either.

Porky took over. "You know, I've talked to so many people through my blog; people are interested in my story because, in their own ways, they are suffering too. I suffered and nearly died— did you know that?" They shook their heads. They obviously didn't. "So many kids are obese because they stuff their faces full every day. Why? Because maybe they're addicted to sugar. Or is it because there's so much available cheap, processed food in the supermarkets? Ready meals packed with additives. People have forgotten how to cook."

"You sound like Jimmy Olives!" offered Greta.

"Yeah, exactly! He was hungry for change in the school meals system, and look what happened!"

"What happened?

"The government wouldn't back him up."

"Why not?" Beaver leaned in, interested now.

"Good question. Because there's so much money at stake. Big deals. Big corporations. Power." Porky was pleased to have their attention at last. He went on, "And it's not just here. I've talked to kids from all around the world. Take Serenity, from the Amazon: you know how much rainforest is cut down to make way for beef farming to provide you with the burgers that you gobble down at McDollar's? Well, one and a half acres of rainforest is lost every second. Then there's Abala, who's from Ethiopia, but now he's in a refugee camp in another country because foreign food companies made illegal deals with the government and just took land that's not theirs. They don't care what happens to the people as long as they can grow crops to feed the beef industry. And listen to Amy's story. She's Chinese. The rice in China has become so genetically modified that it's now diseased. Now there's famine because the crops keep failing. There's no rice left." He was walking up and down while delivering this rant, waving his arms in the air.

"Hey mate, you're shouting," interjected Beaver.

Porky stopped. He looked at their startled faces. "You know, something's happening to our world; it's almost out of control. And I want to do something about it!" He sat down. He was out of breath. He realised he was still holding onto the little seedling in its pot. Gripping it so hard, in fact, that his fingers had made indents in the sides. His fingers were impossibly hot and tingling. The tingling was spreading up his arms. Beaver looked at his friend in amazement. He'd never seen him like this: so serious, so impassioned, so strong.

143

It was kind of hard to think of anything else to say after that, so the three visitors decided it was time to leave. As Porky watched them walk away, he thought it unlikely they'd visit him again after his performance. How much had they understood? Hadn't Allie just munched down that packet of crisps without a care in the world, even after he'd told her they were *carcinogenic*? He couldn't imagine himself going back to school and being able to relate to people any more. Let alone sitting in lessons. He'd learned so much just by himself; he never stopped researching, reading, getting amazed by new and sometimes terrible facts.

Bina tapped him on the arm. "What?"

"Oh! Just thinking. Sorry for getting so carried away."

"No—you were great!" She was smiling up at him, flushed with pride.

"Let's sit over here." He took hold of her hand, and they sat among the larger shrubs, letting their fingers entwine, uncoil, and entwine once again.

The sunflower watched over them like a guard. The large bison lying under the stairs raised its shaggy head and took note.

"See how nobody understands? They're lost to their own greedy habits." He let out a long sigh.

"I know," murmured Bina. "I know all about it."

"You *do*, don't you?" he said, studying her face intently. "Bina, can I ask you something?" She nodded in the Indian way, saying no instead of yes. "Remember when we opened the parcel and pulled out the horn?" She nodded again. "You looked at me . . . what I mean is . . . did you feel it too? The tingling—the tingling in your hands?"

"Of course. I thought you knew."

"Okay," he laughed, as if hugely relieved.

"I think the horn is making you well. It has power. You are getting strong and . . . a little bit slim!" She shook her head in her cute way, trying not to laugh.

"I thought it was because of *you*!" Porky squeezed her hand, making Bina blush.

"No. The horn is your gift. Like me. Look." She took the nutmeg out of her bag. "My fingers made like so . . ." She fluttered her hands in the air. "when I was given this in Karna."

"Karna?"

"Yes, the village I told you about," she explained. "There I knew something, something new, like a gift. I always keep this nutmeg with me." She stared at it then, turning it over and over in her hands.

"What happened in Karna?"

"It is hard to explain. An amazing place. With no disease. The people there are different, healthy and strong. They know things . . . things about food. What to eat and when. They know without learning. Do you understand? I do not know the word in English. Like an animal."

"Oh—yeah. It's called . . . instant . . . no—instinct!"

"They have *ins-tinct*?" She said the word slowly, practising. "About food. And now I have it, and my aunt, of course."

"Wow!" Porky was impressed.

The two friends weren't aware of it in the dim light, but as they sat and talked, the sunflower seedlings lining the paths were growing— and fast! They grew until they were at least two metres tall! The magical growth was accompanied by a tinkling, a tinkling so delicate that it was only discernible if you were on the right wavelength. Kitchi heard it, and his hairy bison ears pricked up. The sunflower not only heard it but vibrated to it, its yellow petals quivering.

"But," she said, lowering her eyes, "there is danger. Something or someone do not want people to have this instinct." She slowly pulled up her sleeve, revealing the ugly laceration which still hadn't healed.

"Wow!" Porky said again; this time shocked. "What happened?"

"My taxi was attacked by a . . ." She didn't know how to describe it. "A kind of creature. It had long arms, like snakes. It wanted this." She raised the nutmeg up in front of his face. Porky was silent; it was all a bit hard to believe. "You know how I know? That it is important? That it has power?"

"How?"

"Because first my hands," she wiggled her fingers in front of his face. He nodded. He understood that only too well. "Then, when I was on the aeroplane and was afraid, I thought of the nutmeg and Karna and I *saw* a garden. I felt better and stronger. And even when Ajit . . . my fiancé . . ." She hesitated.

"Go on," Porky urged, pressing her hand tightly.

"When we met that first time, and he would not look at me at all, I held the nutmeg and knew what I should do."

"And what was that?"

"Come here."

"Come here?" Porky was whispering now, his heart beating louder than his words.

"Yes, come here and meet you."

The light in the garden was fading fast. Porky gently stroked Bina's wounded arm, and before he could change his mind, he pulled her quickly towards him. He kissed her lips, lightly. And again. This time harder. Bina pressed in. They stayed like this for almost half a minute.

Kitchi saw it first. The tiny, dark shape. Shooting through the branches, fangs poised, ready, aiming for the side of Bina's neck, so vulnerably exposed, while she was lost in a kiss. He pulled his great shape up and leapt; the bat met him in mid-air, smack in the middle of his chest. It fell to the ground. The bison placed his hoof on the little vampire and rammed a horn through it. Then he picked it up with his horn and tossed it over the wall and into a garbage bin. Then he lay down, pressing himself into the ground, and waited. Maybe there would be another.

"What was that?" Bina was frightened.

"Probably a fox. I always hear them. They come to feed from the bins."

"I should go. It is late." They stood looking into each other's face, holding hands.

Now Kitchi was getting frustrated. He had a message to give Porky. Looked like he should have given it before now.

The couple walked out of the garden towards the main road to hail a taxi. The time was now, decided Kitchi. He'd intercept Porky on his return. He waited in the shadows.

On his way back, Porky walked slowly, marvelling at the stars, marvelling at all that Bina had told him, but most of all marvelling that she loved him. Him. Fat boy Porky! He was so star-struck, in fact, that he did a very stupid thing. Again, Kitchi saw it coming. But this time, he was too late to stop it.

Porky spied a can. Red with white lettering. He knew what it was. It had been left on a wall, close to the stairs. It was half full, and Porky was thirsty. He knew he shouldn't drink it, but he was heady with love. It was a product Porky now hated. But it beckoned him. And he felt invincible. It would be all right. He was on a new diet now. Just a sip or two. He picked up the can, raised it to his mouth, and poured. The poisoned drop splashed onto his tongue just as Kitchi knocked him over.

Flat on his back, Porky stared into a massive, foul-smelling, hairy face, a hard object holding down each of his arms. Through the steam of its breath, Porky heard a boy's voice, sharp and clean, say:

> *You are a Keeper, my friend. You and Bina. Keepers. You must leave this place. Tomorrow at nightfall. I will take you. Wait by the sunflower.*

But Porky's tongue was swelling up, fast. He made choking noises. Kitchi couldn't be sure if he had even heard him. For now, that didn't matter. The bison released him and galloped off to show himself to the security guards. Porky writhed on the ground, clutching his throat. Then, just in time, there came the sound of running feet.

CHAPTER 17

Sergio Goes off the Radar

Serenity's dad was furious when he found out that she had released Sergio without his permission; he nearly cancelled the trip to Africa that he'd promised her. But after a week or two of doing special favours and going out of her way to please him, he started to soften up a little. Serenity knew how to work her father.

She kept him company as much as possible in his office, cleaning and even emptying the rubbish bins. Then one morning—two days before her dad was to leave for Nairobi—something happened. She entered his office as usual, carrying a tray of red berry tea (good for his blood pressure and hand-picked that morning), and found him half-sitting, half-standing at his desk, staring at the computer screens before him. "What?" she heard him yell.

"What's wrong? What is it?" She ran up for a closer look.

"Sergio's gone way off course!" he said. "I can't believe this!" He turned and looked at her, his face full of shock and worry. "He's heading for Yemen."

"So now I'll have to come with you, right, Dad?" She tugged at his arm as he turned to examine the screen again.

"Yes. We leave tomorrow."

CHAPTER 18

Abala in Trouble at the Camp

These days, wherever Abala went, he was showered with goodwill. Everyone who passed by either smiled, waved, or slapped his shoulder. Children called his name in a chant as children do: "Ab-a-la! Ab-a-la!" Sometimes people clapped when he entered the dining tent. It embarrassed him. He took to spending longer and longer in his tent. He didn't want to be thought of as a saint or a prophet.

He told Sally he didn't know what to make of what had happened that day in the dining tent. She confided that her father had said nothing like that had ever happened before at the camp—or any camp—or anywhere else he knew, for that matter! He had also said that the leaders of the camp, or the committee, as they called themselves, were *concerned.*

"Concerned? What does it mean?" asked Abala.

"It means they are thinking seriously about it," Sally said, putting it nicely.

"Thinking about what?"

"I don't know." But really she knew.

"Seriously? What does it mean?"

"It means that it is important," Sally said, putting it nicely again.

"Yes, it is important," Abala echoed, deep in thought. He felt disturbed. *Concerned.* The word niggled at him.

149

Later that evening, while taking his usual stroll around the perimeter of the camp, he passed by an assembled group of men drinking coffee. One stood up and called out to him. He was wearing a long robe, and a round white hat was perched on the top of his head. Abala recognised him immediately. They had travelled together. He was the tall man who had found him. The cook. They embraced heartily. "Join us, join us, Abala!" he urged.

"What's your secret boy?" one of the men joked. "Are you the next prophet?" They laughed and teased him good naturedly. Abala felt at ease. He relaxed. The men were complaining about the coffee. "It is that instant stuff, from a jar. You know—from the West." Abala smiled. Everything from the West was bad, in their opinion.

"This prayer of your grandfather's?" asked another. "Did food ever appear before when he said it?"

"No," answered Abala. The men murmured amongst themselves, occasionally staring at him intently.

"Want some coffee?" his friend offered, pouring some in a little cup. Abala took hold of the cup. Instantly, his fingers were tingling. *Uh-oh, here we go!* he thought. Just from the powerful aroma, the men knew that something had happened to Abala's coffee, that it wasn't the same as theirs. It smelled strong, but sickly sweet, like rich Ethiopian coffee. They were jealous! They wanted some too! Abala grinned and poured each of them a cup of coffee from the pot. Cheers went up then as each of their coffees were transformed. They planted loud kisses on Abala's cheeks; he thought he'd better leave before the singing began.

On his way back to his tent, Abala went over and over it in his head. *Why did that happen?* Just to give the men some coffee or to show him something? If so—what? That this was his gift and not his grandfather's? That he had to use this gift for others? He was beginning to make more sense out of it. *Concerned.* The word made him angry. How dare they? This was obviously a good thing. He quietly crept back inside the tent. The family were already sleeping. He snuggled down under his blanket, the taste of coffee still pleasantly in his mouth. He lay there for some moments thinking about the gift—his gift.

A shadow. A shadow he had come to know. It was close by. Inside the camp this time. It circled the tent two, three times. The outline of the beast was clear. And terrifying. He knew what it wanted. But this time he was wrong.

Abala Alemayehu Zerihun—so you like to make the people happy? it snarled. **What if I snatch up and devour one of the little ones asleep beside you now? That would only be a snack for me, and then I would be hungry again. No need for your gift—there is plenty of food for me here.**

Suddenly, *concerned* was applicable. Now the love people felt for Abala would turn to hate. He knew that he had better be leaving this place.

CHAPTER 19

Amy at the End of the Line

Amy peeked out from behind the curtains for the umpteenth time. It was still there. Even though the car was parked in the shadows on the opposite side of the road, the light from the street lamp shone on the driver's glasses. This was the second week running. She hadn't left the house for days. She'd used her mother's accident as an excuse at first. But as Mom had gotten better, she was beginning to run out of reasons for not going to school. But she hadn't been idle. She'd arranged everything. It had meant stealing her mom's credit card, but Amy suffered no guilt after seeing what Mom had gone through.

She went through the plan yet one more time:

She'd take the midnight Overnight Express to Chengdu. She'd booked a sleeping berth online. She hadn't quite decided how she was going to get to the train station. She couldn't take a taxi, because she didn't want a car arriving in front of the house while the surveillance car still sat there. But the last bus into town from her district was at 10 p.m. So, no good. She was still thinking about it, but she'd have to think fast because she was leaving tonight. Then she had to pick up her renewed passport from Chengdu Town Hall after it opened at 8.30 a.m. (She'd had to forge her dad's signature for this.) Next, she had a seat booked on a long-distance coach to Macau Special Administrative Region from Chengdu Bus Station.

After that, she had to make her way to Macau Port. Her boat ticket had been harder to secure online. You had to be there in person. It was an international border, and there was a visa to obtain. It was settled. She had worked it all out. She was going to the Philippines.

She went through the contents of her backpack one more time too:

One change of clothes (she had to travel light), her computer tablet and cable, her phone and cable, credit card, birth certificate and other identification papers, a map of southern China and a city centre map of Chengdu, and finally some fruit and sandwiches.

All she had to do now was double-check her bookings and post a note of thanks in this guy Porky's blog. He had told her about the Philippines Rice Institute, about the research they did there, and how they had samples of all kinds of rice. He'd been so helpful. Unlike Seung-Yub, who had disappeared off the radar completely. She'd emailed him after her mom's accident, but he hadn't replied. It was strange and dreadfully disappointing. After all—he'd sent her on this mission, hadn't he? It was as if suddenly he didn't care. But she had no doubt about what she should do. Not after she saw the danger her family was in. Would leaving protect them or leave them unprotected? She consoled herself by remembering it was her they were after. The wild rice had been entrusted to her. She had to honour that. She decided to check the contents of her backpack again. It was too heavy. She took out the tablet and cable. And the maps. They were too bulky. She had Internet on her phone; it would have to do.

Although Amy herself was a flurry of activity, the rice grains were silent. Neither were there any voices on the wind, no tingling or throbbing fingers. Amy was about to make her second terrible mistake. She still had to learn to trust the signs. And she had forgotten one tremendously important thing: she hadn't waited for the message.

So instead, as leader of her own mission, Amy climbed out of the small bathroom window at the back of the house. She shimmied down a drainpipe, unrecognisable with her hair tucked up inside a boy's baseball cap. She knew the timing was right; she'd spotted the evening garbage truck doing its rounds in the street behind the row of back gardens. She'd hitch a ride and be outside the station in no time, with twenty minutes to spare before the night train departed. Hanging on the back of a garbage truck was not at all romantic or dangerous, but exhilaration surged through her; she felt like a character in a movie. She wished she'd thought to tie a scarf over her mouth and nose, though—the smell was disgusting! At the brightly lit station, her first job was to pick up her ticket and then take out some money. The ticket clerk remained impassive, obviously thinking there was nothing strange about a young girl embarking on a journey alone at midnight. Good. Next—money. Yes! The ATM whirred into action, accepting the PIN number. No problems so far.

Just at the moment the ATM spat out the wad of notes into Amy's hand, a little bird landed on her bedroom windowsill. It was perfectly white all over, except for a red head and tail. It had flown all the way from Nepal, resting in a cypress tree in the park while it waited for the designated time. It tapped on the window pane. After about thirty seconds, it tapped again. After a third attempt, it flew off and settled into the dark branches of a tree to watch and wait. Meanwhile, Amy boarded the train just as the whistle sounded. She couldn't help squinting from side to side to see if the other passengers were watching her. They weren't. She also refrained from counting her money over and over, just in case people sensed her nervousness. She was also aware that there was a lingering smell of garbage hovering over her. But her fellow passengers hadn't noticed that either.

The night was long. Everyone slept but her. She thought of the note she'd left for her parents: *It is for your own good that I do this. Our family is under threat and it is my fault. Only I can fix this. I will be in touch. Please do not worry.* Around five in the morning, she eventually nodded off, so when the train pulled into Chengdu Station an hour later, Amy was very tired indeed.

Chengdu Town Hall was not hard to find. She found a café opposite and downed coffee after coffee in order to stay awake till the doors opened at eight-thirty. She checked her phone. Twenty-two missed calls from home! She'd call when she was boarding the ship. Waiting in line, Amy started to feel dizzy; she was not used to drinking coffee. Her passport was ready and waiting. No questions asked. *So easy!* she marvelled to herself, skipping down the stairs into the morning sunshine. Right—what next? The bus station was on the other side of town—a forty-minute walk. After munching down a light snack of green bean and chestnut noodles from a street vendor, Amy walked it happily. She felt like she was riding the crest of a wave. Everything was going according to plan.

It was the same at the bus station: the ticket agent barely glanced at her as she collected her ticket. "Macau coach leaves in twenty minutes. Stand nine." Amy sat at stand nine and closed her eyes. She digested the events of the last ten or so hours. She thought she'd done well. Here she was, on her way to the port. Soon she'd have left China! Yes, she was pleased with herself. The driver arrived then and opened the coach doors. She boarded and sat at a window. They'd be off in two minutes. She saw a newspaper stall and wished she'd bought a magazine. The driver started up the engine. *Too late.* The coach began to slowly pull out from its stand, but then stopped as a late passenger got on. She looked out the window at the newspapers displayed at the stand. A strange and horrible sensation gripped her chest and rose into her throat. Unmistakeably, Seung-Yub's photo was on the front page, accompanied by the words: *"Mayor's son caught and found . . ."* And that was it. The coach's engine roared in her ears. They were off.

Amy laid her head back on the head-rest, her mind racing. *Found what? Guilty? In possession? Armed? Or . . .* she hardly dared think it . . . *dead?* The five-hour journey passed in turmoil; her emotions were swirling: doubt, regret, confusion, and slowly creeping all over her—fear. Finally, exhausted, she dozed for a while, only to be lurched out of her slumber by the coach screeching to a sudden stop. "Passports!" shouted the driver.

Craning to see ahead, Amy made out a checkpoint manned by at least five policemen. She knew she shouldn't wait around to see what was going to happen. As quick as a flash, she pulled herself up and miraculously squeezed through the narrow space offered by the coach window. There was an agonising moment as her backpack got jammed, but she managed to tug it free. But she'd been spotted. Two policemen were after her at once. And onto her. Amy turned and kicked the closer one under his chin. In that brief moment, she noticed he looked not much older than her. He reeled backwards, losing his balance.

And next, a crazy thing happened, one that Amy was to regret for a long time after. The young policeman had his gun out, and it was pointing straight at her. She stared at it, frozen in time. The other cop was almost ready to grab her arm. She hadn't expected this, but she was ready. Pulling out a handful of red-hot ground pepper, she aimed at his eyes. He fell over in shock, and she was off! A street market lay ahead. She could get lost in there easily. She charged into the mess and the bustle, rolling under a stall before you could snap your fingers.

A face appeared upside down under the table. It was the rough face of an old man, wizened through years of a hard life. "You in big trouble, missy. Want visa?" Why was he helping her? Her hackles were still up. Or maybe it was just a scene he'd seen so many times before. She nodded. "Last stall on the right. Potatoes. Say Yan sent you."

First, she secured the remainder of the pepper. Who knows? She might need it again. She took her cap off now, letting her hair flow freely; a girl instead of a boy. She bought pink candy floss and licked it, walking nonchalantly past the chaos of the heavily laden stalls and cries of the vendors. But up in front, a policeman appeared—scanning, searching. Amy panicked, lost her cool, and let her eyes meet his fleetingly. He sprang into action. She dodged him successfully, weaving between the stalls for about twenty seconds. Then she saw a rickshaw pass and jumped on.

"Where to?"

"On," which in Chinese means "just a little further."

No one followed. She leaned back. She had no idea where she was going to go. She suddenly realised she could smell the sea. A pang of emotion hit her chest. She reached onto her back to get out some money to pay. But . . . her backpack wasn't there! She couldn't even remember losing it. So there was nothing left to do but jump. The rickshaw driver yelled out but didn't bother to chase her. Perhaps he was used to it.

She ran and ran. She wanted to be away from all this. Away from the mess she'd made. Away from the image of the boy policeman with red hot eyes. She ran for about fifteen minutes. The land gave way ahead. *What was this?* It was a cliff, of course. She was so exposed here. She wanted to hide. A swelling on the head of the cliff edge revealed a bunker, half sunk into the ground. It would do for now, she supposed, and scrambled down inside. There were slits in the concrete, looking out over the South China Sea. She covered her face with her hands. Somewhere, a young man lay, inflicted with burns to his eyes. How had this gone so horribly wrong?

A great tiredness came over her. Her head spun. She hadn't eaten or drunk anything for hours. But she wasn't hungry. She felt nothing, only numbness—the numbness of regret. She'd failed. *At what?* She wasn't sure of anything any more. She felt for the pouch still in her pocket, took the rice out, and looked at it. *All because of this?* She'd failed Seung-Yub. He'd trusted her. And then suddenly, out of somewhere far away, she remembered his words: *You're a Keeper, Amy. And remember, wait for the message.* "Noooo!" she hollered aloud till it trailed off into a deep and pitiful groan. What had she done? She had been too impetuous. Too headstrong. *Why, why, why?* Tears fell then, and her body kept shuddering long after they'd stopped.

Amy lay listening to the sound of the waves crashing far below. The sky was darkening outside. Fireworks sounded not far off, maybe at a wedding. She jumped; everything sounded like gunfire to her now. If she hadn't been too upset to take a stroll outside, she'd have seen a little bird, perfectly white with a red head and tail, fly from the mainland and settle on top of the grassy mound. But it wouldn't have mattered much, because Amy had yet to learn to read the signs.

As darkness settled in, she saw the car headlights. Heard one door close and then another. This was it. She was at the end of the line.

♦

Mr. Corporate was sitting behind his mahogany desk and checking his emails. His partner, Mr. Deal, was paying him a visit and reclining on the leather sofa. He was puffing on a fat cigar. Mr. Corporate let out a loud chuckle, "Ha! They got her—I knew they would. Now we've got the answer."

"The answer?" Mr. Deal asked, looking up sharply. "Don't ever presume you've got the answer, that it's all sorted. Because, usually it isn't. You've got to push—use force if you have to."

"Little Miss Wong will be locked up and we'll create new hybrid rice, stronger than before. The crop yield will double—no—triple! We won't even need to continue with GMOs for a while. This is great news!" Mr. Corporate answered.

"You fool!" Mr. Deal retorted scathingly, "Don't rest on your laurels; don't assume victory. Take the Ethiopian for example—where is he? Have you brought him in?"

"I've got a plan in motion," Mr. Corporate said.

"A plan?"

"Yes, a plan." Mr. Corporate confirmed.

"Let me see . . . does it involve a certain hocus-pocus crystal?" Mr. Deal asked, guessing correctly.

"Mr. Big's been talking to you."

"You're right there, Buddy," Mr. Deal said, taking a puff on his cigar. "Look at me a second, will you?" His tone was menacing and not to be messed with. Mr. Corporate obeyed him instantly. "This is serious. These kids are likely more dangerous than they look. They could be runners, just pawns—know what I'm talking about?" Mr. Corporate nodded. "When I go into countries and make deals, like in Ethiopia, people always get in the way, you know, threaten action that sort of thing." His eyes narrowed as he continued, "You have to take them out."

"Take them out?" Mr. Corporate echoed.

"Yes, take them out. They're nobodies, they don't matter. Call it collateral damage. Call it what you want." Mr. Deal said, waving his arm in a dismissive manner. Mr. Corporate's chest tightened.

"I've got it covered," he said, remembering the beast which had lain in the very place his partner was sitting now.

"You better have it covered," Mr. Deal replied. His steel grey eyes meant business. He got up to leave. At the door he turned around and said, "One phone call is all it takes. Remember that, Corporate."

Mr. Corporate's heart beat quickened. A musical note announced the arrival of a new email in his inbox. It was from Ms. Grayling and the subject read: *Bison.* A deep furrow appeared between his eyebrows as he read the letter. He rested his head in his hands for a moment before getting up and walking purposefully over to the window. The box was open; he looked down at the crystal which lay inside.

He knew it would have the answer. He saw a creature. A long-legged thing with a huge mouth. Through the murky purple glow he watched it tear up a sheep and eat it. Then he could have sworn he heard a voice:

"Let the ancient monsters deal with those who are foolish enough to believe in them."

♦

CHAPTER 20

Porky Leaves the Garden

Bina turned round, an agonised look on her face. She was wearing her national costume; it glittered all gold and pink. He approached her through the garden, which looked beautiful that evening; coloured lanterns adorned the trees. A frown appeared on her otherwise perfect face, just above a red dot painted between her eyes. With an outstretched arm, palm turned towards him, she mouthed, "No." Strangely, he couldn't hear her voice. All around him, people were laughing and pointing. But still he couldn't hear anything. He looked down at himself. He was barefoot and was wearing pyjamas. Worse still, he was his enormous self again. A handsome, dark young man in a white turban, from which a gold feather bounced in the air, came up to Bina's side. He observed Porky with a look of distaste. He mouthed something at Bina. She shook her head. "No," she said silently and turned her back to Porky again. Petals were flying in the air, cascading down, fluttering, landing on everyone's heads and shoulders. Silently, like snow. The wedding guests laughed and clapped in slow motion. The moment a man began to blow a trumpet, the sound came on. Its shrill blast rocked his ears. With a shout of protest, he woke up. Pain stabbed the back of his eyes. He had a headache. The monster of all headaches.

"Uhhhhhhhh!" he gasped, raising his hand to his forehead, only to find a mass of tubes dragging along with it. He saw that he was attached to a drip once again. There were tubes in his nose too. How long had he lain here like this? Had he missed the afternoon? Caught between dream world and reality, he wondered if Bina was already married. A panicky feeling rose in his chest. He lay there, horror engulfing him—eating him alive. In the dim room, patches of sunlight fluttered on the wall like butterflies; like the petals falling down at the wedding. Porky struggled to regain control. *Stop! Stop this!* He urged himself to breathe. *Slowly. Deeply. It was a dream—okay? Only a dream.* He willed himself to get up. *Only a dream,* he said to himself, over and over. He got up and shuffled, swaying slightly, over to the window. He had a vague feeling that seeing the garden, and especially the sun, would make things all right again. The sun would tell him what time it was, for one. *Instinctively.* Somewhere deep inside, he smiled, strangely comforted at the word—Bina's word. And then an amazing sight met him. Down below were row upon row of tall spindly sunflowers waving gently in the soft breeze. His little kid seedlings had grown up overnight! They were "teenagers"! He almost laughed aloud. He had to get down there *tout suite,* as they say! He did laugh then. (Porky loved his own jokes.)

He whirled around just as a nurse entered the room. She looked angry on seeing him standing at the window. "You should be in bed," she said. "You had a nasty accident."

"Did I?" Porky tried to remember. "I think . . . I only took a sip of cola." But she had taken hold of his arm and was guiding him roughly back towards the bed, a little too fast for his liking.

"No, sonny boy—you fell down those iron stairs. No more gallivanting in the garden for you, young man!" She had a harsh accent, which Porky couldn't place. Could have been from Northern Ireland; it always sounded strange. But it also occurred to him that he'd never seen this nurse before, and he knew all the hospital staff well now. He was brought back from his musing by what happened next. For, losing patience, she shoved his big weight onto the bed.

"Hey!" objected Porky. "Don't push!" He was going to say some more, maybe even swear at her, when he saw the syringe in her hand. A cold wave of fear broke over him. "Wh—I don't usually get injections. Wh—" But she wouldn't let him ask any questions. Her large pork chop hands pushed him again and pulled at his pyjama trousers. "Hey!" Porky struggled, moving his big bottom from side to side uselessly. He was scared now. He tried to pull a punch, but the gruff nurse gripped his hand. Fully fledged fear took over. "Mum!" cried Porky involuntarily.

"Calling for Mum at last, are we?" came her accusing voice, like steel. He felt the needle go in. As he drifted off into a blurry slumber, he was sure he could hear her opening cupboards and going through his things.

Bina tipped the taxi driver and stepped out into the early November chill. Soon they wouldn't be able to spend their afternoons in the garden. Still, it was amazing weather for this time of year, so people kept telling her. An Indian summer, they called it! Must have brought it with her, they said. Anyway, so what about the weather? All she cared about was seeing Porky. She thought about him all the time. She knew other people wondered why. Sure, by most people's standards he wasn't good looking. That was just because he was fat, she told herself. Most fat people looked ugly. But Porky's face held great promise. He had vivid green eyes, like emeralds. Not the pale wishy-washy green most people had. And golden hair, not red or ginger, as it was often described. And freckles. Freckles were cute. Above all, though, he was passionate and strong. She loved this about him. He had fought his illness, and he was winning. But apart from all this, didn't they share something else, connect in another way too? He had been given a gift, like her. She had felt alone in her knowledge before meeting him. Why had she been attracted to him—in a *garden?* And she'd been there when he got his gift. She knew it. It was meant to be. The only question she couldn't answer was *why*. Ajit's face entered her mind. And now—now what?

Sister Gandhali came into view in front of her. Bina pushed her thoughts aside. She didn't want to think of Ajit right now. "Look at this!" her aunt said, turning round and round, spreading her arms out like wings, indicating the sunflowers which, by now, were almost as tall as her. She turned to Bina, radiant, as if she had seen a religious vision. But her look also indicated that, somehow, Bina was involved. She and Porky. And she looked uncertain, even afraid; a reverent kind of fear. She wasn't sure what to say, either.

Finally, she asked, almost accusingly, "Were you and Porky in the garden yesterday after I left?"

Bina thought of the kiss and stayed silent. Mercifully, her aunt's mobile rang just then.

Sister Gandhali spoke in Urdu. "Yes, she is here," she said, looking at Bina nervously. "No, no—do not come. No need. Bina is with me. We are having tea. Yes, in half an hour. Of course, brother. Goodbye." They looked at each other. A look that meant time was running out. "Bina, my sweet, you have half an hour. And I cannot keep covering for you. You must decide." And as an afterthought, she added, "Oh, Porky is sick—poisoned!"

She was running then. Flying through the garden and up the iron staircase. Her bright green scarf fell down the steps and onto the bison's head. Kitchi raised a sleepy eyebrow and gave a heavy sigh. *Those star-crossed lovers had better get it together for tonight,* he thought. He hated to admit it, but he was doubtful.

A drowsy Porky groggily put his hand down his pyjama bottoms and felt inside his underpants. It was still there. He'd cleverly hidden the horn in a place the pseudo-nurse hadn't been rude enough to look. What else could she have been looking for? He wasn't a drug addict or anything. It had to be the horn. The next burning question was, of course, *why?* At that moment, Bina ran in, looking like she was about to cry. She fell headlong on top of him as he half lay, half sat up in bed. She showered him with clumsy kisses, almost pulling out his nose tubes. And then she sat up and perched on the edge of the bed, like a bright green tropical bird. They both laughed at how ridiculous they must look, but Porky sobered up quickly, the events of the last few hours overshadowing his mood.

"What is it?" Bina asked, noticing his odd look. "And what happened to you? Aunt Gandhali said . . ."

He touched her mouth gently to stop her. "Bina, something's wrong here," he spoke in hushed tones. "I don't understand what exactly, but first I was poisoned, then forcibly put to sleep while my room was searched."

"For what?" But immediately she knew. "For the horn." She remembered her own ordeal as she had left Karna. "Is the horn safe?" He nodded and willed himself not to blush as he gripped it tighter between his thighs. *Please don't ask to see it,* he prayed. He sat up and offered her juice instead as a distraction. He was still sleepy and struggling to think straight.

"If . . ." he began. This time, Bina stopped him.

"We have to leave," she said; her face had gone pale. "Or soon, something worse may happen."

"Leave?" Porky looked grim. "To where? And why? I don't get it. I just don't get it. What does all this mean? Horns. Nutmegs. Tingling hands. Sunflowers growing like a speeded-up film. This is nonsense!"

Suddenly, he felt just like he had when he had been in the ambulance, rushing to hospital with his mother. Afraid, like a little child. Bina stared at him, watching the strong man in him deflate. She started to feel alone. What had Aunt Gandhali said? She had half an hour. Half an hour to make a decision that would change her life forever. She jumped off the bed and walked to the window. The garden. *Oh, what did it all mean?*

Porky looked over at Bina, looking out of the window. Were they meant to be together? Did he really want to selfishly take her away from her family? She might regret it all her life. And it could be dangerous. He'd heard about those honour killings such families carried out. Porky was, metaphorically, having cold feet.

Bina glanced over and saw it in his face. She looked back out at the garden. She noticed a movement near the biggest sunflower.

Porky felt confused; he was still fuzzy from the drugs. A vague memory was stirring deep inside of him. Emotion rose up with it. He saw himself lying limply on a bed in an operating theatre. Nurses were pushing at his chest. He felt angry. A powerful force pushed up from where the horn rested in his loins, rushed up through his chest and exploded out. A huge hairy face came into focus, and he heard a boy's voice. "We're Keeeeeeepers!" he shouted, elongating the word so that he sounded like a crazy football fan at a match.

At exactly the same moment Porky yelled out, Bina said, "There is a bison in the garden."

He was out of bed now and bounded over to where she stood. Kitchi looked up as their faces appeared at the window. He sat under the sunflower, ever patient. Porky gripped Bina by the shoulders. He was yelling in her face. "We're Keepers! Bina—we're Keepers! It . . . He . . ." He pointed at the bison down below. "told me. A boy, it's a boy! He told me!" Bina was shushing him, flapping her arms in a placating manner.

"*Who* told you *what?*" she asked, but she was smiling. This was the Porky she loved: strong and passionate. Of course, somewhere deep down, she knew already what he was struggling to grasp.

"He did," he answered, still pointing at Kitchi, getting breathless now. "You and me are Keepers, Bina! We have to leave here. He . . . it . . . I dunno . . . will take us. He said it. And tonight. Bina—it's tonight!" She studied his face intently. The clock on the wall said five minutes to six. She had five minutes.

"But—what *is* a Keeper?"

"Um . . ." Porky was so elated he could have laughed and cried at the same time. "We both have something. We know this. This something has power. We know this too. Someone doesn't want us to have this power. We both know about *this!* Right?"

"Right."

"So we have to hold onto what we have, what we've been given—we have to *keep them safe*," he said the last three words slowly, savouring them, loading them with meaning.

Bina was nodding vigorously. "What do Keepers keep?" She kissed him and whispered in his ear, "Secrets!"

For the first time ever, during the course of a whole working day in cities around Britain, not a single customer entered McDollar's. Thousands of defrosted burgers went to waste.

There was a sharp knock at the door. Quickly, they both stepped apart, guiltily. Ajit stood in the doorway. Without a word, he strode forward and took hold of Bina's wrist. He threw Porky a look that said, *I want to kill you.* Porky stood motionless, looking foolish in his pyjamas and bare feet. Ajit pulled his fiancée to the door, where they paused. He said something to her in Urdu. She shook her head. Porky started to say something, but Bina stretched out her arm, her palm turned towards him, and mouthed, "No!" She turned her back on Porky and was gone.

"Bina!" he was yelling now. "Tonight—under the sunflower. Be there!" *Oh my God, please be there.*

He let out a choking noise as he tried to conceal his sobs. He remained sitting at the window, where Bina had stood, looking out at the garden and watching the sky grow darker. He was nervous while waiting for nightfall. *Would she come?* His preoccupation with Bina had caused him to overlook other important things. He thought suddenly about the fire escape door. Would it still be open? He didn't know if it got locked at night. And what was he going to wear? And take? That would depend on where he was going, and he had no information on that. It didn't worry him, though. Under normal circumstances, it would have, but these were no longer normal circumstances. He realised that Bina knew something he didn't. She had *instinctive* knowledge. She believed in it, or rather *trusted* was a better word. And he had to trust too. He wasn't religious, but here in this place, he'd become aware of another dimension to things. *Something* had communicated with him, had *connected* with him. He didn't know how to put it yet, he didn't have the words. But the sunflower which spoke to him, the seedlings Sister Gandhali taught him how to plant, the horn's power which made him stronger, meeting Bina—these things were *real* and mattered in a way that nothing ever did before. His parents, his school, other things he used to live for, like video games or Facebook, had faded away into insignificance. But not only that, there was something at stake; he felt it when he talked to all those other kids who were facing horrendous problems: Abala, Amy, and Serenity. And what about him? He'd been obese and nearly died. It was time to trust. *Hungry for change*. He gave a small smile—that was it—that was what it was all about.

A clattering noise at the nurse's station announced the arrival of the dinner trays. He jumped; he wasn't ready, and he hadn't checked the fire escape. He quickly laid out some jeans (new, and two sizes smaller!) and a long-sleeved sweatshirt. A jacket too? He wasn't sure. The food trolley was making its way down the corridor. Better check the fire escape first. He looked out—all clear. He dashed all the way to the end of the corridor. It was open. Of course it was open; it was a fire escape! On his way back, he heard voices up close. The dinner trolley had reached his room. Shouldn't be a problem. He sauntered along matter-of-factly. Then a really strange thing happened. Two nurses made towards him. Slowly, not aggressively, but their movements weren't normal—kind of jerky. He looked at their faces. They wore no expressions. Like dead people. *What?* A chill covered him with goose bumps, and he forced himself to move, because a moment later and he'd be frozen with fear. He was out of the fire escape door and down the iron stairs like lightning. And hid beneath them till his eyes became accustomed to the dark.

There was the bison, dozing under the sunflower. Porky thought it had better wake up fast. But he remembered that they had to wait for Bina. His great protector, the sunflower, turned to him, using the same words that he had heard on that very first occasion when he had become aware: *"Don't worry, Porky. Don't worry."*

Okay, he whispered in his heart. The bison raised its head. Porky saw for the first time that it had only one horn. *So it's yours, not mine.* A question flickered in his mind. *What about me—my secret?*

The sunflower was to provide him with the answer in the nick of time. The zombie nurses had made it onto the top of the fire escape. The great sunflower rotated its head to face them. And fired. Hundreds of tiny seeds shot out of its round, brown disc of a face. The nurses were squealing in pain, arms flailing, trying to protect their faces. They fell down the iron stairs and disappeared. Kitchi got up then, approached the space where Porky hid, and bent down on four knees. This was it—he had to go. As Porky climbed onto Kitchi's back, he realised he was still in his pyjamas, clenching a horn between his legs! And with a sunflower seed in his pocket. He retrieved it from the place he'd hidden it on that very first day he'd found it in the garden. It had been with him all along. Had it healed him too? Tingling started up in his fingers as if to say, "Yes, of course!"

The sunflower loomed over them and bowed very low to the ground. A regal, Japanese-style bow. Porky felt strangely honoured. He had a lump in his throat. He stroked its head and heard it speak, for the first time, out loud, saying, "You are Head Keeper. A good and strong leader. My seed contains your secret. Keep growing things, Porky!" Its gravelly voice sounded just like a sunflower's should. "Don't worry; we will look for the girl."

We? thought Porky. A large bird fluttered down then and stood on a branch, as if listening. It was the northern lapwing again. After a moment or two, it flew off again into the night.

As the bison started walking forward, Porky clutched onto the shaggy hair around its head. It picked up speed quickly and went in the direction of the helicopter pad. Porky wasn't afraid in the least. Instead, he *believed* in the impossible. If you did that, he reckoned, it became possible. He touched the little seed in his pocket, and his heart swelled. So much so, that he forgot about Bina not turning up. He *trusted.* And the power of that trust warned the legion of vampire bats lined up in the shadows not to attack. Because they would surely be beaten.

CHAPTER 21

Abala Secretly Leaves the Camp

Sally was the only person to know. Abala didn't want to tell her, but he had no choice. So he explained everything. She had to promise him she wouldn't tell her father. He made her vow the Ethiopian way. Behind the wash tents, they crouched in the long grass and mingled blood. He was impressed: she didn't flinch at all when the knife sliced through the thick skin of her palm. They pressed hands together with the fervour that accompanies a shared secret, him with his wide, white smile, her face pale, lips pressed together, trying not to cry. They had been planning for two days now, whispering together in a corner of Sally's living area. Sally hoped her father would just assume she had a crush on Abala. They used the computer as a decoy, although it was often useful, for getting in touch with Porky, for one.

Abala was glad Sally had Porky to talk to. There was nothing worse than being alone with a secret. Porky's response was clear and direct: "Leave," he'd written, saying that he, himself, had been told to do the very same thing. *Been told?* ruminated Abala. *By who?* He thought Porky was lucky to have that kind of guidance. He felt so alone in this next step. Abala delved into the past. Who had always directed him? Who had he turned to? *Grandfather, of course.* But now, wasn't it because of Grandfather's prayer that he was being victimised? Then Grandfather was with him in this, he reasoned. He wondered what Porky was running away from.

"He says that it's the monster of consumption," Sally reported. They both looked at each other, perplexed.

"What? A monster?" But wasn't he running away from a monster, too? His enemy didn't fit the description of any animal he knew. So Porky and he had something else in common. He felt comforted. He remembered their poems, both entitled "I Am Hungry." Was it more than a coincidence? Were they connected in some way?

"Maybe it's a metaphorical monster," suggested Sally.

"What?" He looked at her, hoping this was his answer.

"I mean . . ." she began. "Oh, nothing." It was too difficult to explain.

They applied themselves instead to the task of pulling resources. So far they had cleverly hidden in Sally's bedroom a sharp knife, matches, a compass (which Abala always took to turning round and round admiringly, wasting time until Sally would grab it off him), and water containers (how many could he carry—full?). He'd need food, surely, but Abala had reassured Sally over and over that he knew how to hunt; all he needed was a weapon. The weapon was proving harder to procure. Abala knew that at least half of the Ethiopian men in the camp had a weapon stashed away, somewhere. The question was how to *steal* one. It was something he wasn't comfortable with. He decided to steal one from the oldest son of the family he lived with, but then he couldn't go through with it. It was a matter of honour. He had to keep himself right if he wanted to succeed. That's what Grandfather would have said. A little while later, he found a child's slingshot, lost in the stony ground. Perfect. He could have a roast bird or two every night for dinner.

Every now and then, Sally would come up with a question that unnerved him. Like just now: "What about bugs? Or . . . snakes?" Her voice was loaded with horror. "Or . . ." She knew there were worse things she daren't mention.

"Hmmm," Abala said, pretending to think deeply, but in reality, he had no clue. Also the question made him think of the beast, which he'd been carefully avoiding. Thoughts of the beast lurked in the deep recesses of his mind. They jumped out at him now. By leaving the safety of the camp, he'd be taking one step closer to . . . what exactly? He didn't know. Let alone *why*. Why? Well, it was the *gift*, of course, if you could call it that. Some gift.

"You know," Sally said, interrupting his train of thought, "we could make something for protection. You could wear it."

"Like a mosquito net?"

"No, more of a cream or something; it would act as a barrier." She showed him a tube bought from a pharmacy: "Keeps insects away."

He nodded; it sounded like a good idea. So they gathered whatever they could think of into a bowl. Sally poured, squeezed, or spooned everything in, while Abala stirred. First the insect repellent from the pharmacy went in.

"Antiseptic cream?" she suggested.

Abala agreed.

"Clove oil?" she asked.

He nodded.

"Hair remover?"

He shrugged, not sure. "Yeah! It smells disgusting!"

Sally chucked it in. She was enjoying this. A load more things went in.

"Bleach?" she offered.

He raised his hand; a definite no. They were finished; they put the thick and grey goo into the camp workers' fridge.

"Bring it this evening," he said, "at six. You know where?"

Sally nodded. She was going to miss him, and she was afraid for him too but tried not to show it. If she was honest, she didn't fully understand all that Abala had shared with her. About this beast thing. Out to get him—or it would attack the camp? There was a part of her that was sceptical; she had heard too much about African spiritual superstitions, voodoo, and so on. But she didn't want to be prejudiced, either—and what about the feast of food that had appeared because of him? And the coffee? She watched him walk away. He was so small. A lot shorter than her. In two hours' time, they'd be saying goodbye. She wished he didn't have to go. Just then, a loud shriek made her jump. It was a white cockatoo; it flew up and sat on the perimeter fence.

The bird stayed there, watching and waiting, for an hour, just before Abala's departure. Then, away it flew over the wild and empty savannah of eastern Kenya. The land was flat and soon sloped slowly downward into a valley. Farther below, the wide and meandering river bed lay cracked and dry. The expected rains had not arrived yet. Trees stood in clusters, their leafy branches held up in worship to the sky. Further uphill to the right, a stream trickled towards the greater tributary of the river, its source high in the hills. The trees and the long grass hid many things. The cockatoo would seek them out.

It first spotted a herd of wildebeest occupying the expanse directly in front of the camp. The bird knew that where there are wildebeest, there are predators. On circling the herd, it soon picked out a strong male, likely to be a leader. After a few minutes of jumping on and off his head and popping its beak in and out of his ears in a most annoying manner, the great wildebeest started plodding south, farther inland. Abala would go west towards Lake Turkana. When the slow plod came to a stop once again, the cockatoo let out a loud cry, unsettling a group of females gossiping nearby. One final menacing tug on the chief wildebeest's ear did the trick—he was off. He jumped round and about for a moment or two, in an effort to shake the pest free of his ear; the others stood, heads raised, staring vacantly. Finally he bolted, the rest following, slow at first, but before long picking up speed—until the whole herd was stampeding blindly on its way to what they assumed must be a better place.

A sleepy lioness raised her eyelids lazily, peeking through the grass stalks. *What?* This was most unexpected. She pulled her body up and stretched to her full length. *Hmmm.* The wildebeest were already dots in the distance. She nudged her cubs impatiently with her huge head, and they were soon up and following Mum. The others in the pride would do just as she said, and so they did, making a pattern in the long grass as they edged forward, an arrowhead with their queen in the lead.

A gigantic grey rhinoceros watched them leave. He stood amongst the group of worshipping trees. He trusted the lions; they knew their stuff. Especially Cleo, that insolent queen of theirs. *Hmmm, what was she up to now?* he thought. *Must be a detour.* And so he duly followed, at a safe distance.

A herd of elephants, caked in mud, were rolling in some short savannah turf, having a late afternoon scrub. Evening was drawing in; soon it would be time to huddle the family together and sleep near the path Abala would be taking; he could bump into them in the dark. The cockatoo landed at the top of a tall shifara tree and had an urgent conference with a long-legged stork. Their cawing and cackling unsettled the mother elephant, making her nervous. Worse was to come. The cockatoo's friend, the stork, went about her evening toilet business on the elephants' heads. When a splosh reached the corner of the largest elephant's eye, she was fuming. She needed to find her family water—and quick! Back to the mud before nightfall, she decided. They moved slowly off.

A rattlesnake, coiled up near the path, awoke from the thudding and couldn't get back to sleep again. She missed the proximity of the elephants, as they guaranteed plenty of food for her babies. How? The abundance of small rodents that had to flee as the huge elephant feet approached was the reason. She always waited a short distance in front of the herd. Better get going too, she reckoned. And left.

The cockatoo surveyed the land. Job done! They had all been on their way to Lake Turkana. But Abala was going there, and now the path was clear.

Sally used her father's wire cutters to help Abala slice through the fence. They shared the task, which took longer than Abala had planned. He kept looking anxiously at the sun. He'd chosen the time perfectly, or so he'd thought; two hours to sunset. By dark, he would be far enough away, yet not too tired. He'd rest a little, ready to start again at dawn. Walking in the heat of the day was foolish. At last, they were through! He had to be quick now. Sally smeared the paste all over his body; he helped with the difficult parts. She'd put everything in a backpack and given him a pair of trainers, too. He had two plastic bottles of drinking water but refused to carry food. "No space—and I can hunt!" They said a hurried goodbye. He disappeared into the bush before she could blink. Abala was gone from the camp.

It wasn't long before he found a track regularly used by animals. A slight furrow had been worn by many feet moving in single file. He wasn't accustomed to tracking; he had no real experience, but he had herded goats and knew, from his cousins' hunting stories, to watch for flattened areas of grass, footprints, and broken branches, but he saw nothing. No poo either. *All good,* he exhaled with relief. This was easier than he thought. His backpack was heavy because of the water. Thank goodness he hadn't taken food too! He drank some now, sitting on a small mound. From here he could survey the entire sloping valley below.

He'd gone a good distance already. But where to now? He took out the compass and stared at it, as if it held the answer. It didn't, so he had to decide. In his haste to leave, he had only formed a rough plan in his head: either make for Nairobi, the capital, or go towards the nearest body of water, which was Lake Turkana. Going anywhere near the border with Somalia was out of the question, for obvious reasons. So was it to be south or west? He fancied seeing a large town, a city even. If he was to be safe from that wild *thing,* surely the city was the place to go? And after that, maybe to Tanzania? Who knows? The sun was alarmingly low in the sky by now; he had to decide. Some squawking made him look up and over to his right. On the crest of the hill, two birds were fighting in the trees: a cockatoo and a stork. Such a lot of thrashing and crashing went on that he went over to look. As he approached, they stopped suddenly and flew off in a westerly direction. *Wow!* gasped Abala. It really was beautiful down there; so many trees! He just caught sight of the two birds disappearing into a small wood. He thought it looked like a good place to spend the night. It was dusk already, and he still had firewood to gather. On entering the wood, he heard the birds' sounds echoing all around him. He realised he had forgotten to hunt. How stupid of him! Now the birds and animals were settling for the night. Soon, after dark, he'd be the one hunted. He had to light a fire. Nightfall came suddenly in Africa. And it did just then.

He lit a fire he had literally thrown together and stayed as close to it as he could. Stretching out on his back, he found he couldn't see the stars, the canopy of branches so dense it was the perfect shelter. How lucky he was to find this place to sleep so close to sunset. He mentally thanked the fighting birds. Yet he hadn't eaten, and his stomach ached a little. Still, his exhausted limbs and the stress of the last few days were enough to knock him out.

The curling twirl of smoke from Abala's fire didn't go unnoticed in the moonlight. Somewhere further on and higher up, two sets of watchful eyes studied him, predicting his next day's route.

CHAPTER 22

Porky and the Bison on Their Way to Yemen

A wind blew up almost immediately. Suddenly—from out of nowhere, and it wasn't a normal wind, either. Porky's first thought as they took off from the helicopter pad, or rather his second thought after he'd *believed* and *trusted,* was that they weren't going to make it. He gripped onto the bison's mane even tighter. Its flying had become more like swimming: a clumsy and desperate doggy paddle, unable to withstand the gusts shifting them this way and then that. But, as well as this, there was a noise. Or was it a voice? Saying something; moaning at them. Only, it was more like threatening than moaning; he could make it out now: "You will not win. I cannot be beaten. Everything is mine." And then he saw it: a skinny creature jumping (or flying) from treetop to treetop, then it landed on the hospital roof. No, not flying; it had legs. Two long ginormous legs. It had huge eyes, "all the better to see you with" eyes. Porky noticed as they flew over the hospital garden that there was nothing left; it had all been torn up. The sunflowers, the vegetables, the trees—everything! Where had it all gone? He craned to see if his sunflower was still there, but he couldn't be sure.

They were level with this *thing* now, edging over the top of the hospital. A dog on the roof terrace was barking at it furiously. The apparition, if that's what it was, opened its big mouth and just, kind of, *sucked* the dog up. The dog was gone; eaten alive. The bison made a brave attempt at trying to get higher, out of the *thing's* reach. Not so easy. The goggle-eyed creature, with the huge mouth, leapt onto an even higher rooftop just ahead of them. The bison scrambled to get away. Not so easy again, because the monster's mouth was widening, its face closing in on them. It repeated its mantra: "I cannot be beaten. Everything is mine. I can gobble you up." And it did so, just then, to a small family having a barbeque on their terrace. Whoosh, they were gone. Slurped up—it was horrible. *Gobble you up.* The words reverberated around Porky's skull. It occurred to him then (or he hoped) that this could be another dream, but despairingly, he knew it wasn't. The same moment the ever-widening mouth reached within a metre of them, he heard the bison groaning, with fear and effort. No, this was *not* an apparition, and they had no way of getting away except just falling out of the sky. In the split-second he was considering jumping, they were snapped shut inside a bubble.

Porky couldn't tell what the bubble was made of—plastic, Perspex, or thickened glass—but it was strong and it was transparent. And they were safe! They sped up as if in a glass elevator in a mall. He saw clearly everything happening below: the creature couldn't jump high enough and leapt down to the ground instead; in its rage, it sucked up a taxi.

"Coool!" Porky said, letting the word draw out; it was so exciting to be free! The bison just stared. Either it was scared or it knew exactly what was going on. Time to find out. They stared at each as the bubble floated up and up, picking up speed. They stared for what felt like a very long time, although probably it wasn't.

Eventually, Porky said, "So, what's this all about then?" The bison stared back at him. "I know you can talk—I heard you." Silence. "Ah—maybe only to give messages?" Nothing. Then, he felt the discomfort of the horn again, still between his legs. Maybe if he gave it its horn back? He drew the horn out and placed it near the bison, which, of course, sniffed at it. *Sorry,* thought Porky. No other reaction. The bison's golden eyes stared into his. They looked terrified.

Finally, a boy's clear voice said, "Wendigo." And it looked away into the night sky hurtling past.

And so they whizzed along in silence, at full speed, although it felt like floating. A bubble in the night sky. Clouds below; stars above. Soft light ahead. *Where it's day,* Porky thought. For the second time that evening, he *believed.* Because you cannot go through an experience like that and not *trust* that something more powerful than you has put you there. He looked over at the bison curled up, asleep. And, tingling all over, he closed his eyes and thought of Bina.

CHAPTER 23

Three Keepers Together in Yemen

In the early morning light, Porky saw the Pyramids of Giza for the very first time. They looked tiny, like Monopoly pieces (if Monopoly had pyramids, that is). He was more surprised, though, by the fact that the city of Cairo was in their back gardens! Egypt. At least he knew where he was now. They hurtled on like a meteorite, approaching the Earth. The bubble cruised over the desert of Saudi Arabia. The bison lay quietly, without looking out, just looking down at the horn. It had seemed dazed since the incident with the monster thing. *Wendigo;* now Porky knew its name.

The sun was up, and it was getting hot inside the bubble. A long strip of the Red Sea was visible on their right. Lower and closer they came to the Earth. Porky started worrying about how they were going to land; it was scary enough in an aircraft. But all of a sudden, they were catapulting out over the sea. So low, he could see ships. He was amazed by the detail; sailors on board were pointing. *Oh, please don't shoot!* He guessed they could be taken for aliens. And then the bubble was turning, round and round, over and over; sky then sea, sky then sea. Till he got a face full of hairy bison. They were slowing down, of course; he braced himself for the plunge, taking hold of the horn and his seed, just in case. And . . . none came; nothing but a gentle splash.

All at once, there was no bubble—just salt and sea! In his mouth, nose . . . he gulped down too much water, went under two, three times. Porky had been an obese boy; he'd never swum. The silent bison came to the rescue and bumped him above water from underneath. Soon he was on top of his new friend again, who turned out to be a good swimmer. They swam towards shore, passing some fishing boats. Men were standing, cheering, waving their hands in the air. Some were already on their mobile phones; what would meet them on the shore? They were maybe more prepared for a press conference than for what actually met them.

Sirens could be heard now at the fishing port which lay ahead. *Probably an ambulance,* thought Porky, squinting to see in the strong sunlight. Rapid movements made him look down into the water. He gasped. What seemed like hundreds of schools of fish, too numerous to swim through, surrounded them. Pushing in all around, encircling the bison's legs till they couldn't go the way they wanted; instead, they were directed up shore to the left of the small harbour. It was a miracle that all those minuscule fish had the combined strength to push against the current, but they did. Mimosas and willows leaned over the shore line and into the water, preventing the assembled welcomers from chasing along and getting a glimpse of the bedraggled bison, holding up an equally drenched fat boy in his pyjamas. A break in the beautiful line of trees revealed a small dark-skinned boy sitting on some rocks, fishing. He got a fright when he saw them; he rose up and instantly abandoned his line, running and yelling at the top of his voice, "Miss Jasmine!"

The fish relaxed, ceased being a set of muscles, backed off, and swam away. "I guess this is it, my friend!" Porky said, patting the bison on its back. "Our destination." And up onto the shore they clambered, dripping wet.

Moments later, a girl approached, holding a camel by a red tasselled cord. The small boy followed, hiding in her skirts. Purple and green skirts and a black head. But when she came closer, they saw a strong face and piercing stare under her long black headscarf.

Her height also gave her an imposing quality. Porky felt himself shrink inside. *She looks very . . . capable,* he thought, unwilling to admit, even to himself, a nervousness rising within.

She looked them up and down and finally announced, in a rough voice, "You are the *others.*"

Was there a tinge of disappointment in her voice? Or had he imagined it? He also noticed it wasn't a question.

"The others?" repeated Porky. Amazed at himself for understanding her. Hadn't she spoken in Arabic? *The Others* was the name of a film he'd seen, and he thought of making a quip about not being dead yet, but, somehow, she didn't look like the kind of girl you could joke with. She looked at him again, sizing him up. She took note of the pyjamas.

"The other Keepers."

"The other Keepers?" Porky could have kicked himself for echoing her *again.* Why wasn't he taking control of the situation? The boy came out from behind her skirts. Even he could tell who was in command. "Um . . ." Porky cleared his throat. "We've come a long . . ." but before he could really get started, there was a commotion behind him. The bison grunted ferociously and lunged at the camel. It succeeded in taking hold of the camel's red reins and tugged at them angrily. "Oh!" Porky said, taking responsibility. "Stop it, Bison! That's enough!" Like a dog owner in a park.

"Does your animal not have a name?" the girl asked; she could obviously understand what he said, too. Without waiting for an answer, she went directly over to sort out the problem. After chastising her camel, which went by the name of Flying Carpet (*How ridiculous,* thought Porky), she turned to the bison. She laid a hand on its neck and just *listened.* A moment later, she glared at the camel and shouted, "How many times have I told you about this incessant flirting? Kitchi is *definitely* not interested!"

Kitchi? Why hadn't it told him that? Porky was feeling really uncomfortable now. At the same time, he realised how tired he was, and wet. He knew he needed to pull himself together. But she was talking again. "My honoured guests—Keepers or not—please allow me to serve you some tea."

"No, actually we *are* Keepers . . ." he said, trailing off and mumbling the words to himself. She had moved ahead anyway, Flying Carpet leading the way. He noticed the camel was limping. The bison plodded along beside him, finding the sand hard to negotiate. Porky wouldn't look at him; he was seething inside.

They followed her to a shelter made of sheets tied to poles; she pointed to cushions scattered on a mat and generously waved her arm, saying, "Breakfast and tea will be served in a moment. Please sit. First, I *must* deal with these animals."

Porky noticed the stress on the "must." As if she had taken over ownership of the bison already. *His* bison. Or was it his, really? He looked over at them. They were talking together continually as she poured water into two buckets, at careful distances from one another. He knew this *Kitchi* was talking, because he was moving his head in an animated way, while the girl nodded or said, "Uh huh?" or "No!" He felt mad but was so tired now—and starving! The boy was nowhere to be seen. He hoped he'd gone off to boil the kettle and rustle up some scrambled eggs on toast or something. It was then Porky pleasantly remembered that today was the first day of his new diet.

The girl came back. "How rude of me!" she exclaimed loudly. Too loudly, Porky thought; there was only him there, not an audience. "I am Jasmine Khaled Ali Hareeb. And you are?" This was his chance. He got to his feet.

"I am the Head Keeper," he said, pausing for effect. "Philip Porky McGregor." He stretched out his hand, but Jasmine kept hers on her chest, getting one up on him again. She motioned for him to sit, watching him carefully. *Head Keeper?* She didn't like the sound of that. Breakfast arrived just in time to break the tension, momentarily anyway.

Two trays were presented, one carrying a plate of one-two-three-four-five (Porky had them counted before the tray touched the mat) dates and a small bowl of yogurt; the other bore three very small glasses of tea. Was this between three people? "We have had our breakfast," Jasmine said. "Please go ahead."

Oh thank my lucky stars! he breathed, trying not to show his enormous relief. He waded in, gobbling the dates hungrily and drinking the yogurt from its bowl. Jasmine looked on in distaste at the so-called Head Keeper. Wiping his mouth on his sleeve, he waited to be offered seconds. No offer came.

Porky's stomach grumbled throughout the conversation that ensued. He began by asserting himself: "Has Kitchi had breakfast?" he asked. "We have journeyed through the night."

"Surely." She nodded, still watching him carefully.

It was hard to think of anything to say: his rumbling tummy, lack of sleep, and burning anger at the bison made him restless and unfocussed. *And* it was getting hot. He played nervously with his sunflower seed. She continued to observe him. "The bison, Kitchi, has lost a horn," she said at last. He sighed and placed it on a cushion.

"Yes, I know." He turned the seed over and over. He suddenly got an image of Bina, the last he'd seen of her, stretching out her palm at him, mouthing "No." His heart was sinking.

"You are . . ." She started to say something but changed her mind. She could read the hunched shoulders and bowed head. She remembered herself when she'd been left behind. She had been going to say *sad,* but instead changed it to "a gardener?" He looked up quickly, surprised.

"Yes." He showed her the seed in his hands, smiling briefly. "Yes, actually—I am! I have a big garden in England. I planted many pots—of these, actually!" He held up the seed again. Then he remembered how the garden had looked from the bubble as it rose away from the ground. And fell silent.

"You have much sorrow," Jasmine finally said. "You must rest. Sleep a little here."

He was grateful, but there was the problem of his nagging hunger.

"Sorry, um, but before that, could I have a snack? Like, a sandwich or something?" Jasmine laughed. She, too, twirled something in her hands. A dried-up date. She held it up in front of his face.

"See this? This is my Lucky Date. It always reminds me not to eat too much. At breakfast, you already had one date too many! No snacks till lunch time. Restricted diet! You look like you need it!"

She laughed again, throwing her Lucky Date onto the cushion where Porky had put the horn. Feeling embarrassed, he curled up on some cushions. He popped his seed onto the cushion too. He lay on his side, just looking at the three objects right in front of his face. Unanswered questions whirled around in his brain, as he drifted off to an image of Wendigo wolfing down the dog.

CHAPTER 24

Amy Rides the Dragon

Amy came out of the hideaway; she was blinded for a second by the car headlights. Then two silhouettes of policemen in their caps came into focus. Before they even shouted the inevitable "Raise your hands!" she felt a billowing movement vibrate up and to the left, close to the cliff edge. Averting her eyes for a fraction of a second, she glimpsed something like a huge hot air balloon entangled in a tree. Although it was dark, the colours were still discernible: red and yellow. As soon as she'd raised her hands, the officers began moving towards her. Her heart pounded, but she felt dead already. How many years in prison could she get for pepper spraying a policeman?

The billowing shape filled more than a corner of her eye by now. In fact, it was moving towards her, faster than the policemen were. She could see that the balloon thing, or whatever it was, was going to hit her. Should she jump out of its way into the restraining arms of her assailants? She thought not. And so she succumbed. She yielded. To something greater than herself, she would explain later, when telling her story.

It engulfed her, this great red and yellow thing. It was hard not to struggle, to try to break free. But she didn't; she let it whoosh over her like a wave. Only the policemen struggled—to find her! One began to viciously swing his baton, and he was getting closer.

Then suddenly she was up, up and away in her beautiful balloon, except it wasn't a balloon at all—it was a cloud of seed spores, thousands and thousands of them, all in the shape of a dragon! This was no surprise to Amy; the Chinese were used to seeing dragons, especially at weddings and New Year. What shocked her was that there was no basket to sit in or ropes to tie her down, and yet she floated in it without falling out. And it was a quick mover! She was way out to sea in no time, the policemen hardly visible on the cliff edge. She thanked the stars they had the good sense not to shoot. A chilly night breeze helped her along, and although she was cold, her heart was on fire: she was riding the dragon! It was considered massive good luck to ride a dragon, and only ever happened to mythical characters. It was more than she could ever have hoped for. Why was this happening to her? She correctly guessed that it had something to do with the wild rice, patting her pocket as a thank you. She had the wonderful feeling of being forgiven and given a fresh start; so exhilarating that she hadn't noticed the dragon had been descending for some time. A dark land mass came into view. *That must be Vietnam,* she thought.

She was correct. And in Vietnam, the dragon landed and transformed into lots and lots of disintegrating seed spores, little dots. Amy sat and looked at them. What was she supposed to do now? The dark and lonely truth—that she had no backpack, no passport, and no money—came back to haunt her. She had only the wild rice; she was the proverbial Jack in the beanstalk fairytale, with five beans in his pocket.

There were only a few hours left till daybreak. She lay on her back and looked at the sky. Her mind drew a blank. A sudden jerking movement under her head caused her to jump up. *Yeuch! I bet it's a mole!* She hated vermin of all kinds. She took a step or two back, just in case. But it wasn't a mole—it was a kudzu. She knew this plant; it was found in south China, but its name came from the Japanese *kuzu*, meaning *climber*. It was considered a noxious weed that was stronger than everything it encircled. Amy had always loved it, though, for its strikingly violet flowers, and something else she couldn't remember. One sprouted just as she thought the word *flower*. The scent was heady in the quiet night. To her amazement, the kudzu continued growing, and climbing, right in front of her eyes. It was growing so rapidly, she could no longer see the top in the dark. It covered everything in its path, every tree and shrub. The whole area was kudzu now.

So . . . was she meant to climb it? Oh no . . . that was just too clichéd. She wouldn't do it. She sat down again in a huff. Although she'd just travelled all across the sea in (come on, let's face it) a *magic* dragon, without as much as a basket to sit in. At the word *basket,* one appeared (of course). Now she remembered: she loved the baskets people made out of kudzu. Amy was feeling a little better; after all, two things she loved had come alive just for her! And anyway: *Have basket, will travel!* Was that a proverb, or had she just made it up? But it seemed to fit, and so she climbed in. A long kudzu arm encircled her basket, and she rose higher and higher, spinning a little, like on a fairground ride. It was daytime now, but real time, in that sense, had ceased to exist. There was light, but it wasn't daylight, because there was no sky above. Amy felt like she was in a kind of dome, like a butterfly dome she'd once visited in a park in Nanjing. As soon as she thought the word *butterfly,* butterflies appeared, flying everywhere. It wasn't so much magical as *beautiful*—truly beautiful. And so she travelled, through a dome-like tunnel in a basket, which was passed from one long, creepy kudzu arm to another, spinning all the time. She never tired of it or felt sick once. It was better than a fairground ride, in that respect. (Amy covered 975 miles this way, passing over Vietnam, Laos, and Myanmar. But, of course, when time and distance cease to exist, this is meaningless.)

In Laos, shy newborn orchids raised their heads to the sun. The rising sun had not seen the like of such fragile beauty for many a decade. Its gentle rays coaxed the sleepy orchids to open their petals to a welcoming world.

Movement ahead caught her eye. From a distance, it was like the perpetual wriggling of maggots. Closer up, it looked instead like a mass of snakes, coiling and uncoiling. The basket was disintegrating from underneath; as it fell apart, in a moment of squeamish disgust, she realised she was going to fall into the tangled mess below. Which turned out not to be snakes, but more creeper plants! Vines, to use a better name. One vine, using two strands, delicately entwined her two feet and ankles, pulling her down out of the remains of the basket. It successfully cradled her to prevent her from falling; she was lying in what can only be described as a hammock. In this way, she was swung from one long creeper to another: creepy vine hands grasping her hammock at either end and passing it to yet other waiting tendrils. It was the weirdest way to travel; she thought it even stranger than the basket ride.

Clumps of blueberries, as big as grapes, appeared now and then, dangling from the vine stalk. She *was* thirsty, but what if they were poisonous? Somehow, that seemed a preposterous impossibility. This was a place all about *life*. Hadn't she just been rescued and absolved? This rung true, and so she tried them; the berries made a welcome delicious, watery snack. The question and answer session on the berries aroused a much deeper debate, however. Two important questions surfaced: *Where am I going?* and *Why me?*

Amy couldn't see where she was going. She saw only an endless domed tunnel of vines. She must have left Vietnam by now. Who knows how much distance and in what time a magical vine (by the name of *Cissus hypoglauca*, commonly known as the jungle grape) could cover? Amy was outside space and time, in an eternal space maybe, but certainly a place of the living, not the dying. (She had, in fact, if this is relevant, just passed by Bangladesh and India.)

In India, some little shoots came up from the ground. They were extinct Kerala legume trees. Within a minute, the strong shoots had become trunks. In two, branches appeared. Leaves next, and it took thirty seconds for their spindly green legumes to sprout. A young girl, on her way home, stopped to pick some.

An old lady, sitting by the side of the road, shook her head in wonder.

So, no answer to the first question; she could be going anywhere. And the second? This was much more difficult. Because attempting to answer this question involved seeing Seung-Yub's beautiful face again; she wondered what had become of him and agonised over whether it was her fault or not. He had trusted her, and so had his grandmother. Amy suddenly remembered Xi. It was she who had called her a *Keeper* in the first place. So . . . she had been *chosen*, somehow, whatever that meant. There was no time for answers to any more questions for now; it was time to catch the next creeper.

She could see it ahead, waiting for her. An enormous thick-stemmed vine lay below. It was a calabash, or bottle gourd vine. The criss-crossed tendrils of her hammock disentangled, and she was dumped at the base of the calabash. Amy was, by now, accustomed to being carried, and the long, steep climb upwards proved quite tiring, although she found her rubber-soled trainers easily gripped on the sides, and there were plenty of short shoots to hold onto. And it felt good to move again. She marvelled that, here she was, clambering eagerly, excitedly—anxious to see what was up ahead, so different from the grumpy girl who had refused to climb the beanstalk in Vietnam. Every so often a gourd appeared, in various shades of green. At one point, while she paused for a rest, panting, one of those gourds tipped up and spouted water! It made her smile, and she lapped it up, most spilling all over her face, wanting to laugh as she did so because it must have looked so funny. The whole thing was becoming funny to her now. She seriously wanted to laugh, really laugh, but it was hard to laugh alone. Instead, her laughter bubbled inside, but it would have to come out sooner or later.

Sliding was to follow. Miles and miles of it, a spaghetti junction of vine slides. From where she stood at the top, the endless twists and turns looked nonnegotiable—how would she possibly know which one to take? Now hilarity was out of the question; this looked dangerous. At this point, Amy did exactly what Porky had done during his bubble ride across a continent: she *trusted.* Was it Amy's trust that caused her to choose the right way, or was there a secret system of signals, like on railways, that shifted the right vine into place just before she reached it? She would never know, but she enjoyed sliding over Pakistan and Iran just the same.

In Pakistan, far away in the quiet mountains, among glades containing fir, spruce, and blue pines, a tiny tree pushed its way up out of the ground. The other trees were surprised to see their long-lost friend back again. *Taxus wallichiana* was pleased to be back too. Before long, it was standing as tall as the others, its bark thickening nicely. A powerful remedy for cancer within that bark lay ready and waiting.

Another vine took over as soon as the slide came to an end. Amy had noticed it in the distance as a purple haze: monkey ladder. Of all the vines in the world, this had to be the most beautiful. Its long, deep purple and dark green arms were undulating before her like strips of seaweed underwater. It was slimy too; a long slippery tentacle wrapped itself around her and moved her through the mass, as if she were entering another room through hanging plastic curtains. Monkey ladder moved forwards, carrying Amy with it. Bright, fluorescent green seed pods sprouted at regular intervals along the vine. She was slithering downwards now, and the end of another slimy tendril helped her into a pod. Even with seeds in it, there was plenty of room. These plants were huge! She was getting tired now. How long since she'd had any sleep? She yawned and curled around a seed, hugging it like a pillow. And she was out like a light, sleeping as she continued to travel; the vine slowed down and carried her gently over Oman and Yemen along to her final destination.

In Yemen, bunches of long green stems topped with purple flowers burst out of the ground on the dry hill slopes. The flowers exuded a pungent odour that had not been smelled here for over two hundred years. Although smelly, *Valerianella affinis* would be welcomed and embraced once more for the relaxation and sleep it provides.

CHAPTER 25

Amy Arrives in a Seed Pod

Porky was woken up abruptly by a shrill sound filling the air all around him. He sat up, rubbing his ears, willing it to go away. He thought it could be crickets singing inside some trees, trying to cool down. But on looking around for the trees, he couldn't find any, just endless scrubby ground and the blindingly bright sea stretched out before him. It took him a while to realise that the singing sound was coming from the objects next to him. Was this another message? Why was he finding it so hard to decode everything? He really had better get a grip. If only he wasn't so hungry. He looked over at Jasmine, busy milking Flying Carpet. He wondered what camel milk tasted like and shuddered. *Yeuch!* He would have to do something about the food situation. Hospital food was bad, but he had an awful feeling that this was going to be much worse.

The camel wouldn't cooperate or stay still. He watched Jasmine struggle to get it under control. He admired her strength, her command, but even Flying Carpet was too much for her. The high-pitched singing and the gathering heat were beginning to make him dizzy. Why had she said *the others?* So she knew something. But didn't he also? The sunflower had made him Head Keeper; but what did that mean? And the monster? And the incredible journey? And . . . he looked over at the bison, laying in the shade of a low, stubby palm. And a bison that talks? Maybe the ringing noise was actually in his head—maybe he was going mad!

What made things worse for Porky was that he didn't have food to turn to as an ally. Okay, the hospital food was liquidised, but it came regularly, and it tasted all right, really. Plus, he had chewed gum in between, and then Bina had given him some lovely violet sweets from some plant or other in India. Bina. Even the thought of her name hurt. He decided to go for a walk before it got hotter.

First, he sauntered along the sea front. Apart from the section of mimosas and willows, the shore was rocky. Perched on a large rock, a little way out in the water, the boy sat fishing. "Hello!" Porky called, waving. "Any luck? Nice big fish for lunch?"

The boy looked round and smiled, but he didn't seem to understand him the way Jasmine did. There was nothing else of interest here, so he turned inland. He surveyed this new country for the first time. It was bleak and made up of different shades of yellow and brown. Occasionally, a palm or two would break the monotony. Far away, there were hills displaying sporadic bursts of green, and behind them, mountains. It occurred to him that he hadn't even enquired of Jasmine the name of her country. Or asked her what she was doing here alone, with only a boy and two camels for company. Let alone talked about the *Keepers* or the *others.* Obviously, she'd been expecting him—*them,* in fact. They hadn't got off to a very good start. He guessed that he could have appeared rude and ungrateful.

But his rumbling, aching stomach took over his thoughts. He knew if he solved this problem, everything else would be okay. He sat down, his head reeling from the heat and lack of sleep. Porky had, after all, just been prematurely discharged from hospital. For a fleeting moment, he wished himself back there, being taken care of. His mum's face popped into his mind, but he banished it quickly before he slid down the slippery slope of self-pity. He had to be strong! He remembered the noises that had rudely awoken him and added that to the list of things to discuss with Jasmine. He rested on a boulder, his surroundings beginning to spin in the rising heat. Round stones covered the ground, looking to Porky exactly like bread rolls. He closed his eyes and imagined them freshly baked and spread with melting butter. *Mmmm . . .*

But on opening his eyes, all that met him was a splattered and decaying cactus fruit—its black seeds looking like chocolate sprinkles. What had Jasmine asked? *Are you a gardener?* He smiled. The thought pleased him, made him feel strong. He picked up the black seeds. Instantly his fingers tingled and soon were throbbing hot. His one and only sensation at that moment was the urge to plant them. He was filled with a purpose then and scrabbled at the ground with his hands. It was too dry. It was nearly impossible to dig up, and Porky felt a pang of foolishness. Until . . . suddenly his hands were wet. Water bubbled up from below, moistening the dry rocky earth till it resembled soil. It crumbled in his fingers, and a glorious smell rose out of it; he thought of a farm from a school trip long ago, of freshly cut grass, of the wind blowing in earthy aromas from the allotments behind New Market Gate. He pressed the seeds into the soil and covered them up quickly, patting down the soil on top, gently, lovingly. And rose up to look at his little garden with satisfaction.

"Por-ky!" He swung around. Jasmine was approaching, carrying what looked like a cup. It had to be camel's milk to taste; he braced himself for the unavoidable. She was waving a white scarf in her other hand. "You must put it on—your head . . ." But her words trailed off, and she was staring beyond him, wide-eyed and open-mouthed.

He swung back round again. "Wow! Hey-ey! Look at that!" A wall of bright, shiny green plants had sprung up when he wasn't looking. It was an impressive vegetable garden: peas, beans, aubergines, courgettes, tomatoes, even a few orange pumpkins sat lazily on the ground.

Jasmine had her hands on her face, unable to speak. "It is beautiful," she murmured, again and again, mesmerised. She turned to Porky and nodded gravely, saying, "Thank you, Por-ky Filip Magreegor. Thank you, Head Keeper."

Porky was pretty speechless too. He was grinning from ear to ear, though. He began to gather some vegetables, fingers tingling all the time; all was right in his world again. Jasmine held out the white scarf, and Porky loaded up with veggies. Before they returned to camp, she offered him a drink of camel's milk. "Thank you. But— no!" And laughed. He'd avoided the inevitable and was now looking forward to a *big* lunch!

The boy, Hassan, got a fire going and was roasting the vegetables in no time. He hadn't been lucky with a fish yet. They sat in the makeshift tent, drinking sweet cactus juice. Porky now wore a white headdress. His face was slightly sunburnt. The sun was getting somewhat lower and cast some welcome shadow. Porky was deep in thought about how Jasmine's people managed here, without a water tap to open or an electrical switch to turn on. If he was honest, he thought a lot of time was wasted, and more importantly, he missed his laptop. He would have been on top of everything if he could just connect. Where was he, for one? Jasmine and he had a lot of talking to do. But first—lunch!

He didn't wait for Jasmine this time, just loaded his plate up, but was careful not to come across too greedy, so he filled it just over half full. On looking for knives and forks, he found only flat bread. No problem—he was too hungry to care. He'd torn off a piece and scooped up some roasted pumpkin and tomatoes before you could blink. But just as he was about to pop it in his mouth, Jasmine announced a need to pray. She requested that he close his eyes. Porky squeezed them shut, visibly annoyed. Jasmine sang a lilting song that went on for ages, or so it felt. And when it was over, Porky was sure his portion was smaller. Less than half a plateful! This time he was visibly dismayed, but felt his hostess's eyes on him, so he dove in without a word.

He made a brave effort to eat slowly, savouring every mouthful, and chewed carefully, allowing the tastes to caress his tongue for the longest possible time. Jasmine was aware of it, he knew, because a tiny smile was making the corners of her mouth quiver. "Delicious! Truly delicious. What a gift you have bestowed on us by your presence, Por-ky Filip Magreegor." She glowed, delighted. Porky felt her delight had something to do with the fact that she was controlling his eating habits.

"Just Porky will do," he said simply, with a sigh. He didn't want to be hungry all afternoon long and was trying hard to stay calm. *Try to think of something else.* "I saw Egypt on my way," he began, "and the Red Sea. This country is to the south of that sea, so it must be . . ." He wanted her to say it, because his geography was really bad. She continued looking at him and waited, because Jasmine could read Porky well and was glad she had the upper hand. "Um . . ." At that moment, Hassan started cleaning up and was placing the plates on an old piece of sacking, which had *Bound for Yemen* printed on it. "Yemen." She looked impressed. "Now," Porky added, breathing easier, "that makes you a Yemeni girl." He paused, boldness rising, "Living alone in a secluded place?" It was a question she didn't know how to answer.

She found a way out, saying, "My tribe, the Hareeb, went on ahead. We are Bedouins, always on the move. But Flying Carpet has leg wounds; she is lame. So I had to stay behind with her. Because I am the tribe's camel expert." She added the last part quickly and in a higher voice. Porky was also quick to sense some tension.

"And is the camel getting better?"

"No, she is not." Jasmine lowered her eyes.

"So you don't know how to help it?" And then he felt sorry for her. Weren't they both in the same boat, so to speak? Alone and stuck; unsure and confused. "Tell me about the Keepers," he said instead.

Raising her head, Jasmine looked relieved and began excitedly, "Yes! You are the others." This time she was sure.

"How do you know?"

"You made the garden appear."

"No," Porky persisted, "first—how do you know about the Keepers?"

Jasmine wanted to explain, but she didn't want to show him the magic carpet. She felt it was much too precious. She held onto it, like she prevented the other tribe members from taking too much water.

"I heard a voice," she said, "telling me that I was a Keeper. And my hands and body tingled all over. And I was holding this." She held up her Lucky Date. It matched Porky's own experience so clearly.

He began to tell his story too. And in the telling, he remembered who had told him about the Keepers. He looked over at Kitchi. The bison was sitting alert, head up, ears erect, hanging onto every word. Porky looked into his eyes and wished he could communicate his gratitude. He was sorry for being angry with him now. But the bison's eyes held only fear.

Porky remembered how the sunflower had bowed to him. But he held onto this part of the story for himself. It was much too precious to share with the others. "Did you hear the singing earlier?" he asked instead. He was becoming increasingly aware, to his enormous relief and pleasure, that he didn't feel hungry at all.

"I thought that it was you singing . . ." But she couldn't finish, because a fisherman had come running up and was saying something to Hassan. The boy brought him closer to the tent.

"Miss Jasmine! We have found a girl in a seed pod floating in the sea!" And then he added, "She is Chinese."

Porky gasped and jumped (very easily) to his feet. Things were becoming clear. He was certain who the girl must be.

"Amy Wong!"

CHAPTER 26

Abala in the Wild

He awoke as the first slivers of sunlight filtered through the canopy above. His limbs felt cold and achy, but sleeping like this, out in the wild, was a trillion times better than the captivity of the refugee camp. Grey paste lay stuck to the earth and the grass where Abala had lain, and he, of course, looked patchy and dirty—but he hadn't been bitten once!

Abala stretched every muscle from top to toe and yawned, just like a great cat in the wild waking up. If he'd looked up into the branches of the trees just then, he'd have seen one such creature, observing him quietly from above. The white cockatoo, who had stuck around, also waited and watched from a higher branch still. It knew the cougar had a stash of gazelle carcass hidden up another tree nearby and did not require breakfast. The white bird had not banked on this complication. The cougar growled back that if it had not been for him, that prowling black beast would have broken every bone in the little boy's body with one gnash of its teeth. Beasts, he had assured the cockatoo, are cowards; they don't like to fight for their dinner.

Not realising all the politics surrounding him, and fancying himself alone in the outback, Abala planned his day. Talking aloud to his compass, he gave all his secrets away to those lurking in the shadows. "Due west to Lake Turkana or south to Nairobi?" As if the compass was a coin he was about to toss. Although he felt an aching desire to go to a great city, a strong pull he could not explain was dragging him in the direction of Lake Turkana. It made more sense too; in less than five days, he would be at a major source of water. There would be all kinds of activity around that lake; fishing for one. Maybe he could get a job? Make some money? He'd never had his own money.

His mind was racing with ideas now, and so he relished the thought of spending the day walking through the savannah, nurturing those dreams and turning them over and over in his mind.

It took only a minute or two to check through the contents of his backpack. He held the slingshot in his hands. *About time I had something to eat,* he thought. The birds were awake and chirping. A squirrel-like creature shot up a tree and then jumped rapidly from branch to branch, as if teasing him. Abala quickly found a small stone for the slingshot and aimed. And missed. He tried again and missed again. *Too many branches,* thought Abala. *Not my fault.* He reckoned on better luck out in the open. So off into the open he went.

Instead of plodding along and conserving his strength, he found himself running instead, perhaps driven along by excitement, but more because it felt natural to do so. He couldn't explain it and couldn't stop himself, either. It was peculiar, but not for one moment had he felt scared of the beast, even while asleep. This land and its smells felt positive to him, and he was propelled on by a strange certainty that a better life lay ahead. But now the sun was up high in the sky. And Abala had nowhere to hide. The savannah was open country, and now, not two but three pairs of eyes traced his little, black figure racing across the pale, yellow grass, leaping here and there to avoid outcrops of rocks.

They knew that sooner, rather than later, Abala would be overcome with exhaustion, thirst, and, if he wasn't careful, sunstroke. All they had to do was follow and wait.

He was hungry, but there was nothing to hunt out in that hot sun. Eventually, he caught a lizard and killed it by smashing its head on a rock. Abala looked at the mess in his hands; was he really going to eat that? He'd have to light a fire, but it must have been past midday by now, and the sun was beating down on him. The priority should have been to find shade and rest, but Abala's gnawing hunger called the shots, and he duly built a fire. He had it going in no time; everything was so dry. He roasted the lizard on a stick, aware that his fire was giving off a lot of smoke. It made a dark, vertical line that reached up into the sky. Abala had just done something no fugitive would ever have done—he'd revealed his position by lighting a fire in broad daylight. It was noticed, of course, by those who watched and waited.

Once he'd quickly chewed the awful-tasting, rubbery snack, he found that the remaining water bottle had leaked; there was only a slurp or two left. Now finding fresh water was urgent—and shade, too. He scanned the landscape; dusty-coloured yellow grass stretched out for miles on all sides, broken only by a few gnarled trees here and there, offering little in the way of protection. The distance was blurred and wavy in the heat; nothing was clear. It made sense that any water source, like a stream, would descend from the northern hills above him. So an uphill struggle ensued, making him both dizzy and sick. At one point, he vomited up the contents of his stomach, retching loudly. By turning due north, Abala was now walking into the path of his pursuers, and he became increasingly aware of it.

First it was a noise. He thought he heard a low growl, just ever so slightly. But it could have been the rumble of thunder far away, the long-awaited rains coming at last. Was that a swishing sound in the long grass above and to the right of him, or was it just the wind? He was feeling so weak now: his throat was parched from thirst, head throbbing from the sun beating down on his head, sharp pains shooting in his belly as a result of the lizard meal, and now fear crept up on him. He thought he saw a black shape pass in front of him, partly hidden by the swaying grass, or was he blacking out? He shut his eyes and swooned; no, that was dangerous. He felt if he lay down now, he wouldn't get up again. Now there *was* a noise—a fast movement from left to right. Abala instinctively crouched down low; his legs were trembling, he really should run, but his legs felt like jelly.

In his fear, he pressed closer to the ground, willing himself to disappear. A vivid picture of the boy in the woods with his tongue cut out flashed into his mind. He was going to be sick again. His heart stopped when something touched his back. Turned him over. Abala looked at a very black face, and two dark eyes stared into his. The face was painted with white markings. Then he passed out.

CHAPTER 27

Four Keepers in Yemen

T he fishermen escorted the Chinese girl with the wild eyes to Jasmine's camp. One of them carried the bright green seed pod on his back. The pale-faced girl had a seed under her arm, like a ball. For almost thirty seconds, they all just stood and stared at each other. Jasmine, who had never seen a Chinese person before, even in a picture, was at a loss for words. Porky, who was of course familiar with Chinese people in Glasgow, stepped forward and extended his hand, saying, "Amy Wong, I presume?"

Amy took one look at the fat boy, with his sunburnt face, a white scarf wrapped round his head, and crumpled and dirty pyjamas, and started to giggle. She still felt slightly hysterical after her long and winding journey. But unlike Porky, Amy had confidence in herself and wasn't going to let feeling disoriented get to her. She shook his hand firmly. And laughed, smiling around at everyone. "And you are . . . ?"

"Philip Porky McGregor." He was about to add *Head Keeper*, but held back for fear of sounding pompous.

"Por-ky." She repeated his name slowly and quietly, drawing it out for as long as she could, giving her the time she needed to process the scene. She took in Jasmine, with her long black headdress, giving orders to Hassan for juice and dates. She saw the two camels tethered together and the bison, untied, lying under

202

the low palm. It had raised its great, shaggy head and was looking straight at her. She saw the vegetable garden resplendent with its abundant, coloured produce growing out of an impossibly dry, stony ground. She scanned the terrain and the hills beyond, and listened to Hassan's dialect as he answered Jasmine. The juice and dates arrived.

Jasmine motioned for her to sit, speaking in a language Amy could understand. She gestured at the array of pretty coloured cushions on the mat, now fully covered by shade.

"Thank you." Amy noticed, with dismay, that there were only six dates, which meant only two each, and she was *ravenous*. The three sat down, cross-legged. She turned to Porky. "So, Porky, how long have you been in Yemen?" And before he could answer, she continued, "Not long, by the looks of things." She pointed at his pyjamas. "Did you escape from that hospital, then?"

Porky just stared at this slip of a girl who, within minutes of arriving, had the whole situation sussed, or so it seemed. Her next comment confirmed Porky's appraisal. "Mmmm," she said, chewing on a date. "So which one of you is going to make more dates appear because . . ." She looked from Porky to Jasmine and back. "methinks there's magic in the air!" And she laughed, a high ringing laugh, like a church bell announcing a festival.

The bison, meanwhile, had drawn closer and was laying belly to the ground, a short distance behind Amy, its nose twitching, smelling the air. Abdul, being a male camel, knew exactly what this meant; he smirked and looked forward to witnessing Flying Carpet having a fit of jealousy.

Jasmine cleared her throat, as if to make an announcement. "Two dates at this point in the afternoon are adequate. It is just the correct amount to prepare digestive juices for dinner later this evening. Eating any more is simply greed and wasteful." After a pause, she said, "I am Jasmine, by the way."

In all the stores of the US supermarket chain *Halmart*, *Stuffed Pancake Ready Meals* were mysteriously halved in

number on the shelves. In Paris and Brussels branches of Donoprix, all stock of *Deep-Fry Crispy Rolls* was reduced by three-quarters.

"Restricted diet, I think it's called!" Porky said, smiling. "And it's working for me." He pulled out his baggy pyjama trousers to indicate how much weight he'd lost. "And that's just since getting here!" Amy looked alarmed. "No, seriously, I feel great—so much stronger, and surprisingly, I don't feel hungry!"

"Okay," Amy answered quietly. Porky noticed that she rolled her second date around in her mouth for a very long time before swallowing. "So," she said finally, "are you Keepers too?"

Porky was amazed that Amy was on top of the very subject he and Jasmine had been trying to work out over the last twelve hours. Jasmine and he simply nodded. "In that case, what are you Keepers of?"

They looked back at her blankly. Amy made a face and said, "You mean you don't know?"

"No, no, we do," Porky said hurriedly.

"Keepers have secrets," Jasmine said in an important voice.

"And . . . ?" Amy looked like she wanted to laugh again. Porky didn't like her tone, treating them as if they were goofballs. For the first time, he felt that he wanted to protect Jasmine.

"Jasmine is the Keeper of the Restricted Diet. We eat too much; she knows the secret of conserving everything while the rest of the world wastes and throws away." He looked over at Jasmine, who was glowing proudly.

In Prague, all sweets and puddings on the shelves of Sweet Savers were reduced by two-thirds. Shoppers in Singapore and Tokyo were surprised that they couldn't find enough pre-packed donuts in the stores. They had to opt for fresh fruit from the local market instead.

Now it was Jasmine's turn to compliment Porky, but before she could begin, she gasped and pointed. They all turned to look. Everywhere on the scrubland around them, small bushes had sprouted, getting bigger by the second. Tall, green leafy stalks topped by long, purple flowers. *Valerianella affinis.* Amy had brought them here, from the past to the present. Jasmine jumped up to inspect them and gather samples.

"And you?" Amy asked Porky. "What's your secret?"

It was to be the first time Porky had put his precious discovery into words. "Gardening," he began tentatively.

"Gardening?" Amy repeated, screwing up her nose. "What's so secret about that?"

"No, wait . . ." It was becoming clearer and clearer. "I have the secret of how food should be grown. The right way. The way that doesn't harm mankind or the Earth, either." She still looked puzzled. "I mean, without chemicals: those pesticides and fertilisers that pollute and poison and deplete the soil."

Amy remembered the empty rice paddies, with their sick and damaged rice shoots, and nodded. "Those vegetables growing out of the scrub over there—so you did it, didn't you?"

Twelve containers of sprayed and perfectly formed French apples bound for Britain rotted and died on the spot. Forty truckloads of green bananas at the Port of Santos destined for Pesco's in the United Kingdom turned yellow in an hour and had to be distributed between the monkey sanctuary at Sao Paulo Aquarium and *favelas* in the city. Pesco's and Larrefour called on local organic farms for emergency replacements. As well as organic apples and pears, tens of thousands of French and Brits enjoyed local asparagus, green beans, and tomatoes for lunch that weekend.

Just then, a shout rang out. The camels were fighting. Flying Carpet was in a rage, grunting and groaning, all the while lunging at Abdul and biting at his neck. Abdul just roared with laughter. Jasmine worked hard at separating them, and once she had tied them a distance apart, Porky and Amy jumped up to see if she needed help. It was only then that they noticed the bison sitting right behind them. In fact, they almost bumped into him. Kitchi stood up suddenly and slunk away. But Jasmine intercepted him and seemed to be giving him a telling-off. "What is this Abdul has been telling me about you and the Chinese girl?" she asked, and then she whispered into his ear.

Amy pulled on Porky's arm, "Is she *talking* to that animal?"

"I'm afraid so, yes."

It was his turn to laugh at her now. Because there was no describing the expression on her face! But he quickly turned serious again. He'd almost forgotten the boy inside the bison. And he remembered how scared the boy had been of the monster. *How easy it is to dismiss an animal as if it doesn't feel*, he thought ashamedly. "What was all that about?" he asked Jasmine.

"Oh, you will not believe!" He noticed she was blushing. Porky thought there was nothing he wouldn't believe any more. Jasmine hurriedly changed the subject, thrusting bunches of purple flowers into their hands. "You know what these are?"

Amy and Porky shook their heads. "Ancient plants!" she said, almost shouting. "Can you believe it?" She called Hassan to make tea with the flowers. "Now we will relax! This plant calms the mind—not seen in Yemen for over two hundred years!" Her dark brown face was beaming, almost shining red. As an afterthought, she called, "Hassan—only one flower per cup!"

Porky pointed at Amy and said, "You brought these plants here. I mean, they appeared after you came. I think I know your secret! It's about extinction . . . or about the lack of it. Something like that—come on, tell us!"

Amy now felt a bit hesitant and shy. She thought about how difficult it was to put words to things you didn't understand fully. But was that really what was wrong? Hadn't she done that already? Hadn't she given a presentation on the wild rice, showing off in class about her knowledge of diversity and how science was twisting and changing things to all look the same? No, if she was honest with herself, she had been questioning the others to check out their credentials before revealing the wild rice again. The reason for her shyness was because she was ashamed of the way she'd behaved as a Keeper already, handling her secret clumsily, almost giving it away.

Jasmine served everyone a glass of *Valerianella.* They sipped the warm, aromatic tea silently. Amy stole a glance at Jasmine. Her face was care-worn through hard outdoor work already, but it had a soft quality too, which showed she cared. Looking at Porky only confirmed what she had read between the lines of his blog: he had a soul filled with passion and anger at injustice.

So she took out the pouch from her pocket, opened it, and spilled the rice grains onto her palm. She knew the secret would be safe with these two special people.

Instantly, the rice tinkled and sang—for the first time since she had been at the rice paddies in Anhui Province. The four Keepers stared at them, mesmerised: Porky, Jasmine, Amy, and Kitchi, too, from under the stubby palm.

In that same moment, *Euphorbia Tanaensis* sprang up from swampy soil between some trees. It had never been seen outside of Witu Forest Reserve, where only twenty remaining plants survive. Now there were twenty-one.

All of a sudden, they were disturbed by Hassan, running up, yelling and waving his arms. "*Samki! Samki!*"

"It means *fish*," explained Jasmine.

A fish at last! thought Porky, imagining a great dinner that night. But Hassan was pointing out to sea.

"*Samki!*"

They all turned and looked. Waves broke urgently against the rocks, indicating something big passing by. And close to the shore, unmistakeably, was berthed a massive blue whale, bleeding profusely.

CHAPTER 28

Lastro and Dobi's Final
Leg of the Journey

Back down in his "cabin," Lastro found that some of the seaweed had empty pods attached to them, which could be filled with rainwater and then stored. He thought he'd try that the next time Dobi popped him up for a drink. And so the days and nights went on, in a kind of routine: sleeping, listening to the whale song, eating seaweed, bathing, and popping up to drink and gather rainwater. For once, Lastro was contented and still; a song his mother sang came into his head repeatedly. *By day the Lord directs his love, at night his song is with me.* He had no way to count the days except to snap off a small piece of seaweed for each day. These he stored carefully in a ridge high up near the ceiling. Not once did Dobi offer Lastro fish to eat; it was as if he knew how much the boy hated those ghoulish dead fish faces. Once, though, a strangely shaped piece of deep pink coral entered Lastro's space with a gush of seawater. When he picked it up, his fingers tingled in a very strange way. Dobi must have given it to him; was he trying to tell him something? On examination, he saw that it was in the shape of an animal; a sheep or a dog, it was hard to tell. What did it mean? But he treasured it and kept it in his pocket, close to him at all times.

The highlight of each day was the ride on Dobi's back out on the wide, wild ocean. It was never the same twice, even although there was only sea and sky; Lastro discovered that there were endless variations. Sometimes beautiful, sometimes scary. Dolphins frequently swam alongside them. It became Lastro's plan to try to swim beside Dobi—if only he would slow down. He wanted to look him in the eye. Face to face. He thought, somehow, this way, he might get an answer. But before that, there came another sign. They had a travelling companion.

A bird. Lastro had spotted it on many occasions, but it suddenly clicked that this enormous white bird with the black wings was accompanying them. It stayed really close by, sometimes far above them, sometimes nearer sea level. It didn't seem to be flying at all, but glided instead, holding its long narrow wings out straight. Once, he caught sight of this feathered giant, floating on the surface of the water near the whale's head. How weird it looked doing that! Was it making eye contact with Dobi? Were they exchanging travel plans? If they communicated at all, Lastro never heard anything.

But still, Dobi's pitiful night singing went on. Lastro continued to wonder about it. It occurred to him that there was never an answer. Usually, whales sang together. Was Dobi looking for his old friends? Or maybe searching for a mate? But why did no other whale respond to his call? They'd been travelling a long time now. At last count, Lastro had fifteen strips of seaweed. Half a month! And no other whales in the South Pacific Ocean? It wasn't possible. And, as always, after all his thinking was done, he'd come back to the last remaining question: what had all this to do with him? (Or the black and white bird, for that matter?)

An unexpected bump, followed by two or three more, woke him very early one morning. Everything stopped. The red light faded, leaving the cavern cold and blue. Lastro waited, alert. Dobi made a loud low sound. Was he hurt? The sounds continued, one after the other, until Lastro realised that this could be the same as himself hollering for water. *I'd better do something!* He was so excited that, at last, Dobi was communicating directly with him. He squeezed up the blowhole tube without the whale's usual help; it was a steep and difficult climb. There was no water spouting out this time, so Lastro could peek over the edge without being seen. It must have been just before dawn; in the ghostly paleness of the morning light, a shape rose up before them. A short distance of water separated them from a small island. He could swim it easily. A new adventure was beginning! He'd wait till daylight for a better look. He lay down then on top of Dobi, shivering. It made his heart jump to see the large bird do the same, not far off. No matter how hard he tried to stop them, Lastro's teeth were chattering noisily. The next moment, he felt something soft and warm press into his back. A latticed black "roof" covered him, resting gently on his skin. He no longer felt the chilly wind; his feathery friend took the strain till the first rays of sunlight touched them, when it suddenly rose up, cawing loudly as if to say, *Time to get up!*

At first sight, the island was beautiful in the morning sunshine. A chalk white beach lined with palms, surrounded by deep green jungle behind. Very inviting. It beckoned Lastro with whispers of fresh water. And promises of fruit. What about Dobi? Would he be all right in the shallow water? He slipped into the water beside the whale and swam up to consult with him. And there, at last, he found the magnificent head and the gigantic eye he'd sought for so long. Lastro crouched on a rock, and they stared at each other for a time. How to begin? *Excuse me . . . um . . . Mister or Sir? Or . . . just plain Dobi?* He thought he saw the eye smile.

Dobi is good. He heard it clear as clear. Not out loud, but he heard it—he knew he did.

And again. *Go—drink and eat.*

Lastro gazed at his friend for a long time. It felt like he was falling off an edge, but with the certainty of being caught. He was falling deep into the Earth, to the source of all things. Where everything was right. They were meant to be together, Dobi and him.

"Okay. I won't be long," Lastro whispered, though he didn't need to. He stroked Dobi. "Thank you." Dobi blinked, meaning, *Don't mention it.*

How good the soft sand felt underfoot! Lastro felt an urge to lie down and roll about in it, to run and jump, maybe do a cartwheel or two. But he felt Dobi's presence watching him and was embarrassed. He was on a mission: refuelling—not larking about! The island was a paradise. It looked beautiful, perfect. But very still and very quiet. Somehow, too still and too quiet. Where there should have been the intolerable noise of buzzing and whirring insect life—there was nothing. No fluttering, either, of colourful wings, no parrots, no butterflies. No screams of monkeys, or branches crashing as they leapt from tree to tree. No rustlings in the undergrowth to be afraid of. Nothing—but a strange and stagnant silence. Lastro felt the island hold its breath as he picked his way through a jungle abandoned. Or was it breathing at all? One look at the state of the trees and bushes was enough to answer that question; the leaves didn't look healthy, mostly pale greens and yellows. And there was a very disheartening absence of fruit. No berries or nuts, either. Lastro's heart was heavy. This might mean there would be no drinking water. He felt inclined to turn back; less light was filtering through the trees above as he moved deeper into the jungle. For the first time since embarking on their voyage, he felt a chill of fear. A loud caw rang out. Above the treetops, he saw their majestic companion flying onwards and upwards. Was it urging him on? The way ahead was getting steeper. Would Dobi be okay for so long in the shallow water? The giant bird called again. Lastro pressed on. Once he got to the crest of the hill, he saw what the problem was.

The whole of the other side of the mountain was covered in all kinds of garbage, mostly plastic. Plastic bottles and bags filled a narrow valley up the hillside, and they were strewn about almost everywhere else. Where there should have been water gushing out of a spring source, there was nothing but decay. With the source of life blocked, the island was choking, suffocating. Looking around,

Lastro felt disgust at the vulgarity of the scene; he scrambled farther up to get a closer look. Everywhere he stepped, there was a crunching, crackling sound. To his horror, he was walking over a hillside covered with bones! Thousands upon thousands of them! He knew immediately what they were—they belonged to migrating birds which congregated on that island to mate and breed. He'd seen that amazing sight on islands close to his own back home. They'd been killed off en masse. How—lack of food? Oil? A chemical spill? There could be any number of nasties in those rusted barrels dotting the hillside and beach. Now Lastro was overcome by anger, a fury so terrible that he began swearing and cursing, using every bad word he knew. He began picking up plastic containers and throwing them down the hill and back into the sea, shouting wildly. And then he suddenly stopped, thinking, *This is useless.* He had to think of something else. He fingered the piece of pink coral in his pocket and felt his fingers tingle slightly. *Dobi—he's big and strong!* So next, he was careering back the way he came, back to the beach, to enlist Dobi in the mission to save the island from its certain death.

The ease with which the whale understood the boy's frantic cries and gesticulations was remarkable. Without hesitation (or complaining), he duly went backwards a little bit till he could comfortably swim around the island to the other side. On his way back over, Lastro collected useful materials they needed. Like long trailers hanging from the trees—they would make strong ropes. He'd even seen a few fishing nets washed up. Being a fisherman's apprentice, Lastro was deft with his hands; he had a knotted contraption conjured up in less than half an hour. He slipped a jungle-trailer harness over Dobi's head and swam underneath him to pull it on snugly. The other part—he rapidly filled the knotted-together nets with as much of the offensive rubbish as he could. "Now—*pull!*" he yelled. Three more hoists, and the garbage had come free. Other bottles and rusted metal cans fell down from above. The tangled mass moved downwards like a mini garbage avalanche.

More work was needed, though. Again and again, Lastro filled and Dobi pulled. He was aware that they were simply dumping it all back into the sea—he hadn't thought of a firm disposal plan yet. And this thought niggled annoyingly at the back of his mind. Dobi hadn't thought of that either, it appeared; he simply kept on following his young master's instructions. At last, a gurgle of water became a gush—the spring was open again! Fresh water spouted out at a tremendous speed, the force of which cleared away the rest of the plastics in its path. Bottles and cans and masses of plastic bags were flying through the air then, and a few of them hit Lastro and Dobi. Nothing could stop this partnership now—they kept on working until the sheer mass of flowing water overcame them. Unbelievably, it had become a waterfall of the most gigantic proportions. Water flowed out on all sides, travelling deep into the jungle. Lastro sat on the safety of a rock and watched, awestruck by the power generated. *Deep calls to deep in the roar of your waterfalls* went the song.

But something happened then that truly gave him goose bumps—a butterfly landed on his forearm! It was purple in colour. As it fluttered away, a nearby cockatoo cried out. He looked up and saw streaks of yellow and blue feathers. The screech of a monkey sounded from high up in the trees. He was sure he could see bananas. Amazed and overwhelmed with joy, he *did* do a couple of cartwheels, and whooping with delight, he ran around, trying to collect as much fruit as he could. Of course, he dropped half as much as he could carry. The island was now teeming with life! A crab scuttled across the sand towards the sea. Watching it caused Lastro to set eyes on Dobi again. He rushed over, splashing into the water. "Look what we've done!" he cried. "We did it! We did it— together!" And he was saying thank you over and over and trying his best to give the whale a hug, which was near impossible. He could have sworn Dobi's eye was chuckling! Next he heard Dobi's voice loud and clear: *Come on, my boy. We have a long journey ahead. Load up.*

Soon, fruit and water were gathered and stored in Lastro's space. *It is time to leave,* Dobi insisted. Lastro's thoughts at last turned to sort out the plastic debris littering the shore and bobbing in the water; they couldn't just leave it there. But where was it? Stupefied, he stumbled about like a drunken sailor in his search for the piles of ugly garbage they'd just cleared. Nothing! Empty white beach! Unbelievable! *It is time,* repeated Dobi, perhaps afraid that Lastro would lose himself in some cart wheeling again.

Laughing aloud, he skipped through the shallow water instead, thinking to summersault aboard . . . when he went under. Bubbling and gurgling was all that could be seen of Lastro. Till he surfaced and let out a shrill scream. An octopus tentacle had hold of one arm and one leg. He desperately scratched at Dobi's side with one hand in a frantic attempt to reach the fin directly above him. No use. He disappeared from view again. Up popped his head; he screamed, "Help! Help me, Dobi!"

The massive whale was moving now from side to side, churning the water up. It began bouncing its giant mass in one direction, tilting over towards Lastro in an attempt to bring the fin closer to the water. And using every last ounce of strength in his body, Lastro grabbed it. Dobi instantly straightened up, snapping the boy free from the octopus's clutches. He was catapulted onto Dobi's back, only to get a full view of the next assault awaiting them. Two killer whales lurked in the shallows, unmistakable by their black and white markings. Orcas. People spoke of them getting so close to shore—but to ambush seals, not the largest mammal in the world! As they drew closer, he got a good look at their faces. What he saw was surely not of this world: the red eyes and snarling teeth looked more like comic strip monsters. Their hideous teeth snapped at Dobi's sides. Lastro saw blood mix with foam on the surface of the water. Once again, the end stared him in the face. Dobi was afraid, he could sense it. And so was he—no—terrified. What could he do to help his giant friend now? *A prayer to the God of my life.* The last line of Mother's song. Lastro screamed the words aloud. Unheard by the orcas, he knew, but heard deep in the heart of the Earth.

In immediate response, a wind blew up. Waves were sent crashing down on top of them. The four—Dobi, Lastro, and the two orcas—were mercilessly tossed high and dropped low again on an oceanic roller coaster. Lastro saw the island receding and separated from them by a dark cloud. And so were the deadly beasts! The last sight he got of them was of their tails sticking out of an enormous wave, pushing north. So Dobi had to turn south towards Antarctica, which Lastro correctly guessed was not part of the plan.

The storm passed over as quickly as it started. The sun came out, and he enjoyed many hours lying on his friend's back, watching cloud formations and eating bananas. He had plenty of time to think seriously about the evil attack. It came directly after Dobi and he had saved the island, and those magical things happened too. If he was right, then what was trying to stop them?

One cold morning, a black dot appeared on the horizon. *A ship!* thought Lastro. It was the first one he'd seen since his life on the ocean wave began. He became quite excited. He felt sure he'd have his picture taken and be on the front of some newspaper. However, if pirate ships were a thing of the past, Japanese whaling ships weren't, and unluckily for the two friends, that was one of them. And it came up close very rapidly indeed. Lastro sensed that there was great excitement aboard. He heard a lot of shouting and cheering. At first, he thought it was because *he* had been spotted, but then it occurred to him that perhaps there were no other whales left in the ocean. The first harpoon struck even before he made it down the blow hole. Dobi dived down very deep and made a sharp U-turn. But not before another hit pierced the giant creature's flesh. Lastro felt the blow. His room was turned almost 180 degrees as Dobi pushed farther and farther down to lose the killers. He thought of the whale's wounds; couldn't sharks smell blood for miles? Was Dobi badly hurt? For now, he didn't know. He stared at the pile of fruit, nuts, and berries, supply enough for weeks, only he couldn't enjoy them now. He was too worried about Dobi.

They moved forward down in the deep, but Lastro knew Dobi was moving slower than before. At night, the red glow from his heart was weaker. Lastro couldn't sleep, and the pool was now too cold for a bath. He lay curled up in a ridge, holding his piece of coral, and waited. Twenty-three days passed like this.

Then it happened. The red light of Dobi's heart flickered on and off, and slowly, slowly the whale turned over onto its back. The water from Lastro's pool fell into his face. The lights went out. No red light. No throbbing. "Dobi! C'mon, get up!" Lastro shouted. "Come on!"

In the hours of cold black silence that followed, he did everything he could think of to revive the whale. He was hoarse from yelling, from praying, from crying. He'd have danced if he thought it would do any good. But what more could he do now? A tingling started up in his fingers; the vibrating he'd felt the first time Dobi had sung so sadly. *At night his song is with me.* He got it. He knew what he had to do. Dobi had sung for him, now he would sing for Dobi. They were a team. With the little strength he could muster up, he reached down inside himself and let out the notes of the whale song he loved so much. Louder and louder he sang. Never pausing. Never giving up. He vibrated like a dragonfly again, suspended in mid-air. Tears flowed down his face, but that didn't stop him. On and on he sang, till he must have passed out from exhaustion.

On waking, Lastro knew the result was good before he opened his eyes. Because he was warm again. He was lying pressed up against the throbbing red light, although it glowed weaker now. They chugged slowly on like this for many more days, while Lastro slept, faint from hunger and thirst. A whole day passed before he became aware that Dobi had stopped moving. Although weak and dizzy, he crawled as best he could up to the blowhole exit. He heard the voices before his head appeared out in the open.

"It's a whale!"

"This far inland? No, it can't be."

"It is—look, it's wounded!"

"See the blood!"

"Poor thing!"

And when Lastro finally looked out, the sight that met him made him sure he had lost it completely. A group of people stood close to the water's edge: a fat boy with a red face dressed in pyjamas, a dark girl in a long green and black dress, and a Chinese girl in jeans. Behind them, a short way off, snorting and pawing at the ground, stood an enormous bison.

"Hello," Lastro said in a very small voice.

CHAPTER 29

Abala with the Maasai

He came round again as he was being lifted up, turned upside down and carried off. He could only see the ground below his head. Another pair of black feet ran behind him, below the curved edge of a shield. As they moved away, he caught sight of a black beast on its side, with two arrows sticking out: one from its eye and one at its neck. He instinctively looked away rapidly and then quickly dared a second look. The beast's body was gone! Only an empty space where it had been—no tuft of grass displaced or blood stains on the ground. He felt so weak, yet his heart beat furiously. What kind of danger was he in now?

Abala covered an incredible distance upside down like that. Eventually, at dusk, they stopped. From where he was laid on the ground, under the shelter of some low scrubby bushes, he observed the two young warriors. For warriors they were, he had no doubt about that. And he knew they were Maasai. Legends were told about these people back home. It wasn't just the long oval shields or arrows they carried, or the white marking on their faces, or the intricately braided long hair; it was everything they did. They were very fast and efficient. They didn't go anywhere without running. They built fires, shot birds, cooked, and built shelters with a deftness and ease that made Abala feel like a clumsy fool. They spoke a language he couldn't understand. And when the hand signs had failed yet again to inform them of who he was and where he was going, the two very tall, very thin, and very black (they were much darker in colour than him) men would flash him brilliant white smiles and pat him on the head.

And yet, he still could not keep any food down. He tried to eat the meat they offered but vomited it up every time. The next day, they ran faster than ever to wherever they were taking him.

Towards afternoon of the second day, sounds of voices in greeting met them, and Abala saw lots of sandaled feet on the ground, all running alongside them. Soon, he was inside an area of low huts, and then he was lying on a soft blanket, with many caring hands reaching out in attendance. He felt weak and sleepy and was aware only of a lot of colour all around him, especially red. A lady sporting many long earrings and rows and rows of coloured beads gave him something pink to drink. And finally he slept.

When he awoke, he had no idea how much time had passed. Was it hours or days? He felt so much better; he could have got up and set off to Lake Turkana right away, or so he thought. But events were about to take another surprising turn. It was dark when he went outside, and a large group of the Maasai were gathered together in a central area. A big fire burned in front, lighting up their faces. Low cheers went up when he was noticed. He heard some clapping too. His two travelling companions, the warrior youths, came across and picked him up, putting him high on their shoulders. White smiles greeted him from out of the darkness. They seated him down, accompanied by lots of friendly back slapping. Now he could see what everyone was doing; they were watching the tribe's shaman, or priest, at work, performing a healing ritual on a young girl who lay writhing on the ground. After some dancing and chanting, the girl became still and sat up, obviously better. Her mother approached, took her by the hand, and led her away to some clapping and singing.

More of the same continued, and there was a lot of music and singing. Someone brought Abala another cup of pink drink. He gulped the lot down instantly—it really was delicious. At some point, he realised that the shaman was staring intently at him. His face was rather scarily painted, and he approached Abala, shaking something long and black directly at his face. There was some low laughter, and then the silence of anticipation. Abala groaned inwardly; it was his treasured carob pod—why had it been taken from him? But then, there was a hand on the medicine man's shoulder. A very old man stood there, almost shooing the other out of the way. The old man leaned right down till he was level with Abala's ear and said one word: "*Zerihun.*" The sound of his grandfather's name was like a bolt of lightning. He just sat there, alert and upright, with a startled expression, staring into the old man's face.

A boy of about his own age drew up beside him. He had a shaved head and spoke simple English. "Man blind. No see you." Abala continued staring. The old man spoke for a long time to the boy, pointing to Abala. The boy began again, "He say he know why you here. Wrong place."

As he listened, his fingers began tingling till his hands were throbbing hot. Stupidly, he felt afraid a banquet would appear now and scare everybody. The man was saying something else and gesturing at the people. "You keep secret. Danger for people." A heavy silence had fallen over the assembly. Another message followed: "Home. Good place. You go home." Then the old man smiled and whispered something. The boy, looking perplexed, translated, "Now—make sweets?"

It was hard for Abala to know whether to feel happy or sad at these revelations. His whole body was quivering now, but he felt himself relax as he processed several things. He had been recognised from deep within the soul or spirit of a blind man, who knew who he was. His gift had been acknowledged and the danger that followed him around. With relief tinged with anxiety, he knew that what he had in him was *real.* And important.

On the old man's instructions, a large container of milk was plonked down in front of Abala, who then poured small amounts into bowls. The bowls became full of honey-flavoured cream and were handed around, amid squeals of delight. The people were smiling, but looked scared of him too.

So Abala had to sleep outside the Maasai village that night with his carob pod and, this time, four warrior friends for company. They took it in turns to keep watch and stoke the fire. But Abala couldn't sleep, due to the excitement bubbling in his chest. He was going home at last.

♦

Let the ancient monsters deal with those who are foolish enough to believe in them. Mr. Deal repeated the line over and over in his head. He was fuming as he stomped along the corridor to Mr. Corporate's office. He barged through the door without knocking, marched up to his partner and grabbing him by his collar, lifted him up off the ground. "You're the foolish one!" he bellowed letting Mr. Corporate fall backwards onto the sofa with a thump. Then he bounded over to the window and banged on the sill with his fist yelling, "I want answers, not gibberish!" The box containing the crystal jumped slightly. Mr. Corporate swallowed hard.

Mr. Deal began pacing the room anxiously, ranting and raving, his voice getting louder and louder until it filled the room. "How can this be happening? How can kids . . . what the hell . . . who are we dealing with here?" He approached Mr. Corporate again, this time raising his arm with his fist clenched.

"Hey!" Mr. Corporate shouted, ducking. "I'm under pressure too, you know. I've got Halmart and Donoprix on my back."

"Yeah, I heard about that," Mr. Deal answered, flopping down onto the sofa. He breathed out a long sigh. He lit a cigar and sat puffing on it in silence.

Mr. Corporate took his chance. "Look Deal—the Indian girl, she's the one to take out." He began, speaking softly. "Without her everything will fall apart, because she's got what the rest of the world lacks: instinct."

"Oh don't start with all that weirdness again. You'll tell me next that crystal of yours told you."

Mr. Corporate tried again. "Without instinct people don't know what food is good for them. She's got the gift and we've got to get it off her," he continued, calmly. Mr. Deal looked dubious but he was sufficiently freaked out by all that was happening on Food Masters Inc's land in the Midwest to listen.

"What if her Indian in-laws got incensed enough to arrange an honour killing?" he suggested.

"No, we don't want her dead—not yet anyway. Once she's been stripped of her instinct she won't matter anymore." He picked up his phone, pressed a button and said, "Ms. Grayling, arrange a meeting with Bina and her aunt, the Sauranine sister, in the hospital garden."

"Good," said Mr. Deal as he got up to leave, "Remember, if you need any help . . ." But Mr. Corporate knew what Mr. Deal didn't: a hit man's bullet could only achieve so much against Mother Earth; the forces he was commandeering emanated from the depths of darkness itself.

◆

CHAPTER 30

The Five Secrets in Yemen
Shake the World

There was no time to say hello back, because Dobi was making a low and terrible moaning sound. It reminded Jasmine of the horns from ships which passed in the night. The small boy who had emerged from the whale's blow hole was in the water now, trying to comfort the giant mammal. They stood on the shore and watched him, feeling helpless. Jasmine thought the boy looked pale and tired, so she sent Hassan to fetch the fishermen to help him, seeing as she was only a camel expert. Amy sensed he'd been on a journey as strange as hers, but he hadn't come out of it laughing. The bison, Kitchi, looked on with interest; he had a feeling that the arrival of this boy was going to be important for him. And Porky felt sure that this was another *other*.

The fishermen came running and, although lacking experience with big fish, did their best to appear confident and in control, especially with an audience looking on. Jasmine guided Lastro to the tent. The others trailed behind; even the bison followed at a distance closer than usual. They sat outside the canopy, for it was cool and breezy, and the sun was falling in the sky. Jasmine called for Hassan. *Please, not more dates and tea,* Amy thought with a grimace. Somehow she felt the bison read her look and smiled. But Hassan had a trick up his sleeve; he was cooking fish, he announced, holding one up and grinning. The fishermen had brought their catch with them, he said. At the sight of fish for dinner, Lastro promptly threw up everything in his stomach, covering the pretty cushions with a green, sticky mess. At that particular moment, as if to save the day, the moving black mass of the Murad tribe turned the bend in the coastline and headed towards them.

The fishermen had come up with a poultice of seaweed and tea leaves and packed Dobi's wounds with it. Lastro had been tucked up in bed hours ago; the speed with which the nomadic tribe had set up camp was unbelievable. With all the *others* settled and being well looked after, Jasmine found herself off the hook and relaxed in the quiet night. After all, it's hard to play host if you have few resources. She'd missed sitting alone with her camels, which she was doing now, stroking their necks and whispering to them. The bison sauntered up and hunkered down on his knees. She had been looking out to sea, checking on the whale, which by now had ceased its baying. She noticed Kitchi then and let out a long sigh: "What is it all about, Kitchi? What is it all about?"

Kitchi looked up at her with his troubled eyes and answered, "Wendigo."

Breakfast was special and marked the start of a new day. They had an omelette made with vegetables Porky had selected from his vegetable garden: green onions, red and yellow peppers, tomatoes, and courgettes (five a day!). He'd given Amy a tour in the early morning and found that the garden had quadrupled in size and was still growing. Two fig trees, a lemon tree, and four ancient-looking, gnarled olives had appeared and were growing nicely, their fruit tiny buds. In addition to vegetables he recognised, there were many strange shapes and colours he didn't know. He wondered aloud if any of them could help the whale boy get better. "Bina would know," he murmured, running his hands over the green beans, which tinkled back at him.

"Who's Bina?" asked Amy.

"Oh, just a girl from home. She's Indian." His voice was laden with sadness.

"Yeah, I know how you feel," she said, thinking of Seung-Yub and banishing his face from her mind as quickly as it had appeared.

As they walked back from the vegetable garden, tens of thousands of acres of maize and soy plants in America's Midwest withered and died. The land underneath them went wild for the first time in decades. Here and there, clumps of flowers dotted the wild grass, and bees and large bluebottles got busy. The land relaxed and breathed easily once again.

The whale boy introduced himself as Lastro, while he gobbled down the colourful omelette. Everyone enjoyed the omelette; Porky had secretly added some chilli pepper in Bina's honour. He guessed they might need the extra spice to fire up the getting-to-know-you process. Jasmine kept her sharp eye on the size of everyone's portions; the Murads only had six laying hens.

Lastro recounted the tale of his journey without a single interruption. They sat in an awestruck silence once he'd finished. It was finally broken by questions on the whale's condition.

"How is . . . um . . . Dobi?"

"Has it . . . sorry, *he* eaten?"

"I have checked, and he is still bleeding," reported Jasmine. "It seems the fishermen's cure was not good enough."

"And he will not eat food that he has not caught himself," announced Lastro, looking dejected.

A tray of sweet tea arrived and, trying to buoy up the mood, Amy told the story of her travels, even curling up in the seed pod and cuddling the seed as an illustration. This caused laughs all around. Lastro took a special note of how the bison was leaning in, ears pricked, listening. It was Porky's turn next; he pointed at the bison:

"Well, believe it or not, I rode on the back of this bison over here, and then flew over . . ."

Lastro didn't let him finish; he blurted out, "That is not an animal!" Everyone turned to look at the bison and saw that it certainly *was*. "That is a boy," he said, approaching the bison, which now had an embarrassed look about it. Lastro touched its giant mane with his tingling fingers and looked into its eyes. "I am sure of it." He stroked the place where the horn was missing. "What happened here?"

There was no answer to the question; the bison began snorting and pawing at the ground with a mad look in its eyes. Lastro had to take a few steps back. It shook its head with such gusto that it looked like the other horn would become dislodged. With one last enormous groan, the bison made a clumsy-looking jump in the air and disappeared—leaving a boy lying in a crumpled heap on the ground. The boy raised his head, looking as if he'd just woken up, and shook his long black hair. Then he stood up and brushed some bison hairs off his shoulders. Treating the onlookers to a dazzling smile, he said, "Thank the Spirit of the sea creature! That was killing me. One more hour and I might have tried flying all the way back home again—believe me."

Porky jumped. It was the same voice that spoke to him in the garden and in the bubble. Of course it was. For some reason, he felt ashamed and thought he'd better say something. But the long-haired boy went on talking; he was so pleased to be free. "Hey dudes—I'm Kitchi!" He turned to Porky and said, "Man—you and that girl! I thought we were never going to leave that garden." But suddenly, at the mention of the garden, his face clouded over and shut down. Only Porky knew why.

Hassan brought a bowl of figs that had just ripened on the trees, and they all sat down again. Kitchi seemed pleased to be sitting next to Amy. "I liked your story," he told her, his eyes wandering over her face, admiring her strong, wild look. "My journey wasn't a bit like that." And he lowered his eyes again.

Amy started the conversation up again, asking, "Porky, what were you saying? About your trip here—with Kitchi? Did you come from a garden or from a hospital?" She looked him up and down and added, "Glad to see you're out of those pyjamas, by the way." Everyone smiled because Porky looked every bit like a desert sheikh in a long white Murad dress, complete with a white scarf coiled round his head. And he had been right about his significant amount of weight loss since arriving at Jasmine's camp; the robe didn't cling around his belly and wasn't tight around his arms. He had a chin now, too; the fat had just rolled off his neck and face. Despite the freckles and the sunburn, Porky was looking strong and handsome. (Bina wouldn't have recognised him.)

In Glasgow, an obese family (soon to be one of many), who were regular customers of Crunchy Fried Chicken, saw in the window that there was a new meal out that day, called Happy Deal. But their fat kids didn't seem impressed and tugged on their parents' hands. They wanted to make Jimmy Olive's fruit smoothies at home instead.

Porky decided not to tell the story, because he couldn't tell it without avoiding the monster, Wendigo, a subject which obviously upset Kitchi. He looked around the circle at their faces, each one so different in race and colour, yet so beautiful all together. But at the same time, he noticed they wore the kind of tired and startled expressions of being in some kind of shock, except Jasmine, because she was at home. He felt a pang of compassion for them at that moment, and a strong impulse to care, or rather *hold them all together* was a better description of how it felt. He knew they were all Keepers—but did *they*? And another question nagged him all the time, a question he might have to answer if he introduced himself as Head Keeper. *What was all this about?* And if he was perfectly honest, he didn't know the answer.

He decided instead to try to lead the group, but keep it at the level of introductions: where each of them was from, that kind of thing. He cleared his throat and said, "Um . . . maybe it would be a good idea to go round the circle, telling the group where you're from."

Kitchi immediately reacted to this, saying, "Oh man! Leave it out—we're not at school!"

Porky began once more; he stood up this time. Jasmine looked encouragingly at him. "Well . . . um . . . Friends . . . Keepers . . ."

"Countrymen!" laughed Kitchi. Only Amy got the joke, but she kept silent and gave him a stony look. They waited. Porky started again. Jasmine was still looking positive, but inside she doubted this Head Keeper. She wished she had consulted the magic carpet about him.

"I want to thank Jasmine for looking after so many unexpected visitors."

Everyone looked over at Jasmine and smiled.

Kitchi raised his glass of tea and said, "To Jasmine!"

The others followed suit, a little awkwardly. Porky pretended not to mind.

"Thank you, Kitchi. The fact that we've all arrived here safely is great news. We're obviously together for a reason and . . ." Kitchi interrupted him again.

"Stop avoiding the truth—great news? But are we safe? Why don't you tell them what kind of danger we're all in?"

The smiling faces turned serious again.

"Well, yes, Kitchi has a point. When we were leaving the garden, there was an incident . . . um, a monster thing . . ."

"Monster thing? Dude—that *thing* you are talking about happens to be a wendigo!"

"Okay—so what's the big deal? We got away, didn't we? In the bubble—remember?"

"Yeah—that time maybe. But what about now? And don't ask me what I'm doing here, cuz I don't know. All I know is that I was a bison and now I'm not, but that's cool—cuz that's an honour. And bison or me—it's all the same, man—cuz we're all one, you understand? But about the Wendigo—I'm not cool. No way—no, man, we gotta sort this out!" ranted Kitchi.

But no, they did not understand. "He is talking too fast," Jasmine complained, looking confused.

"I know, I know," Porky said, taking over and going slowly. "When we were leaving the garden, Kitchi and I, we were followed by a monster. It kind of ate everything in sight . . . and it wanted us. I mean, it nearly got us, and then we flew away, kind of miraculously." He drew *miraculously* out slowly, still incredulous himself.

Kitchi started up again, saying, "We saw it eat a whole family, for gods' sakes!" He had his head in his hands. "Look, I know about this thing. It's from my tradition. All Native Americans, even adults, even old people believe in the Wendigo, cuz it can take you away. It just consumes everything. And now I've seen it!"

"Maybe we are safe here," Lastro said.

"Huh! If it was in Scotland, there's no reason it can't come here." Kitchi was getting more and more worked up. Porky looked around the group for some inspiration.

"The Head Keeper will help us," Jasmine said encouragingly, nodding towards Porky.

"Head Keeper?" Kitchi asked, sounding aghast. "You gotta be kidding!" Kitchi had got up and was standing over Porky. "You mean, *you* are going to lead *us*?" He sounded really angry and made a movement to leave. The others all looked at Porky, waiting for his response.

"Look," Porky said, realising he only had this moment to put things right; he desperately scrambled his thoughts together and added, "I didn't ask to be . . ." No, that wouldn't work; he went down another route. His fingers tingled slightly. "It all started with the sunflower."

"The sunflower?" Kitchi stood stock still.

"Yes, when it started speaking to me in the garden. I knew it was telling me something important."

Kitchi saw the wall again, outside his classroom window. *Every time you look at a sunflower, the whole world starts to smile.* He remembered the moment it had spoken to him too, in a way, and then he'd just left school and walked away into a new life. He looked around at the others; each one had arrived here using no known means of transport, carrying nothing with them—for what reason? Kitchi was confused, and he had a blinding headache. Porky didn't have a chance to remind him of the horn he had gotten from the Native American, who, Porky now realised, had to be Kitchi's uncle; the bison boy walked away then, towards the sea, where he sat down to do some gazing.

These were only the teething troubles, the real trouble would come later, and it was all because of what was happening to Bina.

♦

Bina lay on a sun bed beside the swimming pool and sipped her third cocktail that morning. She had taken to ordering banana and cinnamon because it reminded her of the fresh fruit juice stall where her father had always taken his family before the disaster. Here at Summer Hills Resort, they were very good at cocktails. If she ordered extra mint or pineapple, it was never a problem; the waitress advised her to try this or that, telling her about where the fruits were sourced and assuring her they were all fair trade. Bina didn't know what fair trade meant, but she smiled politely all the same, feeling sure it was important and that Porky would explain when he got there.

When he got there. It had been days already. His letter hadn't been specific but had said *very soon.* So, very soon was almost now, wasn't it? She hadn't been surprised at Porky's attempts to rescue her from the arranged marriage with Ajit; it was just like him to do a thing like this. Despite his appearance, he was brave and strong, she knew it. She closed her eyes then and stretched out in the sun. What a perfect place! The gardens were so beautiful, if a little too clipped for her liking, but that didn't matter; Porky would be here soon and . . . She imagined his arrival again, as she did almost twenty times a day. Most of all, she imagined kissing him again.

She knew she would throw herself into his arms the moment he walked through that door.

The waitress arrived with the lunch menu. As always, it included dishes from her country; they were so thoughtful here: braised lamb's livers in pomegranate juice (her favourite), with saffron rice (yummy), followed by an ice cream sundae called Bombay Bomb. She smiled up at the waitress and said, "Perfect, as usual."

"Will madam be requiring the use of the spa this afternoon?"

Bina smiled an even wider smile and answered, "You bet!" She would dream of being married to Porky during her massage, she thought, as she tucked into her fifth chocolate from the complimentary box.

♦

Amy made to go after Kitchi, but Porky grabbed her arm and said, "Let him go—he's got a lot of thinking to do." Two Murad tribesmen had approached and were talking with Jasmine. "Look, why don't you come with me? I'm going on a tour of the mosque gardens with these guys."

So they went off together while Jasmine and Lastro got down to the serious business of saving the whale.

Dobi's breathing was shallow and urgent. He wouldn't eat anything offered him. Blood still oozed from his wounds. The two waded in the bloodstained water, whispering out of respect for the giant creature in torment. Lastro stroked the whale's head, gently murmuring all the time. Then he stopped, listened, turned to Jasmine, and said, "He thinks he cannot hold on any longer."

"So he really does talk to you. Like the camels. It is a great gift, Lastro."

"We cleared an island together." Lastro's eyes were brimming with tears.

"Cleared?"

"Yes. Full of rubbish. Of plastic mostly, swept up by the sea. The island nearly died. But we saved it; we worked together—a good team." He sniffed as he spoke, holding back the tears.

"Wait! You said the whaling ship did this, but before that . . . the orcas and what was the other thing?" Jasmine was beginning to see a link with Porky and Kitchi's story.

"An octopus. But no ordinary octopus. It was huge. Really scared me."

"Hmmm. I think they wanted you gone. Because . . . because . . . you are an *other*. So you have a secret, too." She looked at him excitedly, her voice raised. Lastro put his finger to his lips. "Sorry—but do you see? This is it. Your secret. You and Dobi." She nodded her head from one to the other. "And how you manage him."

Lastro gave a short nod and sadly laid his head on the whale's side, willing him well.

At a huge chicken farm outside of Brussels, the large doors, locked from the outside, began shaking. The interior infrastructure also shook violently and fell apart. Great numbers of fowl went flapping and screeching towards the massive bolted doors. Any human in their path would have been clawed to death. Their combined weight forced open the doors, and the tens of thousands of inmates flew out to freedom and a new life.

After the sea gazing did not yield any answers, Kitchi made towards a series of small hills. It suited him to be alone; in some ways, he'd enjoyed being solitary when he was a bison. He never seemed to be able to think like other people. He was always angry. The hills had enough trees on them to hide between, so he sat down among them; the day was getting hotter, and any shade was welcome. The air was noisy with the sound of cricket songs. His head was clearing now, and he lay down and closed his eyes. So he'd wanted to fly away, and he had. And ended up here, doing goodness knows what. That sunflower story had surprised him. *Me a Keeper, too!* What was that fat boy talking about? At the words *fat boy,* Kitchi's memory was jogged. He remembered the words of the bison at the Buffalo Dance which had, yet again, eluded him. *The brave boy in pain* who would *lead the Keepers.* He guessed Porky could have been in pain; after all, he'd been in hospital. And so he *was* a leader. Fat boy Porky had been introduced as Head Keeper. Meaning the rest of them were Keepers too? They had to be, he supposed. Keepers of what? *What do Keepers keep?* he wondered, but instead of finding an answer, he heard a noise.

He sat up suddenly, with a start. Something was moving through the trees, making the dry ground crackle. Still on edge, Kitchi expected the Wendigo to be hiding around every corner; he pressed himself close to a tree trunk and peered out. The source of the crackling was standing only a short distance away. It was a wild goat, munching on a sage plant. And Kitchi was hungry. Maybe because he'd been thinking about secrets, or maybe Kitchi was, in fact, in tune with his secret without realising it; he reached behind his back for that arrow, which he knew would be there. And shot it from the bow he held confidently in his hands. In an instant, the goat was dead. As Kitchi picked it up, two hooves in each hand, and threw it over his shoulders, his fingers were tingling and burning, and he remembered that sensation too. He smiled and congratulated himself. *Secrets*: he formed the word in his mind. *Keepers have Secrets.* And, with that secret stored safely in his heart, he trotted back to base to prepare a big barbeque.

Animal rights demonstrators in the hundreds stormed beef farms in Ohio and Brazil. Their combined fury scared the farm workers, who jumped in their cars and went home. The police were called, but they were outnumbered. Once the demonstrators had broken in and the cattle were released, everyone was outnumbered. The tens of thousands of animals, once weakened by drugs and food that fattened them up, regained renewed vigour once out in the open country and had the strength to stampede onwards for hours.

Amy and Porky looked at the rows and rows of qat trees with dismay and disgust. "Why all the same crop?" she asked. They were visiting the terraced hills far above the coastline below.

"Why all the waste of water?" Porky said, realising the madness behind this kind of growing. "This whole system is spelling death for a country. This way, they'll run out of water that's meant for other crops and start fighting over it."

"What do they need qat for?" Amy tore off a leaf and smelled it.

"Addiction," Porky said in a hushed tone. Some farmers had seen them and were approaching. One of them was holding a purple flower in his hand, and as he got closer, the incredulous look on his face became evident. The flower was from the plant *Valerianella Affinis,* which the farmer must have known was an extinct species. He spoke to them in Yemeni Arabic, but neither of them understood a word. However, his gesticulating caused them to look behind and retrace their steps. All along the way were the purple-topped bushes and many other unusual plants as well. The farmers were puzzling over them, intermittently glancing over at the two newcomers. Their expressions held fear. It crossed Porky's mind that they might be arrested for being witches. Once the farmers left, he breathed easily once again and smiled as he looked at Amy, because he knew her secret.

"Your wild rice," he began, "is the last remaining remnant, right?"

"Right—or so I was told."

"And you trust whoever told you?"

"Yes," she said; after a little pause, she added, "Of course I do." Her voice betrayed an unmistakable sadness.

"And . . . um . . . should we say *just a boy?*" Porky said hesitantly.

Amy smiled. "Yeah," she said, and then she shivered. "Come on—let's get out of here. This place's giving me the creeps."

"I know. But just give me a minute. I think something should be done here, don't you?"

"Sure—like what?" But Porky was already busy. He pulled out the little sunflower seed that he always carried, took a handful of earth, and rubbed them together. Then he sprinkled the mixture over the ground; he kept on repeating the same procedure until all the qat terraces where they stood were covered. Then he took Amy by the hand and walked away.

After ten steps, he said, "Now look back." So they did. And gasped. More at the colour than the spectacle itself, for the terraces were now cascading with vegetable plants and fruit trees, more than they could count. And all organic!

The acres upon acres of fields in the Midwest that had been allowed to run wild had already reached optimum levels of health, and now a diverse multitude of crops grew abundantly. Each acre yielded hundreds of different kinds of produce. In between and at the edges of the fields, wild weeds had freedom of expression, and butterflies and bees pollinated freely.

An hour later, as they approached the camp, they were laughing about the look on the farmers' faces when they saw the extinct plants. "They could have burnt us at the stake!" Amy joked.

"You know, your gift is amazing," Porky told her. "The opposite of extinction—what is it?"

"I guess diversity. But it's not mine. And it's not a gift as in *talent*, either. It's a secret."

"That no one should know?" He was trying to put the pieces together.

"I don't think so. Because it's knowledge that's good for the Earth and its populations. But . . ."

"What?"

"I think they're secrets because they're dangerous."

He mulled it over and knew she was right. He and Kitchi and Lastro had been in danger. "What about you?"

"Me?" She knew what he wanted to ask and bit her lip nervously.

"Yeah, on your journey—were you in any danger?"

"Only initially." He waited for an explanation, but none came. She wanted to say *it was my fault,* but she was too ashamed. She had sensed correctly that Porky was not only brave but compassionate and essentially *good,* and there were some things she didn't want him to know about her.

"And by the way, I think you'll see your guy again. I mean, whoever gives you a secret is someone special, right?"

"Right. Okay, I'll believe you."

"What about your *just a girl?*" she asked, smiling coyly at him.

"You mean Bina?"

"Yes. Bina? That's a strange name."

"Yeah, she's Indian. And she's a Keeper too."

"She's a Keeper?"

"Yes."

"So—where is she?"

"If I only knew," said Porky. "If I only knew."

And they continued on in silence until they found the others on the beach.

Kitchi had got a good fire going and was roasting the meat on a spit. Jasmine and Lastro sat watching and peeling vegetables. "Hey!" Kitchi called out, obviously in much better spirits.

"Hey!" Porky called back, glad they were friends again. He tried a joke: "It could've been you on that spit!"

"Could well have been," Kitchi retorted. "All one and the same!" An answer that made no sense to anyone.

It would have been a happy party if it were not for the background music of Dobi's low moaning. The whale was obviously dying. Lastro squatted on a rock with his head on his knees, crying. Amy sat down and began to play with the sand. Crabs ran to and fro near the water. A head poked out of the shallow waves, bobbed up and down, and popped up again. But no one had noticed it yet. It took a few minutes of being battered and splashed backwards and forwards by the incoming waves before the head and its shell finally emerged—a large and very majestic sea turtle crawled up the beach.

Kitchi was the first to be aware its arrival; he said, "Hey! Welcome, welcome! Another guest for dinner!"

Everyone turned to look, except Lastro. The sea turtle's entrance was immediately accompanied by many exclamations: *Wow! Would you look at that! Awesome!* (befitting the arrival of an ancient mariner). Lastro was forced to look up. It was he who saw the phial hanging from its neck, and he wandered over to talk to the newcomer. He sat crouched beside the turtle's head, in silence, just listening. The others went quiet and exchanged looks, but there was a charged feeling in the air, like electricity, which is one way of describing *wonder.*

With the others looking on, Lastro took the phial from around the old sea turtle's neck and waded into the water. He splashed about as he rubbed the phial's contents over Dobi's wounds. Back on shore, he held it up and cried out, "All the way from the Amazon!"

"Amazon?" Jasmine repeated, screwing her nose up, as she did when she didn't understand something.

"Cheers to Mr. Turtle!" Kitchi took him over some crabmeat. "You sure do deserve this," he said, patting the creature's old, wrinkled head. They all ate dinner then, the breaking waves the only sound. The whale's moaning had stopped, and water began spurting out of its blowhole, slowly at first, but then faster, until it gushed upwards like a glorious fountain. (More beautiful than those in the grounds of the Taj Mahal, Porky was to tell Bina later.)

Lastro was so happy that he began crying again. Porky surveyed the jubilant, albeit strange, scene; he looked into the glowing faces of the Keepers, and the puzzle was clearer to him than ever. Jasmine was watching him, and she, too, felt a moment had come. She left the group to go and fetch her magic carpet from where it was hidden. It was time the Keepers knew the next step.

As she hurried back to the camp in the pink light of the evening, murky shapes flitted between the shrubs and the branches of the mimosas and willows. As Jasmine passed by, one of them slithered up behind her. She let out a yell as its teeth sank into her foot.

CHAPTER 31

Ghouls

But the teeth were well and truly in. The jaws of the disgusting, slithering beast clamped shut and twisted sharply. Jasmine's scream pierced the night air. The creature suddenly made off—with her foot clamped in its mouth.

They all came running, and it was Amy's turn to scream, before she clamped her hand over her mouth at the horror of seeing so much blood spouting from where Jasmine's foot had been. They crowded around her at the same time as Murad members arrived on the scene. But there were attackers to fight off. Most of the tribe fled at the sight of them. Only a few brave souls stayed to face the onslaught of ghouls, which were infamous for consuming human flesh.

Little Lastro courageously ran forward to where Jasmine lay. He poured the remainder of the potent clotting potion over the bloody mess that was now the remains of her foot. The bleeding stopped instantly, but her foot did not reappear, as her friends looking on had hoped. She was quickly carried to the safety of a tent, however safe that would be, nobody really knew. Legend had it that ghouls could easily wrench off a man's head and crunch it to pieces. And just at that moment, Kitchi saw that happen to a Murad tribesman. Lastro didn't have enough potion to go round; the phial was empty. Blood was all over the ground. The ghouls were tearing at the tents as people screamed and ran.

Porky did his best to protect the *others* in the face of such a ferocious attack. His heartbeat was so fast he thought his heart would burst, and it flashed through his mind that it would have done so had he still been obese. And how would he have moved as swiftly and powerfully like he did now, as he herded the Keepers onto the beach and into the water? Lastro was already there, guarding Dobi and the turtle. Though what good he could do was debatable. Later, Porky couldn't explain why he thought the water would be safe place—he just did. Like anyone would think of water if he was facing a fire; it was the same with Porky at that moment. All he could think was the word *water,* and it turned out he was right.

The tribesmen were fighting the ghouls with their enormous Yemeni swords, but it was no good. No impact was made at all by any weapon; not a scratch was inflicted upon any of the beasts. Because as any Yemeni should have known, ghouls are the undead; they can't be killed. But worse, these were a new kind of ghoul; a modern off-shoot from the legendary, formed out of toxic waste dumped in Yemen by richer nations. Fortunately, most families had quickly fled on camels, but a trail of dismembered bodies led out of the camp, and the cries and wails of the inflicted were pitiful.

But it was the Keepers the ghouls were really after; this was obvious. The poor Murads had simply got in the way. Time after time, the sickly corpse-like creatures tried to enter the sea but couldn't. An invisible barrier prevented them; even when the beasts ran at full speed and leapt at them from above, they hit a transparent wall at full speed and fell, *splat,* to the ground, stunned. Not one was able to enter the water. The four clung onto each other and shook with fear; Amy covered her ears to block out the terrible screams of the injured. Porky was anxious about how they would leave the water. It occurred to him that they could somehow leave with the whale, but that didn't solve the problem of Jasmine. Jasmine, on the other hand, was thinking differently. She looked upon the scene on the beach from her tent and seethed.

All at once, the ghouls retreated and disappeared into the shadows where they came from. Any remaining person with two legs took to their heels and ran. All others needed help and slowly moved off. Some tribe elders went to Jasmine's tent. Porky saw them go in and felt trouble brewing. He knew he had to go up there. "Don't leave us!" begged Lastro.

"Don't worry—those guys have got enough body parts to feast a whole night on," predicted Kitchi. "It's time to get out of here—now or never, dudes. What's the plan, boss?" It was the first time anyone had tested Porky on his authority—what timing! He had no idea what the plan was—even *if* there was a plan. There had to be a plan.

"I'm going to get Jasmine," he said in as firm a voice as he could muster. That was the first step of the plan. "You wait here." They nodded and crouched low behind Dobi. He ran up the shore easily; there was no barrier now. He kept himself bent double as if in combat (which he was), but in this stance, he looked even odder in his Arab dress. A Murad stood guard outside Jasmine's tent. He looked hatefully at Porky, pushed him roughly in the chest, and started growling at him in Arabic. Jasmine's voice sounded inside, and a curtain was pulled back. She was sitting on a pile of cushions, the end of her leg wrapped in cloth, glowering at him.

"You have to leave," she said, almost spitting the words out. "Look what has happened to my people because of you!"

"Me?" he asked. "No, *we* have to leave. And right now." He made a move towards her. A tribesman grabbed his arm and squeezed it so tight Porky thought it might break off. Through clenched teeth, Porky exhaled and said (trying not to squeak), "*You* are a Keeper, too. We're in this together—remember?"

She didn't seem to care, saying, "Kitchi was right to be scared. You, the so-called leader, should have warned us about the dangers."

"How do I know about the dangers until they happen? Kitchi's coping well now—don't you see the change in him? I . . ." But he could feel this exchange was going nowhere, and the angry man holding his arm looked ready to silence him. He was running out of time and grappled to find something to say that would make a difference, something *key*. He got it. "Jasmine—tell me! How did you know we were the *others*?"

He gasped as the grip on his arm tightened. She opened her mouth to speak and let out an "Ahh," but nothing more. She had remembered why she left the beach. A few moments of silence followed. Porky broke it by yelling, "Let go of my arm!"

Jasmine conceded. She called for Hassan and begged the men to leave them alone. Hassan ran in, with a tear-stained face Porky noticed, and Jasmine whispered in his ear. The boy rummaged under some bedding and pulled out a small rolled-up piece of carpet. He spread it out on the ground between them. And withdrew to a corner, whimpering. "He's terrified and saw the camels getting slaughtered," she told him, her voice hard with anger.

The beauty of the carpet drew a blanket of calm over them however; even Hassan found some solace in edging nearer to look. The carpet depicted a colourful map of Yemen. A golden orb (or a droplet of liquid gold was perhaps more accurate) appeared, hovering closely above the carpet. It stopped on the coastline at the place where they were camped and split into six smaller teardrops. Five remained over the camp, while the other one flew up and out, as the map itself enlarged to show the surrounding area of Saudi Arabia and east Africa. Each country lit up in hues of colour; the sixth drop split and became two; one hovered over Ethiopia, and the other Djibouti.

"More *others*," Porky whispered. Hassan watched wide-eyed as the five gold droplets moved from Yemen across the Gulf of Aden to Djibouti. *The next step of the plan*, Porky thought with relief. There *was* a plan. "You see?" he said, pointing to the map and looking at Jasmine. "We *all* have to leave." She sat, staring at the obvious, with tears running silently down her cheeks. "And that means right now!"

Porky got to his feet, picked up Jasmine (who didn't resist), and called out for Hassan to follow with the carpet. He duly scampered after them because he had nowhere else to go.

They moved as fast as they could down to the beach, where the four still stood, shivering in the shallows. But exactly how were they going to travel? After seeing the magical carpet, Porky knew he only had to *trust*. He thought he had better explain first and lay Jasmine down; Amy rushed to her side and held her hand. He rolled out the carpet, which instantly became huge—as big as any carpet in a house! It had lights too, which flashed on and off, as if to say, *Speedy boarding for immediate take-off.*

Porky didn't need to give an order; all he had to do was nod. They all jumped on; Kitchi carried Jasmine this time. Another nod to Lastro, and he was off down the blowhole. Dobi gave out a snort of water and moved slowly out to sea. Into the Gulf of Aden, to be exact. The carpet rose directly upwards, like a helicopter, and then flew slowly, trailing Dobi's path in the dark. It was to be a short trip, only a hundred nautical miles. So they took it slowly, there being no rush.

♦

"I'll protect you from the Hooded Claw; Keep the Vampires from your door," the singer whispered through the speakers, before launching into "The Power of Love." Bina listened to the love song, feeling unsettled. She had taken to munching far too many chocolates. Formed in heart shapes, she would pop one in her mouth and wish for the imminent arrival of Porky. The sweet taste, though overpowering at first, now soothed her and fed her patience. They would spoil her dinner, though. She rang the small bell, which summoned the waitress, and asked for dinner to be set out on the terrace; after a pause, she requested candles too. And then she asked for the table to be set for two persons.

Though tired and feeling irritable, Bina was still alert enough to detect a slight quiver in the serving girl's cheek before giving her the usual polite smile. "Is madam expecting a visitor?" she asked.

"Yes, madam is," Bina answered somewhat nasally, making sure the sarcasm in her voice was evident.

The girl maintained her professional smile, but her eyes didn't, and her step away was too fast. Bina noticed all of these things and felt uneasy. *"Love is danger, Love is pleasure."* A knot formed in her stomach. She absently reached out for another chocolate and raised it to her mouth. Then stopped. What was she doing? She never ate chocolates. She found herself looking at the grand, glass front doors opposite. Doors she fixated upon daily, mentally pulling Porky towards them. But no one *ever* came through them. And . . . why were there no other guests here? The knot in her stomach tightened. She watched the activity outside through the glass. Cars were passing and people walking by, even a dog or two. The streetlights came on, and it got dark. A little . . . too quickly? Her concentration was interrupted by the waitress, who had returned and stood directly in front, blocking her view.

"Dinner is served on the terrace tonight madam," she said. "Here's the menu for your perusal."

As usual, there were no choices on the menu; you had to have what was offered and that was it. All the excitement had gone out of eating for Bina. She liked choosing, because it was important to her to read her body and know what was best for it at any given time. This way, she couldn't do that. She'd loved the food when she first got here, but now? So what was there . . . mmm, chicken in red wine sauce (a bit heavy late in the evening), roasted potatoes (a bit fatty but sure to be delicious), and some broccoli (well, that was healthy) in cheese sauce (oh, that was fatty). She didn't really want to eat this kind of food, but she was hungry; what did it matter—she'd swim it all off tomorrow.

She went out onto the terrace and inhaled the night air. Beautiful. An emotional surge hit her, and she immediately felt she wanted to cry. The table had been laid for two, with candles. Where was Porky? What was happening to him? Why had he let her stay all alone here? Her meal arrived, and she ate it too quickly, because she was unhappy and alone. The rich food was absolutely delicious; the roast potatoes salty but yummy. Soon, she was full and didn't feel so bad afterwards, just felt like sitting and enjoying the view. Did she want dessert? Sure, she did! A piece of rich cherry chocolate cake arrived, which she also ate rapidly. Normally she would have just tasted such a rich dessert, had enough to enjoy something different, maybe with friends. She knew she wasn't making healthy choices—but she wasn't able to do anything about it.

Completely stuffed now, she was comforted and not sad any longer. In fact, she was too sleepy to think of missing Porky and didn't feel worried at all. Time for bed—after all, tomorrow was another day.

CHAPTER 32

Djibouti

The freight ship docked in Djibouti Port with a loud clunk and a shudder; its hold doors opened wide. Serenity crawled out of her hiding place into a ray of early morning sunshine. A monkey, certainly also a stowaway like her, peered out from behind the opposite container, its head rotating rapidly from side to side, checking for a way to make a safe exit. Serenity immediately knew that shadowing her fellow passenger was the best bet. But she would have to be fast.

Moving on all fours comes naturally to a girl raised in the rainforest; Serenity had the skills if not the speed, but she only needed to borrow the animal's instinct to get out of that place without being seen. It sure would have been a funny sight if they had been spotted; the little monkey, convinced it was being followed, moved all the faster, throwing objects back at her (only paper trash, luckily). As the agile monkey scaled high container tops and then made momentous jumps, Serenity waited in the shadows or crawled along the floor. And suddenly they were out. They stood immobilised by the bright sun, which hit them like a floodlight, and within a split-second, the monkey was gone, leaving Serenity to face the hazards of Djibouti Port alone.

Massive containers were being moved in every direction: hanging from cranes above, being pulled by dinky trucks on the ground, and sometimes hauled by human hands. Traffic was everywhere, and she had to get out of there. She made her way to the exit, edging slowly between gigantic truck wheels. She had nearly made it and was held up just for a minute beside a container entering the huge iron gates. The strangest thing happened then; Serenity looked up to see a row of dark brown eyes staring at her through a space in the container. How many? Twenty? Thirty? Were they on the run like her? She didn't think so; they looked sad and pleading. But as soon as they appeared, they were gone. But that sight was to haunt Serenity for many a year to come.

Now out in the city, Serenity didn't feel safe. In Nairobi, which her father knew well, they had always known which direction to go in, which bus to take, or how to talk to the taxi drivers. This place was different, more chaotic. For a moment, she regretted giving her dad the slip when she did. Sergio's radar beeper had put her into a panic, and she knew Dad wouldn't understand. It was the first time she'd ever disobeyed him. But she knew that this mission, *her* mission, was ultimately more important than his and the migrating turtles. *This* was world changing—she could feel it. After wandering aimlessly, Serenity realised she was attracting a trail of beggars; this became a spectacle, causing people to stop in their tracks and stare, point, or laugh—or all three! She guessed with her long sun-bleached blonde hair, chocolate-brown skin, green eyes, sparkly tee-shirt, and backpack, she could have looked like a rich tourist. Never mind the bright pink phone with the radar screen that she kept consulting. She had Djibouti francs but had already given far too many away. Enough was enough. But how to lose the crowd of beggars? They soon reached an open-air market, with stalls filled with tasty things to eat.

Some of the kids approached a man selling fresh baked bread, shaped something like pizzas, but with crushed chillies and oil on top. He shouted roughly for them to go away, so the kids were all over Serenity now, pulling at her tee-shirt and reaching into the pockets of her jeans. "Stop it! Stop!" she called out in Portuguese.

None of the beggar children paid any attention to this, but a stall owner shouted at them and then said, in French, for Serenity's benefit, that he would call the police. This scared her, because her father didn't know she was here. But then screams and cries sounded above the market noise; one of the kids had been burnt on the pizza seller's fire. The dirty little girl's flood of tears was ignored by the townsfolk. Serenity guessed that if she kept that screaming noise up, she'd get a beating as well.

There was a phial of soothing ointment made from the crushed flowers of a creeper at the bottom of her backpack. So out it came, and Serenity set about treating the small child's burns, which were now blistering into big bubbles. The little girl, named Pica, was crying the frantic cries of a newborn baby, she was in such agony. Serenity spied some bunches of leaves on a vegetable stall that she recognised. Her aunties at home chewed them before applying the pulp on burned skin. So she bought some and started chewing, and she got the other kids to chew too. Then she gently patted the spat-out green patties on top of the balm. Pica stopped crying as the cool medicine of the plant pervaded her blistered skin. All of the beggar children sat quietly now, in a kind of awe of Serenity and her healing skills. She bought them all cartons of juice and chilli bread to share. And so they sat in a little circle, eating and drinking.

In a patch of cleared rainforest in the Amazon basin, a creeper plant, the leaves of which contained an amazing antidote to migraine headache, started growing again. It hadn't flourished for years; every time it tried to spread, it got cut down again or burnt. Such destructive activity was never to come near that area of the forest from that moment on, and in the quiet and freedom that remained, many other plants stretched out their stalks and produced leaves that would help countless millions to regain full health.

Serenity's beeper went off just then. It told her that Sergio, her turtle, was back on the radar. The children were still munching, and it was a good opportunity to make a hasty retreat back to her original mission: finding Sergio. So she skipped off into the narrow streets behind the market before anyone could follow her. The screen showed a red dot flashing in a line approaching the coast, somewhere north of Djibouti. Some fishing towns lay in that direction, according to the map. Serenity had to get there fast. She didn't know how to get a bus, so it would have to be a taxi. As a tourist, she was bound to be swindled; her year's worth of hard-earned cash was disappearing fast. Twenty minutes and minus thirty francs later, she was in the outskirts of a place called Tadjoura, looking out at sea. Nothing to be seen. There was an old rundown café at the side of the road. It looked dirty and unappetising, but Serenity was tired and famished. How long since she'd eaten? She sat on a wooden bench at a table that looked out to sea. As she waited for her tea and sandwich, she studied the graffiti and carvings on the grubby table top, trying to make sense of the multiple languages. Just when she thought she recognised *J'aime Maro*, she dozed off, overcome by tiredness and heat.

And so she didn't see a large blue whale approach the shore, accompanied by a deep green turtle at its side, bouncing along in the surf. Likewise, she didn't see a carpet glide slowly to the ground, slowing down by going first one way and then the other, till it settled on a patch of yellowed grass at the roadside. She was awoken by her mug of tea crashing to the ground; it had slipped from the hand of Tante Renee, the café owner, who was bringing the tea to her table and saw the carpet land.

At first sight, Serenity thought the group were sitting, having a picnic. A group of tourists, obviously. But then she noticed Jasmine's bandaged foot, stained with blood, and their strained faces, dishevelled hair, and crumpled clothes. Something was wrong here, and her first thought was that it had to do with the dark girl's bleeding foot. And, as usual, Serenity felt that it was her job to put it right. She dug deep inside her backpack and rummaged about, a frown on her face. It wasn't there, the phial of ointment she needed. *How come?* she wondered, but no time for that. This girl was in trouble for sure. Only one glance at her pale face, screwed up in pain, was enough to suspect the worst. There had already been too much blood loss. But nothing prepared her for the gruesome sight of a severed foot.

Tante Renee went over and invited them into her not-very-inviting establishment. Her small children played barefoot in the dirt, wearing only tee-shirts. She groaned loudly when she saw Jasmine's foot and ran inside to boil some water. Kitchi and Porky carried Jasmine to a bench at the café, while the others followed. Hassan rolled up the now shrunk carpet and placed it under his arm. The café comprised of a wooden shack for a kitchen, while the tables and benches were scattered outside, under a shabby and torn awning. They congregated around one of the tables. Serenity surveyed the bunch: they were all around her age but couldn't have looked more different. *Like the United Colours of Benetton,* she thought, smiling wryly. Except that they looked nothing like models at that moment. As well as looking dirty and tired, their faces looked haunted, like a great shock lay hidden behind each. Hassan was whimpering again and wiping his nose on his hand. "He misses Flying Carpet," Jasmine said, the first to break the silence.

"Your carpet?" Serenity asked.

"No. My camel. She was torn to pieces." Jasmine still couldn't hide the anger in her voice.

"Torn to pieces?" Serenity looked from one to the other. "By what?" But nobody offered an answer. She studied them carefully, and an impossible thought came to her mind: "Are you some of the *others?*" *They can't be,* she thought at once; *they look too weak.* Serenity had been expecting something else, something magical, like she'd seen in her dream.

"I know you!" It was Porky who spoke. He'd been puzzling over the sudden appearance of this girl, whose face he was familiar with. "You're Serenity from the Amazon! I'm Porky. My blog, remember? You sent me your picture. You and your dad, outside the turtle sanctuary."

"My turtle!" she screamed, remembering the reason for being there in the first place. Everyone looked up at that, some animation in their faces at last. She pulled out her radar phone, but its battery was dead.

"He's here," Lastro said, pointing from the rocks where he was perched, checking on their animal companions.

"Oh Sergio!" she cried, scrambling down to hug his withered old head. The others managed smiles at that, even Jasmine, who, of course, completely understood the love of animals.

"Sergio," Jasmine repeated, sniggering.

"Flying Carpet?" Kitchi said, raising his eyebrows. At which Hassan began crying aloud again.

Jasmine made a face at Kitchi. Porky felt the tension and, although exhausted, made an effort to order a meal. The group needed their spirits raised. So he asked for a menu; at the same time, it occurred to him that they had no money at all between them. He couldn't expect this poor woman to provide food for them for free. Unless Serenity . . . she still looked like she inhabited the world. Unlike them: homeless, possessionless, and penniless. He wondered what she thought of him, dressed like an Arab nomad, his white dress horribly dirty now. He decided he'd have to ask her for money, after asking the group to order some breakfast—or lunch (*What time was it anyway?* he thought). He walked over to Serenity, who was laughing with Lastro. Lastro was always happy around the animals.

"You know, I've followed him all the way from home. I even left my dad . . ." But she stopped mid-sentence. "The medicine! Sergio's got a phial of medicine round his neck."

"No, we used that for the whale," Lastro said.

"No, there are others. Look here—under his shell." She put her hand all around under the rim. "Just a likkle bitty tickly-wickly, Sergio old boy!"

Amy and Kitchi stifled giggles, and Jasmine snorted. Serenity pulled out four plastic phials of potion, one of which she hoped would stop Jasmine's bleeding. As she attended to the gruesome task of cleaning and dressing the wound, Jasmine winced in pain. The others discussed the abysmal menu, for there was nothing on it except for a watery noodle soup, which was obviously from a packet, or tinned meat sandwiches. Porky glanced into the kitchen, and his heart sank. There was no fridge; nothing was fresh. The place was well stocked up with the well-known red and white cans of fizzy drink, though. Well, how would that sustain anybody? No fresh food, but plenty of soft drinks! The familiar anger was rising up in him, which at this point in their journey was exactly what Porky needed to feel—before it was too late.

Tante Renee was apologetic and embarrassed about her menu (or lack of it), while Porky squirmed over having no money. Finally, he had to say it in front of everyone. "No money?" asked Serenity. *No money?* thought the cafe proprietor, her heart sinking. "No money," Kitchi said, shaking his head with his hands outstretched, palms up. *Like Big Eagle,* he thought. *Like Buddha,* thought Amy. *Like Gandhi,* thought Porky.

Like always, thought Lastro. "I can catch some fish!" he piped up.

Tante Renee looked encouraged. The Keepers mostly didn't care one way or another about the money, because when you've faced vicious monsters who want to take a bite out of your face, or flown by night on a magic carpet, or had your foot wrenched off, issues like *money* cease to exist.

"I can handle it," Serenity said, shaking her sparkly purse in the air. *All saved up for a moment like this,* she realised deep down and felt immensely satisfied. "Not much to buy, though," she added, screwing her face up at the menu.

"I think we'll have to sort this out," Porky decided. "Okay guys?"

Everyone nodded, even Jasmine. Lastro was already fishing. Kitchi went for a walk across the road, looking for a bird or two to shoot. Porky himself was eyeing the pots of yellow, dried-up herbs that lined the terrace. He took out his sunflower seed . . .

Less than an hour later, they all sat down to a meal of barbequed fresh fish and wild pheasant, accompanied by a salad of green leaves of all descriptions, asparagus spears, and sweet yellow tomatoes. All prepared with Tante Renee's help and without money. The meal nourished them out of their tiredness and despair, their faces cheered, and Jasmine was laughing with Serenity and Amy, her foot cleanly bandaged using some of Porky's robe (now much shorter.)

As they ate, Tante Renee told them her story. Her husband's small farm had gone out of business due to rising cotton and corn prices in the world market. He now worked in a local factory in Djibouti City, packing containers with products from African countries that foreign companies owned. As they sat round the table, she suddenly jumped up and asked for a photograph; she wanted to remember this day forever, she said. Pulling out a camera from a drawer in the kitchen, she asked everyone to smile. And—click— the Keepers were immortalised on film.

After the mass escape of imprisoned animals across the United States and Europe, people were now aware of the cruel and miserable conditions found inside industrial farms. They stopped buying beef, pork, and chicken from supermarkets and began to only buy meat from farms that raised animals humanely.

Later, that photograph was to become one of the most sought after in the world. It was the only known photograph of the Keepers altogether (well, six of them, at least). The president of Djibouti would be reluctant to let it leave his country, despite many generous offers. It was said that he had put it in a heavy gilt frame and hung it in his office, and after his death, it was placed in the Djibouti National Library.

Porky and his fellow Keepers enjoyed that unexpected pocket of rest and contentment, as things in Bina's world were getting infinitely worse.

♦

Breakfast was completely different the next day. Bina awoke to find that in the dining hall, for the first time, she had a choice.

An agonising choice. For laid out on the long table, covered with a white linen tablecloth that was embroidered with wild flowers, was a tantalising array of delicious morning food. A deep bowl containing all kinds of fruit was the centrepiece, surrounded by freshly squeezed orange juice, bowls of oats, cinnamon and milk, boiled eggs, wholemeal bread, and various brightly coloured boxes, each claiming wondrous health benefits: *energy all day; enriched with calcium and vitamins; lose pounds the special once-a-day way.* One box had pictures of luscious, deep purple berries splashed all over its front, their goodness the kind of pick-you-up she needed right then. But she told herself that they weren't real, only a picture, and the berries inside the cereal were dried up and probably months old. Not fresh, like she'd have picked at home.

Some fruit and an egg was the best choice for her, she knew it. But she couldn't do it. She couldn't make the right choice; her thoughts felt weak and far away, like voices calling from a distance. She wanted the red berry cereal, because those berries contained antioxidants and were good for her. She could do with losing a few pounds for when Porky arrived, and the cereal would taste so good, so comforting; she might have two bowls, not just one, because it was for dieting and good for you. So she filled a bowl from the cereal box and added milk (low-fat, of course, because it was good for you). She scoffed down two bowls of the sweet and satisfying stuff before going to the TV room, where she spent an hour watching day-time chat shows and not missing Porky at all.

When the waitress came in to announce that the spa was open, Bina hardly looked up. Her head felt heavy, and so did her limbs. It took all of her brainpower to ask if Porky had called. The waitress smiled as she shook her head; Bina was distracted by something about the young woman's teeth. Were they longer at each side or just crooked? But the waitress had noticed something about Bina. The old laceration on her arm was oozing blood ever so slightly. She bent down, took Bina's arm in her hands, and licked it from one end to the other, smiling as she did so and licking her blood red lips afterwards before letting the arm fall with a thud on the chair.

Shocked and revolted, Bina's head was spinning, but she remembered something, something important. Something that had been taken from her; she knew now that she was becoming lost without it. She drew in a deep breath and pulled that thought up from the chasm it had fallen down into. "I want my nutmeg," she breathed out.

"What?" the young woman said, swirling round.

"I want my nutmeg!" Bina shouted.

♦

After the meal, Porky was in a bad mood. He felt irritated at everyone suddenly, but he didn't know why; it wasn't like him to be like this. Lastro went off to swim with Dobi, and Serenity curled up and slept with her turtle among the long bulrushes. Porky thought they were being lazy, but at the same time, there was nothing else for them to do. Amy and Jasmine were sitting close together and chatting, almost whispering, he noticed. Jasmine hadn't even thanked him for getting her out of that dangerous situation. Kitchi was cleaning his arrows and checking the bow out. Where did he get that thing? He was such a show-off with it. He thought of how Serenity had mentioned her father. She was lucky to have support, unlike him—all alone. Just then, Bina's face filled all the space in his head, and his eyes flooded with tears. Why had she chosen Ajit over him? He couldn't take this any more; he had to get away somewhere by himself. He got up and announced that he was going into town. No one moved. Typical. So he turned his back on them and left.

A minute down the road, he heard footsteps running after him. "Hey—I'm coming with you!" It was Serenity. "I need to email my father. Better to let him know I'm here. Don't you think?"

Porky didn't answer. He stopped a passing bus, and they got on. Serenity had to pay, of course, which only increased his frustration. *Her and her sparkly purse,* he thought, feeling annoyed with her, but for no good reason. She sensed this and kept quiet. She had wanted to talk about what it meant to be a Keeper, and the amazing magical meal they prepared, and why they were travelling together, and what they should do next. But she didn't even try. Porky wasn't like he'd seemed in his blog: strong and passionate and ready for anything. She thought maybe he was worried because they had no money. Maybe he was going to the bank. They sat in silence and watched the busy Djiboutians go about their business, dressed in their brightly coloured clothes. As the bus entered the town, an imposing billboard looked down at them: *Queen Burger—Fastest Growing Fast Food Chain. Now 6 Branches!* Something did a somersault inside Porky, but he didn't know what it meant.

He left Serenity at an Internet café. She slipped him some money and sat down double-quick before he could refuse. Catching sight of himself in a shop window, he got a shock—he looked awful. He had to get out of this robe. There was a clothes shop round the next corner. He liked the stuff there, but it wasn't all that cheap, so he made to leave. A television blared high up in the corner; he was almost out the door when he heard his name: *Philip McGregor.* He looked up so fast, he cricked his neck. It was an English-speaking news station, and his parents were on the screen. His mum's face was blotchy from crying, while his dad was making an appeal: "If there's anyone out there that knows anything, anything at all, please come forward."

His latest school photo was in the corner of the screen. His mum added, "We love you, Philip," and she covered her face with a tissue. Porky froze like a statue when he heard her next words: "Bring Bina back, Philip; her fiancé's very worried and upset." The camera moved over to show Ajit and Bina's uncle, sitting at the table next to them. They were nodding sincerely, and then Bina's uncle said, "We do not blame you. Just come home—both of you. Please."

Porky gazed at the screen in shock, even though another news item was being reported. Then, suddenly scared that someone would recognise him, he fled and started walking the streets manically. A bright, shiny new Queen Burger appeared. Without hesitation, he entered, sat down, and ordered the biggest beef burger they had, complete with supersize fries and cola. It took him less than five minutes to finish the lot. He ordered the same again.

Serenity saw him through the glass as he raised his third burger to his lips; she screamed, "Stop! What are you doing?" She ran inside. "You big fat fake! You fraud!" Now she was hitting him with her sparkly bag and shouting some more. Some other diners, amused, tried to calm her down; finally, she sat opposite him. She stared, suddenly hostile, and hissed, "You're not the Porky of the blog, are you? How many burgers have you eaten? How many trees does that make?" He stared at her as if she was speaking another language. He couldn't even begin to understand what she meant. "How many? Around twenty trees per burger! You were the one who said burgers were killers, remember? In your blog!" And to Serenity's dismay and complete surprise, Porky began to cry.

♦

"Vetala, tell Ms. Grayling she can come in now."

Vetala, the pseudo-waitress, lingered at the door.

"My dear, pretty little thing—you *shall* have blood. Patience, child, patience. The girl will soon be yours. Give me one more day."

Smiling in anticipation, Vetala left. Ms. Grayling took her place at the door. She looked a little scared.

"Come in and sit down, Grayling," the man behind the desk said, his tone changing. "Do you know what happens if we fail?"

"We lose the race, sir?" Ms. Grayling replied, not sounding too sure.

"No. You lose the race, if that's what you want to call it. And Vetala wins. By that, I mean she wins you. Or rather, your

256

delicate-looking neck. Or any other part of you that she fancies." Ms. Grayling's face was sheet white. "Now you are chief psychologist here, so what do we do next?"

Ms. Grayling straightened herself up and said, "The girl is weakening, that's obvious."

"She's asking for that infernal nutmeg!" the man thundered from behind his enormous desk.

"The nutmeg has yielded nothing in our laboratory. It is harmless."

The man stood up and walked round his desk till he faced her, standing uncomfortably close.

"You and I both know that is bullshit," he said, growling out the words. "She has a power that can change the world. Alone, she's proved herself weak—but with that magical nutmeg, it's a different story. You failed with her lover-boy, remember? Or have you forgotten already? Well, I haven't!" Now he was roaring. "He and his precious horn and sunflower outwitted Wendigo! And that's a first!"

Ms. Grayling was silent. He walked over to a world map on the wall and flung his arm in its direction. "You see this?" He was indicated the shaded purple areas that covered almost 80 percent of the land mass. "We're nearly there. The rest is almost negligible. And we don't want to lose it. The Food Masters will hold you responsible if these kids change the balance of power."

"Mr. Corporate, sir," Ms. Grayling began, finding her voice at last, "they're only kids. I mean, what can they really achieve? I don't think . . ."

"Only kids?" he bellowed. "You have no idea, do you?" She looked bewildered. His voice became a strangulated, tortured whisper. "No idea about the power of Nature?" Mr. Corporate brought his fat, suntanned face up close to hers till she could smell his tobacco breath. "Nature," he said, breathing into her face (now she could smell what he'd had for breakfast), "always fights back—don't you see?"

His voice sounded twisted. Ms. Grayling felt chills go up and down her body; she decided she would leave this job now, today.

"Now," he said, moving away from her and sitting back down behind the shiny, mahogany desk, "what have you got to say?"

"I suggest you switch to salt," she said. "Bina has responded to sugar, but not enough. The taste receptors on her tongue need more confusion."

"Okay," he smiled. Because he'd just decided Ms. Grayling's fate. "And the nutmeg?"

"We can give her a GMO replacement. And see if she notices the difference."

"Oh thank you, Ms. Grayling," he said, gracing her with a beaming smile.

She breathed out again slowly. Maybe she would stay; after all, the salary was excellent, and she was saving for her around-the-world honeymoon trip.

Once the door had closed, Mr Corporate picked up the phone. Little did she know he had done some genetic experiments and created genetically modified vampires; he would put them to full use. He had some arrangements to make; he had just consigned Ms. Grayling as Vetala's prey. He and his business partners at Food Masters Inc. would enjoy watching a bit of afternoon sport.

♦

It took half an hour for Porky's sobs to subside. Serenity had guided him out of the fast food restaurant, with its fatty smells, to a smaller, quieter café. Some lively African music gently drifted around them. Serenity laid her hand on his and whispered, "It's okay to cry. It just means that you've had to be strong for too long."

He looked up, a hopeful glimmer in his eyes at those words. And it was true. Porky could no longer bear worrying over Bina's absence. Nor could he face the hard task of leading the Keepers; he felt he had no strength left. Worse still, he imagined they were turning against him. He thought Jasmine hated him, and Kitchi despised him, and Amy? She was okay—for now—but the others could poison her and Lastro, too. *The others.* He sighed deeply. *What's happened to the others?*

Serenity looked enquiringly at the sound of that sigh. He saw the look and gave out another. "It's not working, is it?"

"What isn't?" asked Serenity.

"The quest, the mission—I don't know what to call it any more."

"Oh." She sat thoughtfully for a minute. "But—you're wrong. It is working—whatever *it* is." She laughed. "Because we're here, all together, and my turtle made it with the medicine I was told to send."

"Told?" he said, tired out, but making a supreme effort to summon up the concentration to listen. An ominous feeling of nausea was building in his chest.

"Yes, in a dream. I saw us all—all eight of us. Flying."

"Flying? Or fleeing?" he said, managing a smile before grimacing and standing up real fast. "Excuse me!" And ran to the toilets. Serenity heard the retching sound of vomiting from inside. A waiter approached anxiously.

"Not your food!" Serenity said cheerfully, pointing across the road at Queen Burger. The handsome young man smiled a wide, white smile and nodded knowingly.

"Bring you something on the house," he said when Porky came sheepishly back.

"Where were we?" he asked, sipping on some bottled water.

"My dream. I saw blood in water and heard moans and cries. I saw Sergio swimming in a deep, broad ocean. And when I woke up, I knew what I had to do."

"You dispatched your turtle with medicine from the plants you know about."

"Right. And while I was doing that, securing the little phials and whispering to Sergio, my . . ."

"Fingers tingled," they said in unison, staring at each other, before bursting out laughing.

Porky was feeling enormously better. Some coriander and aubergine salad dotted with pomegranate fruits had just been delivered to the table. He nibbled it slowly. It's always encouraging to hear another's story when you've doubted your own. Serenity continued talking. She'd also heard a voice telling her she was a Keeper. And that was it. She told him about the turtle sanctuary and how it wasn't uncommon for her father to travel to reclaim a stranded turtle. But this time, she'd begged to come along, and then she ran away from him when the radar showed Sergio was on his way to Djibouti. And here she was. "Look," she added, "what about all that happened back at the roadside café? The food we provided from nothing. Don't say it's not working, when it obviously is."

"And your medicine," Porky said, "the Amazon's amazing plants curing the whale—bringing him back to life. And the flying carpet—we escaped the ghouls! And the bubble—snatching us from the Wendigo!"

Serenity wanted to know more about the dangers they were in, but Porky's face was looking weird. He was back in the garden, and then he was back further; he was in his hospital room, and there was the moment he'd last seen Bina when she had turned away from him and was gone. But now . . . if she wasn't with Ajit—where the hell was she? She wouldn't have left him, run away or something. No. No way. Someone had kidnapped her. It had to be that. Who—and why? But of course, he knew why. With dread in his chest, he knew why.

"Porky?" It was Serenity, trying to bring him back.

"Wait a minute . . . what did you say back just then? How many Keepers? You saw *eight* of them?"

"Yes, that's right."

"What did they look like? I mean . . ." Porky was grasping desperately in the air for answers.

"I don't know, I didn't see their faces." Serenity looked worried about him again. "What is it? What's wrong?"

"Eight. But there were only seven droplets." He stood up. "C'mon, we've got to go." He pulled her by the end of her sparkly purse to the bus stop. He had to see that carpet again.

♦

Bina clutched the nutmeg to her chest. For the first time in her life, she prayed; a real prayer, not an empty ritual. She said simply, "Thank you." And waited, looking out to the garden, feeling confidence return timidly. And rush away again. Because nothing happened. No tingling in her fingers—that was the first and certain sign. She felt she was being watched, too. She was sure of it. It was now blatantly obvious that this place had nothing to do with Porky, that he wasn't coming, and more frightening still, that he didn't even know she was missing. The cloudy effects of the sweetened breakfast cereal had worn off; her mind was clearing. He probably thought she was with Ajit, maybe even married by now. She would put them to the test: if she tried to open the front door, somebody was bound to stop her. She casually walked over to the glass doors, outside of which she suspected was nothing but a film screen.

Vetala appeared before her, looking bigger and taller than usual. She had a self-satisfied smirk on her face, and her lips were a deep red. She had the audacity to caress Bina's forearm, lovingly. When she put up her other hand to touch her neck, Bina suddenly recognised her as *Vetala,* from her home country. Vetala, queen of the vampires, who possesses the uncanny knowledge of confounding humans. Bina had been tricked. But she was waking up from this strange delusion. *No longer,* she thought. But just as she was contemplating how to compete with her opponent, the front door opened, revealing a busy, lively street outside with real people passing by. Bina was confused again. A couple walked in to the check-in desk; behind them, a smiling, suntanned man strode up to her, reaching out both hands and cupping Bina's in his. "My dear Bina," he said. "Please excuse my late arrival. I'm the manager of

Sunny Hills. Mrs. Luta, from Karna in your home country, arranged this wonderful spa break for you. She heard you were going to be married soon and wanted to make sure you married the right person. Ha ha ha!" He laughed so pleasantly that Bina believed him and began to think that if this had something to do with Karna, then of course Porky would be part of it too.

He led her to a sofa, patting her hand all the time. They looked at photos of Karna together on his phone; Vetala, who looked simply like a sweet black-haired girl now, brought two large bowls of potato chips. "These are freshly made in our kitchen," he said.

Bina had never tasted savoury snacks like these before. At first, they seemed overly salty, but then, she couldn't stop herself. She downed handful after handful, all the time remembering Karna and Mrs. Luta and her wonderful courtyard. Somehow, this place reminded her of Mrs. Luta's courtyard. Yes, that was it; the tranquillity and natural colours in the garden and on the walls. The manager had a telephone call to take, so Bina waited. A fresh bowl of tomato sauce-flavoured chips arrived, and she reached out for a handful and stuffed them into her mouth. She felt so full and satisfied; she thought she might have an afternoon nap right here on the sofa. The manager wouldn't mind; he was such a nice man.

◆

But the more Bina succumbed to the Food Master's brainwashing—or should we say *taste-washing*—of her instinctive gift, the more her secret slipped out of her hands and into theirs, the worse the tension between the other Keepers became.

CHAPTER 33

Keepers in Trouble

Porky saw them even before they got close: Jasmine and Kitchi were hunched close together over the carpet: examining, pointing, whispering. He quickened his pace with an urgency to intervene, but when he drew near, he encountered a barrier, almost tangible, so much so that he had to make an extra effort to push against it. At the same time, his heart began to fail him; he imagined the contemptuous look on Kitchi's face, and the gleam of burning hatred in Jasmine's eyes. He felt afraid. More afraid, for some reason, than he had been of the Wendigo in the garden. Porky, due to his enormous size, had been bullied at school all his life, and it still remained his greatest fear. He had combated it then by playing the clown, but he couldn't do that now. A leader demanded respect. He was at a loss; he didn't know what to do or say. To his surprise, Serenity, whether she knew how he felt or not, filled the gap by blurting out, "Porky saw his parents on TV!"

They all turned round at once, opened-mouthed and silent, because each one in that moment thought of their home and who they had left behind. Porky at once decided to tell them all about Bina; they had a right to know. She was a Keeper too, wasn't she? They had to find out where she was, and the carpet could tell them. But Kitchi spoke before he could get started. From the expression on his face, it was obvious he'd run out of patience with the situation and wanted to hold Porky responsible. "Yeah well, Mr. Head Keeper, I wonder if you'd let me know when I'll be seeing my family again. Cuz maybe I'd like to go home soon."

Jasmine smirked, almost wickedly. "And I need to see a doctor. It's ridiculous, just leaving me in pain like this—my foot could get infected!"

Lastro woke up when he heard their voices and listened, growing more uncomfortable by the second. Amy looked down and played with her hair. Porky, his heart pounding, cleared his throat and said, "Serenity's medicine is bound to be enough for you. You see, it was sent specially."

Kitchi snorted and didn't let him continue. "Um, maybe you could just have an ambulance *sent specially* . . . and pronto, dude. The girl's gonna bleed to death."

Jasmine's face turned pale at the thought. Amy looked up, horrified. There was a momentary silence. Then Lastro broke it.

"The potion stopped Dobi's bleeding, and it was much worse than Jasmine's." On cue, Dobi spouted some water, which splattered noisily on the ground next to them. Lastro grinned, and Porky soaked up some courage.

"I saw something else on TV," he began. "Bina's relatives are looking for her. She's missing, and we need to locate her." This didn't exactly work.

"Who's Bina?" Jasmine snapped, at the same time pretending to grimace in pain.

"She's his girlfriend," Amy said, looking guilty at breaking Porky's confidence.

"What? Now you want us to put out a search party for your lost love?" Kitchi said. "I don't think so. We have enough problems of our own." He turned to the others and added, "Listen up! He can go off and search on his own. We've got to find our way out of here. Any ideas?"

Jasmine took over, saying, "We've checked the carpet again but didn't see the lights like the first time. So maybe we should just get on it and see where it takes us?" She looked around encouragingly.

Kitchi nodded, jumped up, and started moving the carpet into the middle. But it was still its small shrunken size.

"You don't understand," Porky said. "Bina is a Keeper, like us. The carpet will show us where she is. We need her. Don't you see? We all need each other!" He sounded desperate rather than strong.

"Oh yeah?" Kitchi whirled round and stepped towards him, menacingly. "Well, from this moment on, we don't need you— okay?" Turning to Serenity, he called out, "Hey, Sparkly Girl—you got enough money in that purse for my plane ticket home?"

♦

Bina woke up and for the first time found herself alone. She rose up from the sofa. The sun was sinking in the sky over the garden. It looked so beautiful; she had to get out there. But she was terribly thirsty after eating all those salty chips. She looked around—no one. Where could she find drinking water? There was a pretty fountain in the grounds, but the water would probably be dirty. While wandering through the dining room, she saw the doorway to the kitchen at the far end. A water dispenser stood inside. As there were no staff members to ask, she went right in and poured herself a glass. Voices sounded in the distance, and as she turned towards them, she glimpsed something familiar. Her nutmeg sat on a shelf, next to a glass jar filled with other nutmegs. She knew it was hers because it was much bigger than the others and had a lighter colour. As she ran over and grabbed it, someone entered the kitchen.

It was Vetala. The small, ordinary Vetala. "What are you doing in here?" she asked, her tone angry, and she began to grow taller.

Bina shoved the nutmeg in her mouth to hide it, but Vetala saw and was immediately upon her, her hands clasping Bina's throat, pressing hard. But the moment the nutmeg had made contact with Bina again, something started happening. Tingling spread over her whole body till she visibly shook. It would take a miracle to release her from Vetala's painful grasp though, and the impossible happened right then: Bina's body became so hot that Vetala couldn't bear to touch her. She let go, her hands badly scorched. "You little . . ." Vetala made to slap her, but Bina was off, running blindly—any direction would do.

But Bina didn't know the Summer Hills Resort as well as the vampire princess, and soon she was heading down what looked like a long corridor leading to nowhere. Vetala slowed her pace to a walk and was laughing. "Where to now, Indian slut?"

The words stung, and Bina winced.

To her left was the door to the spa swimming pool. Maybe there was another way out; she pushed through it.

"Wrong choice!" Vetala laughed loudly, following.

Bina glanced behind at those words, only to see the tall shape of the strange girl become even stranger: she condensed into a black swirl, out of which started flying ten, twenty, then a hundred black vampire bats. They just kept on coming until the huge room was full, their screeching and fluttering echoing wildly. One scratched her face. There was nowhere else to go but down. Bina dived into the swimming pool, keeping her mouth firmly shut. Once under the water, it was impossible to come up; the multitudes of screaming bats were soaring back and forth over the surface. Bina swam up and down, but she was going to need air before long. Blood flowed from the cut on her face, floating up onto the surface of the pool. Scores of greedy, scrabbling bats were on it in a second, and a noisy fight broke out. Another minute went by. Now Bina's lungs were bursting; above her, only waving black shadows, and below her, the concrete bottom. There was no way out.

◆

Porky sat looking out to sea at the container ships entering and leaving Djibouti Port. Dobi was berthed nearby, and Lastro was attending to him. He was crouching down in the water near Dobi's head and nodding. Porky envied him his secret. Relationships with animals were so much easier. Why had *he* been made the leader? He couldn't do it. He didn't have the charisma or strong presence that other leaders had. He couldn't see a way out of this. The others weren't going to listen to him any more. His confidence was sinking by the minute: how could Bina have ever seen anything in him at all? A snort of water emerged from the whale's blowhole and splashed on top of Porky, soaking him completely. He removed his white headdress and wrung it out, managing something that looked like a smile. Lastro was laughing and said, "That's him telling you to stop it!"

"Stop what?" Porky asked, his spirit still heavy.

"Stop what you are thinking, because it is not true." The quiet, thoughtful boy patted Dobi's magnificent head.

"That's what he said?"

"Yes, that is what he said."

Porky saw Dobi's eye looking directly at him. He stared into it, wishing he could hear the whale's voice like Lastro did. Looking into his eye was like falling into a deep, deep place, from before all time began. It wasn't exactly like being hypnotised (although Porky had never been hypnotised), more like being aware of all *goodness* that inherently resides in everything on this Earth. And it didn't surprise him that this particular whale would want to give out such a message. Hadn't Lastro told him that he was the last whale in the seas of this world? All the others had been killed by whalers. Was Dobi trying to point him in the right way? The only *true* way?

He looked at Lastro; how brave he was to have made that journey inside the whale, without even questioning it. Such *trust*. He took out his sunflower seed and twirled it between his fingertips. He remembered when his fingers had tingled every time he'd handled this little seed. They weren't tingling now. He'd had trust once, not long ago. In the garden, he'd trusted the sunflower and climbed onto the bison to make a flying journey, goodness knows where to, and look what that trust accomplished: they were saved from a gruesome death by a bubble appearing from nowhere. *And flying through the night over a continent. It was incredible really.* Unbelievable. If you took the time to think about all their stories, each one was amazing. And not to be dismissed—or forgotten! He had to reach the others, make them listen. He thought of poor Jasmine's foot. But *listen to what?* Maybe that was the problem; they didn't fully understand the importance of their secrets. Or their power. Someone was very afraid of that power—that was obvious.

Another soaking on his head from Dobi caught him out again. "Okay, okay," Porky said, raising his hands in mock surrender. "I can hear you!"

He knew what he had to do—he had to convince them, but not just him. The secrets could do that by themselves. He was almost on his feet when he realised he hadn't solved the problem of Bina. But what was there to solve? She was missing and that was that. What could he do? He sat down again. He looked towards Dobi. *Any more answers?* Now his fingers were tingling, and strongly. Lastro called up unexpectedly, "What does Bina most admire you for?"

Porky thought about it for a minute or two. Okay—got it. *Thank you, Dobi,* he whispered to the deepest of the deep. Bina loved his passion.

Encouraged, he wandered back over to the café and let out an audible gasp of amazement that made the others jump. "Look at this!" he said, spreading his arms out to indicate their surroundings, which had been transformed into something new and really beautiful.

Next he ran over and gave Tante Renee a big hug. The old wooden tables had been transformed into brand new ones with small vases of flowers on each. The renovated kitchen gleamed and sparkled, stainless steel pots and pans stacked up on the shelves. Outside, long strings of onions and red peppers as well bunches of herbs hung from a red and white awning. Now the place looked pretty and inviting. The land all around the family's establishment heaved with fresh produce, ready for harvest. The Keepers walked around open-mouthed and sat down together, awestruck and, somehow, a little afraid. Tante Renee's husband returned from the factory just then; after turning round in circles with his hands on his head, he shook hands vigorously with Porky, who was the only one still standing. And so he stayed standing before them all—and ordered food. Mouth-watering, nourishing, and delightful food:

Starter: Fresh scallops in ginger and cream sauce with a fennel and dill garnish.

Main: Spicy fish cakes dotted with red berries and served with dollops of fresh yogurt plus seaweed and stir-fry cabbage.

Dessert: Fresh peaches and baked bananas topped with grated nutmeg. (Porky himself grated it.)

Drink: Water with a squoosh of squeezed orange juice and brown sugar.

Porky made himself useful by helping the couple serve at the table, all the time making announcements about the courses and their ingredients. He wasn't taking any credit, but he was taking control. He oozed with confidence, and his delight was catching. After a lot of praising of Tante Renee's wonderful cooking and the oohing and ahhing, a silence settled on the company as everyone got down to the serious business of eating. The food warmed and comforted and eased the tensions between the kids. Lastro winked at Porky.

♦

Bina could hold on no longer and felt herself falling downwards. She closed her eyes and said goodbye to her life and to Porky (she was to tell him afterwards when they compared their near-death experiences). If she had looked down, she would have seen a plug hole open up at the bottom of the swimming pool. The water was swirling rapidly round and round into it. Bina also became a liquid swirl of girl and the nutmeg a golden droplet suspended in her throat.

◆

During dessert, Porky mentioned the liquid food he'd had to bear in hospital. They listened in shock as he told them about his collapse in the school canteen and the dash in the ambulance. There was a hush around the table as he recounted the moment his heart stopped and how he'd seen himself from above and yelled, "No!" His account of the sunflower petals waving and speaking to him was met with wide-eyed nods.

Kitchi was the first to speak up. "So really, this whole thing started with you?"

"Maybe—yeah, I guess so."

"Hey dude, I'm sorry for what I said earlier. Of course we need you. We all need each other."

"We all make mistakes, Kitchi," Amy said, knowing only too well what it feels like to mess up.

"Porky," Jasmine said, "I am sorry, too. This pain is just too much to bear, but now I know you had pain too. Let us find this Keeper, Bina; we need her."

"Yes, good," Lastro said, smiling at Porky and winking again.

The carpet was dragged out and passed over to Porky. When he touched it, the lights came on, and everyone murmured approvingly. The golden droplets appeared once more. Again, six on the coastline of Djibouti, and there was one other. It was hovering above some mountains at the southern border of Ethiopia.

"That must be your Bina," Kitchi said, pointing. But just then, another droplet appeared high above their heads; they all said a collective "Wow!" It circled slowly downwards till it joined the other one on a mountain in Ethiopia.

"Eight," Porky said decisively, glancing at Serenity, who nodded.

Amy called out, "Hey look! The six are moving." The six droplets became one and were on their way to join the other two. They all looked silently at each other and got up without a word. Since the carpet remained its small size and, having nothing to pack, they did the only thing they could do. They hitched a lift.

CHAPTER 34

The Food Masters and the Zulu Climate-Change Monster

M r. Corporate slammed the phone down. Who was going to pay for this? He turned to his partner, Mr. Big, who was gazing out of the window with a tense look on his face. "The girl's missing." He paced the room a few times, cursing under his breath. "Have you any idea what this means?"

Mr. Big pushed his white Stetson to the back of his head and scratched his forehead. "I thought the mind-change process was complete?"

"*Almost* complete." Mr. Corporate lit another cigarette. "*And* she got that wretched nutmeg back."

"C'mon, you said yourself the lab tests revealed nothing."

But Mr. Corporate wouldn't be consoled. He sat back down at his desk and took lengthy drags on a cigarette, his face black as thunder. Picking up the phone again, he pressed a few buttons and said, "Block all exits and have the swimming pool area pumped full of toxic gas. I want the bats killed as well. No buts. That's an order."

"Hey that's more like it. Something needs to be done around here—and fast." "Maybe you're fixating on the wrong kid. What about that boy who went missing from the refugee camp in Kenya? You know, the Jesus-freak who was multiplying all the food?"

"I know the one," Mr. Corporate snapped; he was short-tempered today. "Well, the Maasai had him for a while. I thought that might have been the end of him—but no."

"Okay—so bring him in."

"What the hell for?"

"Well, you've been messing up all along, Corporate. I've had enough." Mr. Big began pacing the room anxiously, ranting and raving. "My farms are in ruins. How did all that livestock get loose? And the poultry—that's an even greater mess! I've lost everything. The Christmas orders—this is a disaster."

Mr. Corporate ignored this comment. He hated failure. He glanced up at the company map on the wall and imagined gaps in his victorious purple covering. His stomach ulcer went into spasm, and his heart arteries tightened. So he got up for another stroll around the room.

At the window offering a panoramic view of the city he paused and let his hands rest on that special box Mr Corporate opened it with trembling fingers and took out the crystal. Mr. Big looked on with distaste; he hated superstition of all kinds, and he particularly hated his partner's stupid attachment to this object. Mr. Corporate gazed into it for some time. His great-grandfather had owned a precious stones mine in the heart of Africa long, long ago. Mr. Corporate's father had seen stuff happen on account of that piece of rock. Stuff that would make your skin crawl.

Mr. Big got up and opened a window; he needed some air. "Don't get all hokey-pokey with me."

But Mr. Corporate was somewhere else now. Mr. Big caught a look at his partner's twisted face and picked up his jacket.

"No, Gus, don't go. I got it. We'll take the boy out. Maybe I was wrong about the ghouls. The Inkanyamba's the one. Zulu legend. It's on the move; Ethiopia's in for a wild time! No more worries."

"Aw—gimme a break!" And Mr. Big slammed the door shut.

♦

Abala and the Maasai warriors had said goodbye only two hours ago, but it felt like twenty. A wind had blown up almost immediately and was going against him, making his pace slow. And it was getting stronger and stronger. He wondered that the warriors hadn't warned him or given him advice about the weather. They usually knew all about these things. They had given him a flask (woven from grasses) of something to drink, though, so he sat down now to have some. The terrain was mountainous and craggy, but it was easy to find his way as long as he could see ahead of him. According to the position of the sun, he headed northeast, roughly towards home. Clouds were gathering; the clouds high up on the mountain tops were like mist. On looking down, he glimpsed a lake, which had been shining like a beacon in the distance. The lake peeked through a white veil of clouds, threatening to obliterate the view.

His refreshment was the familiar pink drink, which he had learned was a mixture of milk and fresh blood. He squeezed his eyes shut as he drank, pretending it was milk and strawberries. But it strengthened him from within; he could feel it working already. Now warm inside, he picked himself up to face the gusts of wind again. But soon, Abala was staggering from side to side, as if on a boat in a choppy sea. The growing veil of mist was making it hard to see ahead, hiding possible places to grab onto: stubby branches or handles of rock. Panic rose in his chest and fear rushed in with it; he'd have to spend the night on this mountain. This was not good. It would be cold, and he had no blanket. He comforted himself with the thought of covering himself with leafy branches; he'd seen plenty of them around. A black hole appeared ahead before suddenly disappearing behind a wall of white cloud. *A cave!* Making for it was now his only thought.

Stumbling along like a sleep walker, Abala felt a sharp ping on the back of his head. Before he had time to raise his hand to investigate, another caught the side of his face. Its sting burnt so bad, he thought he'd been hit by an arrow, till lumps the size of ping pong balls started bouncing everywhere on all sides. Balls of ice like Abala had never seen. The black hole of the cave received him now like a mouth; he didn't know which to be afraid of more: the deep blackness or the weapons being thrown down on him from the hand of the storm. Exhausted and panting wildly, he threw himself inside, scraping the length of his right leg. His groans of pain were drowned out by the tight popping sounds of the hailstones as they pinged off the rock face for the next hour.

When the assault was over, the thick whiteness of the sky cleared somewhat, and from where Abala lay, bruised and grazed, he watched the sky moving and changing. Black and white and grey swirling clouds took on shapes and mesmerised him; he thought he saw two birds flying round and round, up and down, and thought of the birds which led him into the wood to rest after fleeing from the camp. His thoughts flew back to Sally, painting him with sticky paste. Then his mother kneading the sweet-smelling *injera* dough, humming gently. Tears welled up behind his eyes. He closed them tight. No crying. No crying. But on reopening them, a more terrible sight awaited. The whole of the darkened sky greeted him with a crooked smile. A black and grey cloud face leered at him; it came in close, so close that Abala put his arm up to shield his face, fearing it would squeeze inside the cave. But it pulled back and widened the length and breadth of the heavens, blowing its pent-up fury over the mountain side till the trees and bushes became horizontal. And then it was breathing his name: *Abala, Abala.* Eerily . . . over and over. *It is the end, Abala. Abala.* Till he could bear it no more and covered his ears and shut his eyes. But shaking in fear, all the same.

Stillness followed. Abala dared to open one eye. The ground outside was white. This time with snow. Every branch and leaf, every boulder was being reshaped into a oneness. A bird landed on a white bush, let out a long low note, and stayed where it was. Abala wondered why it didn't fly away, when it fell to the side with a light thud, frozen through. He lay and watched a slug labour towards him, only to meet the same fate and become a sliver of ice. He sat up then and pulled his legs to his chest, shivering. If he ventured outside, he could get lost and freeze overnight, like the bird. If he stayed inside the cave . . . but he had no covering and he was hungry; would he become . . . like the slug?

So he sat and thought of the piping hot and spicy Ethiopian coffee he had poured out for the laughing men in the camp. How he wished he had a small cup to warm his hands on now. There was no sound outside, only a low whistling of the wind in the distance. He heard the sound of his pulse next to his eyes, like a drumbeat. So loud. The sky was darkening outside. He remembered the smiling faces of the Maasai as they licked their bowls of sweet honey milk. His pulse became a drumbeat. The beat of the drum the refugees played at the feast in the dining tent; he saw himself being bounced up and down on the shoulders of one. The scene became slow motion; everyone was smiling widely. Sally came into view, mouthing something at him. What was it? Oh yes . . . *I'll tell Porky.* Porky? Who was Porky? The drumbeat slowed. He saw himself slowly, ever so slowly, raise his hand in a thumbs-up. He was cold and numb. His mind became an aching question mark, and then he saw Grandfather sitting far away in the distance, against the wall of their hut. Grandfather raised his stick. And then blackness.

Bina dropped with a heavy thud and a splash outside the entrance to the cave. The night sky was alive with the whirling of silent snowflakes. She immediately saw the cave and scrambled in its direction for shelter, but she tripped on something and fell inside instead. She slid on the icy cave floor and collided with the back wall. On spinning back round, she came face to face with a large block of ice. Inside the block, reflected in the whiteness of the snowstorm outside, a face could be clearly seen. A dark boy looked out at her, eyes wide open, staring. The shock made her whole body jump, and if it had not been for the nutmeg lodged in her mouth, Bina would have screamed blue murder. She spat it out in case she choked. It rolled over to the mouth of the cave. She knew she had better get it back, because it was precious, but she was afraid to move. At the same time, she wanted more than anything to get away from those two dark, staring eyes. A fluttering noise broke her rigidity; it was a bird struggling to get free from something. Crawling over, she saw what the problem was: its legs were held under a carob pod, which her nutmeg was resting up against. Where the objects lay, the ground was hot and steamy. Bina removed the nutmeg and shards of ice fell from the bird's wings as it flew up and away.

Picking the two objects up and dared a glance back inside the cave. Abala sat, soaking wet and rubbing his eyes. He saw the carob pod in her hand. "That is mine," he said with a weak and faraway smile.

The Inkanyamba retreated down the valley, crouched behind a mountain, and waited.

CHAPTER 35

The Eight Secrets Together at Last

T he first vehicle bound for Ethiopia that came along was a truck piled high with watermelons. It was on its way to Addis Ababa. The driver must have been a man of great patience; number one: to have stopped in the first place, and two: to have waited so long as they all clambered aboard. He kindly carried Jasmine and placed her comfortably in the front compartment with him. They tried to get settled on top and in between the round green melons, but it wasn't easy. The Keepers were each left to their own thoughts as the truck bounced up and down on the rutted roads and the scenery of Djibouti went by.

Lastro was perched in the highest position, just behind the driver's cabin, which gave him a good view of the sea, so he could pick out Dobi setting off on his homeward journey, Sergio by his side. He wished them well and went over those days spent inside his giant friend's belly in silent wonder.

Jasmine closed her eyes and rested. The terrible pain in her foot was now reduced to a warm throb, and she found relief at last from the burning anger that had consumed her since the ghoul incident.

Amy was glad to be travelling on four wheels after her flying and sliding adventures. She remembered the last leg of her amazing escape when she hugged a big seed in the giant seed pod. She put her arms round a melon and did the same again.

Serenity clutched onto the piece of bark stored in her pocket. She was keeping it for emergencies; she feared that Jasmine's foot would not recover if she didn't find some suitable medicinal plants soon. Scanning the countryside, she was doubtful; poor and scrubby farms occasionally appeared, but mostly the land looked barren and dry. There were no woodlands or forests under which those special plants and bushes could nestle. The main highway was lined with billboards advertising all kinds of things. One had the cheek to announce: *To the graduating students of Djibouti University: Congratulations from Queen Burger! Come and celebrate with us.* Serenity hoped Porky hadn't seen it.

Kitchi looked at little Hassan, swaying backwards and forwards while nodding off to sleep, still holding tightly onto the rolled-up carpet. He was pleased he'd made up with Porky. He stole a glance over at him and noticed he was deep in thought. Probably thinking of that girlfriend of his. A huge wave of pity came over Kitchi as he realised, for the first time, how painful that separation must be.

And Porky—reinstated as leader—was hugely relieved that they were on their way again. He *had* seen the sign for Queen Burger and felt revolted. And, of course, angry. Supersized angry, even! He was shocked at what he'd done back in the town. Going back to those old habits just like that. He puzzled over it; something had made him do it, he knew it. Something had made him fall out with the others, and they had become hostile to him. The more he thought about it, he was convinced the same force behind the ghouls and the Wendigo was responsible. And that made him all the more concerned that Bina (one of the golden droplets) was in some horrible danger, now that he knew she wasn't with Ajit. How strange that she was in Africa too . . . but who was the eighth?

The Inkanyamba, even in a crouching position, could see over the top of the rocky peak and far beyond across mountains and lakes to the coast road winding slowly inland. The truck load of melons and its other precious cargo was easily spotted by this monster of the Zulus, with the power to change the climate. And it could change its size just as easily. A look of cunning flickered across its wide grinning face, which suddenly became a narrow twist of smoky wind that turned to face the valley and whirled, moaning loudly and creepily, down to its destination.

Night fell soon after they crossed the border (hidden under a tarpaulin cover), and the truck drearily ploughed onwards through the darkness. The six all slept, slumped over the melons in the back of the truck, which was little better than lying on boulders or rocks. About two hours before daybreak, a wind blew up, which was unusual for that time of year. The truck driver was very experienced; although he knew the road like the back of his hand, he began to feel nervous. Especially when he saw a dark twist in the sky in front of them, coming down from the mountainous country beyond Addis Ababa. The twist thickened until it filled half the sky with a black swirling mass of dark wind, screaming like a freight train in the night. They stood no chance and joined the other casualties of the night: cows and sheep, vehicles, and many wooden buildings minus their roofs; planks of wood spun wildly in the air. One narrowly missed Porky's head.

"Whoa!" he yelled. "Get your heads down!" But it was doubtful anyone heard him. Their ride skidded over to the other side of the road and overturned; the melons split on impact, their pink innards spewing onto the tarmac. Porky knew a bash like that would mean certain death and screamed for everyone to take action: "Roll to the side!" he yelled.

As light oozed gently from the horizon, he counted five Keepers safely curled up in tight balls; he pulled himself up to go and check on Jasmine.

Looking up at the sky, he could have sworn he saw a leering face swoop in as if coming to get him, perhaps scoop him up with its long tentacle-like arms. But off the cloud went, calmer, not so loud but still eerie, moaning as it twirled and unfurled on its way southwest again. To where? Jasmine was all right, just some cuts to her face and head. But the driver took one look at the damage, gave Porky a terrified look, shook his fist at him, and ran away fast.

Amy and Kitchi were helping Jasmine slide out of the truck's window when Porky saw it: a tattered remnant of a Queen Burger advertisement, wrapped around a bent electricity pole. He could still make out the fluttering words: *Fastest Growing Fast Food Chain,* and he burned with anger. It was them; he knew it was them. All that was behind that industry and others like it wanted the Keepers stopped or, worse still, killed. Because the Keepers had the secrets that, if the whole world knew . . .

But someone was calling him: "Porky! Porky!" It was Kitchi. "C'mon—this is no time for sitting and thinking—we've got to *do* something!"

Kitchi's eyes met his knowingly; the tense look of a warrior under threat—waiting for the command.

What to do? Porky thought hard but didn't know what to do next. His eyes followed the line of black clouds leading towards the mountains. *Bina!* His chest nearly caved in.

Jasmine saw his upwards gaze and said, "We're *not* going anywhere near that thing again. C'mon, we've got to go back to Dijbouti, to a town, a safe house—something!"

"No. No—we have to go up there. The last two Keepers are in those mountains. Remember what the carpet told us? They need us. They need our help."

"*They* need *our* help? *Really?*"

Jasmine opened her mouth to start again when Amy spoke up. "Porky's right," she said. "We've got this far. And we've followed the signs all the way. I know what will happen if we do it our own way—or worse still, give up now. I did it once—messed up, I mean. Don't. We have to follow the signs." Her face was flushed with a passion not expressed before; Kitchi laid a hand on her shoulder. She squeezed it and smiled at him.

"Okay, okay . . . so where is the sign?" Jasmine asked, turning both palms up to the sky. The sky, now clear of all storms and clouds, was, in fact, bright blue. And it was getting very, very hot. Sweat glistened on their faces.

Serenity was turning over her piece of bark in her hand; she said, "Porky, you know that seed that you carry? And Jasmine—what about your date? What if we . . ."

But there was no time for what she had to say next—if they could listen, that is. Because no action was needed, Mother Nature had it in hand, as she had all along. For the sky was filling up with birds, birds of all shapes and sizes. Birds from Norway and Germany. Some from Britain and even Canada. All migrating birds needing to fly farther than they had two years ago; birds with issues too. The noise was unbelievable! Chirping, singing, squawking, and screeching of all sorts silenced the six as they stood craning their necks upwards.

The birds made the usual V shapes that they do when they fly long distances. They made a V around each Keeper (two around Jasmine, for extra support) and hovered above the ground, surrounding them all. And up they went, flying magically without any real support—but *something* kept them up! They travelled this way for nearly four hours with no storms or winds opposing them. However, there was a new challenge: the heat from the sun, which beat down on them mercilessly.

♦

Before Abala and Bina could exchange names, the sound of running water, from the melting snow and ice, reverberated all around and began rushing down the mountain side. And as Bina passed the carob pod to Abala, he gripped onto her hand and mouthed, against the loud background of water gushing, *Thank you.* Bina pressed her hands holding the nutmeg into his and squeezed tight; and they stood smiling into each other's faces like complete idiots—too delirious for words at finding each other, at being set free, at sharing secrets from the beginning of the world (which deep down they both knew). And had they known what was happening in fields across Africa, and other poor nations where people's livelihoods had been seized, they would be hugging each other tighter still. They set off slowly down the mountain, the brilliant white light of the moon guiding them, to a warmer place.

In nearly every area within Ethiopia itself, in some parts of Sudan and Somalia, and even in Uganda, fields were delivered back into the hands of the farmers who had once owned them. Families started planting straight away; the crops grew to dizzying heights almost immediately.

♦

Slowly, slowly the giant throng descended; Porky could see people tending their fields, their heads covered from the burning sun, looking up at them and pointing. He was surprised at how many small farms there were in the area; he'd somehow always thought of Ethiopians as poor and needy. He squinted through the sun's glare to where they were heading. Further inland to where he believed Bina was—and the other golden droplet. But what was that? White smoke puffed up in several places from woodland on the distant hills. Fire? His brows creased; he stretched himself up and squinted again. Maybe someone would put it out. But who— up here? A sharper descent now; Porky worried about the fire, remembering the line of black clouds leading to the mountains and the terrifying face that had taunted him.

They swooped down suddenly to land. Kitchi caught his breath and winked over at Lastro, saying, "How's that for a thrilling ride through the world of Nature!"

Lastro, having never travelled except by sea, could only raise his eyebrows. They all jumped out of the sky, landing on both feet (except Jasmine, who rolled) on some very dry and brittle grass. At first glance, the place was a complete disappointment. Mainly because there was nothing there; nothing that was any good to anyone, that is, and they were all very hungry. Each went searching around but only came face to face with damage from the hot, scorching sun. Where there weren't briars and thorns, the only shrubs had yellowed leaves and dried-up berries. Porky felt the soil; it was hard and couldn't yield anything worth eating. Lastro came running back, glum-faced, and announced that he hadn't found any running water. They all knew what this meant and, desperate to get out of the burning sun, crouched despondently together under a thorny bush, whose branches spread out like low wings. Nobody spoke, but they all knew what they wanted to say. Porky could feel it, but his first concern remained the forest fire, and he kept one eye on the now billowing smoke some distance above them.

Eventually, Jasmine broke the silence, saying, "Does that crackling noise mean the fire is getting closer?"

Porky felt his stomach muscles tighten; he would have to decide on a plan within the next few minutes. He had five Keepers to lead to safety out of the hot, burning sun in a place where nothing would grow, with a rapidly approaching forest fire and no water in sight. Great. What next?

Serenity piped up, "Look—I was trying to say before the birds came, that . . . well, things keep happening . . . I mean, it's about the objects we've got. You know, Porky's sunflower and Jasmine's date . . . We could . . ."

"It's not about making magic!" scoffed Kitchi. "What're you going to do? Wave that piece of bark in the air and say, 'Pibbery-Pobbery-Poo'?"

Lastro and Hassan sniggered. No one else offered a comment, mostly through feeling unbearably hot, but also because the birds, which had been resting after their long journey, began making a terrible racket. And then put on an incredible flying show. The six even ventured out of the shade to fully appreciate this amazing display of diving and swooping, coming together and making huge, yet beautiful, shapes before breaking up and shooting out in opposite directions, then coming together in a massive cone or diamond. It went on for five full minutes, enough time for Bina and Abala to notice from the place farther up, where they were also taking shelter from the sun.

♦

"What does it mean?" Bina asked Abala, for she knew by now that this was his country.

He shook his head; he didn't know. "But I think it is a sign. We should follow. Birds have helped me before." And he told her about his long walk in Kenya. It was then that they, too, saw the smoke as the fire spread around the side of the mountain towards them.

"We can't go that way—there's a fire!"

Bina was shocked, and for a moment or two, they both contemplated how to get out of this one.

"If the power that your nutmeg has melted the ice, it can put out the fire too," Abala said confidently, smiling.

"I think it is more about both of us together. Being together, I mean."

Abala looked at the approaching fire. "Okay. So . . . ?"

"Let us go." And she took his hand. They walked towards the heat and the crackling, the smoke beginning to make their eyes smart. In his mind, Abala heard the words *Share this bread as a symbol of our bonds.* He said it over and over to himself, just as Bina thought of Karna and, for some ridiculous reason, the way she had first understood her secret: *Just like the cats in Mrs. Luta's garden.* Within fifty metres of the edge of the fire, a whooshing noise made them jump. A falling sheet of water flew above their heads; the water that had melted from the Ice Age on the top of the mountain had been diverted to come their way. It quenched the fire in no time and then made its way downwards as a gurgling, innocent-looking stream.

♦

The others saw the smoke change colour and heard the hissing as the water quashed the flames. Porky whispered a million thank-yous. The noise of running water could be heard near them too;

Lastro led the way to the stream. They all lay down and lapped up water like animals at a long-awaited watering hole, and then they sat up and laughed at how funny they looked. Porky was smiling broadly at last, and an idea came to his mind. Cupping his hands in the stream, he poured fresh water on the hard ground; taking some of the dried-up berries, he scooped out a hole and buried them. The result was instantaneous: the berry plant became a young bush in no time, yielding almost fluorescent green leaves and bright red berries the size of small apples. Everyone was upon them at once, their hunger pushing aside all manners. A few minutes passed, during which all that could be heard was crunching and then slurping, and they all laughed at Hassan, sucking his fingers.

Thousands and thousands of acres upon acres in North America's vast empty spaces and Europe's farming heartland were transformed from monotonous rows of corn and soya plants into patches of land boasting over two hundred species of edible plants each: peas, beans, potatoes, carrots, onions, asparagus, pears, cherries, kiwis, apricots, peaches, melons, and berries: blueberries, strawberries, mulberries . . . and trees too. There were oak, olive, apple, and chestnut, to name but a few. At the side of the road, massive tractors (worth $250,000) began to rust.

Only Porky saw it, the Inkanyamba, as it fled downwards, losing strength and power, turning round and round on itself like a deflating balloon, leaving pathetic wisps of white mist trailing behind.

Sitting and lying on the hard, parched ground became easier for the friends, as tufts of softer grasses emerged, growing quickly. The blazing sun went behind a cloud and reappeared again as a soft, yellow disc; cool and welcomed breezes ruffled their hair. Hassan noticed him first. He let out a kind of yelp and pointed, making everyone turn around. At the opening to the little glade they were resting in stood an Ethiopian boy.

♦

They had argued about the place. After the fire went out, the *others'* voices could be clearly heard. Abala wanted to go to them immediately, but Bina felt the need to go in another direction. "That is not the place," she stated, becoming agitated, for the first time her voice slightly whining. Abala couldn't understand.

"There are people there—we should go to them," he said.

But Bina was feeling a pull, a strong pull, leading her in the other direction. A tangible pull that she couldn't resist. Images of Karna were flooding her mind: how Mrs. Luta had called out, *You need this* and thrown her the huge nutmeg, how her body had warmed up and her head swum when she ate the fragrant dish prepared just for her. Just as her body was hot and throbbing now, and her fingers tingled as she clutched tightly to the nutmeg. She turned around and started walking, Abala following obediently behind (*Just to see,* he told himself). They padded along single file, like two great mountain cats, sometimes passing a rocky outcrop or two, heading it seemed to Abala towards a sparse-looking wood growing on a headland jutting out slightly from the mountain face. Bina stopped suddenly; she had seen something. And she knew. "This is the place," she said to Abala, pointing. "I will wait here."

He said, "And I will bring the *others.*" She nodded and smiled, suddenly looking really happy. Abala was to wonder afterwards why he had said "the *others.*" At the time, it had felt like the right thing to say, and as he retraced his steps in the direction of the voices, he had the odd, but pleasant, feeling that this, at last, was the culmination of all he had been through, from meeting the group of villagers fleeing danger like him, to being in the camp, escaping and meeting the Maasai, and finally the girl who rescued him. And he also knew that he was host to these newcomers, strangers in his own country, that he was Abala Alemayehu Zerihun, and this moment was destined to make his grandfather proud.

♦

On seeing Abala, Porky couldn't help himself—but he was instantly and so crushingly disappointed that he bounded over, all quivering strength and muscle, and found himself shouting, "Where's the other one! Where is she?"

"Calm down, man!" Kitchi said, clapping a hand on each of Porky's shoulders, steadying him.

Porky towered over Abala and looked close up into his face; he asked, "Is she here?"

Abala could feel Porky's body shaking through the ground; he looked into his frantic eyes and understood. He didn't know Bina's name, so mimicked her distinctive dress using hand movements.

"What *is* he doing?" Serenity asked, exchanging glances with Jasmine. But Porky had told Amy that Bina was from India, so it clicked with her as she watched Abala draw out a sari around his own body, flicking the long scarf backwards over his shoulder as Bina repeatedly did.

She jumped up and called out, "Yes, yes . . . Bina, Bina!" She clapped her hands in the air and attempted (rather badly) to perform some Indian dance steps.

They were all smiling and relieved for Porky, patting him on the back. Abala, observing the band of *others,* noticed that, despite the smiles, they were extremely dishevelled and wearied. His glance took in Jasmine's bandaged leg. Perhaps it was not such a good idea to introduce them to the seriousness of Bina's place quite so soon. They had needs, and he was host, after all. It occurred to him how much they all needed the sustenance of the Maasai drink of pure blood and milk, but not having that to hand, he tried something else. He'd already spotted an abundance of tall crimson-stalked plants capped with umbrellas of tiny white flowers. He knew that his mother and aunties used to make sweets from the stalks, for celebrations like weddings. Not knowing how to make sweets, Abala simply picked some stalks, broke them into small pieces, and smiling around at everyone, started rubbing them between his palms. The resulting pieces of candied pink stalk, miraculously sprinkled with a dusting of sugar, caused squeals of delight.

Over all of Ethiopia, Somalia, and many of their neighbours, there was great merriment as families sat down to a feast from their harvest. The first harvest from their own fields for many a decade.

Now it was time to follow him, in single file (except for Jasmine, who hopped, held up between Porky and Kitchi's shoulders). Slowly upwards they went on a winding path, scrubland burnt by the fire on either side; even the trunks of the sparse trees were scorched. They could see a small wood of shifara trees ahead, looking welcoming. They felt the welcome in another way too; the closer they got, the more they felt the *pull*. Just as Bina had tried to explain; they all felt strangely pulled forward till it was impossible to resist, and they had to run. Poor Jasmine—it was a struggle for her—so the two boys lifted her up and swung her like a small child.

They almost tumbled and collapsed into the space—a copse it was, really. Running water could be heard nearby, and strange, pale rocks of varying sizes stuck out of the ground at weird angles. In the middle was a huge, brown tree stump. They stood, turning round and round, looking up and down and all around—expectant. No one dared speak, but Kitchi, catching the wild-eyed and desperate look on Porky's face, marched over to Abala to demand Bina's whereabouts. But before he could do so, Porky saw a giant nutmeg sticking out of a hole on the face of the stump. Hassan was running his hand over it and all the other odd-shaped holes. Amy, Serenity, and Lastro crowded round. Serenity squealed, "I told you! I was right!" But she was ignored, because at that moment, Bina appeared.

She had approached them from behind a small, raised mound; through some overgrown honeysuckle and jasmine bushes, their white and fragrant flowers were still clinging to her hair and falling onto her shoulders. She looked surprised to see so many people and surveyed them back and forth at speed, looking for someone. And she found him. His green eyes pierced hers. His face was red and tense, and he looked different in other ways too: he was slimmer, much slimmer, making him look taller and stronger, but he was still unmistakably her Porky. And he was wearing a short Arab dress, complete with a white headdress! She didn't want to think about why now. She only wanted to be safe in his arms again. And now he was close to her, picking her up—so easily! Now she was suspended in the air but held tight—crushed against him. He covered her face and neck with kisses.

Lastro and Hassan looked away, embarrassed. Kitchi tried to look at Amy, but she avoided his gaze and turned away too, with a pained expression on her face. Serenity was closely examining the tree stump and then turned to the others, smiling a deeply satisfied smile.

The Inkanyamba began whimpering and retreated farther down the mountainside.

Serenity, exhilarated by her find, charged towards Porky and Bina, grabbing handfuls of leaves, berries, and blossoms as she did. Showering the happy couple with petals and leaves and leaping excitedly round and about them, she was screeching, "I know why! I was right!" She skipped back to the girls and shoved green stuff at them too. Soon everyone was throwing foliage and flowers onto the beaming Porky and Bina. Hassan and Lastro overcame their embarrassment by throwing berries at each other.

When all the hilarity had finally calmed down and introductions were made, Serenity pulled Bina towards the tree stump and pointed to the nutmeg. "Look, your nutmeg! And there are places for all of us." She pointed to a tiny sliver of a hole. "There's the one for Porky's seed—and over there, that's the one for Kitchi's horn. What do you think? And—why?"

"Because this is the place," Bina answered simply.

"I knew it! Yes, this is *our* special place!"

Bina began again, "Well, maybe not just *our* . . ."

But Serenity wasn't listening; she'd started pulling the others towards the stump, and everyone placed their symbol in its appropriate hole.

Abala had been feeling uncomfortable because, as host, it was his responsibility to make sure everyone had proper refreshments and rest. It was customary to make a real feast for any strangers visiting an Ethiopian village, and he was a little nervous about how he was going to provide it. *Would saying Grandfather's prayer be enough?* he wondered. When he placed his carob pod in the hole in the face of the stump, his feeling of urgency increased.

On popping his horn into the tree stump, Kitchi could see that the symbols together were making the shape of a tree. He pointed this out to Lastro, as he laid down his coral, which fitted perfectly too. "Yes. You are right. A great tree, too," he agreed, looking around for one the same shape. But there were none to be seen.

Once all of the other Keepers' objects—the seed, horn, carob pod, date, wild rice, bark, coral, and nutmeg—had been deposited, the shape was intact, the puzzle complete. Together they made a picture of a huge and strong tree; with the nutmeg as the stump and roots, the carob pod a trunk, and all the other objects in the branches.

"Wow!"

"How beautiful!"

Everyone *Ooooohed* and *Ahhhhhed* over the tree picture for some time, until gradually, a wearied silence overtook them, and they all sat looking around at each other as if to say, "So what now?"

They had little idea that for the first time ever, huge supermarket chains around the world—in New York, Montreal, London, Rome, Cairo, Beirut, Mumbai, Lahore, Bangkok, Singapore, and Sydney—had empty shelves. Crowds of people flooded the streets, looking for another place from which to buy food.

It was Kitchi's idea to build a fire; they all busied themselves with finding wood, and poor little Hassan was given the tiring job of rubbing sticks together to make a spark, as the sun was far too low in the sky to be used. But eventually it worked (it took him over half an hour), and soon a good size bonfire warmed the friends. The girls found some low nut bushes and returned with their hands full. They munched on nuts and gazed silently at the bright fire against the darkening sky. Abala remembered the last time he sat around a bonfire: at the dinner with the group of refugees he joined. There was dinner then; now there wasn't. He burned with shame and wondered what to say next. For some reason, the enormity of being back home, in the centre of Ethiopia, had made him forget about Grandfather's prayer. The Keepers sat in silence, exhausted. Only Porky noticed that the tree shape made up of the symbols was glowing. Blue.

CHAPTER 36

A Neolithic Village

D usk was gathering; it would soon be dark under the shifara trees. The Keepers continued to stare into the flames. Porky waited, holding Bina close to him, aware that this was an important moment, the culminating moment of a long and treacherous journey. He thought he might just creep over and peek at the glowing tree stump, but then Abala said, "You know, Porky—I never thanked you." Porky tried to answer, but Abala stopped him. "No, really. You brought everyone here—to my homeland." Porky nodded strangely, Bina style, humbly, wanting to shrug off recognition. Abala continued, "I have been alone, going from place to place. My land is gone, you see. My family killed. They grabbed our land from us. We have nothing left." In the quietness, the *others* listened intently.

As Abala described the details of that fateful day, all were thinking of what they had escaped from and of the signs that drove them onwards. "Soon there'll be nothing left of the rainforests, either," Serenity added.

"No wild rice left," Amy murmured, nodding. "Only GMOs. That must be true of so much else as well."

The *others* offered low grunts of agreement. Everyone was too tired to say *Well, what are we doing here?* or *What now?*

"Like whales," Lastro piped up finally. Bina was shaking her head firmly, meaning yes, when she let out a gasp.

"Look!" she whispered. A blue light was approaching the copse. Then followed more: two, three, four droplets of light, similar in shape to the golden droplets, but blue in hue. Porky counted fifteen in all. They flitted to and fro, between the trees.

Bina and Porky roused the others with hushed tones. They rubbed their eyes only to see the blue droplets elongate and become shafts of pale blue light, moving in and out of the trees and circling the stump. Porky felt his fingers tingle; clutching Bina's hand, he whispered, "Can you feel it too?" She nodded, her face serious.

"This is it. This is the meaning of it all," she whispered back and held tightly on. She felt Porky's whole body quivering slightly.

They all stared, not daring to move. It was then that the music started, music like the tinkling of little bells or chimes. What with the flitting light shafts and the magical music—the result was mesmerising. The nine kids were entranced, their eyes wide, now and then glancing at each other nervously. But nobody spoke.

The whole copse had become sheathed in blue light, the shafts of light undulating and darkening till they took on shapes—human shapes. Amy let out a gasp. Serenity and Jasmine were holding onto each other, and Hassan looked like he wanted to cry. The blue and slightly transparent humans were shorter than average, partially clothed, with small heads and bodies that were a little hunched over. They were all busy at tasks: fetching, carrying and chopping, and banging away at things. Abala thought the banging was an action that looked like crushing wheat. Some entered the copse from the left, carrying animals over their shoulders. *Coming back from the hunt,* murmured Kitchi to himself. Others, with water pots on their heads, came from the direction of the gurgling stream. The music changed; the tinkling bells became higher pitched, as some children ran in and out of the scene. Their movements were so fast and playful they appeared like wisps of blue smoke. Other shifting shapes looked like animals, maybe goats, chickens, and ducks. In the Keepers' minds it was clear: it was a family scene . . . and they were making food.

Serenity was sure she saw small rounded shapes in the background, like dwellings, somewhere near the strange-shaped rocks. Amy noticed them too. Some drumbeats started up, and the chatter of these ancient people filtered in through the music. Porky wondered, with his heart beating fast, if the strange humans could see them. Abala had a lump growing in his throat. Smells wafted over: roasting meat and the sweet, sweet smell of *injera* bread baking. Abala held his breath as he realised he was watching his ancestors, who knew the secrets, who had always known the secrets.

The drumbeats intensified as the pre-historic people sat around the feast spread out on the ground. Lastro glanced up through the shifara branches; the sky was black, and he could see the stars twinkling. Then she came. Gliding out of the woods, a tall, regal figure sat on the still glowing tree stump in the centre of the gathering. She wore her hair coiled round and round on top of her head, like a curved pillar. Her face still had the pale blue hue of the others, though it was decorated with engravings of leaves and flowers. The others, who had ceased all activity since the regal lady had joined them, came forward in twos and threes and offered her some of their prepared feast. Next, she lifted her decorated arms, as if in worship, palms upwards, and said, in a voice that was like chimes blowing in the wind, *Thank you that we live another day and share this bread, which you have ordained the land to freely give, as a symbol of our bonds.*

Abala looked down at his hands—they were shaking. Tears pricked at his eyes. He had understood every word of her ancient tongue. Grandfather's prayer, which had become his own, had come from the beginning of civilisation itself, from Neolithic times. His ancestors had passed his secret down through the ages to his own family. And now to him, and to his friends, the Keepers. And it was soon to be released to the rest of the world.

A woman approached and wrapped a poultice of sticky leaves around Jasmine's foot. And then food was brought to where the Keepers were sitting and laid on the ground. What wonderful smells! Abala recognised the dishes immediately: *Quanta fir fir* (made with game, not beef), chicken in *berbere* sauce, spicy beans in ginger and red pepper. Telba drink was poured out for them. If there was any doubt that the people were real, there was none about the food! It was real enough, and they devoured it as if they'd never seen food before. Until something happened to make them stop, mid-mouthful: The woman began to sing.

Her voice was like no other ever heard before: warm, earthy, and rich. The words rang out in time with the drumbeats:

Beautiful, Beautiful;

The Earth yields its fruit.

Bountiful, Bountiful;

The soil knows its worth.

Abundantly, Abundantly;

The Earth gives variety;

For All, for All,

Enough for All.

Healthily, Healthily;

Earth's leaves heal our bodies.

Together, Together;

Animals and humans survive,

Because food is alive;

Food is alive.

The Secrets come together;

As One, as One;

No more bondage, no more slavery.

The eight come together;

One Truth, one Truth.

You Are What You Eat,

You Are What You Eat,

You Are What You Eat.

The refrain echoed for some time among the shifara trees, along with the wind rustling their leaves, sounding like rushing water. But it was replaced by a rumbling; the ground was vibrating under them. The friends looked at each other, looks of angst replacing their dreamy expressions. The vibrating was growing; shaking was a better word. Panic seized the girls, and they clung to each other, yelping like scared animals. The copse was still bathed in blue light, but the figures were gone. Flocks of sleeping birds woke up, fluttered anxiously out of the branches in flurries, and made off into the night sky. The sight of the birds leaving them caused Amy's heart to thud deep into her stomach; she could read the signs, and this looked bad.

As they huddled together, huge raindrops began to descend on them, making huge plops on the dry ground. Within a minute, the drops had become a sheet; it was as if a waterfall was cascading right in front of their eyes. Soon they stood knee deep in water and had to stop Hassan and Lastro from sliding away down a slope. But a strong light shone into their faces at the same moment the wind and rain stopped. It was blinding.

But only for a moment. In the subdued light that followed, that hung in the air like a screen, a beautiful tree appeared. Massive. Ten times bigger than any tree Abala had ever seen in his country. It was made of incredibly bright colours; the branches were colours that the kids thought they recognised and then, in the next second, realised they didn't. It was covered in fruit of enormous proportions. Perhaps each one could feed a village. It was breathtaking and, in the same moment, petrifying to behold. Jasmine was shaking so much she heard her teeth chattering.

Then a voice came, neither male nor female: "Look upon the Earth. Look—take and eat!"

The Inkanyamba writhed on the ground in horror. It screeched in pain. It made one contorted shape after another, moaning terribly till it shrunk up and withered and lay on the ground like a piece of black ash that flutters out of a dying fire.

♦

Somewhere in a capital city, Mr. Corporate sat, with his head in his hands, looking at the shaded purple area on his map, moving inwards towards the centre; his empire was shrinking before his very eyes. Phones were ringing on his desk, then going to answer machine. He heard Mr. Big bellowing, "There are no animals in my farms!" Above the din, Mr. Corporate could make out a knocking at his office door, which quickly became a fist banging. He pulled himself up from his chair, walked out of the double doors that led to the balcony, and just kept on walking. He wasn't as lucky as the Inkanyamba, though. His jacket got caught on a flagpole, fifty floors down.

♦

Finding no food in the supermarkets and shops, people turned back to the land. They explored the countryside and found real farms, with fields holding free and healthy livestock and brimming over with fresh produce ready for harvesting.

And suddenly it was dawn; they had been awake all night! They heard shouts. People were all around, real people this time, local Ethiopians. But they hadn't come to see the visitors—they had come to see the tree. The huge and magnificent and mighty ash, which had been missing for hundreds of years, could be seen from a distance all around. It had grown overnight from the stump. There was no trace of the ghostly Neolithic village. The pale stones stood sticking out of the ground at right angles like before. But the site was now as busy as any tourist spot. Coffee was being passed out by the local villagers. Someone else had brought spicy fruit-filled bread. Children picked up ash keys from the ground for their mothers to roast at home. Abala conversed with his people at full speed, all the time sporting a wide, toothy grin. He brought his friends over some spicy bread and warm coffee, which truly warmed their hearts as they listened to him introduce a cousin or a neighbour, and then as the cousin or neighbour told the story (for the umpteenth time) of the great tree and how it had been felled hundreds of years ago by a wealthy landowner, consumed by greed.

And later the same day, volunteers and whole families helped pick strawberries, raspberries, and blueberries and apples, peaches, and apricots from orchards and fields across small farms all over the world. Others worked together to distribute locally harvested vegetables and fruit into marketplaces to be purchased. Everyone had just enough.

Bina took hold of Porky's arm and whispered that it was time to leave. And so it was time for goodbyes. Abala stood in the middle of the group, and they all put their arms around him. It was hard to let go again. A hush fell over the crowd as they looked on. Abala wept. Not in sadness, but tears of joy and relief. Lastro caused a ripple of laughter when he high-fived Kitchi, calling out, "How was that for an incredible journey through the world of Nature?"

The little group broke up suddenly to Amy's yells and squeals:

"Jasmine—your foot!" When everyone looked, they saw that Jasmine had been walking normally since waking up. She pulled off the bandages, and there it was, complete and new: her beautiful foot. And so Jasmine was hugged by the group this time, but not for long, as she was in a hurry to show off her running skills.

Masses of new trees, bushes, creepers, and flowers grew in abundance in the once-cleared tropical rainforests of the Earth. Packets of pharmaceutical drugs worldwide reached their expiry dates and became obsolete.

Soon, they piled into the back of a local farmer's pick-up and drew slowly away from the scene, all waving furiously at Abala and his kinsfolk. The road on either side was lined with fields, growing a multitude of different crops: wheat, peas, legumes, onions, sweet potatoes, yams, maize. There were orchards, too, and gnarled olive and nut trees lining tracks up to simple farm dwellings. What had the song said? Porky tried to remember the exact words: *Abundantly, abundantly; the Earth gives variety. Enough for all.*

As he looked back over his shoulder up at the promontory, he could still make out the tree, the massive ash, the great World Tree in Norse mythology, standing head and shoulders above the shifaras below it. So his gaze lingered on it for the last time, and he said goodbye to the tree at the centre of the Earth. And he looked forward again at the dirt track ahead—to the beginning of a new life.

EPILOGUE

On March the fourteenth, at exactly midday and ten minutes and nineteen seconds, Porky and Bina sat with Maureen and Alexander McGregor and arranged the date of their wedding with Bina's parents via their computer screens. Now that Bina's sister, Mira, was well again, the whole family were to travel to Windhorn in Scotland, where Porky's parents had lived and worked since the time he had gone missing. They had contributed to life in the most important eco-village in Britain, and Porky was extremely proud of them. Sister Gandhali was invited too, and Porky couldn't wait to show her the massive vegetable garden he was in charge of there. Not only that—a nationwide chain of inner-city Green Spaces had adopted organic vegetable and fruit gardening as part of their project, calling them Porky Pea Gardens. They produced fresh food for school meals in every major city in Britain, cutting down on transport costs too. Now Jimmy Olives wanted Porky as a guest on his television show! Porky decided that he would wear his McGregor tartan kilt.

But first they had to plan their huge Indian wedding. Bina insisted that the starter on the wedding menu be *Nutmeg Karna Kale*. It would be so delicious, she persuaded. Here's how it's made: fry some shredded curly kale in butter, add crushed garlic and a squeeze of orange juice; then stir in some stringy cheese, and top with some freshly grated nutmeg.

On March the fourteenth, at exactly six o'clock and thirty minutes and twelve seconds, Kitchi and Etchemin called out to Grandmother that it was all right. The latest editions to Wind

River Bison Ranch were safely delivered and doing well. The two baby bison stood shivering as their mom licked them all over. Grandmother had prepared some hot boiled bone broth, which she always fed to female bison after delivering. It gave them strength, she said. The brothers both knew that Grandmother would now go home to her tepee and drink some herself, as she said she had a strong connection with the animal. *When I look into the eyes of an animal, I do not see an animal. I see a living being. I see a friend. I feel a soul,* she would repeat over and over. She didn't have to tell Kitchi that any more; he knew. Folks throughout the land had heard about Kitchi's prowess at rearing bison, and they travelled hundreds of miles to buy from his ranch.

On March the fourteenth, at exactly three o'clock and fifteen minutes and twelve seconds, Abala was on his way back from the market in the nearby town. He drove the pick-up slowly through the throng of people, trying to get back home early; he picked up those who needed a lift as he went. He'd sold all his prize goats for a good price today; Grandfather would be so pleased. He'd reached a good position at a young age on his family's farm; he'd been training young goat herders on medical issues concerning their animals for nearly six months already. He took the long route back for the simple pleasure of driving through Grandfather's land. The two acres of grassy fields hosted sheep and cattle as well as the goats. He saw the shepherd boys were out and waved. Closer to home, the apple trees were full to bursting point; Father would have hired the pickers by now. He'd go out and help them tomorrow. As he pulled into the dirt drive leading up to the farmhouse, he spotted a familiar sight. There he was, leaning against the wall in the afternoon sunshine. And Grandfather raised his stick.

On March the fourteenth, at exactly eight o'clock and thirty-two minutes, Amy and Seung-Yub were sitting around the large table in the kitchen of Peace and Plenty Farm, sharing an enormous welcome meal for Amy and her parents. The long wooden table was spread with dishes of wild rice, spiced delicately with saffron, spring onions, and water chestnuts; serving bowls were brimming full of pork, leek and celery stew, and lamb in mint and green chilli sauce. Every ingredient was hand-picked from the farm that very morning. The centrepiece was a bowl of lotus flowers (*Nelumbo nucifera*), which had been extinct in the region for a century. Grandma Xi was ecstatic that the rice crop in China was flourishing like never before, and she didn't have to bear the heartbreak any longer of having to turn away lines of starving people she couldn't help. No one came begging any more. Under the table, Seung-Yub held Amy's hand and squeezed it tight. He was proud of his warrior queen.

On March the fourteenth, at exactly seven o'clock and forty minutes and six seconds, Serenity and her mother walked slowly and carefully through the rainforest near their home. They'd been out an hour already, collecting leaves and barks, and sometimes roots; their shoulder bags were already full. The abundance of species was literally amazing; there was now so much that Serenity's mother simply could not identify. They would spend the rest of their lives discovering everything that was new to them. Parts of the forest were impenetrable; no one had ever been there. Every now and then, a strange bird, dressed in wonderful colours and markings, would fly out into their path and astound them. They meandered slowly homewards, elated that thousands of new remedies were out there; the potential for the relief of mankind's suffering was immense.

On March the fourteenth, at exactly five o'clock and fifty minutes, Jasmine was pleased to announce that her stringent measures for rations on water could now be slightly relaxed. There was more water available since the qat growers had gone out of business. More crop variety on the slopes of Yemen's hills could be clearly seen from afar as a multitude of colours, presenting themselves like a tapestry. Towns followed the example of the mosques and reused their water to irrigate voluptuous green gardens. Jasmine was considered a heroine by those who heard about the ghoul attack, and she was given more camels as a present. Hassan served her from his heart and frequently consulted the carpet, hoping for further adventures.

On March the fourteenth, at exactly the same time, Lastro returned from a trip with his new whale family. All the whales who were mates with Dobi had reappeared, and many more besides. They frequently took Lastro farther south, as close to Antarctica as they could get without it being too cold for him. Why? Because the penguins were back—hordes of them. It was a joy to see those southern islands inhabited by penguins again, due to the abundance of healthy fish in the sea and cooling of temperatures at the Poles. Lastro could have sat and watched them for hours (they were his extra special favourite animal after the whale), but he always obeyed Dobi when he said it was time to go home, because his special friend knew the seas better than he did.

Mairi McLellan has been a teacher and storyteller for most of her life. She is passionate about puppetry and animals and loves to combine the two. She spent twenty years living in the Middle East, but now lives in her hometown in Renfrewshire, Scotland.

Shadi Hamadeh is the director of the Environmental and Sustainable Development Unit at the American University of Beirut. He works on sustainable food systems, and his major challenge is to reconcile the chaos theory with the bitter realities of food security in the Middle East and North Africa region.

Lightning Source UK Ltd.
Milton Keynes UK
UKOW05f0042080114

224165UK00001B/1/P